Nightshade

By

A. Turner

Of Misfortune and Malevolence Book 1

A. Turner

Everyone is the villain in someone else's story. Even if they're the hero in their own.

Playlist

Nightshade (Of Misfortune and Malevolence Book 1)

Rewrite the Stars - Zac Efron & Zendaya

Sparks Fly (Taylor's Version) - Taylor Swift

Nervous System - Taylor Acorn

Pretty Little Poison - Warren Zeiders

The Death of Peace of Mind - Bad Omens

Figure You Out - Viola

Long Live the king - I Prevail

Face Down - The Red Jumpsuit Apparatus

Guilty as Sin? - Taylor Swift

Dancing on My Own - Calum Scott

I'll Be Waiting - Cian Ducrot

Burning Down - Alex Warren feat. Joe Jonas

Please Please Please (Acoustic) - Sabrina Carpenter

Let the World Burn - Chris Grey

Don't Blame Me - Taylor Swift

Haunted (Taylor's Version) - Taylor Swift

Content/Trigger Warnings

Listed below are a few trigger warnings for this book. Please take these into consideration before reading and be sure to take care of yourself first.

- Violence and Death (on page and mentioned)
- Physical Abuse (on page)
- Emotional Abuse (on page)
- Verbal Abuse (on page)
- Sexual Harassment (on page)
- Child Abandonment (mentioned)
- Mutilation (mentioned)
- Sexual Themes (on page)
- Alcohol and Drug Use (on page)
- Racism (on page)
- PTSD (on page and mentioned)
- Anxiety/Panic Attacks (on page and mentioned)
- Nightmares (on page and mentioned)

Pronunciation Guide

Listed below is a pronunciation guide for many of the more difficult names in this book.

People

Ashten Desai (Ash-tin Dee-sigh)

Renlin Desai (Wren-lin Dee-sigh)

Esmerelda Desai (Ez-mr-el-duh Dee-sigh)

Elion (El-ee-on)

Evelien (Ev-ah-lin)

Reyland (Ray-lund)

Sarphi (Sare-fee)

Lyra (Lie-ruh)

Malon Tranelis (Male-on Tran-ell-iss)

Axilya Raloven (Axe-ill-ya Raal-oh-venn)

Rael Dronvakh (Ray-el Drawn-vock)

Galen Windwalker (gay-len)

Dragons

Nyzirth (Nigh-zearth)

Cyphis (Sigh-fiss)

Iressei (Ear-ess-eee)

Zothim (Zoh-theem)

Zynnos (Zen-nos)

Places

Xeswal (Zess-wall)

Arvandor (Are-van-door)

Asballicuo (Az-baal-ick-yo)

Deities

Bacha (Baa-kuh)

Enwerel (In-wear-el)

Laserie (Lass-err-ee)

Illyrie (Ill-ree)

Aliel (Uh-leel)

Arar (Uh-rawr)

Prologue

Ashten

Anger

Fear

Pain

These feelings rushed through me as I held the dagger to his throat. I carefully studied the man's blue eyes. His pupils were shaking with what I *hoped* was anger. What I *hoped* was fear. What I *hoped* was pain. I wished with all my being that he was feeling every emotion I had felt for the past year. At the very least, I found comfort in knowing, without a doubt, that he could feel the dagger I was holding against his throat. His quickened breath and the trickle of blood down his neck confirmed this.

"Please," The man begged. "Please don't kill me. I'll tell you whatever you want to know."

I looked down at the man. His dark, previously tidy hair was now a mess across his face. Scoffing, I straightened my back. I kept the dagger at the man's throat and applied pressure in the direction I wanted him to move. He stood up slowly and I led him to the head of the dark dining table.

"No." I said, a smug smile creeping across my face as I pulled up a chair beside him. I dug the dagger a little deeper into the man's neck, finding satisfaction in his held breath. "*I* am going to tell *you* a story."

Chapter 1

Ashten

I looked in the mirror, taking in my reflection. My dress hung loosely off my thin frame. I hated the way I looked, but my parents made it difficult to change.

Large meals are not befitting of a lady.

My mother's words echoed in my head, causing me to scoff as I swept my long, straight hair behind me. I ran my hand down my soft cheek. My violet eyes were in stark contrast to my raven black hair, but they matched the dark purple dress I had decided to wear perfectly. Purple had always been my favorite color, much to my father's chagrin. My eyes and hair, along with my pointed ears and pale skin, were proof of my Solar Elf heritage. I turned around, looking back over my shoulder at the open back of my dress. My father would disapprove, but when did he not? I straightened myself in the mirror, running my hands down my bare arms and down the lace that covered the front of my dress, making sure the slit that ran down the side was not too revealing. I wanted to upset my father, but I didn't want to give the man I was meeting the wrong idea.

The blankets on my bed rustled, and I turned to see Deyka sprawled out on her back. Her mostly black fur nearly blended in with the blankets. Her brown, stubby legs stuck straight up in the air and her floppy ears were plastered against the bed. I walked over and obliged her with a belly rub that caused her to thump her foot in appreciation.

There was a sharp knock at the door and Deyka to flop back over onto her stomach, a low growl sounding deep in her chest. The door cracked open slightly and a gruff voice with a thick accent sounded from the other side.

"I'm here to escort you, Princess." Finn stuck his arm through the door and gave me a thumbs up.

I stifled a laugh. "I have clothes on, Finn. You can come in." I walked over to the door and opened it to see Finn standing with his back to me. "Ever the gentleman, I see." I poked him in the back of his head and he turned around, giving me a cheeky smile before walking past me into my room.

"I didn't know you were back already. How was your trip to the Mistymoon Glades? Did the Wild Elves treat you well?" I frowned when I noticed his short hair. "What happened to your hair?"

Gone were the messy locks that I had grown to love. His rounded human ears were no longer covered. He wore a uniform typical of his station as my personal guard. His red tunic and pants complemented the tan complexion of his skin well. The golden dragon in the center of his black chestplate stood out proudly as the symbol of my house. A long, white cape flowed over one shoulder and a beautiful sword hung at his hip.

"It was just too much trouble to take care of." Finn waved me off. "The same as usual. No one paid me much mind as long as I kept the king's envoys safe." His green eyes looked me up and down, his smile widening a little before he bowed slightly at the waist. "You look positively wonderful, Princess." He tipped his head towards the ground.

Deyka took this as her opportunity. She leapt from the bed and raced across the floor. Her long body stretched up towards his face, using his leg as support. She licked Finn's nose before he could stop her. Her tail was wagging so hard that she was nearly hitting herself in the face with it as he scratched her head.

I looked both ways down the hall to make sure the coast was clear before I shut the doors to my room and turned back to them both. Finn was still entertaining Deyka, but he smiled at me when I approached him.

"The coast is clear, Finn." I motioned to the closed door.

He stood up straight and wrapped one arm around my waist. "Good," he said as he kissed me gently. "Because I don't think I could have gone the entire dinner without doing that."

"You better get it all out of your system now. This dinner is with the man my father wants me to marry," I teased. I turned back to the mirror to fidget with my hair and dress once more. I don't know why I cared so much. It wasn't like I was particularly enthused about this dinner.

Finn appeared in the reflection behind me and wrapped his arm around my waist. He planted a kiss on my neck before meeting my eyes in the mirror. I usually recoiled from physical affection, but I found myself leaning back against Finn as he pulled me closer.

"We will just have to see about that, Princess." His grip on my waist tightened. "I don't intend to give you up that easily."

I rolled my eyes. "And what did you have in mind to do about it?"

Finn shrugged and let go of me, walking towards the door. "Oh, I have no idea. I figured you would think of something." He held his arm out towards me.

"Let's get this over with," I mumbled. I gave Deyka one last head scratch before taking Finn's arm.

———————————————————————————————

All eyes were on me as I walked into the throne room. Finn followed behind me close enough to look like he was doing his job, but not too close. I took a second to admire the seven beautiful tapestries hung perfectly throughout the throne room. Six of them were depicting the symbols of the Watchers, the deities that most of the inhabitants of Xeswal worshiped.

A sun surrounded by many flames. The symbol of Bacha, Goddess of the Sun.

A crescent moon on a star-filled night. The symbol of Enwerel, God of the Moon.

A towering tree wrapped in vines. The symbol of Laserie, Goddess of the Land.

A. Turner

A barren landscape flecked with green flames. The symbol of Illyrie, Lord of Death.

A galaxy with two purple eyes peering out of it. The symbol of Aliel, Lady of Chaos.

A solid black tapestry with a single grey path. The symbol of Arar, Lord of the Lost.

The final tapestry, which hung right behind my mother and father's thrones, depicted a large dragon with wings spread wide. The symbol of House Desai. Though the dragon was surrounded by the bright golds and reds of the Solar Elves, the darkness of the dragon itself still stood out against the gold wood that the Alterwood Citadel had been built out of. The dragon loomed over the giant, golden throne. The glint in its eyes was eerily similar to the one in my father's blue eyes as he glared down at me now.

On either side of my father stood his personal guards. Drakewardens, they were called. Historically, the highest honor in Xeswal was to be chosen as a Drakewarden for the royal family. These days, it was a position in title only since dragons had not been seen in centuries. I looked down at the white marble floor, taking in my reflection once again. The reflections of the magical orbs that lit this massive room ominously perfectly framed my face.

"Look at me, Ashten." My father's commanding voice boomed throughout the throne room. I looked up, straightening my shoulders and smoothing the front of my dress. I inhaled deeply. It was obvious from the look on my father's face that I was about to receive an earful about something.

My father leaned back and propped his arm up on the side of the throne. His black hair was combed off to the side, highlighting his pointed ears, and he wore a dark red and gold ceremonial suit. He let out a loud sigh before leaning forward once more to study my appearance.

"I thought I told you to wear something presentable. Not whatever *this* is." He gestured wildly in my direction, shaking his head in disdain.

"You said today was the day I was to meet the man you so *desperately* want me to marry, right? I figured I might as well make a good impression." I gave the dress a sarcastic twirl and ran my fingers through my hair.

"You could have at least worn one of the family's colors," He said as he gestured towards his own suit. "Did you consider wearing your hair up with your grandmother's broach?" He raised an eyebrow at me, practically begged me to argue with him.

An argument that I was ready to indulge him with. My blood began to boil, but the sound of footsteps behind me cut my response short. I turned to see my mother in a beautiful, long, gold dress. She glided across the marble floors towards the thrones. The sleeves of her dress were just slightly covering her hands and flowed behind her as she walked. Her long black hair was pulled back into a tight bun, once again accentuating her pointed ears. Her blue eyes were focused on me.

"Oh Renlin! She looks beautiful! Can't you two just get along for once?" My mother stopped and kissed me on the cheek before gliding up the stairs to her throne. I couldn't help but smile.

"Of course, my dear Esmerelda." My father stood as he extended a hand to his queen and led her to her throne. "I was only suggesting that a different dress would have been more fitting."

I struggled to hold back a laugh as my mother gave him the meanest look. She started to tell him off just as a guard entered the throne room.

"Excuse me, Your Highnesses. They have arrived." He gave a quick bow before quickly exiting.

"Come, darling." My mother extended her hand towards me. "Take your seat."

I took my mother's hand and stepped up the stairs to the throne that was at my mother's right. I sat down and took a deep breath, straightening my back. Finn stood beside me, back straight and eyes focused on the doors to the throne room.

The picture-perfect princess.

I looked at the entrance just in time to see a young man walk in. He was tall, slender, and dressed in a dark green formal suit. His long, red hair was pulled back into a messy bun, revealing pointed ears. Proof of his Elven heritage, though his tan skin leaned more towards being of Wild Elf descent. His dark green eyes were focused on me, and there was an unsettling arrogance about him. Like he had already won me over just by walking into this room.

He stopped a few feet short of the thrones, cutting his gaze back to the king before kneeling. "Your Highness." His voice was young, but firm, and he had a thick accent.

My father motioned for him to stand up. "You must be Elion Windwalker. I trust your travels were well?"

Windwalker? Why did I find that name familiar?

"Yes, Your Highness." Elion's gaze fell back towards me. He ran his eyes up and down my body before making eye contact with me again.

I could see Finn's fist tighten out of the corner of my eye. My father cleared his throat and looked at me expectantly. Of course he would want me to go greet him. I closed my eyes and inhaled deeply before standing up and striding towards Elion. My dark purple dress flowed down the stairs behind me. I stopped in front of the Wild Elf and held my hand out towards him.

"Ashten Desai," I said, bowing my head slightly. Elion took my hand in his and pulled it up towards his lips. He kissed it gently before letting it fall back to my side.

"M'lady. 'Tis a pleasure to meet you." He locked eyes with me once again.

This time, I held his gaze, refusing to be the first to look away. I had a reputation for making life difficult for the males in my life, and I didn't plan on stopping now. I would do almost anything to make potential suitors think twice about marrying me. It also served as a way for me to undermine my father, which was a bonus. Elion, however, did not back down, a sly smile creeping across his face.

I sighed deeply and made a show of rolling my eyes before I walked back to my throne. A smirk peeked out from under Finn's helmet, a complete contradiction to my father's glare as I took my seat and leaned into my throne.

My father stood and walked to Elion, engaging in a firm handshake. "Come, boy. You and I need to have a chat before dinner." He wrapped an arm around Elion's shoulder and led him out of the throne room.

I slouched against the back of my throne, voicing my displeasure with a loud sigh. I used my hand to prop my head up on the arm of my throne. My eyes fluttered shut in a poor attempt to will Elion from existence.

"You know. This one isn't *that* bad." I felt a hand on my shoulder. I opened my eyes to see my mother standing in front of me, smiling softly. "Just once, could you at least *act* excited about meeting a potential suitor?"

"But that would make me a liar." I offered my mother a big smile before frowning just as deeply.

Well, maybe not a complete liar.

I wasn't opposed to meeting a nice male and getting married. As a matter of fact, I had already met one. One I could never convince my father to let me marry. A Solar Elf could never marry a human, especially not the princess. Why did I have to spend today, my birthday, meeting some rich, spoiled male that I had no intentions of marrying? Why couldn't I spend my birthday with my friends like everyone else my age?

Princesses don't spend all of their time with the servants. Especially the humans.

My father's words sounded in my head. All my father ever allowed me to do was eat, sleep, and read. Though I loved reading, I had grown tired of looking at the books my father provided. He only ever brought me endless scrolls and tomes about the other elvish societies and the politics behind dealing with them. All so I could become his perfect little lady. What I *wanted* to read about was adventures, magic, and the journey of finding one's place in this world. That was why I particularly enjoyed the few books that Evelien brought me. They were always full of fun and adventure. Of risks and rule breaking. One couldn't forget the brooding males that the ladies always fell for. I always found the ones with dragons to be particularly interesting.

That was the life I wanted. Going wherever I wanted, doing whatever I wanted, and not having to care about what anyone else had to say about it. Sure, I would probably die at the first sign of trouble, but I didn't care. I didn't want to be the princess.

I wasn't sure how long I had sat there mentally complaining about my "horrible" life, but before I knew it, my father had come back to collect me.

"Come, child. It's time for dinner." There was little emotion in his voice as he turned back out of the room. He quickly made his way down the hall, not even stopping to make sure I was following him.

I gathered myself and made my way down the hall to where the dining room was, Finn following close behind. I hadn't even noticed that he had stayed in the throne room with me. The beautiful summer sunlight was glowing through the windows, and my magic hummed in response. I caught a glimpse of long, blonde hair rushing the hall towards me.

"Good morning, birthday girl!" Evelien practically shouted as she all but ran to catch up to me. She stopped beside me and curtsied slightly. "Princess."

When we stood this close to each other, my almost six inches that I had over the human was very obvious. I was average height for a female Elf, but six feet was still taller than any human female I had ever met.

I swatted her shoulder and gave her an incredulous look as I motioned for her to keep walking. "First off, you said that this morning when you woke me up at an ungodly hour to get ready for this ridiculous meal." I couldn't help but chuckle as she tried her best to look offended. "Secondly, you know you don't have to call me princess, Evelien. I would actually prefer it if you didn't."

"Sorry!" She gave me an apologetic smile. "I just worry about what the other servants might say... and I definitely do not want to upset your father, Ashten."

I rolled my eyes. "I don't particularly care what my father has to say about it."

"*Soooo.* Who do they have for you today?" Evelien mocked, putting her arm around my shoulders in an attempt to change the subject.

Finn rolled his eyes. "Another young, rich male. This one's from the Wildelands, though." I swatted him on the shoulder and he shrugged innocently.

"He's fairly cute, but he has the same entitled look about him." I stopped walking for a second, turning to Evelien. "The way he looks at me is very unsettling. It felt like he was looking at every single piece of me, and I don't just mean the dress." I sighed, putting my head in my hands.

Finn leaned towards us, speaking just loud enough for both of us to hear. "I could take care of it for you, Princess."

I pinned him with a glare over my hands. "Be careful about what you say, Finn. If someone other than Evelien would have heard you say that, I don't think I could do anything to help you."

"I'm not worried." He shrugged nonchalantly.

Evelien quietly waited for my glare to fade before grabbing my hands and lowering them back to my side. "Relax. I'm sure he was just nervous. I mean, you are beautiful." She waved her hands towards me.

"If he continues, just tell your father. No matter how he acts, no father wants someone mistreating his little girl." She wrapped her arms around my shoulders and gave them a soft squeeze.

"I wish I could believe that." I leaned into Evelien's embrace. This elicited a surprised gasp from the young lady before I felt her grip tighten even more. "I better go now. I'm already late. Don't want to make the lecture any worse." I pulled away, smiling flatly before continuing my walk down the hall.

Chapter 2

Ashten

The dining hall was beautifully decorated with the colors and symbols of my house. Red and gold tapestries depicting dragons of various sizes lined every wall. The dining table was made of a dark ebony wood. Around it were eight ebony chairs adorned with red and gold accents. I never understood why we had so many chairs. I was an only child, and my parents rarely invited anyone over for private meals.

The queen sat in the chair near the head on the right, and Elion sat one space over from the head on the left, leaving one chair open on that end of the table. The one at the head of the table, which my father sat in, featured a large dragon carved into the back. Its unfurled wings perfectly encapsulated his shoulders as he leaned back. The king's signature frown settled on his face when he saw me.

"How nice of you to finally join us." He spoke flatly. "Come. Sit." He pointed to the chair on his left.

The one between him and Elion. Great.

I quietly took my seat, trying not to think about the fact that I was now stuck between the two males that I despised most in this room. I tried to force a smile at my mother, but it didn't seem to work. My mother sighed, lowering and shaking her head. Finn stood against the wall behind my chair, the picture-perfect guard. I could feel his gaze on the back of my head and I took some small comfort in knowing that he was here.

"So." My father's voice echoed through the mostly empty room. "Shall we begin dinner?"

He then signaled for the servants who had been standing at the door. They all turned back into the kitchen and quickly returned with plates for everyone. They walked around the table, filling everyone's glasses with drinks. The food looked delicious. It was roasted lamb, something we only had when my father was trying to impress someone.

The king and Elion droned on and on about politics and the military. I looked up at my mother, who looked equally bored. She was nodding quietly, only looking up any time her name was mentioned. I took a sip of my drink without looking and nearly spit it out as the tart wine hit my lips. My father rarely served wine at dinner. He always spouted nonsense about how we needed to stay sharp and keep our minds clear. I carefully placed the cup back down, hoping no one had seen my reaction. I returned to my meal in silence, hoping the evening would be over soon.

I was very quickly brought back to reality by someone saying my name. My head shot up and I looked in the direction the words had come from to see Elion calmly sipping his glass of wine. He was locked in conversation with my father. Apparently, a conversation about me.

"I am sure Ashten will make a wonderful wife, Elion." My father sipped from his wine passively, as if he wasn't trying to trade his daughter off like some prized horse. "Though she can be a little... *difficult.*"

"I'm sure I could change that." Elion gave my father a crooked smile. He took a sip from his glass, and I felt a hand rake across my thigh.

I froze.

"Good luck with that." The High Lord of Arvandor shook his head, laughing gently.

My father's words had apparently given Elion a newfound sense of entitlement. He ran his hand along the outside of my leg, stopping where the dress ended and holding it there. The touch sent a wave of nausea over me. I looked over at him, trying to make eye contact. He didn't meet my eyes, but a smile curled at the edge of his lips.

He knew exactly what he was doing.

Elion continued his conversation with my father, all the while never taking his hand off my leg. I tried to reposition myself without making too much of a scene. He moved his hand with me, tightening his grip on my thigh. I tried to brush his hand away, but he caught my fingers under his, holding them down. Panic began to cloud my mind. I looked over my shoulder at Finn, whose eyes were pinned on Elion. His hand was tight on the hilt of his sword.

Please don't. I hoped he could somehow hear me. The last thing I needed right now was him attacking a guest. I turned my attention back to Elion.

"Enough." The word came out as more of a whisper. Less forceful than I had intended. My hands were shaking and my lungs were heavy.

"What was that, m'lady?" Elion leaned in closer to me, fake concern lacing his voice. It did nothing to cover up the look in his eyes as he finally made eye contact with me.

He knew exactly what he was doing.

He was practically begging me to call him out. Because, *somehow*, he knew who my father would side with. Little did he know that I couldn't care less about what my father had to say. I could feel the panic in me slowly dissipating as it was replaced with a new emotion.

"I said," I took a second to steel my nerves and level my voice. "That's. Enough." The words came out louder, but the nerves in my voice were still evident. I swore I heard Elion chuckle as my mother's face changed from an expression of worry to an expression of confusion. My father, on the other hand, just seemed angry.

Like always.

"Enough of what, Ashten?" My father's voice was laced with annoyance. I was used to it, though. I didn't break eye contact with Elion as the king leaned forward in his chair, asking his question again.

"Get. Your. Hand. Off. Me." These words sounded much stronger and demanding, and I was grateful. I finally felt like I had gotten the point across. I let out the breath I didn't know I had been holding when Elion finally removed his hand from my leg. He, too, never broke eye contact.

"Sorry, Ashten." Elion's accent drew out the syllables of my name. I shuddered and hoped that I never had to hear him say my name again. My reaction caused Elion to smirk as he laced his fingers behind his head and leaned back in his chair.

I looked back and forth between my mother, who looked mortified, and my father, who seemed unphased by the confrontation. I opened my mouth to speak, but my father held up his hand, cutting me off.

"It's no big deal, Elion. I'm sure it was just a misunderstanding." He waved his hand in a dismissing manner, intent on just resuming his meal and conversation.

No big deal.

I couldn't believe what I had just heard. My father and I didn't necessarily get along very well, but I couldn't believe that he was dismissing this without at least asking what had happened. I could feel my face flush, but not out of embarrassment. The panic I had felt earlier had been completely replaced with a new feeling.

Anger.

I stood purposefully from my chair, trying to keep my emotions in check. "Please excuse me." My voice wavered slightly, much to my disappointment. "My appetite has left me." I clenched my fists at my sides and walked away, not waiting for Finn to follow.

I had almost made it back to my chambers when I heard heavy footsteps behind me. Glancing over my shoulder, I saw my father quickly gaining. I mumbled a curse under my breath.

"I don't want to hear it." My sentence was curt, not giving him the chance to speak as I continued to walk. I was unable to out-stride him and he caught up quickly. He forcefully grabbed me by the arm and pulled me to a stop.

"I didn't ask what you wanted to hear, child." My father jerked me around to face him. "You're going to stand here and listen to what I have to say." I rolled my eyes but braced myself to weather the storm that was rolling in. I pulled my arm from his grasp and crossed both of them across my chest.

"I invited this young man here as a guest. He is here to meet *you* and get to know *you*. Yet you storm out of the dinner like a spoiled brat." My father's voice rose as he spoke.

I could feel the anger I had just gotten under control threatening to boil over again. "Did you stop to consider why I left? That I may have a good reason? Or were you too concerned with your reputation and what Elion may go home and tell whomever it is you are trying to impress by getting me to marry him?" My breathing was a little uneven as I tried to keep my anger in check. I really didn't want to garner any more attention than I already had.

My father straightened his shoulders and looked down his nose at me. "There is going to come a day, child, when your life will depend on *my* reputation and what the other societies think of us." He grabbed my arm again, pulling me close as he whispered, "Because this, *your blood,* will not be enough." He raised his hand, summoning a small yellow flame. The marble statues that lined the golden halls seemed to hum in response. "Your powers will not always be enough to keep you on that throne." He dismissed the flame and pulled away, straightening his suit.

Then, without so much as a cursory glance, he turned on his heels and walked back towards the dining hall.

Chapter 3

Ashten

I stormed into my room, slamming the door behind me. I stood there for a moment, my thoughts racing. My eyes scanned the room for a distraction to take my mind off of the evening. Something to help calm my pounding heart. Deyka lifted her head from the bed, whining softly as if she could sense that something was wrong. It felt as if I was looking through someone else's eyes as I walked across the room to my bed. The walls of my room were a bright golden color. The same as the rest of the castle, since it was all made from the same rare wood. My bed stood as a beacon of darkness in this room. It was still built in an elvish fashion, but was not decorated in the colors of my family. The dark purple silk sheets were inviting, but before I could crawl into them, there was a loud knock on my door.

"Can it wait until morning?" I asked in the direction of the door. "I'm not particularly in the mood for visitors."

"I would rather it not, Princess." Finn's voice was low and quiet.

I cracked the door slightly to see Finn standing there, his helmet tucked under one arm.

"May I come in?" He looked left and right as he spoke, giving me a subtle thumbs up. Our signal that the coast was clear. I opened the door just enough for him to walk through and then quickly shut it behind him.

Finn placed his helmet on my desk and began pacing across the room. He ran his hands over his head as he moved. He continued until I walked into his path. I grabbed his hands and led him to the couch that was under the window, motioning for him to sit down. He hesitated slightly before obliging. I sat down next to him and turned so that my knees were touching his.

"Do you want to tell me what's wrong? Or are you just content to wear out the beautiful rug that decorates my floor?" I placed my hands on his knees and he looked up at me. The look on his face was a mixture of anger and sadness, but I couldn't tell which emotion was winning. "What's wrong, Finn?"

He waited a moment longer before responding. "I can't do this anymore." I raised my eyebrows and tilted my head, hoping my face accurately portrayed my confusion. He placed his hands over mine, squeezing them tightly. "This." He motioned wildly to nothing in particular before grabbing my hands again. "Sneaking around behind everyone's backs. Playing the perfect protector. Keeping my mouth shut while the spoiled, rich males come into this citadel acting like they are entitled to you!" His voice rose with those last words and he took a deep breath. Deyka leapt off the bed and ran over to us. Finn exhaled through his nose and stood up, ignoring us both by turning his back to us.

I stood up and pulled him to me, wrapping my arms around his waist. My forehead rested against his spine, letting his pine scent ground me before speaking again.

"We have been over this, Finn." I felt his arms close over mine. "There are rules that I, as Princess of Arvandor and Heir of the Desai Dynasty, have to follow. One of those is marrying an Elf of high standing. Someone that my people would look up to. I'm just as unhappy about it as you are."

Finn's chin hit his chest, and I felt my heart fracture a little.

It was my turn to take a deep breath. I exhaled gingerly as I walked around to face Finn. He was at most a half inch taller than me, but I still had to reach up to touch his face. I rubbed my thumb across his cheek and he leaned into my touch, closing his eyes.

We stood in silence for a few moments, both of us content to simply exist in each other's presence. I leaned up and placed a soft kiss on his cheek.

"I know it is hard now, but there is a light at the end of the tunnel." My voice was soft.

"And what might that be, Princess?"

I couldn't help the smile that spread across my face. "Well, you see, when I am High Lady of Arvandor, I can do whatever I want." I met his eyes. "*Whoever* I want." Though I was whispering, I made sure to enunciate, and, judging by the look in Finn's eyes now, I had definitely made myself clear.

He grabbed me by the waist and pulled me into him. He pressed his forehead against mine, his dark green eyes never leaving mine. "Is that so, Princess?" he whispered, kissing me softly.

"If not, then I will make it so." I broke the kiss only long enough to speak before kissing him again. This kiss was harder and rougher than the first. Finn tightened his grip on my waist, a small growl escaping him.

We kissed for what was simultaneously too long and not long enough before breaking away from each other. We were both panting, and I could feel the heat creeping down my neck. I placed a hand on his chest and pushed him back slightly.

"Until then, we shouldn't get ahead of ourselves." I reluctantly backed out of his grip and tried to regain control of my breathing. "Now, if you will excuse me, I need a bath." Finn made no effort to move, so I made a mockingly grand gesture toward the door. "Alone, commander."

Not that the idea didn't interest me. That rumor was just the last thing either of us needed. Emotions settled deep inside me as the thought crossed my mind. Finn's eyes were glued to me and I half expected him to argue. Instead, he bowed his head and chuckled softly.

"Of course, Princess. I wouldn't dare." He gave me a chaste kiss before grabbing his helmet off my desk and walking to the door. Deyka ran up to him and nudged his leg with her long nose. Smiling, he leaned down to pet her.

Finn cracked the door and looked both ways. Satisfied that the coast was clear, he turned back to me. "I have tonight's watch. I will be just outside if you need me." The smile he gave as he put on his helmet and walked out only served to intensify the emotions that were currently wrestling with my logic.

I sighed once I was confident that he wasn't coming back and turned to go to the next room.

A bath.

I was tired, but I needed a bath first. A warm soak would make me feel better. And hopefully take my mind off of everything. Both the good and the bad.

The adrenaline of the entire day began to wear off, making my legs feel impossibly heavy as I made my way to the bathtub. I hadn't even realized that I was in such a state, though it didn't really surprise me. Most of my life had felt that way, even though I had never left the confines of Arvandor. I noticed the tub had already been filled and made a mental note to thank Evelien in the morning. I absentmindedly lit the fire in the furnace under the tub, letting the water heat. My fingers fumbled with the lace on the back of my dress and I let it fall to the floor. I didn't care if it made it to the clothes basket or not. I could pick it up later.

Instant relaxation coursed through my body as I stepped over the edge of the tub into the warm water. I slowly sank down, stopping when the water was just below my chin. My eyes fluttered shut as I laid my head back against the tub. I attempted to take a relaxing breath as the events from the dinner replayed over and over in my head.

How could my father not care? Was he just oblivious to what had happened? Or was he choosing to ignore it? Surely he didn't believe I would marry someone who acted like that. Mother wouldn't allow him to force me to marry someone like that... right?

These thoughts and more consumed me as I laid there, listening to the soft rumble of the furnace. I wasn't sure how long I had laid there, and I definitely didn't remember turning off the furnace, but I opened my eyes again sometime later. The water in the tub was now lukewarm, and the room was eerily quiet. I looked up at the skylight window that was positioned over my tub. The moon was high in the sky just over the window, so I could assume that it was probably close to midnight.

I took a second to bask in the moonlight, lifting my hand and summoning a small orange flame. The statues that decorated my washroom hummed. As a Solar Elf, I had the innate ability to wield fire magic. Solar Elves were believed to have a strong connection with the sun. Some scholars even speculated that was where the Solar Elves originated before coming to Xeswal. I was never given an explanation for the Moon Elves or Wild Elves, though. My instructors refused to even speak about the Dragonfolk and Daemonfolk. They called them "unnatural" and always warned me to stay away from them.

I watched as the fire in my hand seemed to fight against the moonlight coming in through the overhead glass. Two opposites fighting to be the brightest light in the room. I willed the fire in my hand to grow dimmer. Despite my heritage, I had always felt a strong connection to the night. My mother always joked that maybe I was meant to be a Moon Elf, and I couldn't help but wonder what it would feel like to wield darkness itself.

The moon could only be seen because of the light from the sun. Without the sun, the moon could not light up the night sky. Without the moon, the night would be eternal darkness, flecked only by stars not bright enough to illuminate the sky. I often felt much like the moon. Weathering the strong light of the powerful sun and trying my best to reflect it in a way that would make the world better. Whatever that meant.

I shook my head, extinguishing the flame in my hand. My legs felt like liquid as I stood and reached for the towel beside the tub. I was getting philosophical, which meant it was time for bed. Black trousers and a red shirt had been laid out for me and I pulled them on. I climbed under the heavy blanket Evelien had specially made for me and settled in. The blanket helped calm me enough to sleep well on most nights. I barely remembered Deyka burrowing under the blankets before the world grew dark and quiet around me.

Deyka's barks were just loud enough to wake me up as the blankets were ripped off the bed with enough force that I was thrown to the ground. I backed up against the bed frame, blinking frantically as I tried to get my eyes to adjust to the room. I threw up my hand and summoned a flame to my palm. It lit up the room enough to reveal four humanoid figures standing in my room. Two at the large white doors separating my room from the rest of the citadel, and two standing over me. I couldn't see the two at the door well enough to make out any discernible features, but the two standing over me became clearer as my eyes adjusted.

They were both human males with brown hair that had been cropped into a short military style cut. They both had brown eyes and their faces were expressionless. Their tan skin suggested that they had spent an extensive amount of time outside. However, it was their clothing that caught my attention. They were both wearing the red tunic and onyx breastplate of the royal palace guards. The golden dragon on the breastplate was unmistakable. These two didn't have their helmets on for some reason, but the ones at the door appeared to. I fixed my gaze back on the guards' faces.

"Can I help you? There must be some explanation for this rude awakening, and it better be a good one." I worked to get my feet under me, standing and keeping my back against the wall.

I looked around the room in search of something I may have missed. Some sort of hidden danger that I was not originally aware of in my groggy state. I couldn't find anything to warrant being thrown from my bed in the middle of the night.

Deyka continued to growl at them, but the guard's expression remained blank as he reached for me. I pulled my arms closer to my body and stayed just out of his reach. They had yet to say a single word to me or each other. I glanced back and forth between their faces. These males were almost identical to one another. One of the guards at the door muttered something in a language that I did not understand. The language was abrupt and gruff, with most of the words seeming to only have one or two syllables. I couldn't shake how familiar the voice sounded. The guards next to me didn't answer immediately, so the one at the door repeated himself. One of the identical guards responded this time, and the guard who originally asked the question slipped out of the room, shutting the door silently behind him.

I stared at the guards in front of me, waiting for one of them to try to grab me again. When they didn't, I tried to walk past them. That was apparently not allowed, and I was immediately shoved back. I lost my balance and fell back to the ground. My anger threatened to rear its massive head again as I clamored back to my feet. I brushed myself off and walked up to the guard who shoved me.

"Look. I don't know who you are, but you seem to have forgotten who I am and where you are standing. You are in MY house and —" I was cut off as the door to my room opened.

"No, Ashten. They are in MY house," my father said as he stalked across the room. He still wore the same attire from dinner. I squared my shoulders as my father approached me. The guards parted slightly to allow him past, and Deyka's growls grew louder as he got closer.

"They are in MY house following MY instructions. These guards are here because I have asked them to be." He stopped in front of me. He was at least six inches taller than me, so I was forced to look up at him to make eye contact.

"It's nice that you have such loyal subjects, Father. I would still love an explanation as to why they are in *my* room throwing me out of *my* bed in the middle of the night." I crossed my arms, glaring pointedly at the two closest guards before fixing the same glare on my father.

He snorted, shaking his head before crossing his arms, mimicking my stance. "Well, child, I would normally say that, as your king, I don't owe you an explanation. However, given the circumstances, I think I can afford you a brief insight."

My brows furrowed. "What circumstances? Do you mean the ones where you and your guards burst into my room in the middle of the night with no warning or explanation? I would think that would afford me a *brief insight,* regardless of the circumstances."

My father waited with an annoyingly calm amount of patience until he decided that I was done speaking. "If you are finished, I would love to speak now." His mocking tone grated against what bit of self control I had left. "You see, child, that young man that you so ceremoniously rejected at dinner tonight was the son of Galen Windwalker. You know, the Sovran of the Wild Elves, High Lord of Anmythyr, and the current Head Chair of the Nemeluna."

Bacha save me.

I couldn't hide the change in my expression as my father spoke. A smirk formed at the edge of his mouth as he continued explaining.

A. Turner

"I think you are beginning to see why I am so angry with you, *child*. The marriage between you and Elion was supposed to help solidify the support of the Wild Elves. They may not live within these walls, but their support is still needed as much as, if not more than, the citizens of Arvandor. Without the support of the other elvish leaders, your life here would be much more difficult than you currently think it is. A lesson I am sure you are going to learn very soon."

I tried to school my features into neutrality as my father finished his sentence.

"And how's that? I asked. The words immediately carried more bite than they should have given the current situation that I had found myself in. "Are you going to force me to marry him anyway? Try to mold me into the perfect princess you have always wanted? Because I won't make it easy for you!" My voice rose as I spoke, matching the rise in my temper.

I was silenced by a sudden pain that shot across my face. The force of the blow knocked me onto my rear. My cheek stung and I could feel my eyes start to water.

He slapped me.

"No." My father's voice was still very calm as he knelt down in front of me, getting close enough that only I could hear. "I'm going to make you grateful for the life I have *allowed* you to live." The words sent chills down my spine. My father stood back up and motioned to the guards. He spoke in that language that I did not understand, and the guards reached for me again.

He turned and walked to the door as the two closest guards grabbed me, one on each arm so I couldn't jerk away. They hauled me off of the floor and I struggled against them as they dragged me out the door. Deyka lunged at them, but one guard slammed the door in her face. When we exited my chambers, my father turned right without a second glance while I was pulled to the left.

I wanted to yell. Wanted to scream. Anything to get someone's attention. But I couldn't. It was as if my body knew it was futile, even if my mind didn't. My arms and legs began to tire from fighting the males who were holding me. They led me down a series of hallways that I didn't recognize and out one of the back exits of the citadel where an unmarked carriage was waiting for us. I didn't fight anymore as they put me into the carriage where two more armed guards were waiting. My body had begun to shut down. Fight, flight, or freeze and it seemed as if I had unwillingly chosen freeze.

After they shut the door to the carriage, I turned to one of the guards, my voice barely more than a whisper. "Where are you taking me?"

The guard didn't even glance my way when he answered. "Asballicuo."

The familiarity of the voice was even more apparent now that the guard was speaking Xeswali.

"Finn?" I whispered, leaning closer to the guard as I tried to look through the eyeholes of his helmet. The eyes I met there were undeniably those of my personal guard. "Where are you taking me, Finn?" I didn't even need him to confirm his identity.

He didn't look me in the eye as he repeated his earlier statement. "Asballicuo."

What? Why?

This answer only gave me more questions. The armory was located on Oshos Island, a volcanic island off the east coast of the continent. It was known to the commoners as the forge that supplied the weapons used to defend Arvandor and the surrounding villages. The island had once been used to house the dragons of the dynasty, but there had been no dragon riders since the last dragon was killed. That was when my father was a child. None of this information changed the fact that I had no idea why my father would send me to an armory. I was raised behind the walls of Arvandor and had no knowledge of smithing or weaponry. There was nothing I could do at a forge that would be even remotely helpful. All of this and more crossed my mind as I leaned my head against the window of the carriage, wincing from the resulting sting of the growing bruise on my cheek.

Chapter 4

Ashten

The sun had set and rose once since we had left Arvandor and made our way down the road that led into the swamps. The Deadlands, as they were called, had been deemed unlivable centuries ago. My boots squelched against the wet soil that made growing crops nearly impossible, and the heat wasn't dampened even though the sun was always obscured by the uneasy mist that covered the land. The trees were few and far between. The only road through here was heavily guarded. There was a guard posted every thousand feet, and ballistas lined the high walls that had been built along this road to keep dangers away. My father very clearly wanted to be sure that this road was well defended against any creature attacks since it was responsible for transporting the weapons that the forge at Asballicuo produced to the royal armory.

The high walls and guards did more than keep monsters out. They also seemed perfect for keeping unwanted eyes away from anything that would happen on this road. Such as kidnapping the Princess.

Not that the guards had been particularly mean to me. They had yet to lay another hand on me since loading me into the carriage and some of them even continued to call me "princess", though, apart from Finn, I couldn't honestly tell you which guard was which. All of them were human, and they all had that same tan skin and short-cropped brown hair. They had slightly different builds and facial structures, but the only easily discernible difference between them was their eyes. The two identical ones that I had initially met in my room had brown eyes. The other one inside the carriage had green eyes like Finn. I had not seen the driver in the daylight, but I could assume that he also had either green or brown eyes.

I had met nearly all the guards around the palace and knew most of them on a first-name basis. They were not all identical. In fact, most of the guards that worked inside the palace grounds were elves of various descents. I had worked hard to convince my father to allow Finn to be my personal guard. We had grown up together. His mother was my mother's most trusted servant. My father had often said that he didn't trust humans to know his secrets. Therefore, most of my father's close guards and servants were elves. So why were these guards humans and how was it they were all almost identical to each other?

I had an unending amount of questions. The guards in the carriage with me refused to answer my many inquiries and often said nothing at all. I was fairly certain that Finn was ignoring me, but I did remember that it seemed as if the other guards did not speak Xeswali very well, if at all. I couldn't help but wonder what language they did speak. Xeswali and Elvish were what I was raised with, but I could read most other languages well enough to gather a basic understanding of what was written. I had always had an affinity for languages, one my father had said would make me a great ruler. Apparently, being able to read a few words of a language did not necessarily mean that you could understand it when it was spoken. Which was unfortunate.

I sighed and leaned my head against the window of the carriage. I winced as my cheek came into contact with the glass. My skin had always bruised easily, but this one was much worse. Thanks to when I had seen my reflection in the polished glass earlier, I was very aware of the large hand sized bruise that had spread across my face. It was already purple and I had a feeling it would be turning blue and yellow before it went away.

It wasn't nighttime yet, but I could no longer deny how heavy my eyelids were feeling. I closed my eyes, letting the rattle of the carriage wheels lull me into a deep sleep.

The carriage came to a screeching stop that jolted me awake, and my arms shot out to keep myself upright. I could feel a faint vibration through the bottom of the carriage and my heart rate instantly spiked as the two guards jumped out, weapons drawn. The vibrations were getting stronger and I was having to fight to keep myself stable. I poked my head out the open door to try to see what the commotion was, but all I could see was the stone wall.

And then that wall exploded.

A. Turner

I was tossed through the air as the force of whatever broke through that wall launched me into the wall on the opposite side of the road. I covered my head as stone and dirt from the wall fell around me. A hand grabbed my arm and jerked me out of the way just as the horses from the carriage barreled past, their harness having been broken from the blast. The arms helped me to my feet, and I looked over to see one of the guards from the inside of the carriage. Green eyes met mine, and it took me a second to register that it was Finn.

"Here." He said flatly, holding out his shield to me. When I hesitated, he held it over his head, miming protecting himself.

"I know how to use a shield." I rolled my eyes as I took the shield. "What's going o—" my words caught in my throat as something slammed into the wall beside us. I glanced over to see what it was and my blood ran cold. The body of a soldier laid in a crumpled heap beside me. Though the force of hitting the wall did him no favors, it was obvious that wasn't what killed him. He was covered in blood and I couldn't make out exactly where the blood was coming from.

Anxiety began to set in as I turned my head in the direction that the body had come from. What I saw there made me freeze in my tracks. A creature I had only seen in textbooks. Mere rumors circulated about their existence.

Dragon.

It stood tall, its four legs straddling the road. Its purple scales reflected the light from the semi-obscured sun, giving the creature an almost metallic appearance. Vast, leathery wings spread out wide behind it, flexing as it let out an ear bursting roar. The dust from the crumbling wall mixed with the natural fog of the area to give this terrible creature an even more ominous appearance.

Much care had been taken to ensure that dragons had been wiped out centuries before I was even born. There were rumors among scholars that dragons lived in the Deadlands, but only the king's guards traveled this far out.

I guess they weren't just rumors.

Purple smoke billowed out of the dragon's nose as it slowly exhaled. A low rumble that I could feel in my chest emanated from it. Its tongue flicked in and out as its head scanned from side to side. It was as if the dragon could taste the fear that lingered in the air. I knew *I* could feel it. My fear only intensified as the creature locked eyes with me.

Fear.

The next few moments felt like they took an eternity. The dragon stalked towards me, the ground shaking with each step. It stopped just a few feet away from me. It was over five stories tall, and its purple, cat-like eyes scanned me as if it was looking for something. Another low rumble sounded from deep within the dragon. At first, I thought it was the beginning of another roar. A warning right before it ate me. I had come to terms with my fate. Maybe it was a better one than whatever awaited me.

The rumble brought a sense of familiarity with it, and my magic seemed to pulse in response. I could feel my magic rushing to the surface, fighting to see whatever had caused it to feel this way. I held my palm out flat to give my flames a place to escape. As I did, a ball of fire appeared in my hand. I could feel that same familiar humming that I had often felt from the statues inside the citadel, and it seemed as if it was originating from the dragon. It was as if the dragon could sense my magic and my magic could sense the creature.

The dragon leaned in closer and lowered until it was eye level with me. It stared intensely into my eyes, and I found myself unable to look away. I finally let go of a breath that I didn't realize I had been holding in, and the creature breathed out in response. Purple smoke flowed from its nostrils.

Interesting.

I willed the flame in my hand to grow and watched as the dragon's eyes widened. It backed up slightly, flaring its nostrils as a low hiss escaped its mouth. It seemed conflicted, as if it was torn between two equally powerful instincts. I used this conflict as an opening to get myself out of this. I shaped my fire into a whip and launched it at the creature. It flicked its tail in response, jumping back and hissing as the flame scorched the sensitive pale scales on its stomach. I lashed out with the whip again, and the dragon slinked even further back, its eyes never leaving mine.

It almost looked sad.

This cycle lasted for a time or two more before the dragon hesitantly flapped its wings. I covered my eyes as dust began to fly up around the massive creature. By the time I looked back up, the dragon had flown deep back into the swamp. I couldn't shake the strange feeling of loss as I dismissed my flame. My magic was no longer humming. It felt as if it was searching for something, searching for that connection with the dragon again. I swallowed thickly and the loss was quickly replaced by uncertainty as I took in the surrounding destruction.

The cart was destroyed and the horses were gone. All of the guards were dead. The wall had a massive hole and the rubble had blocked the road. I jumped as I felt someone grab my arm and spin me around. I was pulled into a tight hug, but the fire of panic was quickly doused when I heard Finn's familiar voice.

"Are you okay?" he asked. His voice was strained, and I sensed he was trying to hide his emotions, but I caught a hint of worry in his eyes before he looked away. He had blood smeared on the side of his face, but I couldn't tell if it was his or not.

"Yeah, I'm fine," I said, dusting myself off. I reached up, wiping some of the blood off of his face with a shaking hand. He seemed to sense my question before I asked it.

He placed his hand over mine and squeezed it lightly. "Don't worry." He smiled. "It's not mine." Finn blew out a long breath between his teeth. "That was a dragon..."

"Yeah..." I lowered my hand back to my side, and we both stood there for a second. I finally looked around at the destruction that surrounded us. Dead bodies were scattered all over the road. My stomach churned when I counted extra arms and legs that didn't have the bodies they belonged to. The cart was shattered and the horses were gone.

We were stranded.

Panic started to take over the more I looked around. I felt Finn's hand rest lightly on my back as my head spiraled. He rubbed gently up and down my spine. He said nothing as I fought to reel in my emotions. It felt like forever before the shock began to wear off. I handed Finn his shield back and looked down the road in the direction we had been headed.

"It was scared of my fire." I stated blankly.

It wasn't a complete lie, but I didn't feel like getting into the specifics right now. Not when I didn't completely understand them myself. Hopefully, giving him an answer now to a question he hadn't thought to ask yet would keep that question from being asked later. I swallowed thickly. "So, what do we do now?"

Finn gave me a small smirk before schooling his features into neutrality. "We walk."

Chapter 5

Ashten

I stood perfectly still as the dragon towered over me, its long tail loosely coiling around my body. When the coiling stopped, I found myself face to face with the creature, its feline purple eyes piercing my soul. I was unable to look away. I felt drawn to this creature and I couldn't explain why. Its nostrils flared as it assessed me. When I breathed, it did the same. When I raised my arm, the creature's gaze shifted to watching my hand. Its gaze was filled with longing and I watched its eyes light up as I felt that familiar humming again. I summoned a flame to my hand, but something felt off. Though the flame did appear, it was much smaller than normal. It was almost as if there was an invisible force fighting against my magic. Not to stop it, but like it was trying to transform it. Like it wanted to show me something else.

I closed my eyes and tried to center my magical energy like I was taught when I was a young child. I pictured my magical abilities as a raging fire inside me, always looking for a way out. It was different this time, though. Something was corralling my magic. I watched as a purple smoke surrounded my flame. It was not snuffing it out, but merely controlling it. I tried again to summon a flame to my hand and watched as the flame pushed out of the lavender smoke, only to be stopped when the smoke raced after it. I tried this a few more times before deciding to give up. The next problem surfaced when I tried to pull myself back into my body. The lavender smoke began racing towards me.

It wrapped around my body, much in the same way that the dragon's tail had. I began to panic as the purple smoke completely obscured my vision. I blinked once, and when I opened my eyes, I was looking into the eyes of the dragon. The creature's gaze left mine briefly and flicked down to my still outstretched hand. I followed and was caught completely off guard by what I saw.

In my hand was not a bright orange flame, like I had willed and done a thousand times, but a small ball of lavender smoke. The smoke ebbed and flowed, but kept its general shape and stayed contained in my hand. I looked back at the dragon just as it breathed out. More lavender smoke left the nose of the creature. It surrounded me before being absorbed by the ball of mist in my hand. A feminine, gravelly voice filled my head as I met the dragon's gaze once more.

"We have been waiting for you."

Before I could stop myself, I instinctively reached out for the dragon with the hand that held the purple ball of mist. The dragon closed its eyes, allowing me to touch it. As soon as my hand came in contact with the creature's cool scales, I felt a surge of energy pulse through my body. It was like the humming, only stronger. I tried to pull my hand away but could not. My hand fused to the dragon as magic surged through us both.

I watched in horror as the skin on my arm began to change. My fair, pale skin that was common with Solar Elves was being slowly replaced by scales. Purple iridescent scales that matched those belonging to the dragon crept up my hand and arm. The feeling was strange. It did not hurt, but instead felt more like a tingle. Like I had slept on my arm all night. That same gravelly voice filled my head again.

"Yes indeed. We have been waiting for you."

I watched as the scales started to spread across my entire body. I fought against the change, squirming and pulling on my arm with all of my might. My hand finally released from the dragon and I fell to the ground with a thud.

It was that thud that jerked me out of my slumber. I sat up, quickly inspecting my hands and finding no scales. My eyes fluttered closed, searching for that purple mist, but all that greeted me was that same flame I had felt inside my entire life. I frantically looked around for any sign of what had just happened, but I could find none. No dragon. No purple smoke. Nothing. I caught Finn staring at me intently, his brow creased with worry.

Had he even gone to sleep?

"Everything alright, Princess?" Finn asked, running his hand over his head and through what was left of his hair. I had to admit that I kind of missed the shaggy hair he had before. He scratched at his face. He hadn't been able to shave, and it seemed that the stubble growing was bothering him.

"Yeah," I whispered, staring into the fire that separated us. "Just a nightmare. I have them every once in a while."

Finn gave me a questioning look before staring back down at the fire. The glow illuminated his face and I couldn't help but notice how different he looked from the Finn that I had grown up with. His green eyes were wary and he seemed tense constantly. I was sure that he hadn't fully slept in at least a night or two. He was always awake when I fell asleep and awake when I woke up. He probably hadn't fully rested since the dragon attack nearly two days ago.

Finn looked up and caught me staring at him. A small smile formed at the corner of his mouth. "Something I can help you with, Princess?" The words were clipped through his accent. Finn's gaze remained on me, his eyebrows raised expectantly until I realized I hadn't answered him.

Why am I staring at him like I've never seen a human male before?

"Oh! Uh... no. It's nothing. Just thinking about my nightmare," I lied. I felt my face redden, and I turned back toward the bedroll we had been lucky enough to salvage from the remains of the carriage. We had only been able to secure one, though, and Finn had insisted that I use it. We had never gone that far in our relationship, and out in the middle of the swamp was not the right time.

Though it would be much easier to hide it from my father out here.

My imagination threatened to get the best of me as I smoothed out the bedroll and cleared my throat before looking back at him. "And call me Ashten. Please. I seriously doubt I'm a princess anymore, anyway."

Finn's eyes softened as what I had said registered. He offered me a soft smile. "Until the king tells me otherwise, I am still the Princess's personal guard. So that means that if I am here with you, you're still the Princess."

My chest tightened at the sentiment and I decided not to push it any further. "You know you need some sleep too, right?" I patted the spot of ground beside me where Finn had set up a sack full of clothing as a pillow, though I had never seen him lay there.

Finn shook his head. "No. One of us must keep watch, and I am used to the lack of sleep." He smiled, but it didn't quite meet his eyes.

My heart dropped at the sudden change in his demeanor, but I couldn't deny that I was tired. The nightmares had been an almost nightly occurrence since the dragon attack. I was grateful that we had stayed near the outside of the stone wall, but we had been trudging through the swamp the entire time. I had heard no sounds from the road the entire time we had been traveling.

"Hey, Finn?" My voice, though barely a whisper, seemed to overpower the lack of sound out here in the swamp.

"Yes, Princess?" He tossed a piece of wood into the fire and smiled at me.

"Why haven't we heard any other carriages since we left Arvandor?" I scooted closer to the fire. "I thought this road was commonly used to transport the weapons that the dynasty needed?"

"It is, but the king only allows one transport at a time. For safety reasons." His smile quickly dissipated. "And, uh, you were the current transport." He cleared his throat. "So the next transport of weapons from Asballicuo is waiting for our arrival."

I tried not to let the idea that I was basically labeled as cargo get to me as I tried to settle back in. "I was just wondering. It would have been nice to see someone else on this road."

"Is my company not good enough for you, Princess?" Finn asked before taking a sip from his canteen.

"Your company is fine, preferred even, but it doesn't help with the fact that I must walk miles to get to somewhere I don't even want to be." I flashed my teeth at him in the largest fake smile I could muster.

Finn rolled his eyes. "Well then, maybe you should get some rest. Might make the walking a little more bearable." I started to protest, but he held a hand up. "No. You sleep, I watch."

I stuck out my bottom lip like a child, which elicited a chuckle from him. "It would make me feel a little less guilty if you at least came and laid down while you kept watch. Just let your body relax, even if your mind won't." I laid down on my back and closed my eyes.

Am I talking to him or myself?

There was a loud *clunk* that I assumed was another piece of wood being tossed into the fire and heard the sack beside me rustle. I didn't have to open my eyes to know that Finn had taken my advice. I heard him sigh as he leaned back against the sack.

"Get some rest," I said, never opening my eyes as I rolled over to my left side to avoid the painful bruise on my right cheek.

"I wish it were that easy, princess." I barely heard him mumble before I drifted off into the beckoning darkness.

Me too.

Chapter 6

Finn

I settled in beside Ashten and waited for her to fall asleep. Once her breathing became rhythmic and it had been a while since she moved, I got up and moved back to my place beside the fire. From here I could see her face much clearer thanks to the illumination from the fire. I knew that she and I were close in age, but she looked so young sleeping here by the fire. Her long black hair fell across her face, providing a dark frame for her perfect, almost blemish free skin. The bruise from her father had darkened into a deep purple and I was sure it would be yellow in a few days.

It had been harder than I expected to restrain myself when he hit her.

Luckily, it didn't seem that she had sustained any injuries from the dragon attack. She wasn't malnourished, but she was definitely thin and didn't have any muscle to speak of. That would need to change, and quickly, if she were to survive for long. One week. She just needed to make it through one week. The problem was that I didn't know if she could even do that.

Ashten thrived on pure stubbornness and an unrelenting desire to break the rules. Our relationship alone was proof of that. She stood up to her father without a second thought. Something I had seen no one do. Then, she actually chased off a dragon. If that strong will didn't get her killed first, she would become the perfect champion for her dynasty. She already had the unbreakable will, and what we were doing at the Asballicuo would help her develop an unbreakable body. Or it would break her and this would all be for nothing.

I couldn't help but wonder why the king had chosen his own daughter for this. King Renlin knew exactly what went on behind those closed doors. I couldn't think of anything that the sleeping female in front of me could have done to deserve this.

I shook my head and ran my hands through my hair. It wasn't my job to decide if someone *deserved* to go to Asballicuo because most people didn't. It was my job to escort them there and back, if they made it that long. I was built to follow orders. That's it.

I just needed to get her to Asballicuo. Then I could go back to my normal life and forget about her. I could forget about how beautiful her violet eyes were. Forget about how she was watching me through the fire earlier. Forget about the way she tried to hide her face when I caught her staring. Forget about how perfect she looked as she slept right now.

But there was one thing that I don't think I could ever forget.

This was the Princess. Heir to the throne of the Desai Dynasty. And I was most certainly leading her to her death.

Chapter 7

Ashten

The next morning came faster than I wanted, but at least the rest of my sleep was free of strange magic and talking creatures. I woke up to the sound of Finn stomping out the fire. When I sat up, I noticed he had on all of his armor and had already packed up our little camp. How long had he been awake? How long had he let me sleep?

Finn glanced in my direction and stifled a small smile before looking away. "Sleep alright?" he asked, continuing to make sure the fire was sufficiently put out. Not that a fire could spread in this swampy land.

I crawled out of the bedroll and stood, straightening my clothes and picking up the bedroll. "Uh... yeah. No more nightmares, if that's what you're asking." I voiced a frustrated huff as I tried, and failed, to roll up the bedroll.

Finn walked over and grabbed the bedroll from the heap on the ground where I had thrown it. He effortlessly rolled it up and tied it to his pack. He grunted as he picked up the pack and settled it on his back. "Are you ready to keep going?"

"Why do you have to act like that was so easy?" I asked, the annoyance in my voice in stark contrast to the smile on my face.

"What?" Finn asked, shrugging and looking around mockingly.

I affixed him with a glare. "You just rolled that bedroll without even looking at it." I motioned dramatically towards his pack.

Finn smiled and shrugged. "The benefits of having done it a few hundred times? I could probably do it in my sleep."

"Well, that only works if you sleep." I joked. "Which I'm sure you don't, seeing as you had the entire camp packed when I woke up this morning."

"Well, at least I don't always look like I just got out of bed," he quipped back. I gave him a quizzical look, and he paused for a minute before clarifying. "You know. Because of the pajamas." He gestured to my clothing, trying and failing to suppress another smile.

I looked down at my body as the realization sank in that I was still in my pajamas from that night. The black pants were covered in a dull layer of gray dust and the sandals I had been given by the guards were covered in mud. My red shirt was frayed at the hem and had a few small holes in it from the dragon attack. I couldn't help the anger that welled up in me as I assessed my current state.

My glare tightened. "Well, I wouldn't still be in my pajamas if *someone* wouldn't have dragged me out of my bed in the middle of the night, stuffed me into a carriage, and hauled me to the other side of the continent." My words sounded harsher than I had intended, and Finn stiffened as they hit home. I reached toward him, fumbling over an apology, but he turned away.

"I'm sorry..." Finn mumbled as he started back on the road. He didn't look back to see if I was following.

My heart dropped. I had meant what I said, but his reaction was unexpected. I couldn't ignore the twinge of guilt that I felt. It wasn't really his fault, was it? He was just following orders.

Orders that my father had given him.

I considered trying to say something to convince Finn that I hadn't meant it, but that would be a lie. Something deep down told me the damage was already done and that lying would only make it worse. I gathered myself and hurried after Finn. He didn't even glance in my direction, and the ache in my chest grew worse as we walked in silence.

The next few days of our journey consisted of a silent routine. Finn had said little since our argument. We had fought before, but we had never gone this long without talking.

We had also never had an argument about him kidnapping me.

I hadn't quit feeling bad about what I said and had thought about apologizing multiple times, but every time I tried to talk to him,

A. Turner

I only got short answers. He hadn't even acknowledged me the last two nights when I woke up screaming after another series of horrible nightmares. I did, however, wake up this morning to a fresh set of clothing that must have been spares for him. I asked him about them, but, true to the theme of the past few days, he only signaled for me to hurry as he turned around so that I could change. The clothing was much too big for me, but at least it was clean. I tucked the shirt in and used a piece of rope as a belt to hold the pants up. Finn silently took my dirty clothes from me and placed them in his pack. I started to thank him for the clothing, but he just turned away.

Our silence had given me time to think, at the least. I had never been this far from the Alterwood Citadel, had never left Arvandor before, and definitely wasn't used to all of this walking. I knew this road through the Deadlands was not often used, but I had expected to find at least one other transport wagon after we slipped through a crevice in the wall and back onto the main road. Finn was right, though, and that had not been the case. Instead, I had to suffer through this awkward silence of my own making. It was causing this trip to feel much like being at home.

Except the fact that if I were at home, Finn would be the *only* one talking to me. I couldn't explain why, but I missed hearing his voice. Missed hearing his accent as he teased me about how out of shape I was. I missed the awkward smile he gave every time I jokingly scolded him for calling me princess. I even kind of missed him calling me princess. The only person in my life that treated me like a normal person and I had seemingly ruined it. My heart ached, and I hated the feeling.

I was pulled out of my thoughts when Finn started talking to the guard stationed at the bridge gate. They were both speaking in that choppy language that I didn't understand. Lucky for me, understanding words had nothing to do with my ability to understand inflection and context. Finn motioned at me and then pointed at the bridge. The guard he was talking to looked at me and hesitated when we made eye contact. I held his stare for a few seconds before Finn shoved his shoulder. Finn made a very demanding statement, and the guard immediately looked apologetic. The guard raised his hands defensively before motioning to the other guard to raise the gate. Finn turned to me and waved me forward. It was the most acknowledgment he had given me in the past few days. I hurried behind him as the gate opened and we walked through.

I couldn't help but gape at what waited on the other side of the massive stone wall and gate that protected this long, stone bridge. To either side was nothing but blue water as far as I could see. It was beautiful and I could see what I was sure were ships off in the distance. They were just little black dots scattered amongst the vastness of the ocean. I had seen nothing like it. It was *almost* enough to distract me from what was directly in front of me. On the other side of the bridge loomed another tall wall and gate, but I could see the looming volcano that stood on the other side of that wall. There was smoke billowing out of its top, causing a layer of black ash that seemed to envelop the entire island. If I could remember correctly from my studies, this was Oshos Island, and that was Mount Wrath. The volcano was beautiful too, but in a way that made the hair on my neck stand up.

I cleared my throat to get Finn's attention. "Have you been here before?" I asked, hoping he would at least answer my questions.

Finn turned his head toward me. "The island? Yeah. I used to be...stationed here." He hesitated for a second. "It's been a few years, though."

"What was it like?" I asked, trying to keep this conversation going. I needed to find the courage to apologize, but right now, I was stalling.

"Hot. Very hot." He let a smile lift the corner of his mouth.

I glared at him, but made sure to pair it with a smile so that he would hopefully know I wasn't truly mad. "Okay, I walked into that one."

"Yeah, well, we've been doing a lot of walking, so I can't really blame you." Finn shrugged and looked at the mountain in front of us as he proceeded walk.

I took this as my opportunity. Grabbing his arm, I pulled him to a stop. I swallowed the lump in my throat as he turned to look at me. "I'm sorry." The words left my mouth before I could change my mind. "I, uh, said some hurtful things that I didn't really mean. Well, I guess I meant them at the time, but then I realized that it hurt your feelings and I didn't want to do that and I know you would never hurt me on purpose and—" The words tumbled out of my mouth unimpeded before Finn held up a hand.

"It's alright, Princess," Finn said, giving me a soft smile. My heart softened at the sight of it. "I should have offered you my spare clothing sooner." He looked me up and down with dark eyes, and my face reddened at his insinuation. I tried to look down, but he gently placed a hand on my chin, lifting my head so that my eyes met his. My first instinct was to recoil at the touch, but a calming warmth washed over me. "I know you didn't mean it, but maybe we will think before we speak next time?" He lowered his hand back to his side and turned to walk away.

I could feel Finn's smirk even though his back was to me. I was completely speechless as he walked up to the guards that were stationed on the island side of the bridge.

Ridiculous.

Chapter 8

Ashten

It was another day-long walk to Asballicuo across the barren desert landscape of Oshos Island. Unlike the past five days, we did not have a stone wall to follow. This left me on edge, and if I was on edge, then Finn was about to fall off. I walked a little behind him and could see the stiffness in his gait. He kept his hand on his sword hilt, and he was constantly scanning the surrounding area. Every few minutes, he glanced back at me to ensure that I was still there, but he made no effort to say anything to me. This silence was different than before. It seemed to be a side effect of whatever was going on inside his head.

We continued in this eerie silence even as the sun began to set. I was grateful for the lower temperature that the sun's absence allowed, but I wasn't too keen on the thought of having to camp out in the open at night. Ahead of me, Finn stopped and looked around the area before silently placing his pack on the ground, untying the bedroll, and handing it to me. I laid it out and sat down. I watched him as he stood with his back to me, silently removing the bulkiest parts of his armor. He never removed all of his armor before resting, and tonight was no exception. After removing his greaves, breastplate, and pauldrons, he laid them neatly aside before gathering what few pieces of brush were available to start a fire. His silence continued as he worked, and I wasn't sure if I should try to help or let him have some space. He started the fire and threw a few more pieces of brush onto it before sitting down on the side opposite of me.

He drew his knees to his chest, crossing his arms and resting his head on top of them. His blank stare was lost in the fire and I couldn't help but realize just how different he looked in this moment. He looked so small, and the way the flames were illuminating his face brought to light just how young he really was. I knew he was my age, but I had always viewed him as just a little bit older.

I cleared my throat, and Finn slowly looked at me. "Everything okay? If you're still upset with me, I understand. I really am sorry, though."

Finn ran his hand through his short hair and leaned his head back, looking at the star-filled sky. He inhaled deeply, holding it for a moment before blowing the air out through clenched teeth. "Promise me something, Princess."

I didn't bother to correct him. Instead, I leaned in closer to the fire. "What's wrong?"

Finn doesn't look down at me. "Promise me you will never change."

"What do you mean? Why would I change?"

Finn finally looked back at me. He clenched his jaw, grinding his teeth so hard I was afraid he may crack them. "Where we are going... I've been there. I've been inside the Asballicuo." He closed his eyes, lost in his head for a moment, before continuing. "I know you're well-learned. You know what Asballicuo is, right? What it *truly* is."

I swallowed gingerly. Sure, I knew what the Asballicuo was. That knowledge being relevant was not something I had considered until now. "Uh... yeah. Yeah, I've heard the rumors," I mumbled, looking down at the ground in front of me.

"They aren't just rumors." His voice was stern now. Like it was when he had taken me from my room in the Alterwood Citadel. I looked back up at him and met his green eyes. The usual brightness in them was nowhere to be found.

"What do you mean, they aren't just rumors? Asballicuo *is* an armory. I've seen the labeled crates of swords, shields, and armor that's been brought back from there. Everything else is all hearsay—"

"It's all *true,* Ashten." Finn stood up, once again running his hand over his head. He began pacing back and forth on the other side of the fire. "The things they do... Just promise me you will follow the rules." His eyes were pleading as he stopped to stare at me.

I let out a small chuckle. "Finn. You can't be serious." I watched, waiting for his expression to change. His green eyes stayed focused on me, and his expression stayed grim. "I think we both know how improbable that is. Not following the rules is precisely what got me into this situation in the first place."

"And it's going to get you killed if you can't control yourself!" he shouted, turning to face me. I flinched, sliding back on the bedroll and throwing my hands over myself. I peeked between my arms as he stalked over to me and knelt in front of me. He studied me for a moment and I waited for him to hit me like my father had. His fists were clenched at his sides, but I watched as his stern gaze softened, showing a little more of the Finn I had gotten to know while we grew up together.

He gently reached out and placed his hand on my arms. I pulled against him, but his grip only got tighter. "I promise I will never hit you, Princess."

I couldn't explain it, but I could feel the tension and fear leave my body as he lowered my arms to my lap.

Of course he wouldn't hit me.

"In all the time that we have spent with each other, I have become very aware of how you feel about authority. Your strong will is what makes you who you are, and it is one of my favorite things about you. But it is also your greatest weakness, and that is what those at the Asballicuo prey on. They look for your weaknesses, and once they find them, they hammer them out of you. The place is a forge in more than just the conventional sense." Finn's expression changed to one of confusion when I smiled at him, raising an eyebrow.

"You have favorite things about me?" I asked, my smile widening.

"I tell you that the place you will be spending an unforeseen amount of your future at is a hard, cold, unforgiving place, and all you hear is that I like you." Finn shook his head but did nothing to hide the soft smile that crept across his face. "I thought that was something we had already established, Princess."

I had grown to love seeing that smile. I didn't have to tell him that I still didn't believe him. "Well, light always shines brightest in the dark, right?" I held my hand out and conjured a small flame. "It just so happens that I have quite a bit of light at my disposal."

Finn hung his head and laughed, and it may have been the best thing I had heard in a long time. When he laughed, he didn't look like the hardened soldier I knew he was. He looked more my age than he ever had. His shoulders relaxed a little as the laughter seemed to force the tension out of his body. He looked back at me, his eyes a little softer now. I dismissed the flame and leaned back, propping myself up with both arms.

Finn stared at me for a moment before letting out another sigh. "Well, you should probably try to get some sleep. It may be the last chance you get for a good night's rest."

"And what about you? Don't you need to sleep?" I knew he would refuse, but I didn't want to tell him the real reason for my offer. Sleep had eluded me since my first nightmare. I had suffered through the same dream every night since.

Finn shook his head and turned so that he was seated beside me. "No. I'll get a few hours after you wake up. Someone needs to keep watch."

I laid down on my back, looking up at the stars above me. Like that night in the bath, I could feel the night calling to me.

If only I knew how to answer.

Just another thought keeping me away from sleep. I rolled onto my side and tried to get comfortable.

"So, you have more than one favorite thing about me?" I asked, smiled in the darkness.

I heard Finn snort and could picture the smile he had on his face. "There are plenty of things I like about you, Princess."

My face reddened at his words, and I waited for him to continue, but he didn't. Instead, silence washed over us both as I found myself drifting off to sleep.

A. Turner

The night was quiet, which meant I should have gotten a good amount of sleep. My mind, however, had a different idea. I had already woken up twice in the middle of the night thanks to my nightmares. Each time, Finn was there, comforting and reassuring me. He offered me water and made sure I was comfortable before urging me to try to sleep again. I had protested both times, but he was adamant that he didn't need any sleep. This most recent time, I had found it hard to get back to sleep. This was probably why I woke up so quickly when I heard the yelling.

I shot up in my bedroll and looked around. The yelling was very loud, and it took me a second to realize that it was coming from Finn. I looked over to where he had settled in last to see him laying on his side with his back to me. The yelling that had woken me up had been replaced with soft whimpering as he lay there.

So this is why he hasn't been sleeping.

I crawled over to him, grabbing his shoulders and rolling him onto his back. Finn woke up with a jolt, his hand flying out to where he had left his sword laying in the sand.

"Hey, hey, hey." I shushed as I placed a hand on his sword arm in an effort to keep him from swinging it at me. "It's just me. It's Ashten. I think you were having a nightmare."

Finn's eyes darted from side to side, taking in their surroundings. I sat back and waited for him to settle as the adrenaline wore off. Finn took a deep breath and finally let go of his sword. He ran his hands through his hair and wiped the sweat from his brow. He took another deep breath before he laid a hand on my leg.

"Thank you," he said. His voice was thick with sleep and he cleared his throat. "I didn't mean to scare you and I'm sorry that I woke you. You should go back to sleep."

I couldn't believe what I was hearing. This man, who had forgone more than an hour or two of sleep a day for at least the past week, was apologizing for falling asleep and having a nightmare.

"There is nothing for you to apologize for, Finn." I reached up and rubbed the side of his face with my thumb. "You never mentioned that you have nightmares. All these years and I've never known it."

Finn offered me an unconvincing smile. "It's never come up." He paused for a second. "They started after I returned from Asballicuo..." Finn inhaled, "but I can't help but feel bad for waking you after you tried so hard to go to sleep."

"I think that, maybe, it was the universe telling us that neither of us need any more sleep." A soft laugh escaped me at the incredulous look Finn gave me. "I mean it. I know it's still dark, but I am not in a hurry to have another nightmare. I think I would honestly prefer to just sit here and watch the night sky. The moon and stars are quite fascinating." I laid on my back beside Finn, lacing my fingers behind my head as a headrest.

Finn laid back down beside me and crossed his arms over his chest. "A Solar Elf fascinated with the moon. Your mysteries are unending, Princess." Finn shook his head in mock disdain. "What's next? Are you going to tell me you prefer winter over summer?"

I elbowed Finn in the ribs as we both laughed. Our banter and jokes continued well into the morning as we packed up camp and began the final leg of our journey. Even through all of the laughter, I couldn't shake the look that was on Finn's face when I first woke him up.

Terror.

Chapter 9

Ashten

Our walk was taking us closer to the volcano, but I had yet to see any sort of building or towers. From what I understood, we were less than a day's walk away from Asballicuo when we set out this morning. It was now midday and there was no sign of civilization. The sun was beaming down on us. The heat was near unbearable and the reflection off of the sand was blinding.

I shielded my eyes with my hand and turned to Finn, who had been mostly silent since we started walking this morning. He was walking a little slower than normal and seemed to be lost in thought.

"Something bothering you?" I asked, snapping him out of his trance. "I mean, other than the obvious." I gestured widely at the desert surrounding us. "You've been quiet all morning and I'm pretty sure that if a dragon was flying over us right now, you wouldn't even notice."

He rested his arm on the hilt of his sword, letting the other hang lazily at his side. "Have you been watching me all morning, Ashten?" He smirked, and I felt my face redden.

Why did I feel like this every time he smiled at me?

"Well, it's not like I have had much else to look at since we've been walking through the middle of nowhere all morning." I tried to cover the embarrassment in my voice.

Finn held his hands up defensively. "I mean, I don't blame you. A lot of work went into looking like this and *I* appreciate that *you* seem to appreciate it." The smirk on his face widened into a large smile, and I rubbed my hands over my face in exasperation.

"How or why I was looking at you is none of your business." I made a show of rolling my eyes. "I just wanted to know if you were okay, but you seem just fine."

"What if I said that how I felt was none of your business, Princess?" Finn looked back ahead of us, but his smile never left his face.

"Well then, forget I asked!" I shouted. "See if I care next time." I dropped back a few steps behind him and crossed my arms.

Finn stopped, shaking his head. "You make this too easy, princess. Just a few sentences to get you pouting like a child. If it is this easy to get under your skin, you won't last long when we get in there." He pointed to the volcano.

I looked at him quizzically. "What do you mean 'in there'? We aren't headed to the volcano."

"You haven't actually seen the Asballicuo before, have you?" He walked back towards me as I shook my head. He stopped behind me and gently placed one hand on my shoulder, pointing with the other. "Look right there. See that cliff jutting out from the side of the volcano?"

I squinted as I looked for what he was trying to show me, but all I could focus on was the rhythmic rise and fall of his chest against my back. The entire mountainside looked the same to me. I was aware of every movement as he slid his hand from my shoulder to the side of my face. He gently grabbed my chin and guided my head to the right, carefully avoiding the bruise on my face. It was then that I could see the cliff he was talking about. Under it, I could just barely make out a small cavern at the base of the mountain. We were probably only a mile or so away from it.

I swallowed loudly and cleared my throat. "That cave? That's where we are going?" Despite my efforts, my voice still betrayed me and I felt Finn laugh softly.

"Yep. A cave in the side of a volcano. The perfect cover for a secret forge." Finn pulled away from me and I hated myself for leaning into where he had been standing. He walked past me and stood with his back to me before holding his hand out. "Come on. We don't have much longer before they will start sending someone out to find us."

I didn't give it much thought before I took his hand and smiled as he pulled me towards the mountain. My chest tightened as the reality of how close we were began to set in. Finn must have been able to tell because he rubbed his thumb leisurely over the back of my hand. I felt myself relax, losing myself in the rhythm of it. I began to wonder if the reassurance was for me or himself when I heard him let out a long sigh.

"So..." I didn't bother to look over at him and instead let myself focus on my hand in his. "Did you really do all that just to try to make me mad?"

Finn's responding laugh washed over me, bringing a much needed feeling of happiness to the unexplainable sense of dread that I was feeling.

As the cave became clearer, I could see that it was barred shut with a large metal gate. On either side of the gate stood a guard. These guards wore the same armor as Finn. Their red shirt and pants stood out against the onyx greaves, vambraces, and breastplate. The dark helmet was shaped like the head of a dragon. Where the eyes should be sat two golden gems that matched the golden dragon, wings spread wide, in the center of the breastplate.

Finn stopped a little bit away from the gate and turned to me. He let go of my hand and reached into his bag, pulling out his own dragon helmet. A helmet he hadn't worn since the dragon attack. He inspected it for a second before looking back at me.

"I need you to understand something, Ashten." I raised my eyebrows at him, urged him to continue. Finn let his arms hang in front of him, the helmet sandwiched between them. "When I put this helmet back on, I am going to become someone you will not recognize. Someone you will not like." He looked down at the helmet once more. "I don't like it either, but I don't have a choice."

"What do you mean?" I waited for him to answer, but he didn't. He just stared down at the helmet. I waited through his silence a few seconds more before placing my hands over his. "Hey. There is *nothing* you could do that could make me hate you."

"You haven't seen the things that I've done with this helmet on." Finn's head was still hanging, and my heart ached at how defeated he looked. He finally looked up and I could see the tears that had started to form at the edge of his eyes. I had known him most of my life and I could count on one hand the number of times I had seen Finn cry.

I reached up and placed my hands on either side of his face. I pulled his head towards me and placed a gentle kiss on his forehead. Something my mother used to do to me when I was feeling down. I kept my hands on his face as he looked back at me. He placed one of his hands over mine as he closed his eyes, leaning into my touch.

"This past week has been the best week that I have had in such a long time. I know it didn't start out great, but I want you to know that if given the chance, I would do it again." Finn stepped back away from me and held the helmet up again. "Kidnapping you may just turn out to be the best thing that has ever happened to me." His voice cracked a little.

He reluctantly put on the helmet and took a deep breath. We made eye contact and I could see the tear that had fallen down his face. "Nothing?" he asked, taking another deep breath.

I reached up and wiped the tear from his cheek. "Nothing."

Finn grabbed me by the arm and started leading me toward the gate. He leaned down and began talking in my ear, his voice suddenly very serious. "Now listen very closely. These people know that you did not come here willingly, but that is the extent of what they know. They do not know where you are coming from or who you are." I jerked my head to look at him, but he quickly grabbed my chin and forced my head forward. "They also do not know how *informal* our relationship is, Princess. My suggestion is that all of that information is kept between the two of us. Especially that last part." I heard him laugh under his breath, but he quickly regained his composure.

"When we get to that gate, you will keep your head down. You will only speak to guards when directly spoken to. And you will, under no circumstances, tell anyone that you are the princess. That is your best chance of surviving there. Is that understood?"

I still wasn't entirely convinced, but Finn's anxiety was infectious. The lump in my throat only grew as I swallowed and nodded my head. I was rewarded with a tightened grip on my arm as Finn jerked me toward him.

"Use your words."

I could feel that little flame of anger well up in me, but even I knew now was not the time. I closed my eyes and inhaled deeply before speaking through gritted teeth. "Yes, Finn, I—"

Finn's grip on my arm tightened. "Not the right words, Princess."

I took another deep breath before continuing. "Yes, sir. I understand." I hung my head down and watched my feet drag through the sand.

"Good." Finn's grip on my arm loosened a little, and he pushed me forward so that I was walking in front of him. "Head down and mouth shut."

Chapter 10

Ashten

I did as he said, keeping my head down and my mouth shut while we approached the gate. Although he would never hear me say it, Finn was right. My best chances sat with swallowing my pride and doing as I was told, no matter how much it burned going down. At least until I could find out what exactly was going on in there and find a way to get home.

I intend to go home.

Finn suddenly jerked me to a stop. I risked a glance upward to see that we had made it to the front of the volcano. I didn't have to look at him to know that Finn was talking to the guard. They were both speaking in that language I didn't understand. I wished I had asked him to teach me some of it. Or that I had at least asked him what it was called. The words were short and contained very few vowels. I must have stared too long because I felt a strong hand on the back of my head. I was pushed forward, the hand keeping my head down while guiding me.

"I said head down, soldier." Finn barked, the loudness of it startling me and causing me to trip. Finn grabbed the back of my shirt to keep me from falling.

I kept my head down and allowed myself to be led through the creaky doors as they opened. We walked a short distance before stopping in front of a desk. There were papers scattered on the desk, but none of them were in a language I could read.

"Name?" a soft, feminine voice purred. I opened my mouth to speak, but Finn's grip on my neck tightened. I sucked in a breath as he answered for me.

"Ashten Ward." Finn paused for a second as she scanned the sheet of paper in front of her. "She probably isn't on the list. This one is a special case. Sent straight from the king."

The woman at the desk sighed, and I heard her get up from her chair and walk around the desk. "Well then, let me have a look at you. I am going to need some defining features to make you easier to identify in the future." Finn released his grip on the back of my neck just as the woman in front of me grabbed my chin and forced my head up. My pulse quickened, but any thoughts of resisting left my head when I saw who, or *what*, was in front of me.

My eyes first noticed the claws on the hand that grabbed my chin. I followed the length of her pale arm to her shoulder and up her neck to her face. She had dark, void-like eyes framed by large, round glasses. Black horns emerged from her short, curly black hair and curled back to just barely touch her rounded ears. Large, black, webbed wings were tucked neatly behind her. She was a daemonfolk. One with human ancestors, from what I could tell. I had only heard horror stories about her kind from my instructors. I swallowed thickly as she continued to assess me.

"Hmmm." She roughly turned my head to the left, pausing for a second before turning it to the right. "Other than this bruise, there is not a single defining feature about you, Elf. And it looks like it will be completely gone in a day or so, so I'm not even going to bother writing it down. How old are you?" She let go of my face and walked back to her desk, sitting down and leaning over a piece of paper.

I didn't answer immediately, and I was rewarded for that by a hand on my back pushing me towards the desk until my knees slammed into it. I suppressed a whimper and turned to look at Finn. His face was blank and his eyes emotionless. I guess the Finn I knew was out for the day. He was all business now.

"Answer the question, soldier." His hand on my back didn't give when I tried to back up.

Trying my best to remember all the rules Finn gave me before, I focused my eyes on the paper with my name on it that this woman was writing on. I could barely see her at the top of my vision. "Just turned twenty-one last week." I watched as the woman wrote that down and started to ask more questions.

Eye color. Height. Weight. The list went on and on, but I answered every single question. I felt like I was watching my life story being written on this paper. The only thing missing was probably the most important thing about me. It wasn't that I had ever been particularly attached to my title. There had just never been a time in my life that I had existed without it. Yet, there I was, watching that exact detail be left out of what was to be my record of existence in this place. The woman finished writing and looked up at me over her glasses.

"Well, Ashten. Welcome to Asballicuo." She motioned to the other side of the room. "This guard will take you to the testing chamber. You will be placed with your unit based on the results of that testing. From there, you will follow the instructions of your unit leader."

I could hear approaching footsteps before I felt someone grab my arm. I looked over my shoulder, careful to keep my eyes down, to see that Finn's hand wrapped around my arm.

"That won't be necessary." His voice was tight. "I have been instructed to personally escort this one to testing and then to her unit to ensure that she arrives there safely."

The daemonfolk woman began to speak, but Finn held up his hand, cutting her off. "This one is *very* important to the king." He didn't give her time to respond before quickly pulling me towards the door. The guard at the door silently stepped out of the way. The latch was lifted and the heavy metal door ground opened, allowing Finn and I through.

Finn finally slowed down once we heard the click of the latch being replaced on the door behind us. I could feel the shift in his weight as he leaned down until his head was right beside mine.

"Continue walking, head down." His voice was low, but softer than it had been just a few moments ago. We walked down a series of hallways, the sounds of steel on steel and billowing fire getting louder the farther we walked.

"What is going on?" I tried to keep my voice low as I continued to look at the dark stone floor. "What did she mean by testing? And what is a unit? Why do you keep calling me 'soldier'?"

Finn stopped, looking around a corner briefly before pulling me around it. I risked looking up to see that we were in a little alcove. It was dimly lit by the golden, magically colored orbs of light that lined the gray stone hallway. He held me out at arm's length and looked me up and down. I opened my mouth to speak, but he spoke first.

"Every person who comes to Asballicuo is tested for magic. This is so that you can be placed into a unit with others whose magical affinity will complement yours. A unit is a group of four individuals with similar magical or combat abilities." Finn leaned out of the alcove and looked around before taking his helmet off and carefully placing it on the ground beside him. "I keep calling you 'soldier' because that's what you are to everyone here."

I had so many questions, but I decided to start with the one that was probably the easiest. "Why can't anyone know that I'm the princess?"

"What do you think would happen if the people here found out that the daughter of the one who sent them to this place is here and up for grabs? Because anything goes here, Princess."

I swallowed the lump in my throat. "What do you mean *anything goes?*" I felt like I knew the answer already, but I needed to hear him say it.

"I mean that *anything goes.* Anything that any other soldier may have to do to survive or gain fame here. It could be something as simple as manipulating their commanding officer, but it often escalates to *much* more sinister things." Finn stopped talking, undoubtedly giving my imagination time to fill in the blanks. Which it was doing. Spectacularly.

I swallowed again. "Also, why did you tell them my last name was Ward? Isn't that your last name?"

Finn smiled devilishly. "Yes it is, Princess. I think it sounds heavenly with your name attached to it." Finn leaned in closer, caging me between his arms. "But. The actual reason is because you need a last name that doesn't scream 'Look at me! I'm the Princess!' and no one here knows my last name."

I reached up and flicked his nose. He snapped at my finger, and I covered my mouth to try to silence my giggle. "So, what now?"

I was caught off guard as Finn leaned in for a kiss. It was rough and quick, but I was left breathless when he pulled away. He leaned out of the alcove and looked both ways before looking back at me.

"We probably have a few more minutes before they start wondering where we went off to." Finn leaned in for another kiss, stopping just as his lips brushed mine. "I'm not sure how long it will be before we can do this again, Princess."

He didn't wait for me to say anything else before kissing me again. He slid one hand down the wall and wrapped it around my waist, pulling my body flush against his. I couldn't help but melt into his touch. As I did, Finn deepened the kiss, using his body to pin me between him and the wall. Suddenly, it felt like we weren't close enough. I reached around his waist in search of cloth, but he was still in full armor. I whined in frustration when I couldn't find anything to grab to pull him closer to me.

I felt his smile against my lips. He broke his pattern of kisses to lean his head past mine, lips against my ear. "Something the matter, Princess?" he whispered, voice low and raspy. He wasted no time peppering my neck with soft kisses.

"Yeah." I was finding it very hard to form full sentences with his lips on my neck. "Full armor is not the best attire for our current *activities."* I leaned my head back against the stone wall. I tried my best to stay quiet when his hand slipped under the back of my shirt. A laugh rumbled from deep in his chest when I failed miserably. His hand splayed flat against my back, a chill running down my spine in response.

"Do you intend to undress me right here in this hallway?" Finn pulled back from my neck, putting just enough space between us to run his gaze over me. "Because I cannot say that I would be complaining, Princess. You can't possibly think that I could resist you wearing my shirt for much longer." He rested his forehead on mine, seemingly waiting for my response.

I felt my face redden and pulse quicken even more at the thought. Most of our times alone were like this. Hasty kisses and subtle touches in hidden hallways. There was something added by the idea that we could be caught at any moment. Rarely did we have enough time to take things much further. However, I wholly believed that he would allow me to undress him right here in this hallway, if the rise and fall of his chest were any indication. I knew that I didn't look much more composed. I was acutely aware of the racing of my own heart and the flush on my own cheeks.

I wasn't given the chance to answer him before I heard the sound of boots on the stone floor coming down the hall. Finn picked up his helmet and placed it on his head. He guided me to the furthest back wall of the alcove, placing one finger over his mouth in a 'be quiet' sign. He smoothed my shirt, smirking as he turned to walk out of the alcove and cleared his throat.

I leaned back against the wall and closed my eyes. Out of all of the times for us to get caught, this would have to be the worst. Though arguably not the most dangerous. I couldn't understand what was being said, but I could hear two voices. Finn's and one of another male. Time seemed to stretch on as they talked before I heard the other man laugh loudly, Finn chuckling alongside him. I couldn't help but roll my eyes.

How could he go from making me feel like this to cracking jokes with some random guard? Males.

One pair of footsteps receded. I held my breath as the second set of footsteps made their way towards me. If it wasn't Finn, I didn't even know what kind of trouble I was going to be in. Luckily, Finn walked around the corner a few seconds later, helmet nestled under his arm. He looked so perfect. Not at all like we had been debating undressing each other in this hallway mere moments earlier. Judging by the way he was looking at me right now, he was probably still debating it.

"Well, Princess, as much as I would like to pick up where we left off, duty calls." Finn placed a quick kiss on my lips. "For both of us. They are waiting for us in the testing chamber." He looked me up and down for the third time in the past hour. "I'll make sure you get to keep those clothes when you are issued your uniform."

I couldn't help but scoff at his forwardness. "And what makes you think you can do that?"

Apparently in some sort of hurry now, Finn slid his helmet back onto his head. "I have my ways, Princess."

I rolled my eyes once again as he grabbed my shoulder and led me out of the hall with him. He placed one hand flat on my back and all I could think about was how that same hand had felt against my bare skin moments before. My imagination wandered as we walked, causing me to involuntarily jump when I felt Finn's lips brush against my ear.

"Best get your thoughts under control, Princess." he whispered as we remained in motion. I started to question how he knew what I was thinking about, but he cut me off. "We wouldn't want any of those wonderful images becoming public knowledge."

My face felt like it was on fire as we walked down the hall in what I could assume was the direction of the testing chamber. Whatever that meant.

Chapter 11

Ashten

We came to a stop outside a large set of iron doors. I kept my head down, but tried to lift my eyes and looked ahead of me to see two guards standing post outside. Finn kept one arm on my shoulder and used the other to push open the doors. He spoke quickly to the guards. Whatever he had said, it must not have been important, because neither of them responded as we walked through the door. We stepped into a dimly lit staircase that wound down. Several stories down if I judged by how long it took us to descend, paired with the fact that I could no longer hear the sounds of the armory. Finn pushed open another door at the bottom of this staircase and led me into the adjoining room.

I honestly didn't know what I was expecting, but this was not it. When they said that I was to undergo testing, I could only imagine some sort of written exam. I don't know why I had thought that would work, but it was the only type of testing that I was familiar with. Instead, before me was a stone room in the same color as everything else I had seen so far. It had the same golden orbs casting their glow. In the center of this room was a singular metal chair. There were two metal rods on the ends of the armrests as well as leather straps hanging from the arms and legs of this chair. The only comforting thing about it was the cushioned headrest.

Behind the chair was a Solar Elf female. Her black hair was cut into a pixie cut that framed her pointed features well. Unlike me, her eyes were a bright blue. She was wearing black trousers with a white tunic and wore a deep red overcoat that ended sharply at her belt. Embroidered in the front of her coat in gold letters was:

"Naerys Laeovyn"

"Welcome to the testing room." The female walked around to the side of the chair, her hands clasped in front of her. Her voice was light and airy as she addressed me. "If you will please take a seat in the chair so that we can begin."

Finn led me to the center of the room and forced me to sit in the chair. He gently wrapped my hands around the metal rods and proceeded to fasten my arms down with the leather straps. I watched as he knelt in front of me to reach the straps on my legs. My heart began to race, and my throat tightened with each notch on the strap. Finn never once looked at me as he finished with the straps and walked to the other side of the room. There, he stood at attention. A vision of the perfect soldier. Silence filled the room until all I could hear was the beating of my own heart.

I nearly jumped out of my skin when a hand was placed on either side of my head and Laeovyn's voice cut through the silence. "Don't worry darling, this shouldn't hurt. The straps are merely a precaution."

A. Turner

Why would they need to take precautions?

My thoughts were cut short as a chilling sensation washed over me, starting where the professor's hands were on my head. My already racing heart picked up pace as my entire body tightened. My hands closed tightly around the metal rods. Everything was tense. My muscles felt like they were one wrong move away from snapping my bones. I frantically scanned the room for Finn. I found him staring at me, his fists clenched at his side. As we made eye contact, he began to take deep, rhythmic breaths. *In and out. In and out.* Just like he had taught me to control my anger when we were children. He always said it was something his mother had taught him to control his emotions. I was beginning to doubt the validity of that story.

Now is not the time for that discussion.

I tried to copy him, but it felt impossible to fill my lungs. I fought against the restraints as the fear of not being able to breathe began to take over.

Then, as quick as the icy feeling came, it was gone. Replaced by a calming warmth. My entire body relaxed involuntarily, and I exhaled slowly. My eyelids were heavy and, though I was fighting it, it became apparent that I wasn't going to win. My head lulled back against the cushioned headrest as my eyes closed and my entire world went dark.

When my eyes opened again, I was standing in front of my bed in Arvandor. I spun around, taking in the rest of the scene. Sun leaked in through the window and bounced off of the golden walls. A few books were scattered on the floor and the chair to my desk had been knocked over. It was undoubtedly my room. That was impossible, though. At least it should be. The last thing I remembered was being in the chair at Asballicuo. This must be some dream. Or a hallucination. That Elf must have done something to me.

A soft sob from the bed caught my attention. Who was in my bed? I gingerly walked over and peered over the top of the covers. A little girl, no older than eight, lay there crying. Tears poured from her violet eyes as she brushed her black hair out of her face and sat up. She looked right at me and I froze. She stared only for a second before getting up and walking to the desk. She opened the top drawer and pulled out a broken wooden doll. She sank to her knees and laid the pieces out on the floor in front of her, seemingly oblivious to my presence.

I remembered that day.

Father had caught me playing with my doll instead of studying that morning. I'll never forget how scared I was when he yanked me up off of the floor and dragged me by my arm to the desk. He slammed a book onto the top of the desk, flinging it open to some random page as he lectured me. I couldn't even begin to recount what he said to me that day. Probably the same speech I had received over the years about how it was the princesse's duty to learn how to run her kingdom, not play with dolls. What I did remember was how my heart shattered just as the doll did when he slammed it against the desk because I asked to hold it while I read.

I looked back at the little girl crying on the floor in front of me. This beautiful little girl. Crying not because of what her father had done. No. This little girl was crying because she did not understand *why* her father had done it. What had she done to deserve to be treated like this? She had only ever wanted to please her father. Did everything he had ever asked of her. And still he treated her with such disdain. Like nothing she could do was right. She was only a child.

I was only a child.

Anger began to swell inside of me like a storm. My shaking hands formed fists at my side as I looked back down at the little girl. After attempting to piece the doll back together a few more times, she stood slowly and looked around the room. Gone were the tears in her eyes. Her small eyebrows were bunched together as if trying to figure something out. She bent down and picked up the pieces of the doll. She put the doll back into the desk drawer and grabbed as many books as her little arms could hold. I followed behind her as she carried them to the metal tub in the connecting washroom. She tossed them into the tub and looked back over her shoulder. I held my hand out towards her and watched as a stream of purple mist flowed from my fingertips towards her. She did not react when the mist touched her. Her eyes were focused on me, but when I moved, she didn't follow. I stepped around to stand beside her and followed her gaze to focus on the door to my room. I could feel the fear welling up inside of me. Like I was a little girl again, dreading every second of waiting for my father to inevitably walk through those doors.

Fear.

The smell of smoke brought me back to my senses. I looked back at the little girl to see a fire erupting from the bathtub. I watched as she formed another small flame in her hand and threw it on top of the growing fire. It was then that the door to my room slammed open. My father stormed in, headed straight for the little girl. I watched as this little girl, no more than four feet tall and fifty pounds, turned to face him. Her eyes were like a violet storm. Swirls of purple mist filled them and she did not look away as my father stood over her.

Oh yeah. I remembered that day all too well. My father wanted a strong-willed princess to be the future leader of his kingdom. He didn't know what he was asking for.

Chapter 12

Ashten

The pounding in my head was unbearable as I was pulled suddenly from the vision. My head slipped from the professor's grip and I slumped forward. It felt like forever before I took a breath and my chest burned with each subsequent one. My vision was blurry when I pried my eyes open. I looked around and was relieved to see that I was back in the testing chamber.

"Well done, Ms. Ward." Professor Laeovyn's voice was garbled and distorted. I shook my head, opening and closing my eyes to try to reorient myself. "You handled that better than I expected, given your apparent background." She walked around me holding a piece of wood with some paper attached to it. She scribbled down a few words before motioning to Finn, who was still standing by the door.

What did she mean by that? Did she see that vision too? I could vaguely feel someone loosening the straps on my arms and legs. I opened my mouth to speak, but my lungs refused to cooperate. It was all I could do to stay standing upright when I was lifted to my feet. The world was spinning around me and I latched on to Finn's arm out of reflex. He wrapped an arm around my waist, steadying me against him as my legs threatened to give out below me.

The professor took one more look at her papers before motioning to Finn and I. "Take her to the sleeping quarters for Unit C. Her uniform and power cuff will be waiting for her on arrival."

Though I wasn't sure what those words meant, I felt Finn physically relax beside me. We exited the room opposite of where we had entered, which meant we were going deeper into the volcano. I kept my focus on the passing stones of the floor to mitigate the nausea that had set in. What I could see of the halls remained the same the further we went. The stone walls were unremarkable as we turned down a few other halls before stopping at a door. Finn opened it and peaked inside before leading me in and sitting me down on a bed that was covered in red bedding.

The swimming in my head lessened now that I was sitting down, and I took the brief respite as a chance to look around the room. There were three other beds in this room, all identical to the one I was sitting on. Each bed frame was made of a dark metal and had a matching table beside it. Some were littered with books, pictures, and papers that I assumed belonged to the owners of the bed. The sheets of the bed were gold, with a red blanket draped over the top. The rest of the room was fairly unremarkable. Rough stone walls matched the rest of the place that I had seen so far, and the room was lit by the same golden orbs, one affixed to the wall above each bed.

A. Turner

A wave of nausea came over me, and I braced myself on the bed. My hand landed on top of something cold and I drew it back quickly. There, sitting on top of a pile of black and red clothing that I could only assume was my uniform, sat a black metal wrist-band. I reached out to touch it again and fire danced across its surface. I picked up the band, holding it between both of my hands. My magic hummed in response, causing the band to react stronger. Purple mist manifested over the flames. I watched in amazement as the two energies coiled around each other before the entire band went blank. I stared at the metal, so smooth and polished that I could see my reflection in it. My eyes were dull and my hair a mess. No doubt the side effects of whatever that Elf had done to me.

I vaguely heard the door shut before I felt Finn sit down beside me. "So?" he asked expectantly. "What's your power assignment?"

I shrugged. "How am I supposed to know? I don't even know what that means."

Finn pointed to the piece of metal in my hand. "Put that on." At my hesitation, he placed a hand on my knee. "It won't hurt. I promise. It's nothing like the testing. It's just an identifier for the rest of the people here." He gingerly grabbed the band from me and held it between his hands. It remained blank and he shrugged nonchalantly. I couldn't help but chuckle at his goofy smile as he handed the band back to me. "It was worth a shot. It just slides over your hand onto your wrist."

I hesitantly slid the band over my hand and watched as the band shrunk immediately to the size of my wrist. The band lit up once again in a beautiful show of purple and orange. I could feel my magic dancing inside me as if it were mimicking the waves of colors in the band. I looked back up at Finn to find him staring wide-eyed at my wrist. A soft curse left his lips.

He slowly reached out, touching the band before looking up and making eye contact with me. "Did you know you were a dual wielder?" My confusion must have been written all over my face because he didn't wait for me to answer him. "This band reacts to the magic inside its wearer. That's why it didn't do anything when I held it. A dual wielder is someone who has two different magical abilities. Yours are fire and psychic, by the looks of it. Did you know about your second ability?"

"No." I ran my fingers over the band.

Second ability.

So that's what had been going on. The purple mist that had been the highlight of all of my recent nightmares was apparently the manifestation of my second power. I wonder why it had taken this long for it to show up.

Finn stood up and strode across the floor at the foot of my bed. "Most dual wielders don't get their second power until something traumatic triggers it. Because of this, some dual wielders go their entire life without even knowing they have a second power." He answered my thoughts as if I had voiced them out loud.

Now it was my turn to curse. "How do you know all of this?"

"I've picked up on a few things being here for as long as I have." He shrugged. He rambled as his pacing continued. "So you've never experienced any signs that you may have a second power? I guess maybe the dragon attack was enough to trigger something."

His voice faded away as I looked back at the band on my wrist. *Psychic.* I had been taught very little about how to control and use my fire magic since I was a little girl. Everything that I did know had come about naturally, and the idea of having to learn to control a completely foreign power was terrifying. What if I was the only person here who didn't know how to control their powers?

Finn's voice cut through my thoughts. "Everyone in your unit is probably a dual wielder. That's how they separate people here. I'm sure they don't all know how to control both powers perfectly. You will have training sessions for that."

"Training sessions? What kind of training sessions?" I pried my eyes from my new wristband to look up at him. "What is this? Some kind of military school?" I stood up and crossed my arms. "I would really appreciate it if you, of all people, would be honest and tell me what is going on here!"

"In a way." Finn motioned absentmindedly to the room around him. "Asballicuo is a forge for the dynasty's weapons. That includes both steel and blood."

I leaned against the bedpost of my bed as what little I had eaten for breakfast threatened to make a grand reentry. Finn wrapped his arm around my waist and guided me back to a sitting position on the bed.

"It's just the adrenaline. That is what Laeovyn's magic does. It forces your body into a fight-or-flight situation in order to determine what magic your body might try to fight with. Since you can only fight with what you have, it has proven to be a foolproof, though rather uncomfortable, method of testing." Finn rubbed soft circles on my back as I leaned forward, putting my head between my knees and focusing on my breathing. "It sucked my first time, too."

"What kind of magic does she have?" I asked between controlled breaths.

"Psychic." The hand on my back stilled for a moment. "And fire, I guess. She is a Solar Elf after all."

I slowly lifted my head back towards Finn. "So, who here isn't a dual wielder? When you saw my band, you acted so surprised that I assumed being able to wield two powers was rare. Yet you tell me that

I have already met one other person who could wield the exact same powers as me?"

Finn shrugged. "I mean, it *is* rare, but the king only wants the best working under him. I'm sure he went to great lengths to find all the dual wielders he has."

I scrunch my eyebrows. "All?"

"Yes. All." Finn stood and held out his hand. "Why don't you come with me and meet some for yourself?"

Chapter 13

Ashten

The sound of chatter and the clanking of silverware on plates became louder as the doors to the hall were opened. Three rows of onyx tables stretched across the center of a massive dining hall. The room was well lit by magical golden orbs, but the light seemed to be swallowed by the grey stone walls. The entire building must have been carved directly into the volcano.

Each row contained five tables, and each row seemed to be populated by similar people. The first row of tables appeared to be reserved for the blacksmiths of Asballicuo. This place *was* an actual forge, after all. The second row of tables was filled with guards and soldiers, all in the gold and red attire of the dynasty. The third row was a sea of red jackets and white shirts. Each table in this row had four people sitting at it. Except for one. This was the one that Finn led me to.

As we got closer, the Dragonfolk was the first person to catch my attention. Her appearance was mostly Solar Elf, pale skin contrasting her wavy black and blue hair that was cut off at the shoulder. Her back was to me, displaying her neatly folded black wings that were peppered with blue scales. The Wild Elf across from her looked up from her plate. Her long red hair had been braided off to one side, framing her soft features and standing out against her tan skin. Her bright green eyes widened as she saw Finn and me approaching. She pointed at us and the Dragonfolk turned around. The Dragonfolk took one look at us before shaking her head and slamming her fork down onto the table.

"Good evening, ladies." Finn waited for me to sit in one of the empty chairs at the table. I looked back at him hesitantly, but his face did not indicate any emotion. *I guess it was all business again.* "Your final unit member is here. Just in time to see that one has gone missing?" Finn motioned to the last empty chair.

The Wild Elf spoke up first. "We have no idea where Reyland is." Her voice was soft. She didn't meet Finn's eyes as she spoke, choosing to keep her eyes on her plate instead.

"You should check to see if any of your guards are missing dinner, Captain." The Dragonfolk's voice was raspy and low. She leaned back in her chair and propped her feet up on the table as mischief danced in her golden, cat-like eyes. "Particularly any of the female ones." A smile lifted the corner of her lips as she took a drink.

Finn clenched his fists before hanging his head and taking a deep breath. "Well, when you do see him, let him know that all four of you are expected to be ready shortly after first light. Someone will be at your door to escort you." He looked over at me, glancing up and down before turning back to the others. "I trust at least one of you can show the new girl how to wear her uniform?"

When no one answered, Finn turned to leave, nearly running into someone. He regained his footing before leveling a glare at the Moon Elf who had just about ran him over. "So nice of you to join us finally. Your unit can fill you in on all the details." Finn gently shoved the man towards us and proceeded to walk away.

The Moon Elf attempted to tidy his shaggy white hair, which was parted down the middle and promptly fell back down to hang just above his dark red eyes. He was fair skinned, but he did have the purple complexion that all Moon Elves had. He looked at me, hesitating slightly before shrugging at the Wild Elf and taking his place at the last empty chair of the table.

"So," his voice was throaty and low, which honestly didn't match his rather lithe appearance. He, much like everyone else at this table, appeared to be a young Elf. Barely in his twenties, if I had to guess. "Now that our little group is finally complete, does this mean that we can actually start doing something other than sitting in our room? I have grown rather bored in the past few days." He made a show of picking at his nails.

The Dragonfolk sat upright in her chair. "Well, Reyland, you will be pleased to hear that we all have to be ready bright and early first thing in the morning. For what, I don't know."

She turned to me. "It seems as if you are what we have been waiting for. My name's Sarphi. Storm and Fire dual-wielder." She held out her hand. Blue scales decorated her otherwise pale skin from her fingertips to the middle of her forearm. She wore a band on her arm that danced with purple lightning.

"My name is Ashten." I shook her hand hesitantly before folding my arms across my chest. "I guess you guys are my roommates?"

Sarphi offered me a soft smile before gesturing to the others. "This beautiful young lady is Lyra, and that insufferable oaf is Reyland."

Lyra held up her hand in a small wave. "Hi." She pointed to her wrist, where she too had a band. Hers was alight with blue lightning intertwined with green vines. "I can wield both Life and Storm magic."

Reyland snorted and shook his head before holding his hand out as well and leaning across the table. His band was swirling with blue and black smoke. "Truly a pleasure to meet you. I'm Reyland. I wield both Dark and Ice magic." When I hesitated, the hint of a smirk played on one side of his mouth. "Contrary to popular belief, I don't bite."

I couldn't help but smile at the joke as I shook his hand. When our hands met, I could feel the flames of my magic quickly rise to the surface. The feeling caught me off guard and I jerked my hand back quickly, a curse escaping my mouth.

"What's wrong?" Lyra's soft voice barely rose over the chatter of the dining hall.

Uncertainty washed over me as I looked around the table at the friends that had been chosen for me. A Moon Elf, a Wild Elf, and a Dragonfolk. It sounded like the beginning of a poor joke. I hung my head and snorted. I ran my fingers through my hair before looking back up at the group.

"I don't have a clue what is going on." I shook my head. "I was told I was going to Asballicuo. Asballicuo is supposed to be a forge." I gestured wildly to everything around me. "*This* is so much more than a forge!" A mixture of emotions began to rise inside of me and I couldn't hide the crack in my voice as I spoke. I laid my forehead on the tabletop to hide my face. "I just want to know what is going on."

I felt a hesitant hand on my back and Sarphi spoke up. "Why don't you eat some dinner? Then we can go back to the room and talk." I looked up to see her pushing her plate towards me. "Some things are better kept between us."

Though I didn't quite understand what she meant by that, I nodded and grabbed a piece of bread from her plate. I ate it in silence, content to simply listen to my new acquaintances talk amongst themselves. I scanned the room for Finn, but I couldn't seem to find him through the sea of people that filled this space. My attention was drawn back to the group and I couldn't help but laugh at the incredulous look that Reyland gave us all when Sarphi mentioned that she may have gotten him into trouble with Captain Finn.

Reyland leaned back in his chair, running a hand down his face. "Now, why would you do that? I am perfectly capable of making my own trouble, Sarphi." He closed his eyes and stroked his chin. "Though, I'll be honest... I haven't considered those specific methods."

"Like they'd sleep with you." Sarphi scoffed.

Reyland raised his eyebrows in question. "The better question is, who *wouldn't* sleep with me?"

Sarphi rolled her eyes as Lyra buried her head in her hands to hide the blush that was spreading across her cheeks. I decided I could try to spare her from any further secondhand embarrassment.

I cleared my throat and stood up. "I, uh, guess I'm ready to head back to the room whenever you guys are."

Reyland shot up quickly from his chair, fumbling to catch it and keep it from hitting the floor. "Yeah, sure! I'll lead the way."

He sat his chair upright and straightened his coat. He turned and walked away, missing the confused glances that passed between Lyra and Sarphi as they both gently slid their chairs back and stood up. Sarphi gulped down the last of whatever was in her glass before motioning for me to follow Reyland.

Chapter 14

Finn

I watched from the other side of the room as the group introduced themselves to Ashten. She flinched as she shook Reyland's hand, and it took all of my willpower to keep my feet planted. To keep from marching right over there and demanding to know what he had done to her.

I needed to stay out of it. The last thing that I needed was someone claiming that I was showing favoritism. They wouldn't be wrong, but it would definitely cause a problem. I couldn't arouse any suspicion.

I watched as Ashten seemed to settle in, eating bread that Sarphi had given her while the rest of the table laughed and joked. She smiled brightly as Reyland hung his head in response to something Sarphi had said.

It was good to see that she was getting comfortable. She was going to need to make friends, and I could think of no better group. Despite everything, I couldn't be happier with her assignment. I had been worried that she wouldn't get assigned to the dual-wielders. That unit was where I needed her, but she had shown no signs of having a second power.

A. Turner

I watched as they all stood from the table and made their way out of the dining hall. Off to get some rest, hopefully. They were all going to need it for what we had in store for them tomorrow.

Chapter 15

Reyland

Trouble.

That's what she was. As soon as our eyes met, I recognized her. But that wasn't all. It was everything I could do to stay in my lane. To keep from crawling over that table to ask her if she could feel it, too. It was a feeling I had only heard of in stories. One I didn't believe was true until now. I had spent most of that dinner trying to convince myself that I was crazy. Being crazy was less scary than the alternative. When she shook my hand, it felt like there was fire crawling up my arm. We had only just met, but the feeling was intense. Too intense. Was that normal? Did she feel that way, too?

I shook my head as we rounded the corner of the hall that led to our sleeping quarters. I had only just met this girl. Learned her name less than an hour ago. I had met, seduced, and slept with girls that I knew more about. But I had never felt the slightest remorse about leaving those girls alone and asleep in their beds as I snuck out in the early morning hours. The thought of anyone doing that to Ashten made my blood boil.

I opened and closed my fists in an attempt to dispel the rising tension in my body. Rolling my shoulders, I took a deep breath.

A. Turner

Everything about what I was feeling was uncharted territory for me. I didn't like it.

And for what reason? What reason did I have to care about this girl at all? Well, you know, except for the obvious. I seemed to be the only one who had put those puzzle pieces together, though.

I pushed open the door to our chambers. Sarphi and Lyra rushed past me to their beds, but Ashten stopped at the doorway and looked over her shoulder. For what, I couldn't be sure. I leaned past her to look down the hall, but I saw nothing.

"Everything alright?" I crossed my arms, using my foot to hold the door open.

Ashten hesitated before turning back to me. "Yeah. I just thought I saw something." Despite her obviously timid body language, her voice was firm. Friendly, but firm. And her eyes shone clearly. I had never seen someone with eyes as purple as hers. They complemented her raven black hair perfectly. There was a slight tinge of yellow that I was all too familiar with coloring her cheek. A fading bruise. I wondered who had done that to her. I flexed my fists once again, fighting against every instinct in my body.

She cleared her throat and smiled softly at me before nodding her head in thanks and walking into the room. *Staring.* I had been staring at her. Like an idiot. I had been staring at her like an idiot and she had caught me. I took a deep breath and exhaled gradually as I pulled the door shut behind me.

Trouble indeed.

Chapter 16

Ashten

I walked past Reyland into the room, gingerly sitting down on my bed. I watched as Lyra and Sarphi did the same thing. The door clicked shut, and I turned to see Reyland standing just inside of it. He was watching me intently, which he seemed to have been doing since he sat down at the table. He didn't break his stare while he walked over to his own bed and removed his jacket before sitting down. The sleeveless white shirt underneath fit him perfectly and revealed that he was much more muscular than I had originally realized. Lean, yes, but definitely muscular. I couldn't help but watch his arms flex as he leaned back against his headboard and stretched out, folding them behind his head.

Sarphi cleared her throat. "So. Where should I begin?"

I blinked and shook my head. "Sorry. Um... how about with what we are all doing here?" I couldn't help but look back over at Reyland. I could feel myself being drawn to him. But why? He was handsome, but I had seen plenty of handsome males before. I happened to be romantically involved with one. One that could walk into this room at any moment and catch me ogling over this Elf.

Sarphi cleared her throat again. "Well. I think Reyland was the first one here. At least he was here when I got here." She repositioned herself on the bed. "I've been here for a few years. Lyra was the last of us to show up, and that was three days ago."

I turned my head to Sarphi, trying my best to ignore the stare from Reyland that was burning into me. "How did you all get here? And why are you here?"

"Let's just say I made a little trouble in Raven's Rest." Sarphi flexed her wings behind her.

Reyland's laugh filled the air. "A little trouble?!" He sat up, pointing at Sarphi. "This one almost single-handedly commandeered an entire shipment of goods from a royal caravan outside of Raven's Rest."

A smile played at Sarphi's lips. "The caravan shouldn't have been full of food that my city needed." She shrugged. "As a first-time offender, they couldn't kill me without causing a major uproar. So I got sent here instead. Said they were sure they could find a use for me."

"So they decided to turn you into a soldier?" Nothing that was being said came close to dampening my confusion.

"In a way, yes. Though I think Reyland is the only one of us to have seen actual combat. Lyra and I are soldiers by name only."

Lyra waited patiently for Sarphi to finish before speaking up. "My father sent me here. King's orders." She looked down at her lap.

Sarphi moved from her bed to sit beside Lyra, stretching a wing out behind her protectively. "She doesn't like to talk about it."

"My father also sent me here, on the king's orders. Been here for a few years now." Reyland looked down at the floor briefly before meeting my eyes.

Here on my father's orders? For a few years?

I held my breath. I didn't want to lie to them. They had been nothing but nice to me so far. However, I wasn't too keen on my roommates knowing that my father was the one responsible for their being here.

"I, um, am also here on the king's orders." I reached up, running my fingers through my hair. "It was an eventful carriage ride."

"Really?" Lyra finally looked up. "What happened?"

"A dragon is what happened."

Everyone in the room turned to look at me.

Sarphi was the first one to speak up. "Well? Care to elaborate? You know, since dragons don't exist anymore?"

"There isn't a lot to elaborate on." I shrugged. "We were traveling through the Deadlands and a dragon crashed through the wall. It ate or killed most of the guards, destroyed our carriage, and then flew away. We walked the rest of the way here." At the quizzical looks I received from every face in the room, I continued. "We didn't see a single wagon, carriage, or even another person the entire time."

Reyland's eyebrows raised slightly as a smile played on his lips. "I guess that would explain the clothing."

My face reddened as I remembered I was still in Finn's clothing. "Yeah. These aren't mine. My clothing got pretty messed up by the dragon. Fi—" I caught myself before I gave away possibly valuable information about my relationship with Finn. "Captain Finn offered me some of his."

"Well, why don't we get you a bath and into some fresh clothes?" Lyra stood up and walked towards what I could assume was the washroom. She turned and smiled shyly at me. "I'll show you where everything is."

"A warm bath sounds wonderful, Lyra." I stood up and sifted through the pile of uniforms that had been placed on my bed. Once I finally settled on what was most likely to be nightclothes, I bundled them in my arms. I nodded curtly to Sarphi and Reyland before following Lyra to the washroom.

Lyra led me through the back door of the sleeping quarters and down a short hall. She pushed open the door to the washroom, and I was met with an immediate gust of warm air. Inside the room was a singular large stone bath carved out of the floor. The water was flowing from a small geyser on one side of this bath. Steam rose from it, coating the floor and walls in a thin layer of condensation. Golden lights lit this room, though they were dimmer than the others that were about the rest of the forge.

"All four of us share this washroom. You can put your clothes over there." Lyra motioned to the benches that lined one side of the tub. "Don't worry. We do all share this washroom, but Reyland usually waits until we've all gone to bed, so it is fairly private." She nodded slightly before turning to leave.

"Thanks." I smiled tightly as she shut the door behind her.

I placed my clean clothes on the rack and quickly stripped out of my dirty ones. I stepped down into the tub, a soft moan escaping my lips as the warm water soothed my tired muscles. This was the longest I had ever gone without a warm bath, and I don't think I had ever appreciated it more.

I sat down on one of the benches that were built into the walls of this bath and sank until the water was just barely below my head. It was odd, not having to warm this water myself. My assumption was that the volcano itself was responsible for this wonderfully warm water. I listened to the sounds of the geyser as I mulled over the day's events. I had always found it easier to think when taking a warm bath. It was often the only time I ever felt fully relaxed.

My thoughts drifted to my new roommates. Lyra reminded me so much of Evelien. I could already tell that she was such a gentle soul. So much so that I couldn't fabricate any reality in which she had done anything to deserve to be here. Not if it was truly as bad as Finn had made it out to be. There was something about her, though. Some familiarity that I just couldn't shake.

Sarphi seemed cool. Cool in a "I'll be your friend but if you even think about hurting any of them, I'll skin you alive" kind of way. I could respect that, though. I definitely didn't have any plans to wrong any of them, so I *probably* wasn't in any danger of meeting my demise in that fashion.

Then there was Reyland. I couldn't quite figure him out. He was quiet, but I didn't mark him as being shy. Not when he had been staring at me since the moment we locked eyes. Not that I had been much better, honestly. I couldn't help it. I had so many questions. My magic had only reacted like that one other time.

My thoughts turned to my nightmares and what they could mean. Just about every night since the encounter with the dragon, I had experienced the same dream over and over again. At this point, it was less of a nightmare and more of a nightly ritual. I went to bed expecting it, and I rarely woke up in a panicked sweat because of it anymore. Not like those first few times.

I filled my lungs with air and plunged my head under the water. Silence filled my ears. Even here, under the water, I could feel the fire in my veins. It burned through me unimpeded. It danced under my skin, constantly looking for a way out. I tried hard to look past it for my supposed second ability. For this psychic magic that the test claimed I had. My head pounded as I searched and searched within myself. I used every technique that I had ever used when learning how to wield my fire magic, but I didn't know what I was looking for, and it wasn't long before my lungs were burning. I surfaced and inhaled sharply, my body thanking me for the air. This was something that was going to take practice. Maybe the others would have some advice.

I quickly washed up and dressed in the soft white and red trousers and shirt that had been left for me. I dried my hair the best I could before leaving the towel and my dirty clothes where Lyra had instructed. I took a steadying breath before heading back into the common room, hoping I could get some sleep before whatever new life-changing event awaited me tomorrow.

I wonder how many of those I have to have before they are no longer life changing?

Chapter 17

Reyland

The room fell quiet after Lyra left to show Ashten to the washroom. I laid on my bed, staring at the ceiling, my mind an endless sea of thoughts. Why were we all here? Why us specifically? I knew why I was here, and I knew at least the surface reason for why Sarphi was here. Before tonight, Lyra was the only one who did not fit the puzzle. She just showed up one day. She's never offered an explanation, and neither did the Captain.

And then there was Ashten. I could not wrap my head around any scenario that would bring her to Asballicuo. What made it even worse was that I seemed to be the only one who recognized her. I seemed to be the only one who realized that her father was the reason we were all here. There was a part of me, deep inside, that was mad at her for it. Mad that she had lived a nice, cushioned life while I was stuck here. I knew it was irrational, but that was apparently going to be a normal occurrence for me when it came to her.

My mind drifted to the vision of Ashten in the Captain's clothes. My blood boiled at the thought. That man had never been nice to any of us. Especially not nice enough to offer us the clothes off of his back. Not to mention that they were apparently out in the wilderness by themselves for however long it took them to get here on foot. The way she blushed at just the reminder that she had been wearing his clothes was enough explanation for me, and I hated how it made me feel.

Jealous.

"If you tense up anymore, you might just explode." Sarphi's voice cut through my thoughts. I looked over at her as she laid back on her bed, her wings protectively cradling her body. A book hovered over her head, the pages turning with a flick of her wrist. "You should read more. Reading is relaxing."

"Yeah right." I scoffed. "I've seen you throw that book across the room because something didn't go how you thought it would. If that's your idea of relaxing, I hesitate to ask what you find stressful."

Sarphi turned another page in her book. "Yeah, well, at least I'm not laying on my bed one bad thought away from self implosion." She didn't look over as she continued to talk. "What's going on with you, anyway?"

"Nothing's going on with me." I lied as I sat up and swung my legs over the side of the bed. "Nothing more than the usual, at least." I stood up and began rifling through the chest of clothes at the end of my bed. I settled on a pair of loose black trousers and matching shirt before heading for the changing partition at the far end of our room.

"Just like I don't have two giant blue wings attached to my back." She muttered something else under her breath. "You're going to have to try again."

"I don't have to try anything." I pulled off my shirt and trousers. "You'll just have to be satisfied with the answer I give you."

"Did you at least figure out something useful?" Another page turned.

"No." I sighed as I caught a glimpse of my back in the mirror. The raised white scars still stood out against my purple skin all these years later. It was almost easier to notice the patches of smooth skin than it was to pinpoint each individual scar. I swallowed the bile rising in my throat as I tied the string on my pants.

I emerged from the partition, pulling the shirt over my head. Sarphi gave me a sideways glance before looking back at her book. "Nothing? Nothing at all?"

"Nope." I tossed my old clothing into the shared clothes bin and sat back down on my bed just as Lyra walked back in. "Nothing at all about when this place was created, why it was created, or who created it."

Sarphi slammed her book down on the table beside her bed. "Which means we still have absolutely no idea why we are here. I mean, why train us for all these years but only send you out?"

"Maybe we will figure something out tomorrow." Lyra sat down on the edge of her bed.

"What even is tomorrow?" I asked.

"No clue." Lyra shrugged. "Captain just said to be up and ready at first light and that someone would escort us."

"Well, that's helpful." Sarphi's voice dripped with sarcasm as she stretched her wings out before wrapping them back around herself. "Guess that means we should get some sleep."

"Yeah," Lyra muttered, already under the covers with her eyes closed.

I silently laid back down on my bed. Sarphi snapped her fingers and the lights in the room gradually dimmed to a comfortably pale yellow. I laid there listening as my companions' breathing leveled out. A good indicator that they had each fallen asleep. Some time passed before I heard the door to the washroom open. I watched Ashten freeze in the doorway before gingerly tiptoeing over to her bed between me and Sarphi. She silently slipped under the covers. I closed my eyes, the sounds of her breathing being added to the others. Hers never did level out before I slipped out of bed and headed to the washroom myself.

Chapter 18

Ashten

A loud knock on the door was what woke me up the next morning. I sat up slowly and rubbed my eyes. I opened them just as Reyland finished pulling on a tight undershirt. He grabbed his jacket and pointed at the foot of my bed.

"Yours is in there." His voice was thick with sleep. He pulled on his boots and began tying them. "You better hurry."

I stumbled out of the bed and opened the chest at the end. There were several combinations of pants, shirts, and jackets inside. I began looking around at my companions, trying to pull out the pieces that matched what they were putting on. A blue scaled hand reached from beside me and pulled out a white undershirt, red jacket, and black pants. I looked over to see Sarphi smiling softly at me.

"Here." She held the clothing out to me. "These are what you need. You can change over there." She pointed at the wooden partition that created a small section of privacy in this room. I noted that her uniform lacked a jacket, with her shirt being cut in a way that perfectly avoided her wings.

There was another loud knock at the door. "I'm only going to knock one more time," a gruff voice sounded from the other side.

A. Turner

I nodded curtly to Sarphi before making my way to the other side of the room. Quickly, I stripped out of my nightclothes and pulled on the clothes I had been given. I stole a quick look in the mirror. The tight undershirt clung to my body, accentuating the fact that I had next to zero muscle. The pants, which were supposed to be form fitting leathers, hung loosely on my hips. I shoved my arms through the arms of the jacket, which did seem to fit fairly well. The bruise on my cheek was a light yellow now. It didn't hurt near as much and would probably be gone soon. I hoped so because I was tired of looking at it.

I rushed back to my bed, pulling on my boots as I walked. Lyra handed me a section of rope, and I quickly tied my hair back. Reyland scanned me before reaching out and straightening the collar on my jacket. He hesitated before lowering his hand and walking towards the door.

"Straighten up. We can't always look like we just survived a dragon attack," he quipped as he opened the door, his voice tight. My face reddened as I let out a breath I didn't know I had been holding. I smoothed the front of my jacket and checked my laces.

Outside the door was one singular guard. "Finally. What part of 'be ready at first light' does this group not understand?" His voice was gruff, but I didn't recognize it. This wasn't Finn. The guard pushed past Reyland into the room.

"Well." Sarphi's voice was sharp. "It would be easier to wake up at first light if we could see some light in here." She gestured to the stone walls of the room. "We don't exactly have the most breathtaking view."

The guard wheeled to face her. "Perhaps I would be more lenient if you had a better attitude, snake-skin."

The snarl that rumbled from Sarphi was so animalistic that I couldn't help but stare. Her wings flared out behind her, forcing Lyra to take a step back with wide eyes. The anger in Sarphi's golden eyes didn't falter in the slightest when the guard, who was slightly taller than her and definitely had more muscle, stepped towards her.

"Last I checked, snakes don't growl." The guard stood over Sarphi, who only stood taller.

A smirk played across her lips. "Only the most deadly ones." Her voice was laced with venom. "As a warning before they bite."

The guard's hand flew to his belt, pulling out a dagger. He pointed it at Sarphi, shaking with anger. The room grew incredibly tense as we watched this standoff. My heart was racing, oblivious to the fact that I wasn't the one with a dagger to her throat. Lyra's eyes met mine from across the room.

"No," she mouthed, her eyes wide.

I shook my head in confusion and followed her eyes to my hands. To my horror, they were wreathed in lavender mist. My head was pounding as I frantically looked over to Reyland, whose eyes went wide for a moment before he stepped between me and the guard.

"Come on, guys. We can get the measuring tape out later." Reyland's voice carried his normal, calm tenor. He backed up until he was directly in front of me, shielding me from the guard's view. "*Everyone* needs to calm down."

I closed my eyes, the scent of peppermint and smoke filling my nose. I took a deep breath. *In and out.* I let my head hang down, involuntarily resting it on Reyland's back. If I concentrated, I could feel the mist swirling around my hands. I took another deep breath as I tried to get myself under control. The pounding in my head began to subside along with the pulsing feeling of the magic at my fingertips. I opened my eyes to see that the mist was gone. My knees were weak as I placed a hand on Reyland's back, righting myself.

"I don't have time for this," the guard mumbled as he sheathed his dagger. "We're already late. I'll never hear the end of it." His voice faded as he walked towards the door without another word to us. Reyland was the first to the door, ushering Lyra out. Sarphi, who had folded her wings neatly back against her skin, gave me a questioning look before catching up to Lyra.

I stood in the center of the room, staring at Reyland. The muscles in his jaw tensed as he looked out the door before meeting my eyes. I swallowed thickly, my heart racing for an entirely new reason as his blood-red eyes scanned me. I pulled my jacket tightly around myself and folded my arms across my body, growing more self conscious the longer he looked at me.

"We better go before Sarphi guts that guard." His voice was rough as he stepped to the open door.

I nodded sharply, walking past him and towards the others, who were quickly disappearing at the end of the hall.

Chapter 19

Ashten

We were all quiet while we followed the guard down to what felt like the basement of the mountain, if such a thing could exist. We all filed into a large circular room that was dimly lit by a few floating orbs of light. The ceiling was just barely visible, and the center of the room dipped down into a wide crater. There was a singular stone pedestal in the middle. Atop this pedestal sat a dark crystal bowl. The door shut behind us with a heavy *thud.*

"So nice of you all to finally join us." An older Elven man with greying red hair stepped out of the shadows from the far side of the room. Finn was on the left of him and a young Elven woman with short black hair was on his right. They both wore the same black pants and red jacket that the rest of us had been instructed to wear.

Finn was not in his normal guard attire. Instead, he was wearing what appeared to be a fine set of fighting leathers. It was almost a shock to see him in anything but his armor or everyday clothes, but these suited him. Very well, too, if I may add. The dark leather complemented his tan skin and clung to his muscular frame. He shot me a tight smirk that caused my face to redden before looking back at the rest of the group.

"We had a slight disagreement before making our way here this morning." Our escort stared pointedly at Sarphi before turning back to the Elven man. Sarphi bristled, and it was Reyland's turn to level her with a glare.

The Elven man cocked an eyebrow. "One that I trust has been handled? Given that you know the gravity of the situation?"

"And what situation is that?" Sarphi asked, her voice still filled with anger from the earlier confrontation.

"Well, let's start with the introductions first." The Elven man stepped forward. "I am Malon Tranelis. I will be in charge of your weapons' training." He motioned to the woman on his right. "And this is Axilya Raloven. She is going to become your best friend *very* soon."

Without further introduction, Axilya stepped forward. "So, this is going to go one of two ways." Her boots creaked in the silence as she walked to the podium in the center of the room. She stopped, resting a hand on each side of the crystal bowl before leaning on it and scanning the group. "Who wants to go first?"

"Do we get to know what's going on before we make that decision?" Reyland crossed his arms. "Or are we supposed to just trust you?"

An unsettling smile inched across Malon's face. "Have I ever steered you wrong before, Reyland?"

Nobody moved to cross the invisible line that had been drawn across this room. I stared at Finn, wishing I had some way to communicate telepathically with him. He met my eyes briefly before looking at the bowl and back at me. He raised his eyebrows, making a subtle hand motion towards the bowl. I pointed at myself, keeping my hands at my side, and furrowed my brows in question. Surely he didn't intend for me to go first? Out of everyone here, I felt like I was the least qualified to go first. I barely even knew what was going on here. Finn leaned over to Malon and whispered something in his ear before looking back out at the group.

"Fine. If none of you will volunteer, I will just have to pick someone." Malon made a show of scanning the group before fixing his gaze on me. "Ashten. Please step up to the dais."

Great. Make a show of the new girl.

I leveled a daggered stare at Finn before stepping forward, stopping a few inches short of where Axilya stood. Nervously, I slid my hands into my pockets, suddenly unsure of what else to do with them. I looked back over my shoulder at the rest of the group. Lyra's head hung low, and I could see that she was chewing on her fingernails. Sarphi stood nonchalantly with her hands in her pockets, making a show of looking about the room. Reyland's arms were still crossed, but he watched me intently. A muscle in his jaw ticked before he met my eyes. He gave me a curt nod and leveled his stare back at our hosts.

"Something that you need to understand before we get started is that this has not been done in centuries. Everything that I— *we* —are about to attempt is based solely on precedents that I have observed in my studies." Axilya held her hand out to me. "I need to see your hand, if you don't mind."

"Am I allowed to ask what for?" I kept my hands in my pockets, running my fingers along the inside hem.

Axilya gave me a soft smile. "I think it's best if you don't know." My feet took a few steps back before my brain could catch up. Strong arms caught me and I looked back to see Finn standing behind me. "Don't worry though! It's not as bad as what Laeovyn did to you when you got here." She reached her hand out further over the bowl and Finn stroked my arm before giving me a soft push forward.

I loosed a long breath. Finn wouldn't push me towards anything too dangerous, and that brought me a little comfort. I hesitantly held my hand out to Axilya. She grabbed me by the wrist, pulling me forward until my hand was over the bowl. With her free hand, she brought up a dagger, holding it over my open palm.

"Prepare yourself. This is going to sting a little." She gave no further warning before she sliced a deep cut along the inside of my palm.

I let out a string of curses as the blade dug into my skin. Blood spilled over the edge of my palm and into the bowl as I wrestled my hand away from the Elven woman, who then wasted no time running back to her associates. I was left standing there, blood spilling from my hand into the crystal bowl. My head began to pound and I could feel panic beginning to rise inside of me.

Not now. Now is not the time.

"Why did you do that!?" I barely heard Reyland shout over my own heartbeat.

My brain was a storm of words, and I couldn't find the right ones to speak as I clutched my bleeding hand. My magic began to swirl inside of me and the roaring in my head continued to grow. I watched as the blood from my hand formed a crimson pool inside the bowl. I couldn't believe my eyes as swirls of orange and purple formed inside the pool of blood. My eyes snapped shut as the pounding in my head grew louder and louder. So loud that I could barely hear the muffled shouts of the other people in the room.

There was a sudden rush of wind followed by a ground shaking crash that knocked me off of my feet. I crawled to my knees, wincing when I used my injured hand to brace myself. I opened my eyes wearily, fully expecting to only see the ground in front of me. No amount of procrastination could prepare me for what I actually saw.

A large, clawed foot the size of my entire body was embedded in the stone in front of me. I crawled backwards on my knees before sitting up and resting on my haunches. My eyes followed the metallic purple scales up the creature's leg, which was easily two to three times my height. The pounding in my head made it hard to focus as I stood up. Even through my blurry vision, I could tell that I only came up to this creature's ankle at full height. Beautiful webbed wings were folded neatly against this creature's back as it lowered its head into my view.

Its head, which was easily the size of a small horse, was decorated with two large, spiral, crystalline horns. Jagged, crystal-like features and sharp teeth caught my attention before I looked into its amethyst eyes. It scanned the room around us before resting its gaze on me. It breathed in deeply before exhaling. A lavender mist poured from its nose, surrounding me and blocking my vision of the rest of the room. My feelings of panic only solidified as I came to terms with the fact that I was completely helpless and standing mere inches from a dragon.

A familiar, feminine voice filled my head.

"*Finally.*" The voice rumbled through me, settling deep in my chest.

Under no circumstances is this happening.

A wave of amusement washed over me. *"This is the exact circumstance in which this would happen, Ashten."* Her voice was a low purr as she studied me.

"How do you know who I am?" I asked out loud, my voice shaking.

A. Turner

"One would hope that I would at least know the name of my rider before I choose them."

Rider?

"Okay. Different question. How are you here?" I took a deep breath, trying to steady myself. "You were all the way out in the Deadlands."

"The Deadlands are only a day's flight from here." She stretched her wings out behind her, beating them in a slow rhythm. The lavender mist dissipated to reveal the rest of the room.

I looked around at everyone else, most of whom had not moved since the mist surrounded us. They all watched me and the dragon with bated breath. Finn's eyes were wide as he looked at me. Reyland struggled against Finn's arms that held him back.

"What do we do now?" I asked, and I wasn't sure if I was talking in my head or out loud.

The dragon leaned her head back down to me. *"Place your hand on my head."* At my hesitation, she continued. *"The bleeding one."*

I picked my hand up, studying it in the dim light before reaching towards the dragon. I haltingly placed my hand on her snout, fitting it perfectly between her nostrils. Her scales were somehow smooth but rough. Warm but cold.

Wait. No. It was me that was warm. Or was I cold? My stomach churned as a wave of power washed through me. A searing pain started at the middle of my spine, spreading across my back. I could only close my eyes and grit my teeth while the pain coursed through me. Gritting my teeth quickly turned into yelling as the pain became overwhelming. My knees threatened to give out just as quickly as last night's meal threatened to make an appearance. It felt like forever before the burning subsided.

"What... was... that?" The words fumbled out of my mouth as I fell to my knees.

"Nyzirth. My name is Nyzirth." Her voice sounded strained, even in my head. *"Don't worry. That was completely normal."*

My head was still pounding as I opened my eyes. I peeled my hand from Nyzirth's nose, leaving behind a bloody handprint. I tried to ignore the squelching as I closed my fist and dragged myself to my feet.

Chapter 20

Reyland

Her cries of pain were by far the worst sound I had ever heard.

Before I realized it, I was moving towards her. Anything. I would do *anything* if I could make it stop. Even if for just a moment. My senses tunneled. All I could see was her and all I could hear were her screams as I started to sprint across the stone floor.

"And where do you think you're going?" I was reminded of the Captain's grip on my arm as he spun me around to face him. He looked over my shoulder briefly before focusing back on me.

"Unlike some people, I am not willing to just sit here and watch her scream like she is being boiled from the inside out." I fought against his grip and craned my neck in a sorry attempt to get my eyes back on Ashten. I *needed* to help her. "Let go of me!"

He frowned deeply at me. "Sorry. No can do. This has to happen." He tried pulling me back to the rest of the group, but I didn't make it easy for him even as a calming warmth began to radiate up my arm.

"Was that really necessary?" I mumbled under my breath, protesting even as the unnatural calmness took over. He stood behind me, wrenching my arm and holding me in place.

I didn't hear his answer as Ashten turned to face us. I couldn't help but stare. The dragon nuzzled its snout against Ashten's back before leveling us all with a dagger-like stare. A low rumble rose from deep in its chest, causing Ashten to turn back to her with an incredulous look. If dragons could roll their eyes, this one would have before it launched into the sky, leaving through an opening in the ceiling that we couldn't see before.

There was something about Ashten that was different. I couldn't quite put a finger on it yet, but this had changed something. Her eyes were a violet storm and lavender mist swirled around her hands and up her arms as she walked back towards us.

I struggled against the hands that were holding me back. "You can let go of me now," I grumbled.

"Only if you go next," Captain Finn murmured as he let go of me and pushed me forward, causing me to narrowly miss running Ashten over.

I caught Ashten's gaze as we walked past each other. The look in her eyes was *incredible.* She blinked slowly at me before offering me a lopsided grin. A sweet cinnamon smell filled my senses as she walked past me. She took her place beside Sarphi, who caught her when she swayed on her feet. Ashten wrapped her arm around Sarphi's waist, allowing for the Dragonfolk to adjust her weight and support her. Sarphi furrowed her brow at me before subtly waving me away.

Great. My turn.

I swallowed the lump in my throat as I walked towards the stone dais. Axilya had already resumed her position and was waiting for me, arm outstretched expectantly. I rubbed my hands together before holding one out. Axilya grabbed it quickly, apparently afraid that I would change my mind. Nice of her to at least act like I actually had a choice.

She quickly ran the blade of the dagger along the inside of my palm before dropping my hand and running off to the side. I closed my eyes and hissed a breath between my teeth as a searing cold pain shot through my hand and up my arm. My entire arm was overcome with cold. It was like I had dipped my arm into a river in Ebony Peaks in the middle of winter. The coldness began to spread to my chest, making it harder to breathe. My chest and throat grew tighter and tighter. I became vaguely aware of the rhythmic flapping of wings that was getting closer. Refusing to be knocked over, I braced myself as the dragon landed in front of me with a crash. I waited for the dust to settle before opening my eyes.

Before me stood one of the most beautiful creatures I had ever seen. Back at my home in Raath Dorei, I had seen plenty of lovely and majestic creatures. But this. This was more than anything I had seen before. The dragon before me was covered in ice white scales. Cobalt claws dug into the ground in front of me as I gathered the courage to look up. I followed the beautiful scales up the dragon's body until I couldn't look up any more. The dragon was looking out over me at the rest of the group. His nostrils flared as he searched the room.

"Hey!" I shouted, surprised at my own, assuredly false, confidence. "I'm down here!" I waved my arms wildly, hoping to get the dragon's attention. My cut hand was heavy and looking down at it revealed that it was almost completely covered in ice.

"I know exactly where you are." The dragon's voice was just short of a growl as it filled my head.

My legs moved backwards without my head's permission as the dragon leaned its massive head down towards me. Jagged scales that loosely resembled icicles hung from its chin and down its neck. Some of them defied gravity, choosing to instead grow upwards and solidify into two beautiful horns. Cerulean, cat-like eyes met mine and encapsulated my entire vision.

"You have my full attention now, Elf." I grabbed the bridge of my nose as the voice rumbled through my head. The dragon snorted, ice crystals forming in its breath. I could have sworn he was laughing as he leaned closer, placing his head in my bleeding hand. *"You better get used to it."*

A. Turner

As soon as I felt the cool scales on my hand, a numbing pain blossomed at the base of my neck before rapidly running down my spine. The cold rippled across my back and over each of my scars, causing my back to arch as I yelled out in pain. My vision went white momentarily before everything came back to me. I doubled over, letting my entire body rest against the dragon's head as I tried to catch my breath.

"Zothim." His voice was even lower and quieter as he addressed me. *"You can call me Zothim."*

"Well, I guess it's nice to meet you, Zothim," I rasped.

"Go. Stand with your friends."

"They're not my—" I was cut off as Zothim shoved me backwards. I was met with the same wide eyed stares that we had all given Ashten as I turned back to the group. Zothim gave me one last nudge forward before becoming airborne.

Chapter 21

Ashten

I leaned against Sarphi, struggling to catch my breath as we all watched the dragon land in front of Reyland. His dragon wasted no time as he shoved his snout against Reyland. Reyland's screams of pain only made the lingering nausea from my experience worse, and I relied more and more on my new friend to keep me upright. My knees wobbled as Reyland's screams faded and he leaned over against the dragon's head.

He turned to face us, and his dragon pushed him away before taking flight. He walked over to us in no hurry, taking his position on my left. A thin layer of ice encased his fingertips as he crossed his arms, resuming his usual guarded stance. He glanced at me for only a second, but I caught a hint of concern in his eyes. Concern about what, I wasn't sure. The list of concerning things was unbearably long at this moment in time.

"Well. We don't have all day and there are still two of you." Malon's voice cut through my thoughts. He looked expectantly at Sarphi and Lyra.

Lyra was looking down at the floor. Her skin had visibly paled and one of her fingers was bleeding, presumably from her chewing on it. She didn't look up as Malon talked. Sarphi looked between me and

Lyra before slowly stepping away from my embrace. I stumbled backwards, my world spinning from the change in my center of balance. A strong arm wrapped around my waist, keeping me from falling on my rear.

I looked over, expecting to see Finn holding me up. Instead, I was greeted with intense red eyes and white hair. Reyland smiled tightly before looking back at the dais where Sarphi was confidently approaching. That intense peppermint and smoke scent filled my nose as I involuntarily leaned against him. My legs were barely working, and I briefly considered wrapping my arms around his waist to keep myself up.

All thought was interrupted when a beautiful red dragon landed in front of Sarphi. This was the third dragon I had seen in the past hour, but the sight would never get old. This dragon was shorter than either Nyzirth or Reyland's dragon, but what it lacked in size it made up for in sheer muscle. Its beautiful scarlet scales stood out against the blue ones on Sarphi's wings. It assessed her with golden eyes that matched the two golden, lightning shaped horns spiraling from its head. Its features were smoother than the previous two dragons, but none less foreboding.

Sarphi's experience was much like ours, and I figured I was going to have an iron stomach before the day was over. After the initial connection was over, she stroked the dragon's snout once before walking back over to us. Flame danced at her fingertips and I could feel the heat emanating from her as she took her place beside me.

Now it was Lyra's turn. She hesitantly walked up to the dais, tears in her eyes as she held her hand out to Axilya. I couldn't watch as Lyra's blood began to pour into the crystal bowl. My head started spinning as nausea reared its ugly head again. My legs were weak and Reyland's grip on me tightened. I heard a shuffling to my right and looked over to see Finn standing beside me.

I took my attention back to the scene in front of me just as a lithe green dragon landed in front of Lyra. She immediately fell back, hitting the ground with a thud as she pulled her hands over her head to shield herself. The dragon approached her lazily, a loud purr radiating through the air as it nuzzled against her body. I was glad that she had gotten a gentle one. An ornery dragon would have made everything that she was probably feeling right now so much worse. The dragon's scales were a dark green, like the pine trees that dotted the edge of the Mistymoon Glades. Dark brown, antler-like horns jutted from the top of its head. Its features were soft and round, unlike the other dragons we had seen today. It had beautiful teal eyes that closed as Lyra stroked its nose.

"Let her go," Finn growled, bringing my attention back to him. He looked past me at Reyland. "She's going to need to learn how to handle herself. She's not always going to have someone to lean on." His voice carried a bit more bite than I was used to.

When Reyland made no obvious effort to move, Finn reached over and grabbed my arm, pulling me away from him. He held on for only a moment before roughly letting my arm go. The sudden movements only made standing up straight harder as Lyra's cries of pain echoed through the room. I doubled over, resting my hands on my knees.

"It's just the adrenaline," Finn stated flatly. "Deep breaths in and out. Try to focus on something else."

Reyland scoffed and I closed my eyes in an attempt to block everything out. "Yes. Of course. Just the adrenaline. Definitely not the gut-wrenching screams. Or the loss of blood. Or the pain that I can only assume was nothing like she has ever experienced before." There was the shuffling of feet as Reyland walked in front of me. "But yeah. It's just the adrenaline."

More shuffling filled my ears as, I could only assume, Finn stepped up to Reyland. Their conversation faded as I finally receded into my mind. The scent of pine filled my nostrils briefly before being completely overtaken by peppermint and smoke. It was an odd combination, but one that I found surprisingly comforting. The smoke reminded me of the fireplace in the library at home. I had spent many hours there, hiding from my father, while I read all sorts of tales. Tales that were mostly about dragons, ironically. I had always assumed those stories were made up. Works of fiction crafted to entertain the masses. My most recent experiences were leading me to think otherwise. I filled my brain with recountings of those stories until my heart rate slowed and the bubbling in my stomach subsided. I thanked the gods for this reprieve, even if it was only for a moment.

Gentle hands hauled me upright, instantly forcing me back into reality. Sarphi's scaled hands were cool against my skin as she rubbed my arm. I gave her a soft smile, one that I'm sure didn't meet my eyes as I folded my arms across my body. I looked past her at Lyra, who was standing with her head a little higher than normal. Ethereal vines wound up her arm.

Malon cleared his throat and stepped forward. "Congratulations to all of you. You are now the first dragon riders that Xeswal has seen in four hundred years. This is a great honor, and I trust you will treat it as such." He gestured to Axilya. "Axilya is our resident dragon expert, and will be instructing you all on the care of your dragon." He motioned with his hand, and a guard stepped forward, handing each of us a pile of folded leathers. "As for flight, that is something no one here has even attempted. It will be up to you and your dragon to figure that out together."

Sarphi held out her pile of clothing. "And these? New uniforms?"

Axilya stepped forward, holding her hand up. "Those are flight leathers. They have been crafted by the dynasty's best leather workers according to multiple diagrams and depictions found in historical documents and accounts."

Malon didn't give time for further questions before speaking up again. "You all are dismissed for now. I expect you all back here directly after your noon meal for your first lesson in dragon riding." He motioned to the door and two guards stepped forward, opening it and looking at us expectantly.

Reyland was the first to leave, and I couldn't miss the nasty looks that passed between him and Finn as he walked past. Whatever had been said while I was busy not throwing up had really left a mark on both of them. Sarphi and Lyra followed next, and I limped after them. They were all three walking faster than I was capable of at the moment, so I quickly lost sight of them down the hall. Finn stuck with me, wordlessly leading me back to our room.

"Hey." There was an air of awkwardness about us as we walked down the hall. "What's wrong?"

"Nothing." He didn't even look over at me. His voice carried that same agitation it had earlier during the dragon choosing. Enough bite that I decided it wasn't worth pushing right now.

Finn wordlessly pushed open the door to our living quarters and everyone was whispering to each other when I walked in. I shut the door behind me and turned to see everyone standing in the middle of the room.

Reyland looked at Sarphi, who nodded curtly before stating. "I think we all have something to discuss."

Chapter 22

Ashten

"Um..." I limped to my bed, desperate for somewhere to sit before my legs made that decision for me. None of my companions moved from their spot in the middle of the room. I winced as I sat down. "I'm just going to sit down, if you don't mind. My *everything* hurts. The trip here was pretty rough, so my body is in full protest after what just happened."

Sarphi and Reyland exchanged another look, but it was Lyra who spoke first. "Are you sure? Do you think she's ready?" She walked over to the door, placing her ear against it. "I mean, what if they hear us? The Captain specifically said not to mention anything to her."

"So what if they hear us?" Sarphi began pacing across the floor. "They can't possibly expect us to live in the same room for *however* long they intend to keep us here and not possibly learn anything about each other?" She walked over to Lyra, taking her hands and holding them between her own. "Plus, if we are correct, we may have much bigger problems."

Reyland, who was still standing in the middle of the room with his arms crossed, looked me dead in the eyes. "Don't worry. I am fairly certain that at least one thing that I have to say is correct." His usually blood-red eyes now had an ice blue ring around the outside of their irises.

A side effect of his earlier dragon encounter, if I had to guess. I could assume that, if I studied everyone else's eyes, I would find similar effects. But I wasn't studying anyone else's eyes. I couldn't even look away from Reyland's as he approached me. My pulse quickened unexpectedly as he knelt down in front of me, never breaking eye contact.

"You know," Reyland took my hand in his. "It has been a long time since I've had to kneel before the dynasty's princess."

No.

"Wha—" The words were caught in my throat as I looked frantically at every face in the room. I shot up from my bed, practically running across the room despite the pain that shot through my head from the sudden movement. "No. Absolutely not. You are insane! Why would you think I'm the Princess?"

Everything that Finn had said came to mind. He was so very adamant about not telling anyone who I was, yet these three had figured it out in less than twenty-four hours. They knew next to nothing about me but had figured out my biggest secret basically overnight. It made no sense.

Lyra was the first to move. She slowly approached me, holding her hands out like she was trying to calm a wild beast. "Because it makes sense. Just let us exp—"

"How?" My voice rose as I spoke. "How, in less than twenty-four hours, did any of you come to that conclusion?" My head pounded, and the room was suddenly way too small as Sarphi also began to inch closer. Reyland hung back, studying me while Sarphi joined Lyra in her efforts to calm me down.

How do you think they would react to finding out that you're the daughter of the man responsible for putting them here?

I stumbled backwards until my back was against the wall, both literally and figuratively. "No. No, no, no." My voice was shaking as Reyland shoved past Sarphi and Lyra. I couldn't explain the gripping fear that had encompassed all rational thought.

"What's wrong, Ashten?" His voice was laced with an unusual amount of concern as he stopped just short of arm's length away from me.

"I — I don't know!" I threw my trembling hands up submissively as I sank to the ground. My heart was racing and my head was pounding. I closed my eyes, waiting for whatever illogical punishment was coming for me next.

"Hey." Reyland's voice was soft. Softer than I had ever heard it before. "I need you to calm down."

A. Turner

I tried my best to slow my racing thoughts and slow my rapid breathing. I pried opened my eyes and peered through my arms to see Reyland, Sarphi, and Lyra all knelt down beside me. There was a lavender mist swirling around the room.

Wait.

No.

There was a lavender mist swirling around *me.*

"Come on, Ashten." Sarphi's voice was nearly a whisper as she slowly laid a hand on my arms. "We really need you to calm down."

I shrank away from her touch. "Wha — what's going on?" I looked from my companions to my hands, which were now almost completely encompassed in lavender smoke.

"It's your power. Psychic powers can be particularly hard to control, especially if you acquire them as a second ability." Reyland offered me a soft smile. "It's kinda like a second language. The first few times you're probably going to say something you don't mean. Especially if you are stressed out."

"Your powers are feeding off of your own emotions," Lyra spoke up. "Try either focusing it towards one of us or turning it off."

This was crazy. I had only had access to these powers for approximately 24 hours and now I was expected to just *turn them off?*

"I — I can't. I don't know how," I admitted. I was still acutely aware of my racing heart, but it didn't feel so bad now that I knew exactly what was causing it. "I don't know how to focus it or turn it off. I've never used these powers before. I was born with fire magic, not this."

Sarphi and Lyra exchanged panicked looks, but Reyland gently held his hand out to me. "Here. Take my hand."

I put my hand in his, the shaking calming a little as he softly stroked the back of my hand with his thumb. I sat helplessly as he used his free hand to lift my head to meet his eyes. His red irises were filled with the softest flicker of smoke. That familiar peppermint and smoke scent danced at the edge of my senses. I inhaled deeply, savoring the scent as it washed over me.

That must be him.

"Now I'm going to need you to focus on everything you are feeling. Just direct that energy into our hands." Reyland never looked away as he continued to give instructions. "Just imagine it like a river. You want all of the water to flow from you to me."

I closed my eyes and tried to do exactly what Reyland had said. I began pushing my thoughts towards him at first, using our hands as the connecting link. As my mind became clearer, it became easier to push the emotions away. Before long, I could feel the panic and fear begin to fade, ebbing like a receding tide. I opened my eyes to find that Reyland was still looking at me. He hadn't so much as moved the entire time.

"There you go." The hand holding mine shook, but Reyland only tightened his grip. The smoke in his eyes only intensified as I felt my magic begin to fade. "Perfect. You're perfect." His voice trembled a bit before he took a deep breath and let go of my chin to run his hand through his hair. He still held on tightly to my hand.

Now that the fear and panic were gone, I was deeply aware of a quite different feeling. One I refused to acknowledge and severely hoped Reyland couldn't feel. The mist surrounding my arm was gone, replaced instead by shadows. The same shadows that danced in Reyland's eyes right now. My face reddened as the shadows caressed my skin, sending a chill down my spine. My magic danced under my skin, matching the pattern of his shadows as they swirled around my arms. I entertained the feeling for only a moment more before dragging my hand away from his.

"Well, we are going to head to the mess hall." I could hear the barely contained nervousness as Sarphi spoke. I hadn't even noticed that she and Lyra had already walked to the door. They exchanged a glance that I couldn't quite understand before opening the door. Lyra walked out in front of Sarphi, who turned back to us. "Just don't lag for too long. Don't want anyone to come looking."

Reyland simply gave her a nod as she shut the door behind her. He walked over to his chest and pulled out a bottle. He sat back down beside me and took a sip before extending the bottle to me. I took one sip, almost choking on the alcohol as it hit my throat.

"You could have at least warned me first!" I shoved the bottle back at him, laughter taking over as the wall of tension came crashing down. I watched as he took two more long swallows before putting the lid back on the bottle.

"Consider it payback." Reyland chuckled as I continued to cough sporadically.

"Payback for what?" I asked between the coughs.

"For keeping you from imploding and taking all of us with you." Reyland leaned his head back against the wall.

"Thank you." The fact that I could have seriously injured everyone in this room chilled me to my core. I reached out and placed my hand over his, uncharacteristically craving physical touch. "Seriously. In case you hadn't pieced it together, I have absolutely no idea what I am doing." I laid my head back, mirroring Reyland.

"Being raised in the confines of a castle will have that effect."

"Speaking of." I leaned forward onto my knees. "How did you know? I feel as if I have been careful, and I honestly thought it would take more than twenty-four hours for me to screw this up."

Reyland leaned forward as well, never letting go of my hand as we sat eye to eye. "If I tell you, can you please not freak out on me like that again? I'm kind of drained right now."

"I can try my best. Honestly, I don't know what came over me the first time." I pulled my hand from Reyland's and placed them in my lap.

"Okay." Reyland looked at the door for a moment before turning back to me. "I knew you were the princess from the moment I saw you. We met once, a long time ago, and your violet eyes are unmistakable."

I studied his face for a second. There wasn't a single hint of laughter or sarcasm to be found. He wasn't joking. "What do you mean we've met before? I've never left the citadel." And I certainly didn't remember a Moon Elf visiting.

"My father brought me to visit when I was a young boy. No more than six." He chuckled and shook his head. "You stayed locked up in that library of yours nearly the entire time. I had to beg you to come outside with me just once."

Who was he that his father would have been invited to visit? It would make sense that I didn't remember though. I didn't remember a great deal of my childhood.

"While that all seems entirely accurate and believable, I'm sorry to say that it still isn't helping me remember anything. Who's your father?" A muscle in his jaw tensed as he regarded my question.

"My father is Rael Dronvakh."

I couldn't believe my ears. Reyland's father was the leader of the Moon Elves in Wrath Dorei. He had a seat on my father's council, but I never knew that he had a son.

Wait.

It all started to make sense to me at once. It's why Lyra looked so familiar to me. Because her brother had been a royal pain in my butt not but a week or so ago. But I didn't know there was a Windwalker daughter.

"And Lyra too?" He nodded in agreement with me but stayed quiet, letting me piece everything together at my own pace. "There is no Dragonfolk leadership, so I know that leaves Sarphi out of the 'discarded heirs' club, but I'm sure we can make an exception." A deep throated laugh escaped Reyland before he took another long drink from his bottle. "The biggest question is *why?*"

Reyland shrugged and offered me the bottle again. I obliged, drinking a comparatively small amount as he answered me. "That's what I was trying to figure out when you got here. I had been in the library trying to find any documents that mentioned elvish heirs being sent out here. The only particularly interesting thing I found was that it had actually never been done."

"And why not just ask us? Why resort to such forceful methods?" I took another drink from the bottle before handing it back to Reyland. "Who brought you here anyways?" Reyland tensed as the words left my mouth. "If you want to talk about it, that is. It's okay if you don't." The words fumbled out of my mouth.

"No. It's okay. I don't mind telling you." Reyland stood up and walked back to his chest. He hid the bottle back under some clothing before extending his hand to me. I grabbed it and let him pull me to my feet. My head swam a little and my skin crawled with a pleasant, warm feeling. I had whatever had been in that bottle to thank for that. "It is kind of a secret, though. Not a big one, just something I haven't told anyone else."

I made a clumsy attempt at drawing an 'x' over my heart. "Your secret is safe with me!" I offered him the biggest smile I could muster.

"I know it is."

The fact that he said it so matter-of-factly made my chest tighten a little. "You don't know me, though."

He reached out and grabbed my hand, and, to my surprise, I didn't pull away. "I don't have to. There's just something about you. I have no doubt in my mind that I can trust you." He stared at me as if he could see my soul, and for all I knew, he could. I had no idea how his dark powers worked.

Reyland inhaled deeply before speaking again. "When I was just 15 years old, my father had Captain Finn bring me here. He had decided that I was not proper heir material and hoped that a few hard days would teach me a lesson. I haven't seen him since." He raked his fingers through his hair.

I was at a loss for words. "I— I don't even know what to say." I tightened my grip on his hand.

"You don't have to say anything. Truly. It's enough to be able to share that secret with someone who isn't going to use it against me." I couldn't help but catch a flicker of uncertainty in his eyes.

"I would never." My voice was suddenly serious. "I promise. I am a firm believer in the idea that your blood means nothing when it comes to who you are as a person. Because trust me, I am *nothing* like my father." He gave me no response apart from a tight squeeze of my hand.

My pulse quickened the longer he looked at me. Not studied. Not stared. Just looked. Like he was afraid I may vanish if he looked away. I felt the warmth on my cheeks as he pulled me a little closer to him. Not too close, but close enough that I could smell the peppermint and smoke that seemed to radiate off of him. The logical part of my mind was telling me this was a bad idea, but my feet were firmly planted on the ground as he leaned in towards me. He stopped mere inches from my face and I could smell the alcohol on his breath.

"I've known you for less than twenty-four hours. Twenty- four hours and you've got me hooked." I didn't miss the way his eyes flickered down to my lips. "You haven't done a single thing, and the bad thing is that you don't have to."

I was speechless for the second time in less than five minutes. The magic under my skin danced where his hand held mine. My skin was on fire and I was trying to convince myself that it was just the alcohol. Just the alcohol making him say these things. Just the alcohol making me believe them. Just the alcohol convincing me that maybe I felt the same way about someone I had just met. But the alcohol wasn't to blame for why I couldn't take my eyes off of him any time he was in the room, and the alcohol sure couldn't be to blame for how my magic reacted to him.

"But." He interrupted my thoughts by stepping away from me. His face was flushed and the rise and fall of his chest was uneven. "I cannot, in good conscience, act upon my current wishes."

"Why not?" I tried to hide the disappointment in my voice.

"Because, Nightshade, I am not entirely sure that everything I just said is not at least somewhat influenced by the fact that I just absorbed a sizable amount of your emotion-altering magic." He offered me a lopsided grin before straightening his jacket. "We better get going before someone comes looking."

"Oh... Yeah. Of course." I didn't know why I was disappointed. I had no right to be disappointed. In fact, I should be embarrassed. I *was* in a relationship. With someone that definitely could have walked into this room at any minute. "I could definitely use some food. Having no self-control is tiring work." The joke sounded about as bad as I expected as it left my mouth. I smiled half-heartedly at him as he held the door open for me.

"You're telling me..." I barely heard him mumble as he shut the door behind us both.

Chapter 23

Reyland

I had never absorbed that much magic at one time. My head was still swimming from the exertion and the alcohol definitely wasn't helping. Not to mention all the stupid things I had said right after. And then telling Ashten it was just because of her magic? While not a complete lie, I had left out one important detail. Psychic magic that us Elves had access to couldn't make someone feel new feelings. It was only capable of amplifying someone's already existing feelings.

Ashten walked in front of me, arms folded across her body protectively. She hadn't said a word since we left the room, and I honestly couldn't blame her. I didn't have enough fingers to count the number of women who had given very similar confessions of love to me only for it to turn out that they were only interested in my father's power. It was why I quit letting myself get attached to anyone. It just wasn't worth the trouble. That's how she probably felt about me, and I didn't blame her.

I couldn't explain why she was able to squeeze past every defense that I had put up over the past six years without even trying. From the second she walked into that room, the entire direction of my life changed. I couldn't tell you how I knew it. I just did. Now I needed to find a way to convince her of it, too. As unfortunately desperate as I felt, I also knew now wasn't the time. Her entire life had been uprooted and the last thing she needed was some brooding male trying to tell her how to feel. I would have to settle for being content with our current relationship. No matter how much I wanted more.

"Soooo." Ashten's voice cut through my thoughts. "How'd you do that? Controlling my magic, I mean."

I took a few ample steps to catch up until we were walking side by side. "It's a way of using my dark magic that my instructors taught me back home. It's perfect for controlling people and it sucks for the receiving person if done without permission." Ashten gave me a questioning look. "I absolutely could have just siphoned your powers without asking. It would have hurt like hell, though."

"Well, I appreciate you asking then." She looked down at my hands and then back up at me. "Would you mind showing me your powers again? Before today, I had only ever seen people using fire magic."

I had never seen anyone so interested in my magic before. I held my hand up in front of me and summoned black tendrils of smoke. They swirled around in the air before curling up my arms and around my torso. Ashten watched quietly. Her violet eyes danced with amusement as I shaped my shadows into a protective shield.

"Wow." Her voice was breathy and quiet as she studied me. She reached out and gently ran her finger along the outside of the shadow shield. I tried my best to maintain my neutrality as her touch lingered. "I've never seen someone with so much control."

Impossible.

"What do you mean? I'm sure the instructors that your father hired were more than capable." I dismissed my shadows and crossed my arms. "Go on and show me what you can do."

Ashten shyly held out her hand and summoned a small orange flame. She closed her eyes, and it grew just a little before disappearing completely. Her face reddened in embarrassment as she stuck her hands into her pockets and shrugged.

"I, uh, didn't have an instructor." She gave me a half-smile. "My father isn't a very trusting man. He didn't want anyone in the citadel to be stronger than him."

I couldn't believe what I was hearing. "Wait. You're telling me that the princess, heir to the Desai dynasty and future protector of the continent, doesn't know how to use the powers that she has had since birth?" I waited patiently while Ashten made a show of thinking.

"Yep. That sounds about right." She stopped at the door to the dining hall. "Maybe you could help? I know that you don't have fire magic, but it can't be too different. Right?"

"I don't know." I shrugged. "But I would be honored, Princess." A smirk spread across my lips as I exaggerated the last word. Ashten shoved my shoulder, and I couldn't help but laugh at the glare she was leveling me with.

"No. Nope. Absolutely not." She pointed a finger at me. "You can call me whatever else you want, but 'princess' is off limits. I can't stand that title. Especially not now."

I threw my hands up and raised my eyebrows in surrender. "Fine. Fine. Whatever you say, Nightshade."

Ashten furrowed her brows. "I'm not complaining, but I have to ask. Why Nightshade?"

"Because." I placed my hand on the door handle, not quite meeting her eyes as I answered. "You're beautiful. Dangerously so."

Not waiting for her response, I pulled open the door to the mess hall right as someone tried to walk through. The string of curses that left my mouth were nowhere near enough to describe how I felt when my eyes met the anger filled eyes of Captain Finn.

Chapter 24

Finn

The day had sucked so far. That's probably why there was no hiding the blinding rage that washed over me when I opened that door to see Ashten and Reyland. Judging by the colorful language that they both muttered, I was probably the last person they expected to see upon opening this door. Believe me, the feeling was mutual.

"Reyland. Lunch. Now." I ground the words out as I stared at Ashten. Reyland muttered something under his breath that I couldn't quite hear as he shoved through the door past me. Ashten made to follow him, but I latched on to her forearm. "Not you. You're with me."

"Can't it wait until after lunch?" Ashten tried to pull her arm away from me, but I tightened my grip and dragged her down the hall. "Where are we going? Finn! Would you just talk to me for a second?"

I proceeded to drag her down the hall, fighting and ignoring her protests the entire time. I could apologize later. I *would* apologize later. Once I had a good explanation for what I had just interrupted, I would apologize. When we reached the door to my room, I quickly shoved the door open and pushed Ashten in before slamming the door shut behind me.

Ashten stumbled to the center of the room before whirling on me. "What do you think you are doing?! A simple 'Hey Ashten, can I talk to you for a moment?' would have sufficed!" Lavender smoke danced in her angry eyes as she crossed her arms. She was gearing up for a fight. One I was honestly in the mood to give her.

"If you are so keen for a conversation, do you care to explain why you and Reyland arrived for lunch so long after Sarphi and Lyra?" I closed the gap between us until I was close enough to smell the alcohol on her breath. "And don't even get me started on the fact that your breath stinks of liquor. I do not know how or where you acquired it, but I know the smell of alcohol better than I should." Her eyes widened as I finished my list of accusations, leaving my most pressing one unsaid, but she didn't back down.

"Well, I was unaware that lunch was a timed event." Ashten gave me a nasty look before taking a step back, putting some space between us. "As for the alcohol, I don't know what you are talking about."

I quickly closed the space between us once again, letting my anger get the best of me as I grabbed her arm again. "Well, Princess, if you are so set on lying to me, then I think you should just let me do the talking for a few minutes."

If she had more to say, she kept it to herself. I let her go and walked to the other side of the room. There was so much I wanted to say. I had heard exactly what Reyland had said to her before he opened that door, and it was eating me up inside. I thought we were done with all of that. Thought that bringing her here would finally end the years of standing off to the side while some other rich, entitled, prick of a noble tried to win her heart. What made this one sting even more is that she didn't seem to mind it.

"The next few months of your life are going to be full of things you never thought you would have to endure." I began pacing across the floor. "Everyone is going to sit back and watch you try and fail over and over again. You are going to be pushed to your limits and there is very little that I am going to be able to do to help you. My one job since I was old enough to wear this armor has been to protect you, but I can't do that here!" I stopped pacing to look directly at her. "I was not aware of just how many eyes the king has here. When we left Arvandor, I thought I would be done with having to stand back and watch you live your life without me. Done with standing off to the side while you entertained suitor after suitor. However, you've been here for less than twenty-four hours..." She started to speak, but I didn't give her the time. "Don't even try to deny it! I heard what Reyland said to you, *Nightshade*." The nickname left a nasty taste in my mouth that only intensified when I noticed the color of her cheeks darken.

"Wait, wait, wait." Ashten put her hands on her hip. "You mean to tell me that you dragged me all the way down here just to complain about some other male calling me beautiful?" A coy smirk spread across her face. "Finn Ward. You're *jealous*."

"Why wouldn't I be?" Her flippant response only fueled my anger. "Why *shouldn't* I be? I think I have earned the *right* to be jealous!"

"You can be jealous all you want, Finn." She waved her hand dismissively at me. "But, jealousy gives you no right to treat me like this! If you think it does, then we have a different problem."

"Well, I thank you for your permission, *Princess.*" I walked back to her, taking her hand in mine. "Sarcasm aside, I am sorry for my treatment of you." I brought her hand to my face, kissing it. Warmth bloomed where my lips met her skin. "I let my emotions get the best of me. I haven't had the best morning." Yes, I was mad. But I wasn't really mad at her. She just happened to be the one taking the fire.

"I feel like bad mornings are just part of the normal around here." Ashten gave me a soft smile and placed her hand on my cheek. "What's got you so upset, anyway?"

I leaned in to her touch and closed my eyes. "Honestly, the list is long. The fact that I have been summoned back to the Alterwood Citadel is at the top of it, though."

"Really?" Ashten took a step back in surprise. "Father doesn't want you to stay here and watch over me?"

"Apparently not." I shrugged. "His summons were not very clear. You know as well as I that asking questions would be futile."

"Yeah." Ashten scoffed. "I guess I had just hoped that he cared enough to make sure I was safe here."

"I shouldn't be gone long, Princess. If I leave tonight, I could be back by tomorrow evening assuming everything goes well." I schooled my face into a sense of seriousness. "I will not be here to protect you, Princess."

Ashten considered my words. "I think I will be okay, Finn. As far as people to be stuck with, Sarphi, Lyra and Reyland are not the worst. What's there to protect me from, anyway?"

"Quite a few things, Princess. This place is a training ground for the dynasty's military. You don't get a strong, calculating, and ruthless soldier by picking flowers and reading books." I rubbed the back of her hand. "There are so many things that you will have to do in the upcoming days. Things you have never done. Things you probably thought you would never have to do."

"Like?" Ashten furrowed her brows.

"Like learning how to fly on a dragon, for starters. Then there's the magic manipulation, the weapon handling, hand to hand combat." I make a show of counting on my fingers. "The list is truly endless. Anything that you can think of as being necessary for a soldier, you are going to have to learn."

Ashten's confused look only deepened. "But why? Why me? What happened that caused my father to suddenly want me to learn these things? I've been begging him for *years* to at least learn how to use my magic for more than just lighting my hearth, but he has outright refused."

I shrugged. "Maybe he had a change of heart. Just promise me that you will be careful. I worry about what would happen should anyone find out. Not everyone in this place will be as understanding about your disdain for your upbringing as I." I placed a gentle kiss on her head.

"Yeah. Sure. Absolutely." Ashten seemed to fumble over the words. "Don't worry. I'm certain that once I figure out how to control my powers, I will be able to take care of myself."

"And until then? Who will protect you until then, Princess?" I tilted her chin up to me. "I don't trust anyone to take care of you like I can." Ashten's arms slid around my waist and I let her gently pull me closer.

"I appreciate your concern. I really do." She stepped up on her tiptoes, giving me a soft kiss. "I will have to learn to take care of myself, eventually."

I gave her another kiss. "I know. But I wish you didn't." I couldn't help but crack a smile. "Because then I will be out of a job."

Ashten slapped me on the shoulder before pulling away. "I am going to go eat lunch now. I have been awake without food for an illegal amount of time." She walked to the door, which I just noticed was slightly ajar. "Finn?"

I raised my eyebrows. "Yes, Princess?"

She pointed a finger at me. "If you *ever* treat me like that again, *you* will be the one who needs protecting."

Without thinking, I rushed to the door and slammed it shut before she had a chance to walk out. I roughly pulled Ashten back against my chest and deliberately trailed a finger down her arm all the way to her fingertips. "How would you like me to treat you?" I felt her shudder as I ran my fingers back up her arm, over her shoulder, and across the front of her chest. I leaned down and placed a gentle kiss on her neck.

"This isn't a poor start." Her voice was breathless as she leaned her head back, exposing more of her neck. I took the opportunity to trail a few soft kisses up her neck and jawline.

I turned her around, kissing her roughly before she had the chance to react. She leaned into the kiss, wrapping her arms around my waist. I could feel her fingers fumbling with the clasps on my armor, but I was content to explore until she figured it out. My hands explored her back, drinking in her moan when I tightened my hands on her waist and used my body to press her against the now closed door. I pulled her hands away from my body and pinned them above her head with one hand. Resting my forehead against hers, I was enamoured by the sight of her darkened violet eyes as she looked up at me.

"Princess." I breathed, the rise and fall of our chests matching in intensity. "The last thing we need is for a rumor to start about our *involvement*." I gently lowered her hands to her side. "Besides, I would hate for you to miss lunch."

"I think they could get over it. I think *I* could get over it." She reached for my face again, but I stepped away before she could pull me in for another kiss. What I could only describe as a whine escaped her lips at the space that was now between us. "Please?" She made a show of pouting, sticking out her bottom lip as far as it would go.

"As much as I would love to hear you beg, I can't have you getting lightheaded and falling off of your dragon." I reached past her and turned the doorknob. "Now, off you go." I planted a chaste kiss on her forehead.

"You're no fun." Her smile betrayed her tone of voice as she turned and walked out of the door.

I stood at the doorway watching until she turned the corner and left my sight. Stepping back into my room, I shut the door behind me and leaned against it with my head in my hands.

"You're an idiot." I spoke out loud as I ran my hands down my face. "An idiot who has gone and fallen in love."

Chapter 25

Reyland

I stormed across the dining hall, narrowly avoiding knocking plates out of several blacksmiths and soldier's hands. Sarphi and Lyra both jumped when I slammed my fist onto the table and plopped down into the chair. I ran my hand through my hair, letting out a loud sigh.

"Lady troubles?" Sarphi didn't hide her smirk as she took a drink from her mug. "You should really figure out how to hide the alcohol smell on your breath, by the way."

"I'm not in the mood, Sarphi." My voice was filled with a bite that I didn't care to apologize for. Sarphi rolled her eyes and leaned back in her chair. She should be used to my bad attitude by now, anyway.

Lyra cleared her throat. "Where's Ashten? Is she okay?"

I leaned back in my chair. "She was fine when we left the room. I can't speak for now, though."

"Why not?" Sarphi questioned.

"Because as soon as we showed up at the dining hall, we were interrupted by Captain Finn. He basically ignored me, but he demanded she go with him." Which didn't settle well with me. Any time the Captain needed to "speak in private," with someone, it never ended well.

"What could he possibly need to ask her that he couldn't ask in front of the rest of us?" Lyra's voice was laced with concern. She knew as well as I what went on behind locked doors here. I was thankful that she didn't have any scars to prove it.

"I don't know." That was the worst part. *I didn't know.* It was eating me alive. "I can't just sit here and wait." I shoved away from the table, ignoring Sarphi's protests as I stormed back across the room.

I couldn't just sit and eat my lunch knowing that there was even the slightest possibility that Ashten could be in more trouble than she even realized. I exited the hall quickly, hoping to catch sight of them before they went too far. There was a flash of black hair and a red jacket whipping around the corner. Ashten's protests made them easier for me to follow through the winding halls of this place. I heard the door to a room click open before rapidly slamming shut.

I crept down the hall, stopping outside each door until I could hear talking on the other side. Talking that quickly developed into yelling. I couldn't quite make out what was being said, but I definitely recognized Ashten's voice. I pressed my ear against the door, trying my best to understand what was being said on the other side, to no avail.

A. Turner

The yelling very quickly died down, and I started to get worried. I needed to get eyes on her. I carefully turned the knob on the door, peering through the crack that opening the door created. Captain Finn had his hand on Ashten's chin. My hands started to shake as Ashten wrapped her arms around his waist. She gave him a soft smile, and I watched helplessly while she kissed him.

No.

I couldn't believe what was happening. My vision went red when he leaned down to kiss her for a second time. I had rushed down here to save her from some horrible thing. Turns out she didn't need my help at all. Didn't want my help either, judging by how she looked at him when he smiled at her.

I had seen enough. I backed away from the door as quietly as I could before stumbling back down the hall. What was this feeling? My head was swimming and my vision was blurry. There was a tight pain in my chest as I rounded the corner back towards the mess hall. I *hated* it. I hated how she looked at him. It should be me that she looked at like that. He didn't deserve it.

I took a deep breath as I reached the door to the mess hall. He didn't deserve her affection, but she didn't know that. That fact made me feel even worse. I took another deep breath and schooled my features into a practiced neutrality. I just needed to make it through lunch with my mouth shut. What I just witnessed wasn't my secret to tell, no matter how badly I wanted to scream.

Chapter 26

Ashten

I hurried back to the dining hall, hoping that no one had noticed my prolonged absence. Sarphi and Lyra waved as I sat down with a plate full of what little was left from the cooks. They dove back into their food, making vague small talk about the morning's events. Reyland sat seething at the end of the table. I risked a glance his way a few times, only to find him staring at his plate. He picked up a piece of meat with his fork before putting it back down. Something was bothering him. I had gathered that he normally kept to himself, but this was quiet, even for him. Thankfully, lunch was uneventful compared to everything else that had happened this morning. It wasn't long before we were all back in our room discussing the implications of what had happened that morning.

"So..." I settled onto my bed cross-legged. "Does anyone have the slightest idea of what happened this morning?"

Surprisingly, Lyra was the first to answer. "According to my limited knowledge on the history of Xeswal, each of the elvish leaders would appoint Dragonriders as their own personal guards. They called them Drakewardens. I know that my father still has Drakewardens." Her shoulders dropped slightly. "And I know that your father still has Drakewardens, Ashten." She gave me a small smile before looking pointedly at Reyland, who looked like he was trying his hardest not to take part at all.

He shrugged as he plopped down onto his bed, stretching out and folding his arms behind his head. "Not a clue. A lot can change when you're not around." He cut his glance towards me. Smoke swirled in his eyes before he closed them, exhaling slowly. He got up with an unnatural quickness, rummaging through his chest for what I could only assume was his bottle of alcohol.

"But a crowned heir has never been a Drakewarden before, correct?" Sarphi cut in. She pinned Reyland with a questioning stare before continuing. "And none of this even begins to explain where I fit into this entire scenario."

"Exactly. All of the Drakewardens in recorded history have been elves of noble standing, but no crowned heirs, and definitely no Dragonfolk." She smiled sheepishly at Sarphi, who waved her off dismissively. "As far as what happened this morning, I can only assume that it was some rudimentary attempt at the ritual they would perform to bind the Drakewardens to their dragons."

"Well, I wouldn't quite call it an attempt." I held out my arm and allowed the lavender mist to swirl around my hand and up my arm. "I know little about bonding with a dragon, but I would say it worked. I have felt different ever since this morning, and I have never been able to summon this magic on command. My magic has always wielded me more than I have wielded it." My face reddened with embarrassment as my earlier freak out flashed through my mind.

"I've always been able to use both life and storm magic, but my control of it has definitely improved." Lyra held out her hand and manifested a singular, nearly translucent, vine. It slithered across the floor to Sarphi's bed, climbing up the side of it. Sarphi giggled as the vine poked at her wings.

Sarphi swatted at the vines until Lyra dismissed them. Sarphi held up a singular, flaming hand. "I have known that I could use fire magic for a long time, but it feels so much stronger now. Like a bomb in my chest."

Reyland finally emerged from his chest with a book in his hand. He walked over and handed it to me, not making eye contact as he sat back down on his bed. I looked down at the book, which was bound in plain leather with a singular dragon shaped stamp in the center.

"I took this from the library. I was going to give it to Lyra to study. It contains the written record of every dragon known to have existed on the continent of Xeswal until the last one was killed a century or so ago." He leaned back on his bed, apparently satisfied that he had contributed enough.

I opened the book and began thumbing through the pages. Sarphi and Lyra sat on either side of me, looking over my shoulders. I wasn't quite sure what in this could answer our questions, but at the very least, I could try to find Nyzirth in all of this. I found the starting page for the purple dragons and began reading off names. Century after century. Name after name. They all started to run together by the time I reached the end. Oddly enough, I didn't find my dragon's name.

"Um... My dragon's name isn't in this book." I skimmed them again, to no avail. She wasn't here. "I double checked everything."

Sarphi reached over and grabbed the book from my hand. I watched as she flipped to the section about red dragons and began skimming the names. A few minutes passed before she looked up at me and shook her head. "Cyphis's name isn't in here either. What's your dragon's name, Lyra?"

"Iressei." Lyra's face lit up as she spoke the name.

Sarphi quickly scanned the section on green dragons, but unsurprisingly did not find that one either. "What about you, Reyland?" She began flipping the pages to get to the section on white dragons.

"Zothim," I blurted.

Reyland froze and his head whipped in my direction. "How'd you know that?" His eyes bore into me, brows furrowed.

"I... I don't know," I stammered. "The name just popped into my mind as soon as she asked the question. I don't know why I said it out loud, honestly." I covered my face as heat spread across my cheeks.

"Well, that name is not in here either." Sarphi began rapidly flipping through each of the sections, muttered under her breath as she scanned the last entry in each. "I think that our problem lies in the fact that the last dragon listed in here was nearly two centuries ago."

"Zynnos." Lyra didn't even have to look at the book to know. "Zynnos was the last dragon recorded because she was thought to be the last dragon alive. A beautiful purple dragon. Not but a few years old. The king at the current time, King Vulmon, ordered her to be hunted and killed." Lyra's face reddened and she hid behind my shoulder. "Sorry... I really like dragons. Always have."

I patted her gently on the shoulder. "Well, I get the feeling we are going to need someone with some dragon knowledge on our team." I placed the book on the bed and stood up. "Do you know why they had ordered her killed?"

Lyra shrugged. "I've never seen a written reason. Just that the king ended up hiring a group of adventurers to undertake the task after losing so many of his men to the endeavor. My father said that the last *true* Drakewarden was well before he was born. His Drakewardens, as well as my grandfather's, simply held the title. None of them had ever ridden a dragon."

"Well, King Vulmon was my grandfather. He died nearly fifty years ago, so I guess asking him is out of the question." Sarphi and Lyra had moved to one end of my bed, so I sat down on the other end. "There is one more thing that doesn't really make sense, though."

"Lyra's powers." Reyland cut in. He had been indefinitely more interested in the conversation since I blurted out his dragon's name. His stare was making my skin crawl, but in a not entirely unpleasant way as he walked over to us. "My dragon matches my second power, ice, not the dark magic I was born with. Ashten was born with fire, not psychic. Sarphi's dragon is red, not blue like her own scales. But Lyra, your dragon is green. Your life abilities got stronger, not your storm magic."

"Exactly," I finished. "I wonder why you bonded with a green dragon instead of a blue one."

Lyra shrugged again. "I honestly don't know much about why or how dragons choose their riders. I doubt anyone alive truly does, as none of them have ever experienced it. All I know is that once bonded, a dragon and their rider were nearly inseparable. Neither could survive being a great distance apart for too long and if one died, the other would go through a long, painful grieving period. Most riders didn't survive..."

"Well, I foresee a library trip in our future." Sarphi stood from the bed just as there was a knock at the door. She strode over and opened it. Finn stood at the door, still in the black leathers from earlier.

"It's time for your first flight lesson. Get changed and I will escort you back to the dragoncave." He stood with his hands behind his back, no signs of his earlier anger as he barked his commands. I did catch his eyes shifting between me and Reyland briefly before he schooled his features.

Reyland stormed past Sarphi. "Yeah. Just give us a few minutes." He slammed the door in Finn's face, grabbed his new uniform off of his bed, and stalked behind the changing divider.

I questioningly looked at Sarphi and Lyra, who both shrugged.

"I was honestly hoping you would know the answer to that question." Sarphi whispered as she pulled off her shirt. Her shirt had buttons down one side that allowed her to easily slide it off around her wings.

I tried my best not to stare, but I had to admit that her physique was impressive. She wasn't brawny by any means, but that seemed to have no effect on the amount of muscle she had developed. The muscles in her abdomen flexed as she reached down to undo her boots. Black lines of what I could assume was a tattoo streaked from her back to the tops of her shoulders. My face grew hot, and I quickly found my own boots very interesting as she started to pull off her pants.

Sarphi chuckled, causing my face to only grow hotter. "I guess I should have asked. Lyra and I have grown accustomed to changing in the same room. Having to use a semi-public washroom will have that effect." I could hear shuffling and saw Lyra's shirt and pants fall into a pile on the ground out of the corner of my vision. "We can both turn around, if that would make you more comfortable."

"It's nothing against you guys," I quickly blurted, not moving my eyes an inch from the study of my own boots. "I am just not used to this, uh, lack of privacy." The snapping of buttons and shifting of leather filled the uncomfortable silence.

"All done," Lyra chimed.

I finally looked up, color still staining my cheeks. The new uniforms that they were both wearing were very similar to what Finn had been wearing. Skin tight leather pants, a dark shirt, and a form fitting leather jacket that buttoned up the front. They both pulled on their usual boots before grabbing the book of dragons off of my bed and settling onto Sarphi's bed, their backs to me.

I looked back and forth between them and the divider that Reyland was behind. The idea of him coming out from behind that divider before I was fully dressed was what spurred me on as I quickly changed into the new leathers. I found the way they hugged my form strangely comforting as I snapped the last few buttons.

"All done." I mimicked Lyra as I pulled on my boots.

"Took you long enough," Reyland mumbled from behind the divider.

I couldn't help but stare as he walked around the divider. Much like the rest of us, his uniform fit him *perfectly*. It accentuated every muscle he had. I swallowed hard and cursed under my breath as my face grew even redder. It took me a moment to realize that he was staring at me, too. His eyes darkened and his throat bobbed as he looked me up and down. On any other day, I would have been appalled. Apparently, my body had other ideas. Ideas that I was trying my best to shut out.

He walked up to me and leaned over so that only I could hear as he whispered, "You look deadly, Nightshade. In all the *best* ways."

My breath caught as his lips brushed my ear before he straightened his back and walked over and opened the door. It was apparently, and thankfully, Lyra's turn to blush as Sarphi leaned over and whispered something to her before striding to the open door, where a furious Finn stood, staring daggers at Reyland, who could not have looked less bothered.

"Let's go," Finn ground out, giving me a short second look before turning and leading us all back down the hall to what I could only expect to be the most eventful part of our day. And that was saying something.

Chapter 27

Ashten

We entered what was apparently called the dragoncave to find Malon and Axilya waiting in the same spots we had left them. We all filed in and stood side by side in a single line across the room. Finn broke away from us to assume his position beside his associates. As soon as he did, Reyland slid over, closing the gap between him and I. I watched Finn's fists tighten, but his face stayed the perfect picture of unbothered as Axilya spoke up.

"I am so glad to see that everyone's flight leathers fit them. If you notice that any adjustments need to be made after today's outing, let me know and I will get them back to the leathersmiths." She began pacing back and forth in front of us. "Before you call your dragons, each of you will be given a set of weapons that have been specifically designed with you in mind." She pointed to Malon, who slid a bag from his shoulder to the ground and began pulling out weapons.

"For Reyland," Malon began. "A singular longsword. Forged from an alloy of both the strongest and lightest metals in the dynasty, it is both lightweight and durable." I watched in amazement as he pulled a longsword from a bag that was half its size. Its silver blade brilliantly reflected the dim lighting and its hilt was beautifully crafted into the shape of a dragon's head. "I have heard tales of how skilled you are with a longsword. I hope to see even more improvement with such a fine blade as this." He held the sword out to Reyland, who took it and gave it a few experimental swings. A wicked smile that sent a shiver down my spine spread across his face, and he nodded appreciatively at Malon.

Malon continued, pulling two shortswords out. "These are for Sarphi. Much like Reyland's blade, these shortswords are designed to be half the weight of normal blades. This should allow you to take advantage of your natural quickness to overcome your opponents." He handed both of them out to Sarphi. She took them, flipping one over in her hand and holding them both up in front of her.

"Oh yeah." She looked over the blades at me. "These will do just fine."

Malon nodded curtly before continuing. "For Lyra, we have a beautiful bow crafted by the best woodsmiths that hail from the Mistymoon Glades." The bow he presented to Lyra was carved in the shape of a dragon's spine, and its silver string seemed to glow. He also handed her a leather quiver that had a few basic arrows in it. "We all agreed that, being the gentler of the group, you would prefer a quieter, less direct weapon." Lyra only nodded as she stiffly took the bow from him. Her throat bobbed as she resumed her place next to us.

"As for Ashten," Malon reached into his seemingly never ending bag and pulled out a bundle of daggers. All of them looked similar in design to Sarphi and Reyland's blades, just smaller. "I honestly wasn't sure what type of weapon would suit you, but Finn here seemed to have some ideas. We figured he knew best, given his time served at the citadel." I felt Reyland tense beside me as this information set in. Information that I had intended to keep to myself.

Finn grabbed the daggers from Malon and brought them over to me. "I felt that, given your small size and lack of combat experience, you would be more suited to something light and quick."

I grabbed one from him and removed it from its sheath. Though I had never held a weapon before, I could tell that this one was nearly perfect. It felt nearly weightless as I slid it back into the sheath and took an awkward step back to be beside Reyland.

"Each of your uniforms was tailored with these specific weapons in mind," Finn continued, addressing the entire group this time. "You will find that sheaths, hooks, and belts have all been sewn into your uniforms. For example, Ashten, you have several slots for daggers in your boots, inside your jacket, and built into the leathers along your ribcage and back. The rest of you will find something similar on your own uniforms."

I watched as my companions put away their weapons. Sarphi's blades fit perfectly between her wings while Lyra's bow seemed to just hang from her back magically. She even jumped up and down a few times, but it didn't budge. Reyland's sword slid at an angle across his back, most of the blade disappearing beneath his jacket.

I unbuttoned my jacket and, sure enough, there were several spots perfect for daggers. Finn approached with the rest of my daggers. I stiffened as he began sliding the weapons into the various sheaths. His fingers brushed against my ribcage with each dagger. I tried my best to hide my blush as he slipped a dagger into the last slot. He held one more out to me and my hand was shaking as I took it. I slid that one into my boot. His eyes darkened as he took one last look at me before walking back to his station.

Reyland watched him walk the entire way back. I couldn't quite place the look on Reyland's face, but I sure didn't miss the smugness with which Finn smiled at him once he turned back around. The only reaction I picked up on from Reyland was the tensing of his jaw.

I wonder what that was about?

"I felt it prudent that each of you had some way to defend yourself before your first flight." Axilya shrugged. "As I cannot guarantee your safety once you climb onto your dragon's back."

They really weren't kidding. They seriously intended for us to climb onto the backs of dragons we had met mere hours ago and just *go for a ride.* Like they were ponies. I thumbed at the blades that were now strapped across various parts of my body. I doubted these would do me any good if Nyzirth changed her mind about me.

A. Turner

"*I would never,*" A low, purring voice cut through my head, causing me to jump. "*We take bonding with our riders very seriously. If I thought I was going to change my mind, I wouldn't have chosen you to begin with.*"

"*Are you always here?*" I couldn't believe this. I was talking with a dragon. In my head.

"*Not always. I mean, I could be if you wanted me to, but I just assumed you wanted some privacy.*"

"*Well, I appreciate that.*" I rubbed my head in a feeble attempt to stave off my growing headache.

"*Don't worry.*" Nyzirth spoke slower this time. "*The headache will go away. Before long, it will be like I'm not even here.*"

"*You speak as though you have experience?*" I questioned.

"*No. But, unlike humans, bonding like this is natural for us. It doesn't strain our bodies like I can assume it does yours.*"

Okay. It felt good to know that at least one of us had an idea of what was going on. Even if it was the one who had the least to fear of something going wrong.

"*So, how do we do this? The whole flying thing?*" I looked around at the other Drakewardens. They all seemed to be lost in thought, undoubtedly having their own interesting conversations.

"Just follow my lead."

The flapping of wings filled my ears as Nyzirth dove through the opening in the top of the cavern. She landed with an unexpected amount of grace, stretching her wings and shaking her head like a dog. She surveyed the room briefly before letting out an ear-splitting roar. I approached her carefully, still not able to completely override my self-preservation instincts.

"Well," Axilya shouted from her new position on the other side of the room. "I guess you're up first, Ashten!"

Apparently so.

Nyzirth lowered her head to me, nearly knocking me over as she nuzzled against my chest. She chittered rhythmically when I stroked her nose before she finally lifted her head and surveyed the room again. I didn't risk looking around for myself for fear that I would change my mind. Instead, I studied the scales that ran along her back. There were a few places, one in particular near her shoulders, that I may be able to settle in to.

"Climb on!" Nyzirth chimed as she did her best to kneel, dropping her shoulder as low as she could.

I climbed onto her foot and felt her shift, lowering her wing for me to use as a handhold. When I grabbed on, the webbed wing was surprisingly cool and leathery. I pulled with all of my might, my arms shaking with the effort of only trying to lift my own body weight.

I felt Nyzirth shift again before feeling myself being boosted into the air. My hands flew back, finding cool scales beneath them. I looked over my shoulder and found myself eye to eye with Nyzirth.

"Careful there." She rumbled as she finished lifting me to her shoulder. *"Just settle down right in front of my wings. Yeah, right there at the base of my neck should be fine."*

I swung my leg over her body and leaned forward like she said. It was definitely more like I was lying on her back rather than straddling her like a horse, but it would have to work. I settled in, finding two spines to hold on to that I could almost wrap my hand around.

"Ready?" Nyzirth stretched her wings and gave them a few test flaps.

"No." I laid my head down against her cool scales. Nyzirth trilled as she flapped her wings a few more times. *"What if I fall off?"*

"Don't."

That was my final warning before she shot into the air.

My heart flew into my throat as we gained altitude. My eyes were closed and I could hear nothing but the steady, heavy flapping of wings as we climbed. There was already a burning in my arms from the amount of strength it was taking to hold on. I was thankful that I had tied my hair back this morning as the loose strands slapped against my neck and face. The drumming of her wings stopped briefly before picking up pace as a bright light seared through my eyelids. We seemed to level out, and the bubbles in my stomach settled slightly as her wings fell into a steady rhythm.

"*Open your eyes.*" Her voice was soft and gentle.

Using the few spines that peppered her back as handholds, I slowly sat up. I kept my eyes closed as I fought to find my center of balance. It only took a few moments for up and down to become discernible. Nothing could compare to what I saw when I pried my eyelids open.

Ocean. Nothing but ocean for as far as I could see. Small waves rippled on its surface, and I could just barely make out a few sea creatures surfacing. The sun was high in the sky this time of day, its bright rays shining through the clouds that were now just barely above my head. Curiosity beat out logic as I leaned over to look beneath us. I could almost see both sides of the massive desert island from this height. Mount Wrath stood massive in its center. From here, it was not nearly as daunting as it had been when I stood at its base.

"Wow," I breathed. "This is beautiful."

"Isn't it?" I could feel Nyzirth's chest rumble in delight as she spoke in my head.

"I could spend my entire life up here." I absentmindedly stroked the back of Nyzirth's neck, feeling her purr below my palm. *"Truly. This is the most magnificent thing I have seen."*

"I have seen it every day of my life, and it has never gotten old." Nyzirth banked sharply as we reached the edge of the island, causing me to slide sideways before painfully pulling myself back up.

"Why don't you leave?" The thought was at the forefront of my mind as soon as it reached my brain. *"You can fly anywhere you want. You flew all the way to the Deadlands, but you're back here on this island."*

"This island is all I have ever known, Ashten. The elves down in that cave were here when I hatched. They have done everything in their power to keep me close. Limiting food sources, keeping me in that cave, refusing to allow me to fly." I could feel her sorrow as she spoke. *"I only flew out to the Deadlands because I could sense you. After you chased me away, I came back here."* She made another sharp turn, but I was more prepared this time. *"I was punished for it, you know."*

"I'm sorry, Nyzirth." I continued to stroke her neck. I risked a glance at her wings behind me. I could just barely make out scars and slashes that I had not noticed before. My hand drifted to where the bruise on my cheek had been. Bile rose in my throat at the thought of what they had done to her. *"The Alterwood Citadel is all I have ever*

known. When I... left, my father was fairly unhappy with me. I think he hopes I will view being here as some sort of punishment as well."

"Do you?"

I pondered her questions. I certainly had at first. Those first few days in the Deadlands with Finn, I spent all of my time wondering what I had done to deserve this. But now? Knowing that I wasn't the only heir that had been sent here. It was feeling less like a punishment already. *"If it is a punishment, it's worth every second."*

My earlier conversation with the others came to mind. Bonding with dragons had never been done by an elvish heir before, much less a Dragonfolk. If giving me a dragon was my father's idea of a punishment, I would love to see what kind of rewards he gave out.

Suddenly, Nyzirth came to an almost complete stop, hovering in the air with slow, methodical flaps of her wings. She lifted her head high as if sniffing the air. Without warning, she dove back towards the center of the island. I fumbled around for something to grab on to as she picked up speed. I assumed we were headed back to the dragoncave until she flew right past the mountain.

"Where are we going?" I pushed my thoughts towards her. I wasn't entirely sure how this mind-speaking worked, but I assumed she wasn't going to hear me over the wind otherwise.

"To your friends. Zothim has apparently shown them where we dragons are kept." She sounded agitated. She slowed down only

slightly before folding her wings against her body. *"You're going to want to hold on tight."*

We began diving towards the ground at a very high speed. My eyes watered from the wind as we got closer and closer to the sandy earth. *What was she doing?* At this rate, we were going to crash into the ground before she could stop. The desert was getting closer by the second and Nyzirth was only getting faster. I had no choice but to close my eyes and accept my fate as we dove headfirst into the sand.

Chapter 28

Ashten

I braced myself for a crash that never came. Instead, I could no longer feel the warmth of the sun as Nyzirth's wings began to flap again, slow and steady this time. I could tell we were slowing down. My heart felt like it was about to explode out of my chest when she landed on the ground with a thud.

"I know it's dark in here, but keeping your eyes closed isn't going to change that." Reyland did not try to hide the amusement in his voice. I faintly heard Sarphi and Lyra chuckle somewhere off to the side.

"Where are we?" I asked out loud. The air was damp and warm, but it was much cooler than I had been used to on the island. I made no effort to sit up or open my eyes while waiting for Nyzirth's response.

"Open your eyes and look. It's worth it, I promise." Nyzirth folded her wings against her body as I slowly sat up.

The first thing that caught my attention was the crystal lined walls. Hundreds, if not thousands, of opalescent, tower shaped crystals protruded from the earthen walls. They all glowed dimly, their light reflecting off of Nyzirth's scales beautifully. We were somehow in some sort of underground cavern.

A. Turner

"You said this is where you are kept? As in, you can't leave?" I patted her on the shoulder and, as if she knew exactly what that meant, Nyzirth lowered her shoulder towards the ground.

I swung my leg over her body and studied the distance from here to the ground. It was farther than I had hoped it would be, and I was sure I would make a fool of myself trying to get down. As I prepared myself for the imminent embarrassment, a hand shot into my view.

"May I?" Reyland held his hand up towards me. The iridescent light from the crystal walls danced through his windswept white hair.

Even with him standing and reaching as far as he could, I couldn't reach his hand. I slid down Nyzirth's leg, latching on tightly to Reyland's hand on the way down. The drop was about ten feet, and every inch of it reverberated through my body as my feet struck the ground. My knees buckled, but Reyland's free arm wrapped around my waist, keeping me steady. He pulled me against him and the scent of peppermint and smoke filled my nose immediately. I looked up at him and didn't miss how his eyes darkened as he looked down at me. I didn't even realize that my hand had drifted to his chest until Sarphi cleared her throat.

"Careful." Reyland's voice was thick as he lowered his arms, stepping away. He gave Nyzirth a sideways glance. "You really are quite beautiful." He slowly reached up to stroke her neck, careful not to spook her.

"They all are." I looked around the massive cavern at all of my companions and their dragons. Iressei was curled against a wall with Lyra settled in against her side. Her bright red hair stood out against the vibrant green dragon and, for the first time since I met her twenty-four hours ago, Lyra actually looked comfortable. Sarphi was stroking Cyphis's nose, the massive red dragon leaning into her touch, eyes closed like a kitten. She gave me a sideways glance, a hint of knowing in her eyes, and a smile playing across her lips. I wasn't sure what she was hinting at, but offered a tight-lipped smile back before feeling my attention being pulled to Reyland again.

I was drawn to him. I couldn't explain it. My eyes followed him carefully as he strode back to Zothim. The white dragon, who was laying in the far corner of the cave, regarded him lazily before resting his massive head on the ground. Reyland ran a hand along his smooth scales as he walked past and leaned against the wall of the cavern. As if he could tell that I was watching him, he looked up. I could just barely make out his crimson red eyes from this far away. He did not bother to disguise his gaze as anything but what it was as his eyes traveled up and down the length of my body. My skin tingled and I could feel the heat rising up my neck. My clothes were suddenly too tight, and I pulled at the neck of my shirt to get some relief. A smirk spread across Reyland's face as he stuck his hands into his pockets.

A. Turner

"So, according to Iressei, this is where they are kept." Lyra's voice interrupted the absolute mess that was in my head right now.

"Kept? As in contained?" I asked again, out loud this time. Lyra, who was still sitting on the ground, looked up at her dragon, and I waited patiently for an answer.

"Sort of." Lyra turned back to me. "They obviously can't stop these guys from doing anything now, but they kept them down here from the time they hatched until they started to fly." She patted Iressei's side. "This natural cavern connects to the volcano if you continue down that tunnel." She pointed to the far side of the cavern.

"How do the dragons get out of here? How did *we* get down here?" I looked up at the ceiling of the cavern. I could see no sign of an opening or crevice large enough for a dragon to fly through.

"There is a natural crevice that leads down here. Laeovyn imparted some of her psychic magic onto a section of that crevice to create an illusion." Sarphi looked over to Cyphis. "Did I say that correctly?" The red dragon nudged her, but Sarphi added nothing to her statement.

Is that something I could do?

"But why do you stay?" I looked at Nyzirth. "They apparently have some powerful magic users, but I can't imagine they can keep you guys here against your will."

"No. They cannot." Nyzirth looked at her fellow dragons. *"Dragons are naturally territorial creatures. We rarely live with others of our species, but we do usually stay very close to where we are born. This island is all we have ever known. And now..."* She looked at me, the crystals reflecting off of her amethyst eyes. *"We go where you go."*

I assumed everyone else was getting similar explanations from their dragons. I waited an appropriate amount of time before responding, not wanting to interrupt anyone's conversation.

"And if we wanted to leave?"

"Then we would leave." There was no hesitation from Nyzirth.

A careful silence settled over the cavern.

"As much as I would love to get out of here, I cannot help but be curious about what is going on here." Sarphi was the first to speak up.

"Besides, where would we go?" Reyland approached us, leaving his perch against the wall. "I know for a fact that I am not wanted at home." He raised his eyebrows at us.

"I don't care if I'm wanted or not, I'm not going home." Lyra's voice was small.

Sarphi gave a nonchalant shrug. "I don't have a home to go back to."

A. Turner

They all turned their attention to me and I realized that I didn't really have an answer. Sure, I could go home, but what then? I would walk through the citadel doors and accuse my father of instructing his men to kidnap me and tote me across the continent, but to what end? Sure, I would have a dragon to back up my story, but one only I could talk to. My father was not only a powerful man, but a persuasive one. He could feed the people some downplayed story about how or why I have a dragon, and everyone that mattered would believe him. The only other person who could back up my story would be Finn, but would he? He was technically complicit in my kidnapping. My father would most definitely pin everything on Finn if he tried to go against him. That's just the kind of person he was.

"Even if I went home, I would need proof to expose what is going on here." I let out a defeated sigh. "And I *know* that something malicious is going on here. There is no other explanation for why he secretly has the Dronvakh, Windwalker, and Desai heirs all here. And against our wills at that. I just don't have any proof."

"So we'll get proof." Reyland placed his hand on my shoulder. "Let's just play along until we have the information we need. If they truly have plans for us, then there shouldn't be much harm in hanging around."

"You, of all people, know that's not true," Sarphi cut in. I gave her a questioning glance. "It's not my story to tell." She looked pointedly at Reyland.

"Yeah and it's not one I want to tell." Reyland's voice was dry. "At least right now." A tight tension filled the air.

"I still think staying is the right choice," Lyra's soft voice cut through. "Together." She reached out and interlaced her fingers with Sarphi.

"Lyra's right." Sarphi gave the Wild Elf a soft smile. "Us working together, with the knowledge that they didn't want us to have. I think we could have a solid shot at putting a stop to whatever plans are in motion here."

"I happen to take great pride in my ability to ruin my father's plans." I couldn't help but smile. "And I have no inclination to stop anytime soon."

"So then it's settled." Sarphi made a show of wiping her hands on her pants. "We stay here and play their game until we can find a way to ruin it."

I turned back to Nyzirth and patted her on the leg. She lowered her shoulder, and I climbed on much easier this time, but still not without a little help from Nyzirth's snout. I settled into the groove between her shoulders and looked out at the group. My eyes were immediately drawn to Reyland, who was now atop his own dragon. His white hair was almost the same color as Zothim's scales. A wicked smile played on his lips, as if he could read my thoughts.

A. Turner

"I don't intend to ruin their game." My eyes never left Reyland's. "I intend to win it."

The sun was setting as we flew back to the mountain. The view was beautiful and easily rivaled anything I had seen from my bedroom window at the Alterwood Citadel. We dove down into the volcano, landing one by one on the open floor of the dragoncave. There was not a single person in sight as we slid off the backs of our dragons. Nyzirth nuzzled her nose against my chest before taking off into the sky, the others leaving shortly behind her.

"They probably thought the dragons decided to eat us," Sarphi joked, shaking the dust off of her wings. The action posed a question in my mind.

"Hey, Sarphi, it may not be right of me to ask this, but..." The Dragonfolk turned to me with one eyebrow raised. "Can you fly with those?" I gestured to her wings.

She stretched her wings out in response, their blue scales glimmering even in the dim lighting of this room. When she gave them a few experimental flaps, I noticed that they didn't seem to stretch out like the dragons did. Now that I was actually examining her wings, I could just barely make out faded scars along the bottom of them close to her body. I caught a flicker of sadness in her eyes as she folded her wings back against herself.

"I, uh, used to be able to." She didn't quite meet my eyes as she clenched her fists at her sides.

"What happened?" I whispered. The amount of scar tissue was massive. I couldn't imagine what she could have gone through that wouldn't have left scars on other parts of her body. Maybe she did have other scars and I just didn't notice them earlier.

"Reyland isn't the only one who knows just how bad the consequences can be for those of us who don't like to follow the rules." Her arms were shaking from how tightly balled her fists were.

No.

I had heard that people who kept birds as pets would trim their flight feathers to keep them from being able to fly away. It never once crossed my mind that you could do something similar to a dragon, much less Dragonfolk. Bile rose in my throat at the thought of how badly that must have hurt.

"They..." My voice remained hushed. "They clipped your wings..." I didn't phrase it as a question. I knew I was right when Sarphi's back stiffened and she turned away.

"Yeah. It's not a big deal," She mumbled, though the way her wings nearly dragged the ground suggested otherwise. "Other people here have been through worse." She glanced in Lyra's direction.

Lyra grabbed her hand, rubbing reassuring circles on the back of it. "We should head back to the room. Maybe we could at least get to bed and get some good sleep before they realize we're back." Her voice was wavering and, judging by the look on her face this may have been new information for her, too.

"Lyra's right," Reyland cut in. He hadn't said a word since we landed, but his movements were stiff as he headed for the door.

I couldn't find the words to say, so I nodded instead. I followed closely behind Reyland, letting Sarphi have her space as we made our way back to our room.

Upon our arrival, there was a guard standing outside our door. He had on a helmet, but I was fairly certain that it wasn't Finn, given that he was supposed to be headed back to the Citadel. He nodded wordlessly at Reyland before stepping aside to let us all pass.

"Really? Now?" Reyland seemed more than a little annoyed.

"Now what?" I stopped halfway through the entryway.

"Um... I've apparently got somewhere to be." Uncertainty danced in Reyland's eyes, but he gave me a look that said not to push it. "I should be back in the morning."

I looked between him and Sarphi, who just nodded. Whatever was going on must be normal, because she and Lyra seemed largely unbothered by it. I swallowed the lump of nervousness that had formed in my throat and nodded curtly at Reyland before he turned and followed the guard down the hall.

Chapter 29

Reyland

Most people wished for something exciting to happen at least once in their life. Me? I found myself wishing for just one normal night this week. Instead, I was now being led down a set of stairs that I had never seen before in the building I had spent the past six years of my life in.

"Where are we going?" Scanning the walls gave me no clue as to where we were. "I thought you got me for a job?"

"I did." The guard didn't slow in the slightest as we rounded yet another corner and descended yet another set of stairs.

"Then where are we going?" I was growing tired of the lack of information at this point.

"This particular job won't take you outside of Asballicuo." The guard came to a stop outside a wooden door with a small metal grate at the top.

"Then why am I needed?" The jobs I was usually assigned to involved going places the king's soldiers couldn't. The door creaked open and Malon stepped out.

"It's not really *you* that we need." TheElf's voice grated on my ears. "It's your abilities that we are hoping can solve our problem."

"What do you need me to do?" I was slowly starting to realize that this wasn't going to be a normal job. I took a deep breath and tried my best to hide every emotion.

"We need something taken care of." Malon looked around to make sure there wasn't anyone else nearby. "Cleanly."

"Cleanly?"

"Cleanly." He turned his back to me and proceeded down the dark hallway behind him. "Without marks."

"I see." I couldn't help the shiver that ran down my spine. Using my shadows was my least favorite way to complete a job. Not that I was particularly fond of any of it. It just felt impersonal and like an easy way out.

The further we walked, the darker this hallway became. Ice settled in my veins the longer I had to think about what I had been asked to do. We passed several windowless doors, each of them with an unsettling number of locks and bolts on the outside, before coming to a stop outside of one.

"We can do this one of two ways. You can stand out here and complete the job without ever seeing their face." Malon stood between me and the door. "Or I can open this door and you can look them in the eyes before taking their life. The choice is yours."

What kind of choice was that? Regardless of how messed up it was, it didn't take me long to make a decision.

"Open the door," I muttered before I could change my mind. "No one deserves to die alone."

A sinister laugh escaped Malon as the clicks of locks filled the air. The door finally swung open and the amount of blood on the floor nearly made me hurl. The shirtless male in the chair was barely recognizable. I couldn't even discern his heritage. He was bound to a chair in the middle of the room and didn't move as I walked in, my feet suddenly too heavy.

"Shut the door." I didn't take my eyes off of the poor male in front of me.

"What?" Malon had the audacity to sound surprised at my request. "Why would I do that?"

"I don't work for an audience." I pointed to the nearly white metal clasps that held the male in place. "Besides, I don't think he is going anywhere. Silencer's Alloy, correct?"

"Correct." Malon began pulling the door shut. "You have five minutes."

I didn't move until the door clicked shut. Immediately, I surrounded myself and the male in shadow. I meant it when I said no audiences. The metal cuffs around his wrists and ankles were so tight that they had dug into the skin. I knelt beside him and looked for any sort of locking mechanism.

"What are you doing?" The male's voice was dry, probably from a lack of water. Or an excessive amount of screaming. "Who are you?"

I tried not to think about the latter part and thanked whatever gods were listening when I found that the cuffs were being held on by a simple latch. Silencer's Alloy was a nasty creation. I could feel my magic being siphoned away in just the few moments it took me to undo the latches. A few hours in the cuffs is enough to drain an Elf to the point of burnout. Any longer than that and the metal feeds off of the wearer's lifeforce. Judging by the state of this male, he had gone through burnout days ago.

"I'm someone who doesn't want to be here nearly as much as you." I shook my head in an attempt to clear the fogginess that simply touching the cuffs had caused. "And I don't think anyone should die alone."

The male looked up at me, his black hair plastered to his face with a mixture of blood and sweat. It was hard to pinpoint his age given the state he was in, but he didn't seem to be much older than me. Blood dripped from the open wounds that covered his body as he shifted in the chair.

"I'm not leaving here, am I?" Dull blue eyes met mine. I swallowed hard, but didn't allow myself to look away.

"No." Shadows curled from my fingertips and snaked around the male's arms and legs. "But I'm going to try to make this as quick as possible."

The male simply nodded and lowered his head again. He took a deep breath, bracing for what I knew was coming next. I hated what was coming next. I closed my eyes and guided my shadows into the male's mouth. He began to cough and I tried my best to block out that sound. He didn't even fight against me as the shadows filled his lungs. It felt like forever before he slumped forward. I caught him before he fell and leaned him back against the chair. I gave him the honor of looking him in the eyes as I slowly pulled them shut.

A. Turner

"May you have the blessing of the Watchers, and may Illyrie himself welcome you." I cared little for the worship of the gods, but it was the least I could do for the male.

Dismissing the shadows that I had used to conceal the room, I stood and walked to the door. I only had to knock once before Malon opened the door.

"Don't you think the shadows were a bit unnecessary?" He peaked past me at the dead body in the chair.

"No." I walked past him in the direction we had originally come from. "Death isn't a spectacle."

Chapter 30

Reyland

Once the door quietly clicked shut behind me, I could not strip out of my leathers fast enough. I needed them off of my body. There wasn't a drop of blood on them, but they still peeled off as if they were soaked. I pulled on some night clothes and stalked quietly to my bed.

I could just barely see Sarphi laying on her stomach on top of her blankets. Her wings were hanging off the edge of the bed, just barely off the floor. The sight of her wings brought bile to my throat immediately. I couldn't believe I had never noticed the white scars before. What they had done to her was terrible. Sure, she could be hard to deal with, but I couldn't imagine anything that she could have done that would have been bad enough to justify mutilating her like that.

You know better than most that the punishment doesn't have to fit the crime. Not here.

The scars on my back began to crawl and itch as memories threatened to resurface. Taking a deep breath, I pushed all of my feelings back down. I had become good at that. I was going to have to keep being good at it if we were ever going to figure out what was going on. I may even end up with a few more scars if we were unlucky. We all probably would, though I would try my best to keep that from happening. No one else deserved to go through what I had already gone through. The tingling feeling spread across my back no matter how much I tossed and turned. My shirt felt like sandpaper sliding across the still sensitive scars.

I couldn't seem to get comfortable, so I quietly slid out of bed. A quick glance around the room revealed that the others had already fallen asleep. I crept across the room, trying my best not to make any noise. I slipped through the door to the washroom, closing it silently behind me.

I wasted no time stripping out of my night clothes and sinking into the warm water. The burn was a welcomed sensation, one that distracted from the pins and needles that were crawling across my back. I sank down until the water was at my chest before leaning back against the edge. I could feel the tension leaving my body as soon as I closed my eyes. I could always count on a soak to help clear my mind. The idea of actually getting some sleep tonight was beginning to seem like a possibility when I heard the door click behind me.

"Oh! I am so sorry!" I craned my neck over my shoulder to see Ashten, her hand over her eyes, doing nothing to hide the flush on her cheeks. "I — I'll just go back to bed. I noticed that your bed was empty, but I just thought you weren't back yet." She fumbled over the words in a way that made me smile, though I couldn't explain why. "I didn't think anyone would be in here."

"Don't bother. I was just about done." I lied as I turned back around. "Couldn't sleep?" Everything was quiet and my heart dropped at the thought that she may have actually left.

"Yeah. Something like that." Her voice was soft, and I may have been mistaken, but it sounded like she was closer too. I didn't dare turn around for the fear of possibly scaring her away. I heard a few footsteps move across the floor.

"Me either." I sat up, careful to keep the lower half of my body underwater. "This is where I like to go when I can't sleep. The warm water helps me clear my mind." I turned around to face her, hopeful that the combination of steam and dim lighting in this room made it hard to see past the surface of the water.

She had moved to the edge of the pool and now stood just in front of me. If she could see *anything*, she made no show of it. She had stripped down to just an undershirt and a pair of shorts in the time I had been talking. Just beside her feet were my clothes. Her sad eyes glanced over at them and back at me before silently turning around.

I could take a hint.

I rummaged through the pile, grabbing my undershorts and standing up just enough to be able to slide them on before sinking back into the water. My skin was crawling again, but for an entirely new reason as I cleared my throat.

"You can turn around now." My voice was strained as I spoke.

I watched as Ashten hesitantly stepped into the water. She didn't look over at me as she walked down the steps until the water was at her stomach. If she did, she would have caught me staring again. I couldn't help it. She was beautiful. The reflection of the water danced off of her pale skin. So pale that you could convince me it had never felt the warmth of the sun before today. I wanted nothing more than to touch it. To touch her. To gently trace my fingers across her body. I wanted to map out every curve and dip. My eyes drifted to the black lines peeking up over her shoulder.

I wanted to start my map there.

I clenched my fists at my side so hard that my nails dug into my skin. I told her I would be leaving. That's probably what she was waiting for.

I took a few steps up the stairs towards the edge of the pool. "Well, I guess I'll let you have some privacy."

"No." Her hand shot to my wrist and I froze. There was a desperation in her voice that I couldn't have resisted if I had even wanted to.

"Okay." I tried my best to keep my voice soft and gentle as I stopped dead in my tracks. "Okay. I won't go anywhere." I slowly turned back around and waded back into the pool.

Her eyes followed my movement carefully. Earlier, when she had lost control of her powers, she had watched me like a caged animal. There was still some of that in her violet eyes now, but there was something else too. Curiosity, maybe? Whatever it was, I didn't get to look long before she averted her gaze.

"I'm sorry," She mumbled. "I just don't want to be alone." She wrapped her arms around her midsection. "I, uh, have recurring nightmares. Makes sleeping hard on a good night and impossible on a bad one." She hunched her shoulders, making herself smaller. As if she was just trying to disappear.

"Tonight's a bad one." She nodded, though I didn't really need the confirmation. I had experienced my fair share of terrible nights in my time here at Asballicuo. Most of them were a direct result of being here in the first place. "I know because I've been there."

"Really?" Her eyes lit up a little.

"I've seen things you wouldn't imagine. Been through things you probably couldn't fathom." I tried to hide the sadness in my voice as memories threatened to claw free of the cage I kept them in.

"Like what happened to your back?" Her words were cautious and careful.

I hadn't considered that she had seen my back when she came in.

I simply nodded.

"Can—" She stared at me for a moment, her violet eyes lost in thought. "Could I see them again? Your scars?" I bristled involuntarily at the request, and she took a step back. "You don't have to. I just—"

I didn't give myself time to change my mind before turning around. I took a deep breath, rolling my shoulders to release some of the tension. Tension that was quickly replaced as I felt the water ripple towards me. With my back to her now, I relied solely on my other senses as she got closer. Sweet cinnamon filled my nose, and I felt her foot bump my heel under the water. I could faintly feel her breath on my back as she ran a tentative finger along one scar. I shuddered instinctively and the touch disappeared. The loss of touch stirred up a mixture of emotions I wasn't familiar with. I felt like I couldn't breathe. I was frozen. Short of the healers who had kept me alive, no one had ever seen what had been done to my back. Not like this.

"Who did this to you?" Her voice was breathy and nearly a whisper.

I swallowed heavily. She wasn't ready for the truth. Not on this, at least. But lying to her felt nearly impossible.

"This is what happens when you don't follow the rules." I danced around the details, hoping it was enough. I still didn't dare to move.

"What rules could you have broken to deserve this?" That tremble was back in her voice. "I can't even begin to count the number of scars here." Another tentative finger touched my skin. It felt like fire as she traced her way across my back. My breathing was uneven by the time her skin left mine, and I held my breath to try to mask it.

128. It started with one. The number doubled for each day I refused.

"They don't keep a *well-bred* Elf like me around here without putting me to use." I recited the words that Malon had beaten into me each day I had refused his orders. "I was assigned to a few *diplomatic* missions for the king. The kind you don't keep in the books." The movement of her hand stuttered. "This is what happens when you refuse."

"Like an assassin?" There was disgust in her voice as I had expected. It caught me off guard, which was probably why I said:

"Yes. Like an assassin."

"For my father." It was less of a question and more of a statement. Like she was trying to put a meaning to all of this.

A. Turner

"Yes," was all I said as I turned around to face her.

"Is that where you went earlier?" There was no judgement in her eyes when they met mine. "Did you go kill someone?"

I wasn't sure how to answer her question. The bluntness of it made me realize just how sheltered she had been. She just asked me if I had killed someone the same way she would ask what I had for breakfast. Like it was a normal thing to ask.

"Ashten, I—"

"You don't have to answer that if you don't want to." She looked away. "I shouldn't have asked that."

"It's not that." I hated that I could barely formulate a full sentence with her standing this close to me. "I just didn't expect you to ask me that."

"I learned a long time ago that mincing your words just wastes time. I guess I got that from my father." She took one step back, and we both took a deep breath.

"Yes."

"Yes?" She cocked her head to the side.

"I killed someone less than an hour ago because the alternative would have meant more scars and I'm just not sure how many more of those I could take." Her eyes widened, matching my own surprise at the admission.

"Well, the tattoo covers them well." She gave me a half smile, crossing her arms across her body.

What?

"You're not...?" I raised an eyebrow at her.

"Not what, Reyland? I'm not a fan of minced words, remember?" Determination set into her features, and I found it intoxicating.

"Upset." I took another step backwards, not for her sake, but for my own. "That I kill people?"

"No." Her statement was very pointed. "You don't have a choice, and you don't seem to enjoy it. So, no, I'm not upset. I'm not put off or disgusted."

"I do have a choice, though." I couldn't believe how quickly my walls had fallen around her. "I could always refuse."

"And then they would beat you again. Either until you agreed to do it or until you died. And if you died, they would just find someone else to do it, anyway." She shrugged, but it was dismissive. "Either way, a life would be lost."

"Where did you learn to think like that, Ashten?" I almost couldn't believe what I was hearing.

"I've spent nearly my entire life training to lead an entire kingdom one day. Damage control was one of the first things my father taught me." Sadness flashed through her eyes, and she looked away again. "Sorry if I was too forward."

"No. It was just a little surprising to see you act like the ruler I know you are." I couldn't help but smile. "I liked it."

She attempted to hide her face again, this time because of the blush spreading across her cheeks. I let her think I couldn't see when, in reality, it was the best thing I had seen all week. I had been so caught up in her that I had nearly forgotten something else that she had mentioned.

"Tattoo?" I raised my eyebrows. "I don't have a tattoo, Nightshade." The nickname tasted like honey on my tongue. If it was the last thing I ever said, I would die happy.

"Yes, you do." She stated very matter-of-factly. "Turn back around." She made a spinning motion with her fingers.

I obliged, turning my back to her once more. Her soft fingers began tracing my back, but not along my scars. I had stared at them enough in the mirror, hoping that they would somehow disappear, that I knew their exact pattern. This wasn't it.

"See?" She traced a finger from the top of my spine down to the center of my back. "It all seems to radiate from right here." She applied a bit of pressure right in the center of my back.

Wait.

"The dragons," I muttered. "When I bonded with Zothim, I felt this burning pain across my back. It all started where your hand is right now." I turned back around to face her. "I would be willing to bet that we all have one."

I watched with bated breath as Ashten turned around, her back to me now, and dragged her shirt over her head. She still had underclothes on, but I didn't miss the way she wrapped her shirt around the front of her body. Like she was hiding herself. Hasn't anyone ever told her how beautiful she was? My pulse was racing as I closed the gap between us with one step.

"Well?" Ashten's breathing was uneven as she spoke.

Sure enough, there was a tattoo there. Though in no particular shape, the black lines and swirls did indeed start at the center of her spine and spread across her entire back, from the top of her shoulders until they disappeared below her waistband.

Before I could think better of it, I placed two fingers on the center of her back. She tensed, and, for a moment, I thought she was going to pull away. Soon, though, her shoulders relaxed. I began tracing her tattoo like she had done mine, taking special notes of the spots that made her breath hitch. By the time I was done, her breathing matched mine. Uneven and shallow.

"Beautiful." I all but groaned in disappointment when she stepped away, pulling her shirt down. That disappointment was short-lived as she turned around, closing the distance between us. Her eyes met mine, and I could see the emotions in them. All the same ones I was feeling.

Nervousness.

Excitement.

Longing.

I placed a singular finger on her chin as she tried to look down. I expected her to back away but was pleasantly surprised when she didn't. Instead, she placed a tentative hand on my ribcage. My chest tightened at the sensation.

"What are you doing, Nightshade?" She was earning that nickname right now. She was beautiful, and it was killing me.

"I don't know." Her words trailed off.

"I think your powers are getting the best of you again," I lied.

If she didn't know what was going on, I didn't want to push her any further. I wanted her to figure this out on her own. It would be better for her, but torture for me. As if she could sense my thoughts, she stepped away and my hand fell to my side.

"I'm sorry," She mumbled. I could see the flush on her cheeks as she stepped out of the water. Her wet clothes clung to her body before she wrapped a towel around herself, heading for the door.

"Wait!" I hurried out of the water after her, nearly slipping on the wet stone. "Let me show you something else. This bath isn't the only place that's good for clearing your head on a bad night." I hated how desperate I was to spend more time with her.

"Okay." I didn't miss the dip of her gaze as she bit her lip. "But only if you put on some pants." She gave me a teasing smile.

"Of course." I gave her a mock salute before picking up my dry clothes. "However, I will not put these dry clothes on without taking the wet ones off." Her throat bobbed at the realization of what I was saying.

"We can both turn around," She muttered quickly as she grabbed her pile of clothes and turned her back to me.

A few beats passed before she began to pull off her shirt, exposing her tattooed skin once again. She looked back at me, but I turned around quickly before she could catch me watching. The silence that filled the room was deafening, only broken by the sound of wet clothes squelching to the floor.

I wasted no time stripping out of my own wet clothes and pulling on the dry ones, my shirt sticking to my still damp skin. I turned around just as Ashten pulled her shirt down over her head. Swallowing hard, I was unsure of what to do with my hands as she pulled her hair to one side, exposing her neck. She was fumbling with a strand of rope, trying to tie her hair.

"Let me help you." I covered the distance between us in two steps, placing a tentative hand on her shoulder. She didn't look back at me when I took the rope from her and pulled her hair back over her shoulder. She leaned into my touch as I gathered the loose strands. Her hair was just as soft as I had imagined it would be, and I couldn't help but run my fingers through it a time or two before gathering and tying it to the best of my abilities. My hands lingered on her shoulders. "There. Better?" I cursed myself for how desperate my voice sounded.

"Better." Her voice sounded little better than mine as she turned around to face me. Her pupils were blown, and she was chewing on her lip. Had this been any other girl, I would have dove in at the first sign she gave me. Ashten had given me plenty, but I still found myself waiting. For what, I had no clue. I didn't mind waiting, though. Not for her.

She cleared her throat, pulling me from my thoughts. "You wanted to show me something?"

I smiled, stepping backwards. "Do you trust me, Nightshade?" I asked as I held my hand out to her.

She took it without hesitation, nodding her confirmation. I didn't give her a second to reconsider before my shadows swirled, enveloping us in darkness.

Chapter 31

Ashten

My stomach tightened as shadows and darkness rose around us. My hand in Reyland's was a grounding presence. I trusted Reyland. I couldn't begin to explain why, but I did. The peppermint and smoke scent that I now knew was him overwhelmed my senses as his magic snuffed out all the lighting in the room.

Then I was falling. Reyland's grip on my hand remained firm as I instinctively flailed, grasping for purchase on anything I could find. He wrapped his free arm around my waist and pulled me to him, pinning my back against his chest. I was grateful that he did, because that was all that kept me upright as we landed. My knees buckled hard, and the nausea hit me almost immediately. My head was swimming and my vision was so blurry that I closed my eyes to chase away the bile rising in my throat.

"Deep breaths." Reyland's chest rumbled against my back as he spoke. He splayed his hand flat against my stomach, keeping me pinned against him as he rubbed my arm reassuringly. "It always sucks the first time, but we can't have you vomiting all over the library."

"Library?" I questioned, blinking slowly and trying to focus on my breathing. It was both a confusing and welcoming feeling to not immediately shy away from his touch.

"Yeah. I told you there was a library here. Transflux is the easiest way to get to it without getting caught." His chin rested on the top of my head. "Before you ask, Transflux is what I just did. It's something users of dark magic can do that allows us to use shadows to travel to places we have been before. The better we are at it, the further we can go."

"How did you know I was going to ask?" Now that the nausea was gone, I was acutely aware of how close we were. His arm was still wrapped around my stomach, and I could feel the uneven rise and fall of his chest against my back. My breath hitched as he leaned down just inches from my ear.

"Because, Nightshade." The way he said that name sent chills down my spine. I leaned my head back against his chest, ignoring every voice in my head that was telling me to do anything but. "I haven't known you for very long, but I do know that you can't stand not being in control. And control requires knowledge."

But I wasn't in control right now, was I? I didn't feel like I was here with him against my will, but nothing that was happening right now was even close to my normal. My breath caught in my throat as the hand that had been rubbing my arm reassuringly wrapped tightly around my wrist. Reyland's lips brushed my ear as he spoke again.

"You're awfully quiet. What's going on in that pretty mind of yours?" His voice was thick. "Or should I tell you what's going on in mine?"

Where had that come from?

I swallowed hard at the insinuation before stepping away from him. He did not try to hold me back as I walked over to a bookshelf. My hands were shaking, and I began fumbling through the books, desperate to put my focus on anything but the man standing behind me.

"Anything in particular you like to read?" My voice was trembling. I pulled out a book titled *The Oaken Legend,* which was beautifully decorated with a golden tree sprawling across the surface. A quick skim revealed that it was about the Wild Elves. "Boring," I chided as I slipped it back on the shelf. I heard Reyland chuckle behind me, and I couldn't help but join him.

"I, uh, rarely read when I'm down here." He leaned against a table, crossing his arms in front of him. "If you are looking for book recommendations, talk to Sarphi. I am willing to bet that she has read just about every book in this place."

"Well, I'll keep that in mind. If you don't read, then what do you do here?" I leaned against the bookshelf opposite of him. I held up my hand. "Wait. If it's anything close to what Sarphi was insinuating at dinner that first night, I don't want to know." I made a show of shaking my head.

"Well, I usually just hang out here because it's quiet." He smirked as he looked in my direction. "But I like where your head's at."

I had finally gotten myself under control, and here I was again, blushing like an idiot. "I, for one, actually like to read in the library."

Reyland made a show of gesturing to the rest of the library. "Don't let me stop you. I'll be right back." He took one step away from the table before vanishing into darkness. He reappeared a few moments later with the bottle of alcohol from his chest. He sat down against the bookshelf and took a long drink. "This is what I do in the library."

"Why do you have to come to the library to drink? Couldn't you do that in the washroom?" I asked as I shuffled through the books some more.

"Because I don't want to drown," He stated matter-of-factly. "Besides, being found passed out drunk in the bathtub is much more embarrassing than being found passed out drunk in the library."

I had to cover my mouth to stifle my laughter as I shook my head at him. I pulled a book titled *Dragons, Werewolves, and Other Rare Creatures* from the shelf and sat down beside Reyland.

"That one looks just as boring." Reyland took another long drink before holding the bottle out to me.

I obliged and handed the bottle back to him. "It probably is, but I figured that, if I can't sleep, I might as well do something productive."

Reyland didn't say anything else as I cracked open the dusty book. I read in silence for what felt like forever before I felt him shuffle beside me.

"What are your nightmares like?"

I snapped my head in his direction, shocked by the suddenness of his question, just as he took another drink. I took the bottle from him, inspecting it with the orb of light I had manifested to read.

This thing is almost empty.

"Okay," I said, snapping the book shut and patting him on the shoulder. "That's quite enough. Let's get you to bed."

"No." His voice was firm as he snatched the bottle back. "I *need* to know."

"Why?" I sat up and placed the book on the floor beside me.

"Just—" Reyland sat up, placing the now empty bottle between us. "Please?" The desperate tone of his voice caught me off guard.

I swallowed hard, turning my body so that I was facing him. He didn't meet my eyes as I began to talk.

A. Turner

"Well..." Why I felt compelled to tell him, I didn't understand. "The first time it happened was shortly after we ran into the dragon on the way here. The nightmares those first few nights only involved me standing there, unable to move, while the dragon spewed nonsense about how they had been waiting for me. In hindsight, those were probably less nightmares and more of Nyzirth trying to contact me. Tonight was different, though." I took a deep breath and closed my hands into fists to keep them from shaking.

"I was back at home, but everything was different. The citadel was different. Darker. The sun didn't shine throughout the windows like it always has." I laid my head in my hands and closed my eyes. "I was stuck in my room, but something was happening in the citadel. It sounded like some sort of attack. I was forced to listen to the screams as they got closer and closer to my door. I didn't know who the screams were coming from." My head was pounding. My stomach was in knots and I couldn't breathe. I grabbed fistfuls of my hair, desperate for anything to keep me grounded in reality. "But then the screams stopped, and I could hear footsteps right outside my door. The door to my room flew open and I couldn't use my magic to stop them. They—"

"Don't." His voice was soft. I felt his hands on top of mine, interlacing our fingers and gently pulling them away from my hair. "Do not finish that sentence." I looked up to find his eyes trained on our intertwined hands that now hovered in the space between us.

"Why? I thought you wanted to know?" I pulled one hand away to wipe a tear I hadn't realized I had shed.

"I thought I did too." His throat bobbed as he looked up at me. His eyes were glossy, and for a moment I could tell he was somewhere else entirely before he continued to talk. "But I can't live that nightmare again."

I furrowed my brows. "What nightmare? Surely you can't mean that you had the same one?"

"Not exactly." Reyland's hand tightened around mine. "My nightmares are usually just different retellings of the same story. It's almost always me living through any of the *assignments* they've sent me on for the king. But—" He took a deep breath, letting go of my hand just long enough to comb his hair out of his face. "Much like your own, my last nightmare was different. I was fighting through the Alterwood Citadel. It was darker and different, just like you had described. I was cutting down guards with no remorse, as I have been trained to do. Then I got to your door..." He closed his eyes, hanging his head, but never letting go of my hand.

"I... I killed you." Reyland's breaths were short and shallow as he pulled his knees to his chest, burying his head between them. "I didn't want to, but they said that if I didn't, they would. They said they would take their time and make me watch. I — I couldn't..." He trailed off.

I didn't know what to say. Was he insinuating that we had lived the same dream, but from two separate perspectives? I had never heard of such a thing.

"It couldn't be the same dream, could it?" I thought back to what had happened earlier with my magic. I apparently couldn't control my magic very well when under a lot of emotional stress. He also had the ability to absorb magic. Maybe that applied to nightmares as well? "Could it have had something to do with my magic? Like what happened earlier?" I placed a tentative hand on his shoulder, relieved when he didn't pull away. His shoulders shook under my touch.

We sat like that for a while before Reyland finally looked up. His eyes were bloodshot, and I could see the wet lines that ran down his face.

"Promise me, Nightshade." His hand was trembling as he grabbed mine again. "Promise me you won't let that happen. If any part of that dream becomes a reality, promise me you won't let me kill you." His voice broke as the last few words left his mouth.

Impossible, I wanted to say. I can't even keep my own powers from hurting myself. How was *I* supposed to stop *him*? I opened my mouth to say those exact words, but the look in his eyes stopped me. Here he was, heart on the floor, pleading with me. He barely knew me. Regardless, he thought, or at least hoped, that I could stop his worst nightmare from coming true. He didn't need to hear the facts.

"I promise."

Chapter 32

Ashten

Reyland and I both eventually relaxed enough for us to actually get some reading done. We sat side by side, the enormous book sprawled across our laps. We focused primarily on the section about dragons. Something that I had found particularly interesting was the list of people involved in the death of the last dragon. The ruling king at the time was King Vulmon, which we knew.

There were four men sent that day to put an end to this beast after many soldiers from all three elvish civilizations had been felled trying to stop it. Three humans named Fern Delaway, Mance Dower, and Nick McLauren, worked alongside a daemonfolk that called themselves Immortal.

I had never heard of these males before, though they had seemingly done the dynasty a great service that day.

All four of them returned to King Vulmon and were rewarded handsomely for their efforts.

That was where the account ended. Nothing else was written about them. At least not in this book, nor the history books I had been given to study by my father back home.

I looked over to see that Reyland had apparently dozed off while I had been reading. His head was tilted back against the bookshelf, mouth slightly open and blowing on the strands of hair that had fallen into his face. I shifted slowly, trying not to wake him as I pulled the book over so that it sat solely in my lap. He stirred only long enough to cross his arms over his abdomen before his breathing fell back into a steady rhythm.

I flipped to the section on dragon riders and their bonds with their dragons and proceeded to read.

Dragons commonly bonded with other dragons for life, and their bond with their rider was no different. In fact, the connection between bonded dragons often carried over to their riders. This meant that the riders of bonded dragons were very close friends. There were many accounts that mentioned these riders being lovers, with some even moving into a lifelong relationship. Unfortunately, many dragons would become aggressive and refuse to take a second rider if anything were to happen to their first one. This often resulted in them being released from their captivity as they became too hard for the dragon tamers to handle.

I began to wonder if losing a rider had anything to do with why the last dragon was hunted down and killed. Maybe she had lost her bonded rider and was inconsolable, lashing out at those who were probably just trying to help. It felt weird to speculate about the emotions of dragons, but I guess that was what my life had come to. I buried my head back into the book, but it wasn't long before the words began to run together, and I found myself fighting to keep my eyes open. I leaned my head back against the bookcase.

I'll close my eyes for just a moment. Then back to reading.

I should have known better.

There was no bright morning sun to wake me when dawn came, which was probably why we both slept long enough that someone had come looking for us. The door to the library slammed shut, causing me to stir enough to remember that I wasn't in my room. The first thing I noticed was a heavy weight on my shoulder. I glanced over to see Reyland still asleep, leaning against the bookcase. At some point in the night, he had drawn his arm around my shoulder, allowing me to lean against him as I slept. The steady rise and fall of his chest was therapeutic, almost lulling me back to sleep. I closed my eyes again, and I was still leaning against his chest when Finn walked around the corner.

The string of curses that left my mouth as I scooted out from under Reyland's arm would have probably made my mother faint. He barely stirred as I pushed the book over into his lap before standing up. The look in Finn's eyes was murderous as he glanced between Reyland and me. I may have been a little sheltered, but I knew what this looked like.

"What are you two doing here?" Finn spoke through gritted teeth. "You are both late for combat training."

I held my finger to my lips and motioned for us to walk around the corner. He opened his mouth to protest, but apparently decided against it before turning and walking away. We didn't make it very far before he wheeled on me again, looking expectantly in my direction with his arms crossed.

"Neither of us could sleep last night." I retorted, mirroring his stance.

Finn's eyebrows raised. "And cuddling in the library after drinking an entire bottle of whatever alcohol he smuggled into here solved that problem?"

"We were not cuddling. We just fell asleep." I looked around the corner to ensure that we had not woken Reyland. "But, yes, I did get a good night's sleep." I smirked obnoxiously. "Thanks for asking."

"I didn't ask if you slept well. I asked why you slept here. *With him.*" Finn ground out the last few words. His stare was drilling into me as we both stood there.

I took a step back, only so that I wouldn't have to look up at him. "I told you. We came over here because we couldn't sleep. We had a bit to drink, and I pulled out a book to read. He fell asleep first, and I guess I dozed off reading the book." I shrugged. "I don't know what you're so upset about. It's not like we were naked and making out when you showed up."

Finn quickly closed the gap between us, causing me to stumble back into a bookshelf. He quickly caged me in with his arms and leaned until his mouth brushed against my ear.

"You better be glad you weren't, Princess." His voice was barely more than a whisper. "I would hate to remind Reyland what happens when you don't follow the rules here."

"Are there rules about the cadets having relations with each other?" I tried my best to keep my voice steady so as to not give away my racing heart.

"No," he growled. "But there are rules about stealing from me."

"And?" I questioned. I tried to look around the corner to check on Reyland, but Finn's arms kept me caged in place.

"You are mine." He grabbed my chin roughly and pulled my head towards him. "You need me. You understand that, right?"

"I—" The words caught in my throat. He had never been like this before. Never so... rough. Possessive. I tried to pull away from him, but the grip he had on my chin only grew tighter. "Ow, Finn! You're hurting me." I tried to pull away again. This time, he pressed his entire body against me, pinning me to the bookshelf.

"Say it." The pressure on my chin lifted slightly.

"Say what, Finn?" My heart raced. I could feel a rising pressure in my head and my vision began to blur. Tears started to fall and before long I was gulping down air. "I don't know what you want, Finn! Please let go of me. You're really hurting me."

"Say. You're. Mine." Finn rested his forehead on mine. "I meant what I said about being done with watching as you courted every rich boy on the continent. I'm *done* sharing."

A calming warmth settled over me. I closed my eyes, and my heartbeat slowed to a near stop. I could feel my magic flowing through my veins, and I deliberately gathered it in the center of my body. It gathered and gathered until I couldn't take it any longer.

Then I exploded.

White light filled my vision as I pressed my hands flat against Finn's abdomen. I felt my magic surge from where it had gathered. It traveled down my arms and burst out of my palms in the form of a white-hot flame. Finn was sent flying back, falling to the floor after crashing into a bookshelf. Books fell like rain from the shelf, piling up around him.

"That should teach him a lesson." Nyzirth's low purr filled my mind.

"What just happened?" I tensed at the mental intrusion. *"I've never done anything like that with my magic before."*

"Well, it seems like you're a natural." I could almost hear the smile in Nyzirth's voice. *"I can't see through your eyes, but I can feel your power. I definitely felt that power surge. We just need to figure out how to channel your powers without emotions."*

My hands were still wreathed in fire when Reyland walked around the corner. His hair was disheveled, and his eyes were wild as he scanned the scene before him. Despite having obviously just woken up, shadows danced and played at his fingertips, ready to fight off any threat.

"What's going on?" He looked wearily between Finn and me. "What happened to him?"

"I happened to him." I absorbed the fire that was still dancing on my skin, reveling in the burst of energy that soared through my body. Finn scrambled backwards as I walked over to him. There were two hand sized indentions in his armor. His throat bobbed as I leaned in towards him. "I meant what I said too. Consider yourself lucky. Speak like that to me again and you won't be able to walk."

My chest tightened inexplicably at the sight of the smirk on Reyland's face as I walked past him. "Come on." I motioned for him to follow. "We are apparently late for combat training."

Chapter 33

Finn

I tried to blink away my blurry vision as I watched Ashten and Reyland walk away. The bookshelf that I was leaning against was barely standing behind me, and the books that were on it were likely ruined now. I sucked in a breath and was rewarded with a sharp pain in my abdomen. I probably deserved that. Running my hand over the metal of my armor revealed it to still be warm to the touch. It was even slightly melted. I stood up, groaning as the armor dug into the already bruised skin of my abdomen. I undid the straps and tossed the armor to the side. My shirt was singed through my armor, and it stuck to my skin as I lifted it to survey the damage. Blood was already pooling to the surface, causing most of my abdomen to appear dark red. There were even a few scorch marks where the fire had burned straight through. I took another deep breath, the sharp pain still there.

Probably a few broken ribs.

I had never seen Ashten display such power. *Raw power.* She had done nothing more than a few simple party tricks. No one had ever taught her more than what she would need to perform everyday tasks. *This* was so much more. *This* could become a problem. She could have killed me. Easily, if she had really wanted to. Could this power increase have resulted from her bonding with the dragon? If so, we were going to have to be more careful when we started teaching her how to channel and wield her magic.

I was going to have to be more careful in the future. I had lost control this time, but I couldn't afford to keep doing that. Scaring her was not something I had meant to do. It was just so hard when I saw her with him. I had spent the past fifteen years waiting. Years of waiting in the background. Years of being told 'just a little while longer.' Years of playing my role perfectly. Enduring every look, sneer, and jab thrown my way. I slammed my fist against the already crumbling bookshelf and watched as the remaining shelves and books fell.

I was done waiting.

I didn't bother to pick up my armor before leaving the library. Ashten was on her way to combat training, and I wanted to be there. I needed to see if there were any more surprises up her sleeve. Besides, I wasn't kidding when I had told her there would be consequences.

Chapter 34

Reyland

I hurried out of the library after Ashten. She didn't say a word as she stormed down the hall, but I could hear the occasional sniffle. I nearly had to run to keep up with her and just barely caught the door to our room as it shut behind her. I watched as she wiped at her face before digging through the chest at the end of her bed. She pulled out her flight leathers and walked wordlessly behind the divider.

I pulled on my set of leathers quickly and strapped my new sword to my back. I closed my eyes and let the weight of it settle between my shoulder blades. There was a welcomed sense of familiarity that came with the feeling of the blade against my spine. Regardless of how I felt about my *job*, I couldn't deny that it had given me a much needed outlet to work out all of my *issues*. Out there, I didn't have to worry about anyone knowing who I was. It didn't matter who my father was or how I completed the mission. As long as I didn't ask too many questions, I was basically leash free. I just did the job and produced results. My skin crawled with anticipation, and I hated it. I took a steadying breath, reminding myself that this wasn't a job. It was just training.

I opened my eyes but didn't see Ashten anywhere. I was just about to leave when I heard it. Soft sobs coming from behind the dressing divider. I walked over slowly, stopping just on the other side.

"Ashten?" I softly called out, not wanting to scare her by my sudden closeness. There was no response, but the sobs gradually reduced in volume until they were nothing but the occasional sniffle. "Ashten?" I asked again. I rested my hand on the top of the divider.

"Yeah. I'm coming." Her voice was barely more than a whisper. There wasn't a hint of the strong-willed, no-nonsense Ashten I had met. She shuffled around for a bit, and I took a step back when she came around the corner. "Sorry. I'm making us even later than we already were."

Her eyes were puffy, and wet lines ran down her cheeks. She wiped her hand across her nose and gave me an apologetic half-smile. None of that mattered once I noticed the red marks on either side of her chin. My blood boiled at the sight of them. The need to make them disappear was immediate and overwhelming.

I took a step closer to her, gently reaching towards her chin. She flinched away from my touch and my heart dropped. "Oh Nightshade..." I let my hand fall back to my side as shadows began to dance at my fingertips. "I would never hurt you... but I would love to know who did."

Ashten averted her gaze downward and wrapped her arms around stomach. It made her look so much smaller than she already was. My stomach dropped at the sight of it. Sadness radiated from her in soul crushing waves. She loosed a shaky breath before looking back up at me.

"This is what happens when you don't follow the rules." She repeated my own words back at me. She offered me a small shrug before pushing past me to her bed. I studied her quietly as she began sliding her daggers into various sheaths built into her uniform.

It all hit me at once.

He had done this to her.

It all played back in my head. She had been careful not to wake me when she got up, but I had woken up anyway. They had spoken in hushed voices. Then there was the loud bang that had forced me to go and check on her. She had apparently blown him across the room and she was already crying when I came around the corner. It didn't make sense, though. If they were in a relationship, which it had definitely seemed like they were, why would he treat her like that? What rule had she broken that had made him so angry? So angry that she had felt the need to defend herself.

"Why?" I asked carefully. "Why did the Captain do this to you?"

Ashten wheeled around to face me. Her eyes were wide and her mouth hung open in shock. She glanced feverishly between me and the door, as if Captain Finn may walk through at any time.

"He didn't—" she began, but I cut her off.

"Don't lie to me. I could hear you two talking before I walked around that corner. You also admitted that you had done that to him. I don't think you would have without a reason." I took a slow step towards her. "If you don't want to talk about it, that's fine, but don't lie to me, Nightshade."

Ashten closed her eyes and inhaled deeply. "I just don't need to cause any more trouble. I don't want to give him a reason to do that again."

"A *reason?*" I tried hard to keep my voice at a normal volume. "What was his *reason* for laying his hands on you like that? For grabbing your face hard enough to leave a mark, Ashten? What *reason* did he tell you to make himself feel better about it?"

"He's just upset," She mumbled, fumbling with a dagger at her side.

"About what?" I took another small step closer to her. My hands slid into my pockets and I made a show of looking around. "Because I, too, am upset right now. However, you don't see me laying my hands on anyone. Though I have the perfect target in mind."

She turned to walk to the door. "He and I have a history. A long one. One that I would prefer not to elaborate on. Can we please just go to training?" I could tell by the tone of her voice that she was done talking about it. I didn't need to hear anything else, anyway. It was bad enough that I knew just what their history consisted of. I didn't need to hear her say it.

I followed her to the door and reached past her to open it. She flinched as my hand moved past her. I made up my mind right then and there. If he hurt her again, I would kill him.

"Whatever you need, Nightshade."

Chapter 35

Ashten

When Reyland and I arrived at the dragoncave, Sarphi and Lyra were already a few rounds deep into what seemed to be a rigorous training match. Maybe this was just what they needed after the heated argument that ensued once we had gotten back to our chambers last night. Apparently, Lyra hadn't known that Sarphi's wings had been clipped. The Wild Elf was livid that her friend had hidden this from her. What ensued was the quietest heated argument that I had ever witnessed. It ended with both of them passed out on their beds, but I didn't miss the few times Lyra got up to check on her friend.

The middle of the cavern had been transformed into a small combat arena. Wooden beams had been set up in an octagon shape to keep the fighters in one area. Sarphi and Lyra both wielded wooden weapons of their choice. Sweat poured down both of their faces, and Lyra looked as if she was about ready to vomit. Sarphi spared a quick glance my way over her shoulders, her eyes widening in surprise. Malon and Finn stood on the outside of the arena, the latter not even bothering to look my way.

"Focus!" Malon yelled. "Lyra, you missed the perfect opportunity right there. Her guard was down and you just let her get away with it." Lyra opened her mouth to say something, but Sarphi shot her a glance that must have made her think better of it. "We're not stopping until one of you can't walk, so you better get to it." Malon continued, sparing me no more than half a glance. "Ashten, you and Reyland will be next. Start warming up."

I followed Reyland off to the side, where he began walking me through a list of stretches and warm-ups. I could barely do most of them, and was completely out of breath by the end of the first set.

"Is this something you guys do often?" I asked between ragged breaths.

"Every day." Reyland didn't sound the least bit out of breath as he finished his set of push-ups. "Do you have any personal combat experience?"

I motioned to my small, skinny, very unmuscular body. "Do I look like I have combat experience? "

Reyland snorted a laugh as he stretched his arm across his body. I shook my head in mock disdain. "Have you seen combat? Watched soldiers train? Handled a weapon before?"

"Does putting them into my sheaths about 10 minutes ago count?" I smiled, though I was sure it looked about as fake as it felt. "I've never had to defend myself before..." I absentmindedly lifted a hand to my chin, wincing when I touched the already tender skin. "That's always been his job." I nodded my head in Finn's direction.

"What?" Reyland snapped his head in my direction.

"Finn is Captain of the Guard." I made another attempt at one of the many stretches Reyland had shown me. "Back home, I mean. He was my personal guard. He was to escort me at all times, as well as making sure that I had adequate protection if he ever had to be out of town for an extended period of time."

"So you must know him pretty well, then?" Reyland didn't quite meet my eyes as he asked the question. "You know, since he had to follow you everywhere."

I straightened my body and shrugged. "I would like to think so. My father didn't really allow me to have a lot of friends outside of the citadel. I mostly just spent time with Finn and Evelien, one of the younger servants."

"Is it still his job?" Reyland stood with his back to the group standing at the arena. "Now that you are here? Is it still the Captain's job to protect you?"

I looked down at the ground, unsure of how to answer his question. I shifted my gaze past Reyland to Finn, who was leaning against the wooden railing. He gestured to the pair in the center and whispered something to Malon as Sarphi landed a punishing blow to Lyra's stomach that caused the Wild Elf to double over. As if he could sense me watching him, Finn looked up.

There was something different about the way he was looking at me right now. Finn usually looked at me with such adoration and reverence, but there was not a single sign of those emotions in his empty eyes right now. He gave me a smile that made my skin crawl, and not in the good way that it usually did. As much as I wanted to, I couldn't look away. Finn made no effort to either as he shouted across the room.

"Okay! That's enough!" He looked to Sarphi and Lyra, who were both panting heavily in the center of the ring. Blood was dripping from Lyra's nose, and Sarphi had a cut on her eyebrow to match. "I am running short on time, and I would like to have the chance to evaluate each of the Drakewardens before I have to leave."

A sense of relief filled the spot where dread had once sat at the mention of Finn leaving, and I tried not to dwell on it.

Sarphi climbed out of the ring and helped Lyra do the same. She apologetically offered the Wild Elf a scrap of cloth for her nose as they made their way to the side of the room.

"Since the point of today is to learn, you will both be supplied with a wooden replica of your weapon of choice to avoid any serious injuries." Finn motioned to a table where several wooden training weapons lay. "Please make a choice and make your way to the center of the arena."

A. Turner

I reluctantly grabbed two daggers and watched as Reyland grabbed a decently sized longsword. He made his way to the arena, climbing over the wooden barrier with ease. I made to follow, opting to crawl under the barrier to avoid making a fool of myself any more than I was about to do. The two wooden daggers felt foreign in my hand as I held them up in what I hoped was a somewhat defensive position. Reyland stood across from me, the sword held lazily out in front of him.

"This is a training match." Finn's voice filled the room. "However, I want you to treat this fight with as much seriousness as you would an actual life or death situation. You can't expect to survive someone trying to end your life if you don't train as if someone is trying to end your life." He pointed at the both of us. "No magic is to be used. This match ends when I say it does."

Neither of us attempted to move as Finn signaled for us to start. I didn't even know where to begin. I made a slow swipe at Reyland's torso, which he easily dodged. Another swing of my offhand dagger yielded the same result.

"Your movements are too slow, Ashten." Finn stated from the sidelines. "It makes them predictable."

"Well, it would help if I had the slightest clue about what I was doing!" I shouted in frustration. Finn didn't even acknowledge that I had spoken. He just motioned for me to continue.

I made another frustrated lunge at Reyland. This time, he slapped my dagger away with his sword, mumbling under his breath as I stumbled off to the side. I slammed into the wooden railing and turned to see him standing loosely in the center of the ring.

"Your attacks do not have any thought behind them. You are swinging recklessly." He tapped the inside of my leg with his blade. "You are also standing up too straight. You need to lower your center of balance." He made a show of widening his stance and bending his knees.

I tried my best to copy his stance. It felt awkward, and I could already feel the burn in my legs, not to mention the ache in my arms from holding up these daggers. I was not built for this. My father had kept me thin, weak, and helpless. Traits that may not have been so bad had I stayed at the citadel and married some rich Elf that would cater to my every need.

"What are you doing?" Finn asked, a glare plastered on his face.

"She's only ever going to be able to protect herself if someone shows her how." Reyland didn't miss a beat as I made another swing in his direction. One that he easily knocked away.

Reyland thrust his sword forward, catching me square in the stomach. The hit wasn't hard enough to seriously hurt me, but that didn't stop me from stumbling backwards.

A. Turner

"You're not supposed to let me do that." Reyland stated very matter-of-factly. The smirk on his face only fueled my frustration as he made another jab at me. I tried to knock it away with my weapon as he had been doing, but it barely changed the direction of the sword before it hit me in the chest again.

"You are learning," Reyland assured me, though I certainly wasn't feeling it. I was already out of breath and the burning in my lungs matched the burn in my arms. "However, given your small size and weapon of choice, you are going to be much better off getting out of the way instead of attempting to block the weapon." He made an "X" with his arms. "You could always try to stop an attacker by trapping their weapon between yours, but I would just focus on getting out of the way for now."

Reyland made another easily telegraphed swing in my direction. I stepped to the side just quick enough to watch his sword swing past me. I was so elated about actually dodging his attack that I didn't notice how far back I had stepped. Before I knew it, my feet were sliding out from under me and I tumbled backwards onto the stone. The impact knocked the air from my lungs and my hands stung from trying to catch myself. I laid my head back against the stone, honestly grateful for the reprieve despite the embarrassment of having fallen. I opened my eyes to see Reyland standing above me with an outstretched hand. He had an apologetic smile on his face that caused my face to redden with embarrassment.

I winced as I took his hand and allowed him to haul me to my feet. Upon inspection, I noticed that the cut from the bonding ceremony had been ripped back open. Reyland must have noticed it too, because he was walking over to Finn before I could stop him.

"Captain. We should at least bandage her hand before we continue." He stood with his back straight and hands clasped behind his back. "She can not properly hold a weapon as it is. The blood would only make it harder for her. It's no way to learn, Captain."

Finn climbed over the railing and approached me. He held his hand out. When I did not give him mine, he reached down and grabbed me by the wrist, pulling my hand up to where he could see it. Blood was pooling in my palm and running down my arm. His face contorted in what I could only guess was disappointment before he reached into his pocket and pulled out a piece of cloth. He roughly wrapped it around my hand and led me to the edge of the arena. I climbed out and turned back to face him.

"Someone bring me a sword." Finn stated, his eyes never leaving mine. "Reyland still needs a proper training session." Sarphi approached cautiously with a wooden longsword, leaning it on the railing beside us when Finn did not acknowledge her. The look in his green eyes was murderous as he leaned in, whispering so that only I could hear. "Let this be a reminder of why you need me."

Chapter 36

Ashten

I could only watch as Finn grabbed the sword off of the railing and walked towards the center of the ring. Reyland stood in a much more rigid stance, his sword in front of him defensively. I couldn't help but be annoyed at how seriously he was taking this now that he was against Finn. At the same time, I guess I couldn't blame him. Finn was a few inches shorter than Reyland, but he made up for that with pure muscle.

"Once again." Finn took a much more open stance, the tip of his sword nearly dragging in the dirt as he spoke. "This match only stops when I say it does."

Finn wasted no time going on the offensive. He surged forward with huge, wide swings. To Reyland's credit, he stopped all of them with his own blade, but it was still enough to keep him on his back foot. He stumbled backward as he took the final hit, and Finn immediately capitalized on the opening. I winced as Finn's sword made contact with the back of Reyland's leg, knocking it out from under him. Finn lunged forward, obviously intent on ensuring that Reyland didn't have time to get up.

Luckily, Reyland's lithe frame meant he was lighter on his feet. Just as fast as he landed on the ground, he was up and on his feet once more. He slid to the right just as Finn's sword slammed into the ground where his head was moments ago. Reyland quickly regained his footing, holding his sword close to his body. Both males stood deathly, still staring at each other. Neither of them appeared to be the slightest bit winded from their skirmish so far.

I had to admit that it was all fairly impressive. Never was I allowed to watch the soldiers and guards train in the yard back home. I knew logically that Finn had to be skilled with a sword given that he was the Captain of the Guard. However, I had never seen it in action before. I couldn't quite wrap my head around how they moved so fluidly and with so much power at the same time. I watched mesmerized as they traded blow after blow, Reyland meeting Finn's power with speed and finesse.

This back and forth went on for what felt like forever. It was quickly devolving from a training session into an all-out brawl. Lyra snuck into my vision on my right with fresh bandages for my hand. I smiled my thanks as she removed the soaked cloth and pulled a vial from her pocket.

"Just a little something that I made. It doesn't work as well as I would like, but it should help some." She smeared a translucent paste on the wound before wrapping my hand with the new bandage. I sucked in a breath as she tied off the bandage.

"Don't worry." I jumped at the sound of Sarphi's voice and turned to find her leaning against the railing on my left. "We'll have you looking like that in no time."

"I highly doubt that." I scoffed, crossing my arms. "I can barely walk without tripping over my feet most days."

Sarphi smiled, shaking her head. "We all looked like you our first time," she continued, as if she could tell I didn't believe her. "Before I showed up here, I had zero true combat experience. Anything I had learned was out of pure survival. Though you'd be surprised what you're capable of when your life depends on it."

"My father taught me how to use a bow, but it's not customary for Wild Elf women to learn hand-to-hand combat," Lyra added.

"Don't sell yourself short." Sarphi leaned forward, looking at Lyra before looking back at me. "She is the best archer I've ever met."

"Yeah and how many archers have you met?" Lyra retorted, though her face was already flushing from the attention.

"I don't need to meet any others." Sarphi smiled at her, which only caused Lyra's face to redden further.

I looked down at my feet to hide the smile on my face. I was just about to excuse myself from this conversation when I heard it. The crack rang through the cavern as Finn's fist made contact with Reyland's nose. The force of the blow caused him to slam backwards into the railing. My head snapped up, thoughts of the guards that had been thrown into the wall by the dragon immediately crossing my mind. I went rigid, frozen by the sight before me.

Reyland was slumped against the railing, his sword just barely out of arm's reach. Blood was pouring from his nose and I was fairly certain he was going to have a black eye, if the current swelling was any indication. He was panting as he looked around frantically for his weapon. Just as he reached for it, Finn stepped on the blade, pinning it in place. Though he was clutching his ribs, probably from our earlier altercation, Finn looked no worse for wear than he had when the fight started. Both males were breathing heavily, and I looked over at Malon, expecting him to stop the fight. He simply looked at me, eyebrows raised, before turning back to the scene that was unfolding. A chill crawled down my spine as Finn knelt in front of Reyland, his back to us. Finn merely glanced over his shoulder as if to check that I was still watching.

Trust me. I was.

There was no doubt that he had every bit of my attention as he pulled a dagger out of his boot. A real, sharp dagger. Sarphi muttered a curse under her breath. It had been so well concealed that none of us had noticed it.

"The fight is over." Reyland spit out a mouthful of blood. I hoped that it was just the blood from his nose. "You've won."

A. Turner

"The fight may be over." Finn spoke loud enough for everyone to hear. "But has the lesson been learned?" He calmly touched the tip of the dagger to Reyland's throat and looked back at me.

I felt my blood turn to ice.

"What lesson?" Lyra spoke quietly. She peeled her eyes away from the two males to focus on me. "What did he do?"

"I — he — we—" There was not a single coherent thought in my head right now. I watched the dagger rise and fall as Reyland swallowed heavily. Our eyes met past Finn's, and I didn't miss the subtle head shake that he gave me. Though he had every right to be scared right now, I did not see one drop of fear in his eyes. But what I *did* see was acceptance.

Acceptance.

Acceptance of what?

"What did you two do?" Sarphi's voice was low, and there was a hint of desperation to it.

"We did nothing." My voice was shaking now, and I leaned on the railing to keep myself upright.

"Has the lesson been learned?!" Finn boomed before dropping to a near whisper. "Or does Reyland need to be reminded of what happens when you break the rules?" Finn pressed the dagger harder against Reyland's neck, and a small trail of blood made its way down onto his chest. "Is there even any space left on your back?"

"No!" I shouted, climbing over the railing before anyone could stop me. My head was pounding and lavender mist began to cloud my vision. I could barely walk and instead I stumbled across the arena to where Finn was kneeling. "What are you doing? You've won the fight!" Finn didn't so much as look in my direction as I dropped to my knees beside them. "What is going on with you?" I pleaded.

"Don't," Reyland didn't move an inch as he spoke.

I ignored him as I turned back to Finn. "Finn?" I slowly placed my hand on his arm, the pounding in my head nearly unbearable. I tried to blink away my blurry vision, but it was to no avail.

"Do not fight it," Nyzirth's voice cut into my head. *"Use it."*

"Use it?" I repeated back to her.

"Yes." She drew out the end of the word. *"Use your abilities. This is what they are meant for."*

The closest I had come to using these abilities was the other day when Reyland had to use his own abilities to calm me down. I tried to focus on that same feeling again. I could feel the magic crawling just under my skin and I tried my best to push that feeling towards Finn.

"Please," I begged once more. "Please stop. This isn't you." I focused all of my wants into where I was touching Finn's arm.

Finn slowly turned to look at me. A smirk spread across his face, and I worried he may not listen. My relief was immeasurable when he lowered the dagger.

"Has the lesson been learned?" He asked for a third time, though much quieter.

"Yes." My voice was raspy with emotion as tears threatened to fall.

"You would do well to remember it." Without another word, Finn stood, climbed out of the arena, and walked out of the dragoncave. Malon was right behind him, not giving us a second look.

For a few moments, the entire room was quiet. Sarphi and Lyra had not dared to move from where they stood, now wide-eyed. Then, I felt Reyland's hand on my leg. I looked over at him, wiping away a rogue tear that I couldn't explain before he could see it.

"I'm okay, Ashten." He gave me a smile that didn't quite meet his swollen eye. He winced as he touched his bloody nose. "I've been through worse. I don't even think it's broken." He laughed for a moment before coughing and spat out another mouthful of blood.

Even as relief washed over me at his good spirits, I couldn't bring myself to smile.

Is there even any space left on your back?

Surely he didn't...

I felt the blood drain from my face as the realization hit me. I was just barely able to take a few steps away before emptying the contents of my stomach all over the cavern floor.

Chapter 37

Ashten

I felt someone grab the loose strands of my hair and pull them out of my face. They rubbed soft circles on my back but the contact only caused me to shy away from them. I wiped my mouth with the back of my hand and stood up. Sarphi was standing beside me, a concerned look on her face. I glanced over to where Reyland was still sitting, swatting away Lyra's hand as she tried to apply pressure to his still bleeding nose. A soft green glow emitted from her hands and illuminated Reyland's face. Bile began rising in my throat again the longer I looked at him. I made my way to the railing of the makeshift arena, leaning against it with my head between my arms in an attempt to fight off the nausea.

"Take your time," Sarphi spoke softly. I could see her feet beside me as she leaned her back against the railing. Her wings hung lazily behind her, just inches from the ground. I could see the scars that ran along them better now that I was closer. Her scars looked a lot like —

Wait. No.

"Did he do that to you?" My throat was raw as I spoke.

"What?" Sarphi stuck her hands in her pockets. She didn't quite turn her head as she looked in my direction.

Fighting the swimming in my head, I stood up straight and looked her in the eyes.

"Did Finn do that to you?" I asked again through ragged breaths.

"Ashten..." The sadness that filled her eyes was all the confirmation I needed. She looked to Reyland, who was standing now and making his way over to us.

"Are you okay?" Reyland's voice was panicked and strained. He reached for my arm to inspect my cut hand. His own blood coated his hands and the front of his shirt. I took a step back, holding my hand up for him to see.

"Physically, I'm fine. Lyra has already tended to my hand," I snapped. Reyland opened his mouth to speak, but I didn't give him the chance. "Mentally, I'm on my last straw." The unfortunately familiar pounding in my head grew, and I raised a shaking hand to the bridge of my nose.

"A week ago, I was pulled from my bed in the middle of the night, loaded into a carriage, and hauled across the continent. The last two days of my life, I have been struggling to keep up with everything that has been thrown at me. On top of it all, I just watched the person who I trusted the most in this world threaten to maim you over the fact that I was spending more time with you than he liked!" I was struggling to get enough air as I continued.

A. Turner

"So no, I'm not okay! Nothing about this situation is okay…" Tears fell down my face, and I hated that I didn't have the energy to wipe them away.

Sarphi muttered a few choice words under her breath as she took a few steps away. Lyra looked away, wiping away a few tears of her own. My own breaths started to come in gasps, and I leaned against the railing as my head started to spin. My skin was crawling, and no amount of scratching relieved the sensation. I sank to my knees, scratching at my arms and head. I closed my eyes and could just barely hear someone shouting over the sound of my own heartbeat.

It was all too much. I covered my ears in a futile attempt to drown it all out. I felt something wrap around my waist, and I instinctively grabbed it, sending a surge of flames down my arms. Whatever had grabbed me quickly let go. Fire crawled down my arms, and it felt as if my power was being siphoned out of me. I had never felt this much power before. A new reason to panic filled my mind as I tried, and failed, to contain my magic. The roaring in my head was skull crushing, but I forced my eyes open.

Sarphi and Lyra had taken several steps back, both of their eyes wide. Reyland stood between me and them, holding one arm close to his body. The look in his eyes was determined as he took a step towards me.

"Help me," I pleaded with no one in particular. Helplessness washed over me in waves.

"Always." Reyland kneeled gingerly in front of me. "You just have to let me." He held his hand out cautiously.

I raised my hand towards him, but paused as it came into view. Bright orange flames still wrapped fiercely around my hands and up my arms. Reyland would get badly injured if I grabbed his hand in this state. There had to be something I could do. Some way to contain my magic.

"What do you mean?" I asked. "How do I let you?"

"I'm honestly not sure if you can." Reyland gave me an apologetic smile. "Eventually you may have that type of control over your magic, but for right now, let's just focus on not panicking. Do you think you could manage that?" He continued to talk, but I was losing the fight against the pounding in my head that was growing louder than everything else around me.

"What?" My skin was warm. So warm. "I can't hear you. My head... It's like someone is knocking on my skull. Everything is so warm..." My words were slurring together and I was struggling to keep my eyes open.

"Not good." Lyra stepped up behind Reyland. "This has gone on too long, Reyland. She's starting to overload. She's going to burn out if she can't gain control of this soon." Lyra gestured wildly in my direction. "You need to do whatever it is you were gonna do, and now." Sarphi pulled Lyra back as another surge of power pulsed through me, causing sparks to fly off of my arms in all directions.

"Just do it," I mumbled. My vision was going blurry around the edges and I fell forward on my hands as another surge of pain filled power coursed through me. "Whatever you've got to do."

"It's not that simple, Nightshade." Shadowy tendrils began to snake out of Reyland's fingertips. "I could just absorb your magic, but with the state you're in right now..." He trailed off, risking a quick glance back at the others before locking eyes with me. "The good thing is that, given how close you are to burnout, this probably won't hurt. However, if you fight me, whether you mean to or not, there's the chance that I will just continue to absorb until you burn out."

"And if you don't try," Sarphi cut in, her voice much more demanding than Lyra's, "She will burn out, anyway. You've never been gentle before, Reyland, and now is not the time to start."

"Do it." It felt as if I had swallowed glass. Anything had to be better than this. Reyland's eyes softened, but he didn't move. "Please," I begged. If he didn't do something soon... I didn't want to imagine what would happen.

"Okay." Reyland exhaled a long breath. "I'm going to start now. Try your best to relax."

Yeah. Right. Relax. I took a tentative breath and watched as the shadowy tendrils slithered along the floor towards me. I tried my best not to panic as they began to snake up and around my arms. My first instinct was to pull away, but I fought against it. Despite the burning sensation that had encompassed my entire body, a chill ran down my arms. The shadows dug into the fire, disappearing beneath the blaze. There was a sharp pain in my arms as the shadows took hold. Reyland's face was twisted in concentration, his eyes closed as he manipulated the shadows with one hand while the other stayed pressed against his body.

"Okay." He breathed. "Here goes nothing."

Under any other circumstances, I would have been amazed. Flames now flowed along the shadows that connected us. I watched in amazement as they ebbed and flowed, perfectly intertwining and weaving in and out of each other before disappearing into Reyland's fingertips. Slowly but surely, the flames around my arms dissipated. I took a deep breath, relieved when it didn't feel like someone was sitting on my chest. All of that relief was short-lived and quickly replaced by a searing cold. It started in my arms, but I could feel it weave through my body, straight to my chest. It was making it hard to breathe, and panic was rising again.

"Now you've got to let go." Reyland gritted his teeth.

"Let go of what?" I ground out. I could feel the cold cutting through to my bones. The shadows were still around my arms, slithering and searching for more power. Power that I didn't have anymore. "I'm not holding on to anything."

"It feels like you have my shadows in a chokehold," Reyland panted. He tried to close his fist, his hands shaking with the effort, but to no avail.

I closed my eyes, searching for that kernel of magic that had always been deep down inside of me. I focused, following Reyland's shadows as they hung on to what little bit of magic was still coursing through my veins until I found it. It was weak, but it was still there. That mixture of flame and lavender smoke pulsed dimly, though now with Reyland's shadows entwined with it. Our magic swirled around each other, flowing in unison. It was less of a struggle and more of a dance. I focused hard on my own magic, fighting against its urge to continue this oddly soothing dance.

My own powers were resisting me as I tried to untangle them from Reyland's. No sooner would I get the fire to yield that the lavender mist would take its place. It was a hopeless feeling. A never-ending cycle. I could hear Reyland's grunts of pain every time my magic would latch back on to him. I had to do something, and quickly.

"Nyzirth?" I asked internally, hoping she could hear me.

"Yes?" Her voice rumbled against my brain. *"Is everything alright? You sound panicked."*

"That would be because I am, in fact, panicking." I tried again to pull away from Reyland's magic, but to no avail. *"Reyalnd was trying to help me control my magic, and now he's stuck."*

"I see... So that's what I'm feeling."

"Do you know how I can stop it? Let him go?"

"Let me take a look." I suddenly felt a surge of power run through me.

Nyzirth's magic was like mine, but stronger and denser. It forced its way into my core and began swirling around the conglomerated mass that was mine and Reyland's powers. The intrusion wasn't as painful as I had expected it to be, but it was nowhere near pleasant. I watched in amazement as she began to untangle Reyland's shadows.

"The problem is that, although your magic is not stronger than his, it is less refined." As if she could sense my confusion, she continued. *"'Less refined' means that it still has a mind of its own. All magic does. We can only control and use it thanks to its willingness to serve us."* She proceeded to unravel our magic, and Reyland's grunts of pain were getting further and further apart.

"Well, mine doesn't seem to be very willing to serve at the moment." I wrestled with a bit of magic and was pleased to feel it yield just enough for the shadows to slither away.

A. Turner

"Because you haven't given it a reason to yet." Nyzirth sounded a little annoyed as she pulled the last bit of magic away from the shadows.

"What does that even mean? How do you reason with something that isn't living?" I breathed a sigh of relief as Nyzirth's magic left as quickly as it arrived.

"Who says it isn't living?" I felt Nyzirth's presence leave with those parting words.

Very helpful.

I turned my focus back to the problem at hand, only to find that Reyland's shadows were finally able to move freely. I opened my eyes just as he closed his hand into a fist. The magic that had connected us slowly diminished, leaving me with an oddly empty feeling. Reyland slumped forward onto his hands and knees, wheezing as he wiped the sweat from his forehead. He looked up at me, giving me a half smile through sweat drenched hair.

"Well, that could have gone worse." He chuckled, leaning back on his haunches.

Lyra walked up to him and handed him her small vial of cream. Reyland winced as he smeared it across his now burned hand.

"Did I?" I couldn't finish the sentence.

"No." Reyland answered quickly. "I reached for you without thinking. You did nothing wrong."

I didn't have the energy to argue with him. "Be truthful with me. How close was I to burning out?"

"Very." Nyzirth's voice cut in as the sound of flapping wings filled the air.

I looked up just as Nyzirth dove into the dragoncave. The rest of the dragons entered shortly after her. They all landed in a circle around us. Four massive dragons. The sight would never get old.

"Come. We have something to show you all."

Chapter 38

Ashten

My entire body felt like water as I tried to cling to Nyzirth's back. The wind whipped through my hair and was causing the sweat on my skin to dry, leaving little crystals of salt all over my body. A nice, long, warm bath would be in order as soon as possible. I laid my head against Nyzirth's back and closed my eyes. It caught me off guard when she took a sharp turn to the right that almost threw me off. I had expected the dragons to take us down to the cavern that they stayed in, but this was towards the north coast. There wasn't anything off of that coast, and I began to wonder where she was taking us. I looked over my shoulder to ensure that everyone else was following.

"Hey. Where are we going?" I laid my head back down, no longer having the energy to hold it up.

"I said I have something to show you." Nyzirth flapped her wings a few times, taking us higher into the sky.

I tried my best to portray annoyance through our mental connection. *"Yes. But where? We are leaving the island in a direction that only contains the ocean."*

I looked past her head at the ground to see the edge of Oshos island pass under us and give way to the open ocean for as far as the eye could see. Under any other circumstances, I would have been mesmerized by the sight. Today, however, I was not really in the mood to be dragged around without explanation. I was just about to tell Nyzirth as much when something caught my eyes.

In front of us was a wall of fog that was roughly half the length of Oshos island. As Nyzirth flew over, it became apparent that this wasn't a wall at all. It was more like a dome. A dome of fog that was roughly half the size of Oshos island. Nyzirth made a loop and began her descent towards the fog.

"The fog is merely to ward off unwanted visitors." I could almost feel the judgment in her voice. *"Your people tend to stay away from things that they can't study before destroying."*

"My people?" I prodded. *"And who said anything about destroying?"*

"They always do." There was a hint of disappointment in her voice. *"I think it goes without saying that you can't tell anyone about what we are about to show you."* Her voice took on a no-nonsense tone, and I simply nodded in response.

Nyzirth's descent became steeper, with all the other dragons following close behind. We entered the fog, and I had to close my eyes to keep from growing dizzy thanks to the hazy sightlines. We descended for what felt like forever before the sunshine hit my eyelids and I felt Nyzirth level out again. I was stunned by what I saw when I opened my eyes.

A. Turner

Below us was the most beautiful landscape I had ever seen. Lush trees covered in amber and gold leaves stood tall against the blanket of emerald green grass that covered this island. A river of sapphire blue water ran through the center of the land mass, somehow brighter and richer than the ocean that surrounded it. The sun was somehow shining through the dense fog and the entire island was glowing a vibrant shade of orange. However, the most impressive thing on this island was the massive stone dragon that stood in the center of it. As we descended towards it, I realized that this stone sculpture was at least twice the size of Nyzirth. We landed in front of the stone dragon, and Nyzirth dipped her shoulder to allow me to slide off. I hit the ground with an unsteady thud, and I had to lean against Nyzirth's leg to counteract the wobbliness of my own legs.

The stone dragon before us was unlike any statue I had ever seen. It was roughly the same height as the Alterwood Citadel. Carved out of what seemed to be white marble, the detail was immaculate. I could make out nearly every scale on the wings that were spread out wide behind it. Lavender crystals were set into sockets where the eyes should be and veins filled with crystals of all different types ran through cracks in the marble. A large, reflecting off of it in a myriad of colors.

"What is this place?" I breathed.

"It's what we wanted to show you." Nyzirth nudged me towards the statue.

I looked around at my companions, who were all standing beside their dragons, eyes wide in amazement. Lyra kept looking from Iressei to the statue, and I could assume they were having some great intellectual conversation about the history of dragons. Sarphi leaned against Cyphis's leg, arms crossed as she assessed the scene. Reyland was gently petting Zothim's leg, his eyes glued on me. I turned back to the statue, swallowing heavily as I stepped closer.

Immediately, my magic responded to the proximity. A familiar hum vibrated through me, and my skin tingled with anticipation. It was the same feeling I would get when walking past the statues in the Alterwood Citadel. I reached out and placed my hand on the cool stone. As I did, all of the veins on the statue began to glow. My magic surged to the surface, warming the statue where my hand met the stone.

"Wow," I whispered. "This statue is full of magic."

"This entire place is," Lyra added. I hadn't noticed, but she had taken her shoes off and now stood barefoot in the grass. "I can feel it."

"The Wild Elf is right, Ashten. It's not just the statue." The ground shook as Nyzirth walked up behind me. *"This island is the most magical place in Xeswal."*

A. Turner

"If it's so magical, then why is it hidden away?" I asked aloud, trying my best to keep everyone informed in case their dragons weren't.

"Because your father doesn't want anyone to know that it's here."

"Why would my father care about some island?" I furrowed my brows.

"Because this island is but a glimpse of the life every Elf on Xeswal could be living." Nyzirth looked up at the sky, the evening sunlight shining off of her scales. *"You are aware of the origin of the elves, right?"*

"Right." I clasped my hands in front of me. "One Thousand years ago, elves of all races, along with Dragonfolk and daemonfolk, were placed on the island of Xeswal by the gods. The Solar Elves were named the ruler of this land, with the other Elven races being allowed to have their own, albeit smaller, governments that answer to the Solar Elves on any of the bigger issues." I continued to recite every textbook and history lesson that my father had crammed into my brain from the moment I could read.

Nyzirth snorted, cutting me off. *"That sounds like just the right amount of truth to make it believable."*

"What do you mean?" I turned around to face her, sitting on the toe of the stone dragon and crossing my arms. "Are you guys getting this?" My companions nodded in unison.

"The pen that writes the tale of history is always held by the hand that won." Nyzirth turned to Zothim, who bowed his head in what seemed like approval. *"I think that it is time you heard the story from those who lost."* The other dragons pushed their riders forward until we were all sitting in a circle in front of the statue. Each dragon curled up behind their rider. It was honestly a sight to behold. *"Don't worry. I can share what I am about to say with each of the other dragons. It will be their responsibility to share it with their riders."*

"You can do that?" I asked in disbelief. *"How?"*

"Yes. What kind of Psychic wielding dragon can't send simple telepathic messages?" Nyzirth stood tall above us all. *"Now be quiet and listen."*

"An interesting thing about dragons is that our history is passed down in the form of memories," she began. *"Once we come of age, we enter a deep slumber. This can last anywhere from a few hours to a few weeks. It is different for every dragon. During this slumber, our ancestors bless us with their unbiased knowledge. This means that dragons are the only creatures in Xeswal who know what really happened a millennium ago."*

A. Turner

"Then why was my grandfather hunting down all of the dragons? You guys are the perfect record keepers." I looked up over my shoulder at Nyzirth.

"I said to be quiet and listen," She mumbled, though I was certain the corners of her mouth were curved into a smile.

"Sorry," I mumbled in return, turning back around.

"Nearly one thousand years ago, all races lived in their own plane of existence. Each one was ruled over by one of the six gods. These planes of existence lived harmoniously and traded peacefully with each other through a council of elders. Hyria, Onaris, Eteria, Neron, Tyrix, and Andos. These lands contained Solar Elves, Moon Elves, Wild Elves, Daemonfolk, Dragonfolk, and Morphers respectively." Her entire demeanor slumped when I raised my hand and turned to look up at her again. *" Yes?"*

"Morphers?" I asked.

"Humanoid creatures with the ability to change their appearance and body composition to assume the form of other humanoids. They are often strong psychic magic wielders," She answered quickly before continuing. *"These lands were ruled by the gods that you now refer to as The Watchers. Bacha ruled over Hyria, Enwerel over Onaris, Laserie over Eteria, Illyrie over Neron, Arar over Tyrix, and Aliel over Andos. Every god and mortal had been living this way for millennia. Us dragons had lived it alongside them,*

allowing them to bond with us. The first Drakewardens existed out of respect, not necessity." The other dragons grumbled their agreement.

"It was only a matter of time before someone became restless. Mortals always do. This time, the restlessness appeared in the form of a man named Crugil. Crugil was a Morpher and a very powerful plane shifter. He was also a very intelligent man. So intelligent that he had discovered an entirely new plane of existence. One that had no elves on it at all."

"I am assuming that the new plane of existence was Xeswal?" Reyland asked.

"Precisely." Nyzirth ruffled her wings at the interruption. I covered my mouth with my hand to stifle the laugh that escaped me at how insulted Reyland was by her reaction.

"A new land full of a race they had never seen before: Humans." The dragons must have been able to sense our shock through the bonds, because each one of them nodded their colossal heads in agreement.

"Yes. Humans were the first ones to settle this plane of existence. They served no gods and had no magic. They lived and were content. Something that your gods could not stand. It was Aleil who first suggested that each god send an envoy to this new land. Evidently, to her and the other dark gods, 'envoy' meant army. When the diplomatic parties from the bright gods arrived on Xeswal, they

were greeted by a land in total chaos. Aleil, Illyrie, and Arar had laid siege to the land, nearly wiping out the human race in the process." Nyzirth paused, clearly expecting a question after having given so much information. She was instead met with a wide-eyed stare from each Drakewarden, sitting as if listening to their parents tell them a bedtime story.

"The bright gods mustered their own forces in order to stop this terrible thing from continuing. The Elves always had a deeper connection to magic. This, combined with the fact that only pure-blooded elves had ever bonded with dragons, meant that the armies of the bright gods quickly felled those of the dark gods. Either by death or submission."

"The problem now was the state of the human race. Every adult human had been killed in the onslaught. This land would not survive if the elves just left it. Instead, Bacha, the self-proclaimed leader of the gods, suggested that every Morpher present would take on the form of a human and raise a human child as their own. This was voted on by the council of elders and found to be a feasible solution. This would be how the Morphers would pay for the crimes of their god. So it was done, and each human child was raised by someone who had killed their parents."

"So did the Solar Elves become the rulers simply because their god said so?" Lyra asked. Leave it to her to be putting the pieces together quicker than she could learn them.

"Sort of. It was still voted on, but it was highly unlikely that anyone was going to oppose the will of Bacha. The rest of the history that you know is accurate, though." Nyzirth seemed to relax, confident that her job was done.

"So why is this not the history that is told? *How* is this not the history that is told?" Sarphi threw her arms up in exasperation.

"It's as Nyzirth said. '*The pen that writes the tale of history is always held by the hand that won.*'" I shrugged. "For whatever reason, the gods didn't want us to know the truth. The elves probably didn't want the truth to get out, either. It was easy to hide it from the humans, because all of the adults were killed in the initial assault. The children probably didn't remember what happened."

"Or they were told they were mistaken." Sarphi shrugged.

"Is that why they started hunting down the dragons? Because they knew the dragons could tell everyone the truth?" Reyland leaned forward with his hands on his knees. "If so, that's kind of messed up."

"That seems to be the most logical answer at this time." Lyra shrugged her shoulders. "We will likely never know the answer."

I looked around at all of the dragons. "Why bring us out here, show us this island, and tell us that story?"

"Because, Ashten. This island is the proof of that story. This island is not part of Xeswal. It was somehow transported here when

your ancestors' plane shifted, though I do not know which land it originated from." She nuzzled against my back. *"As the first true Drakewardens in centuries, you four are likely the only mortals who know the truth."*

"Then that means it is our job to tell it, right?" I stood up and crossed my arms.

"Wait." Lyra stood, followed by Sarphi. "While I don't particularly disagree with you, we have to be careful. Someone was willing to wipe out an entire species to keep this a secret."

"Which means they will likely have no problem at all *taking care* of us if we just start telling everyone we know," Reyland added. "I know firsthand what they are willing to do to anyone who opposes them." A solemn look flashed across his face.

"I guess you're right. This is not something we can take lightly." I looked around at my companions. "I can't believe I'm the one saying this, but this is not something we can rush into. We need to take time to think."

"I agree." Sarphi crossed her arms decidedly. "Let's focus on the smaller stuff first. Like why they have us all at Asballicuo in the first place."

I looked around at the beautiful forest that surrounded us. The sun had just set, and the stars that were visible despite the fog were otherworldly. I could feel my body relax the longer I looked up at them.

"Do you think they would miss us if we spent the night out here?" I asked as I leaned back against Nyzirth's side.

"I will ensure you are back before sunrise," Nyzirth purred, sleep apparent in her voice.

Chapter 39

Finn

I wasted no time marching back to my room. I was furious. My hands were shaking with anger as I slammed the door behind me. I quickly undid the belts and buckles on my leathers, sliding them off and tossing them across the room. I sucked in a breath as my undershirt peeled away from the bandages wrapped around my abdomen. Standing in front of the mirror, I observed my various injuries. We had been using wooden weapons, so my only concerning injuries were the ones from Ashten. These injuries weren't going to be easy to hide, but I would try my best. While the king rarely had a problem with me losing my temper, I wasn't keen on having to explain *why* I had lost my temper this time.

Though I'm sure he would understand why.

It was true that the king had experienced no shortage of troubles when raising his daughter. I had a front-row seat to much of it. Until recently, I had thought him a little overdramatic in his reactions to his daughter's antics. I couldn't help but be a little more empathetic now. She just wouldn't listen. I had done my best to try to convince her to just keep a low profile and keep to herself. Yet, only two nights in, I caught her asleep in the library with *him*. Not only was she out of her room at night, which alone should make her grateful that I found them and not some other guard, but I couldn't help but be suspicious of why she was with him. How had they all become so close so quickly? So close that she was literally on her knees, *begging* me not to hurt him. Then there was the fact that she tried to use her magic to manipulate my mind. I was surprised that she even knew that she could do that. My anger reached a boiling point, and I punched the mirror out of frustration. The surface rippled in response and I cursed under my breath.

Stupid magic mirror.

I thought that we had grown close enough over the years that it would have overridden the little bit of tension this time in our lives would cause, but I guess I had been wrong. I needed to find some way to convince her I wasn't a bad guy. Some way to prove to her I loved her. That was my entire reason for doing this. I loved her, and I want to keep her safe. The easiest way to do that was by keeping her close. Which was going to be hard to do now that she had gotten so close to *him*. I pulled on my red pants and tunic and began fastening my dark citadel guard armor. I took one more look in the mirror, straightening my white cloak so that it laid perfectly over my shoulder.

"Alterwood Citadel." The rough syllables of the Ansir language clawed at my throat. I watched as the surface of the mirror shifted before showing the inside of the king's war room. It was with great foresight that the king had this mirror enchanted in the ancient language of Andos. No one that opposed him knew enough of the language to use it.

I schooled my features into neutrality before walking through. My skin tingled as the magic contained in this mirror pulled me forward. Within two steps, I was inside the war room. Everything was dark, with only a few candles being left lit in anticipation of my arrival. I began to make my way to the door, hoping to catch some others before they retired for the night.

"You're late." King Renlin's voice broke the silence, causing me to startle.

In my hurry, I hadn't noticed him standing on the far side of the war table. On either side of him stood the other two Elven leaders. To his left stood Galen Windwalker, High Lord of the Wild Elves, dressed in a deep green suit with his long red hair pulled back into a neat bun. To his right stood Rael Dronvakh, High Lord of the Moon Elves, dressed in a deep grey suit, his white hair cut close to his head. The king was dressed impeccably, as always, in a dark red suit. His icy eyes cut through the darkness like a knife, and I dipped into a bow to avoid them.

"Apologies, my king." I rose slowly. "There was a, uh, problem that I needed to attend to before I left." I hoped that was enough information to satisfy his need for an explanation.

The king nodded and motioned for me to sit. I knew better than to deny the request. I took the seat directly across from the king and High Lords. We all sat in silence for what seemed like forever before Galen spoke up.

"We are running into a bit of unrest in the Mistymoon Glades." Galen's voice carried a thick accent, like his son's. "Many have asked where Lyra is. They are concerned for the safety of their heir, and I don't think that vague explanations are going to suffice much longer."

"Has your son not taken on those responsibilities, Galen?" the king questioned.

"He has, sire, but the Wild Elves are a stickler for tradition. They know that his position and power is only, if all goes well, temporary." Galen raised an eyebrow at me. "This charade isn't going to hold up much longer. The last thing we need is a Wild Elf rebellion."

Before I could speak, Rael interjected.

"I am running into a similar problem, My Lord." Rael's voice carried a low tenor that seemed to vibrate through the air. "It has been six years since I sent my son away. It is not unusual for Moon Elves to go on long journeys when they come of age, but many are demanding I send out search parties for him. They say that five years is too long."

"Something I too tried to tell you all those years ago, Rael." The king raised a brow at the Moon Elf, who held up a hand defensively. "However, I must admit that there is a bit of unrest here in the Citadel, as well. Many of the servants, as well as some of the more influential families in the city, have asked where Ashten is. I have tried my best to quell their worries, but rumors spread quickly." He rapped his fingers across the wooden table. "I can only *dispose* of so many servants before the others begin to get suspicious."

"What do you propose we do, my King?" Galen leaned back in his chair and crossed his arms behind his head.

"That depends on what kind of report this young man has for us." The king waved his hand in my direction, his way of giving me permission to speak. I nodded my thanks.

"Well, my Lords, I am pleased to announce that all three of the Heirs have bonded with a dragon." Delight lit up the face of each man before me. "The process was strenuous on their bodies, but they seemed to recover well after a good night's rest."

"That is wonderful to hear, Captain." King Renlin leaned forward in his chair. "Am I correct in understanding that there is a fourth bonded rider, though?"

How did he know about that?

"Yes, my King." I tried to keep my voice level. "A Dragonfolk by the name of Sarphi. She was taken in at Asballicuo many years ago after she raided a Royal Caravan, but only recently showed signs of being able to wield two different magics. We honestly didn't think the bonding would work for her, but saw no harm in letting her try." I shrugged. "The only downside was that the bonding might kill her. Thankfully, that was not the case."

"And their training?" The king seemed uninterested in talking about Sarphi, so I quickly answered his question instead.

"Well, as you know, Reyland and Lyra were both trained from birth in the arts of magic and weapons. They have both progressed nicely in their time away. Reyland, in particular, has proven especially helpful." Rael gave the king an approving nod. "Ashten, however, has no such training. It has only been a few days, sire. She can barely point a weapon in the right direction, and her use of magic is arguably worse. She cannot control her magic and that problem is amplified when she loses control of her emotions."

"Which I know is quite often." The king rolled his eyes, a frown appearing on his face before I could even confirm his statement.

"So what I am hearing is that they are not ready?" Galen looked to me for an answer.

"The bond is in place. It should work well enough for our purposes." If I had my say, Ashten's bond wouldn't matter, but I decided to keep that fact to myself. "With all of my experience being taken into consideration, it would be best to take care of business now. Before they get too strong."

"So, what *will* we do?" Rael echoed Lord Galen's earlier question. "The elves grow less and less trusting by the day. We cannot keep up this charade much longer."

"Then let us give them what they want." The king stood from his chair, everyone else quickly following. "They want proof that the heirs are still alive, no? Why don't we just show them?"

"And you propose we do that how?" Rael cocked an eyebrow.

"With a celebration." A smile spread across his face at our obvious confusion. "Ashten's birthday was only a week ago. We could disguise this as a ball being thrown in her honor. We invite the lords and ladies from all across Xeswal. Once everyone is gathered, we introduce our heirs in all of their newfound splendor. Drakewardens of the Desai Dynasty. It is the easiest way to get everyone we need in one place."

"And how do we get them to go along with this idea? I'm sure they aren't particularly happy about their current living arrangements." Galen began pacing the floor.

"The heirs and I have an understanding," I began. "They know that there are certain rules and expectations. They also know that there are certain *consequences* that come with breaking those rules and expectations."

"Captain Finn is more than capable of maintaining control of his soldiers," the king added. "Rael, Galen, you may both return to your people. Spread the word of the coming celebration." Both males nodded before walking to the mirror, speaking their command phrases, and disappearing into its silvery surface. "Captain, I need you to return to Asballicuo and prepare the heirs."

"At once, my King." I gave a curt bow and walked over to the mirror. "Asballicuo." I muttered in Ansir, waiting only a moment before stepping through.

Chapter 40

Reyland

The cool weather that greeted us once nightfall came was a refreshing change from the constant dry heat inside the volcano. I couldn't remember the last time I had spent a night out under the stars, and I didn't realize how much I had missed it until now. Being so secluded from the night had been harder than I wanted to admit at first. Moon Elves draw their powers from, well, the moon, so it had taken me a while to even be able to use my powers inside Asballicuo.

Here, laid out in the grass under the night sky, I had never felt more in tune with my powers. I threaded my fingers through the thick grass and shadows danced involuntarily. Everywhere that the shadows touched was turned to ice thanks to my bond with Zothim. I was still trying to master those new powers. My hands traced circles along the ground, and I was mesmerized by the potency of my own magic.

Hours passed in the span of minutes until I heard rustling in the grass beside me. I glanced over to see Ashten sitting there cross-legged. There was a sleepy smile on her face as she leaned over towards me.

"I didn't take you for the artistic type." Ashten gestured to the circles I had drawn in the grass. "How long have you been awake doodling?"

"Maybe a few hours?" I shrugged. "I haven't actually been to sleep yet."

"Me either. I don't want to waste our time outside of the volcano, on this beautiful island, by sleeping." She looked up at the stars, and I loved how they reflected off of her violet eyes. "I've always been mesmerized by the night sky. There's just something about it." She leaned back on her arms and smoke, both purple and black, formed in a thin layer on the surrounding grass. She must have felt the magical energy because she looked down at the ground around her, a wide smile on her face. I couldn't help but notice that the smile didn't quite meet her eyes.

She was beautiful, and I wasn't sure she knew that. I wondered if she truly had no idea how beautiful she was. How powerful she was. I had never seen someone with a well of power as deep as hers, and I had siphoned magic from plenty of very powerful people. She had more power than most magic users even dreamed of. Yet here she was, awestruck by the littlest bits of magic this island drew out of her. I couldn't help but smile as I watched her. The light from the moon hit her face, and I was reminded of one reason she probably didn't want to sleep tonight.

"Are you okay?" I asked. My voice was nearly a whisper. I tried to convince myself that it was just so that I didn't wake the others, but I think there was also a part of me that didn't want her to hear me. A part of me that didn't want to hear her answer. I knew that once I heard her answer, I would want to do something about it. Every fiber of my logic wanted me to stay as disconnected as possible, but it felt like there was a little thread attached to my heart that was constantly pulling me in her direction.

She paused as she regarded my question. Emotions danced in her eyes. She leaned back, looking up at the stars again. "I don't know. These past few days have been a lot. I'm honestly not sure how many more life-changing revelations of knowledge I can take." Her laugh was like music to my ears. "At the same time, there is this little ball of emotions inside of me that I can't quite place. Like a tension sitting in my chest and I can't tell if it's excitement or nervousness."

I knew exactly what she meant. That same feeling had been driving me crazy for nearly a week. It has taken all of my restraint not to act on it. I just couldn't wrap my head around why she didn't understand it. She could obviously feel it, but she very obviously didn't know what it meant. That didn't sit right with me. How could she not know about something that was part of our being? Something so natural? Should I be the one to tell her?

"Hello?" She cleared her throat, and I realized I had just been staring at her. "I think I lost you for a second."

"Sorry. I mean, I was asking about your face, but..." I couldn't help but smile as I scooted a little closer to her. "Can't it be a little bit of both?"

She mirrored my smile with a half one of her own, her eyes not leaving the night sky as she reached up to touch her face. "My face is fine, I guess. I might ask Lyra if she could perform a little bit of healing in the morning." She turned to face me, her head cocked to the side like a dog.

"The first twenty-ish years of my life were dreadfully uneventful. Until a week ago, I was just your typical sheltered princess, and I hated it. Look at me now. Sitting on an island that was supposedly transported here from another plane of existence, listening to the sounds of my friends and their *dragons* sleeping, and contemplating the intricacies of my emotions. Then, you've got the fact that every bit of history that I have ever learned about the land I am supposed to inherit has been at least a partial lie." She sighed heavily and hung her head. "Oh, and did I mention the dragons?"

She gestured to where Nyzirth and Zothim were sleeping. The larger white dragon had his body wrapped around that of the smaller purple one. His wings were stretched out over her, as if protecting her from some unseen danger.

"Well, at least he can be nice to someone." I scoffed and Ashten covered her mouth to stifle her laughter.

"I heard that, Moon Elf." Zothim's raspy voice rumbled in my head, and I startled at the sudden intrusion. *"Perhaps I could say the same about you."* I shook my head, choosing not to have this

conversation with him tonight. He sighed and I knew I hadn't heard the end of this.

The moonlight reflected off of the large, white dragon statue in a way that caught my eye. Something that I hadn't noticed earlier. There were flowers growing all around the bottom of the statue. I stood up and walked over, inspecting a deep purple bell-shaped flower. I had never actually seen it in the wild before, but I recognized it immediately. Maybe it was from another plane of existence. Just one thing that hadn't been wiped from the record.

"What are you looking at?" Ashten half yelled, half whispered from her spot in the grass.

"Nightshade," I whispered back, pointing at the flower below me. "I've never seen it growing in the wild like this."

"Which one is it?" she asked as she stood and walked over to where I was standing.

The one that's the same color as your eyes.

"It's that purple one right there." I pointed at the flower. She knelt down beside it, and I grabbed her arm just as she reached out to touch it. "It's poisonous."

"To the touch?" She furrowed her brows. "It's that potent?"

I knelt down beside her. "I'm fairly certain that you wouldn't die just from touching it." I let go of her arm and rubbed my suddenly sweaty palms against the leg of my trousers. "If you were to touch the plant and then touch your eyes or mouth, though... I just wouldn't risk it. It's not a fun experience."

"How do you know so much about a plant you've never seen before?" She cocked her head to the side again. The sight made my heart jump.

"I didn't say that I had never seen the plant before." I smirked. "I've never seen it *in the wild* before. My father had plenty of it in his greenhouses back home."

"Why would your father have so much of this deadly plant?" Ashten looked back down at the flower. The moonlight reflected off of her hair, giving it a deep violet sheen that I had never noticed before. "Though I will admit that it is quite beautiful." She smiled as she looked back up at me.

"The most dangerous ones always are." My voice was thick as I spoke. I cleared my throat before continuing. "Besides, we learned that nightshade could be used to keep some animals away from the plants that we could actually eat. Rabbits love the berries, but deer avoid the plant altogether."

"So rabbits can eat it, but we can't?" Curiosity filled her eyes. "What would happen if we were to ingest it?"

"It only takes ten to twenty berries to kill an adult male. The symptoms range anywhere from blurry vision, nausea, and vomiting to lethargy, delirium, and eventually death as it slows down your heart." I monitored her facial expressions as I spoke. I expected to find disgust and aversion, but I saw nothing but pure inquisitiveness as she studied the flowers while I spoke. "My trainers showed me many ways to use it."

She turned around and leaned back against the statue, careful not to touch any of the flowers around the base. I walked around her and settled in on the opposite side. We both sat in still silence, and I worried that I had said something that might have upset her.

"I've never used it before," I decided to add once the silence became too much. "It never felt right. If someone has to die, they deserve to see it coming. To have a chance to fight back." I exhaled through my nose as a wave of unsettling emotions washed over me. "No one deserves to die that kind of death without knowing what caused it."

"Did the people you've killed deserve it?" Her voice was low as she spoke.

Her question caught me off guard. I whipped my head in her direction to find her still staring up at the night sky. I slowly settled back against the stone, as if moving too quickly would scare her off.

"I want to say yes, but..." The words caught in my throat. I swallowed hard, fighting against another wave of emotion. "I don't know. Sometimes he would send the Captain to arrest them. If the

Captain returned empty-handed, then it was my turn. I didn't ask questions. Not after the first time." My hands began to shake in my lap. "Maybe I should have..."

The idea that I had killed innocent people had never occurred to me before. The face of the Elf in the cell at Asballicuo filled my head. My vision began to blur at the edges and I felt the sudden need to be anywhere but here. I stood up to walk away, but Ashten grabbed my arm before I could get too far.

"I'm sorry I asked... I have a bad habit of asking too many questions," she whispered, pulling on my arm. A silent request for me to sit back down.

I obliged, sitting back down in my previous spot. I leaned back against the cool stone of the statue and closed my eyes. Ashten's hand pulled away from my arm. I nearly reached out for it, but thought better of the idea. After a long while of silence, I opened one eye and glanced in her direction.

She was lying on her side in the grass, arms folded under her head. Her eyes were closed and her breathing was deep and even. She had fallen asleep. I caught myself staring at the way the moonlight reflected off of her hair as it fell across her face. I tried not to think about the finger shaped bruises that her hair was covering. Instead, I pulled off my jacket, folded it, and carefully placed it under her head. She stirred slightly before her breathing evened back out. I leaned back against the statue and closed my eyes. My heart was still racing, but the steady rhythm of Ashten's breathing calmed me and it wasn't long before my own fell into a similar rhythm.

Chapter 41

Ashten

"Wake up." Nyzirth's purring voice pulled me from what was no doubt the best sleep I had experienced in at least a week.

I laid there with my eyes closed, taking in the sounds around me. Birds were chirping. A light breeze was blowing and leaves were rustling along the grass. Warm sunlight was hitting my face, shining brightly through my eyelids. I opened my eyes, blinking slowly as I adjusted to the brightness of the morning sky. It took me a few moments to realize what I was seeing.

I was lying on my side with my head propped up on something soft. The first thing I noticed when I opened my eyes were the two booted feet crossed over one another. I lifted my hand to wipe the sleep from my eyes and it brushed against cool leather. The current situation still hadn't quite registered until my pillow shifted slightly. I bolted upright, immediately scooting a few inches away from where I was laying.

"I was trying not to wake you." Reyland groaned as he hoisted himself into an upright position. "I know how much you needed the sleep." He cut a glare in Nyzirth's direction. "*Someone* wasn't supposed to wake you up." The purple dragon huffed as she stood and stretched out her wings.

A. Turner

"He's just upset that you aren't laying in his lap anymore." Nyzirth's voice purred in my head.

"Wait... Was I?" My cheeks reddened as the realization hit me. I *had* climbed into his lap. "I am so sorry. I didn't mean to invade your personal space like that. I didn't realize..." I buried my head in my hands, muffling the continued string of apologies. Flopping down backwards onto the grass, a part of me hoped the ground would just swallow me up and save me from the embarrassment.

"It's fine." Reyland waved me off as he stood and dusted himself off. "We didn't start the night off like that. I guess at some point you rolled over. When I woke up, you were laying there. Everyone else was still asleep, so I didn't see the harm in letting you lay there." I must have looked mortified because all he did was laugh as he offered me a helping hand off of the ground. "You're not upset that I let you sleep, are you?"

"You should be." Nyzirth stretched. Her mannerisms reminded me of a cat. A massive cat the size of a house. *"We needed to be back before daylight if we didn't want them to notice us missing."*

"No. It's not that." I ignored her and took Reyland's hand, letting him haul me to my feet. "I'm embarrassed, not upset. I really shouldn't have..." My voice trailed off as memories started to resurface and the puzzle pieced itself together.

I had a slight recollection of rolling over in the middle of the night, but it wasn't Reyland that I remembered reaching out for. The heat on my face spread, my embarrassment only deepening as the details came to light. I had reached out for Finn. My subconscious self had thought that it was Finn's lap I had been laying in. I should be mad at him. I should have no desire to be anywhere near him. It seemed that my subconscious had other ideas.

"Don't worry." Reyland picked his jacket back up off of the ground and slipped his arms into it. "I won't tell him."

"Him?" I asked, cursing how my voice cracked under the feigned ignorance.

"The Captain." Reyland looked past me as he spoke. I followed his eyes to see Sarphi and Lyra stroking the sides of their dragons. Sarphi's eyes met mine just as I looked up and she twisted her back to me. "I saw you two the other day. When he got upset and dragged you off." He looked down to meet my eyes and there was an emotion there that I couldn't quite pinpoint. "I was worried that he might... Well, I think you know now what he's capable of. I just didn't want you to get hurt. It had never crossed my mind that you two might have been *involved*."

"I appreciate you trying to look out for me." I answered a little too quickly. An unexplainable warmth settled in my chest at the thought of Reyland being concerned about my wellbeing. We had only just met. He had no reason to care what happened to me, but he did, and that meant a lot to me. For some irritatingly inexplicable reason. "I also appreciate you not telling anyone else. Everything is complicated enough as it is."

A smirk spread across his face. "How do you know I haven't told *everyone* else, Nightshade?"

"Have you seen these guys?" I gestured to our companions, who were *terribly* bad at eavesdropping. So bad that Lyra had to stifle a laugh when I threw a pebble in her direction. "They are sitting over there like we can't tell that they are one hundred percent listening in on our conversation. Which means I guess they know now." I raised my voice a little to get their attention. Lyra turned to me with a sheepish smile and offered a small shrug.

"I mean, you showed up on that first day wearing the male's clothes. That was enough of a sign for me." Sarphi cleared her throat as she turned around. "Not to mention the way you watch his every move any time you are in a room together. Anyone could read those looks from a mile away."

"That's enough," Reyland snapped, and Sarphi raised an eyebrow at him. I mirrored her expression.

"She's nearly as bad as you, Reyland." Sarphi let out a chuckle and started her climb on to Cyphis's back.

"We get it, Sarphi," Reyland ground out through clenched teeth as he, too, turned to face his dragon.

I gave Lyra a questioning glance, but she only shrugged back at me, her face still a little red from being caught. I mirrored her shrug before walking over to Nyzirth. The purple dragon rubbed her nose against my stomach, nearly knocking me over in the process. A low rumble akin to a cat's purr emitted from somewhere deep in her throat.

"Well, someone is in a good mood this morning," I couldn't help but tease even as I struggled to climb onto her back.

"It wasn't just you who needed a good night's rest. I think it did all of us some good." She used her head to point toward Zothim and Reyland.

I watched Reyland run a hand along Zothim's neck. He must have said something to the dragon, because the next thing I knew, Zothim had knocked him over with a flick of his tail. I didn't even try to hide the laugh that burst out of my mouth. It was a real, genuine laugh. The first one in at least a week, I realized. Reyland looked in my direction, smiling as soon as our eyes met. That same warmth from earlier blossomed in my chest, and I covered my face with my hands. Zothim clapped him on the back with his tail again and Reyland muttered what I could only imagine were a few choice words before climbing onto the large white dragon's back.

"See?" Nyzirth affirmed.

"Yeah. I do." I gave her a few pats on the neck before she launched us both into the sky.

"So..." Sarphi slowed until we were walking side by side at the back of our little pack as we made our way down the hall to our living quarters. "You and the Captain?" She raised a brow. "Really?"

"Why do you sound so surprised?" I stared at Lyra and Reyland ahead of us, trying my best to seem casual and unbothered despite the fact that I didn't want to have this conversation right now. Or ever, if I was being honest.

"For starters, he's a human. You're the Princess."

"I am aware." There was a bite to my voice that I hoped gave Sarphi the message.

"Also..." She drew out the word awkwardly. "I didn't take you for the kind of person who was interested in males like *that.*"

"What's *that* supposed to mean?" I nearly came to a complete stop, tripping over my own feet.

"Only that he doesn't seem like your type." She shrugged. "He's rough around more than just the edges." I didn't miss the way her eyes dipped to the bruises on my chin. I was going to have to get Lyra to work her magic just so people would quit looking at me like that. "I just took you for more of a knight in shining armor type of person. You know, the type of male who shows up and saves the day, not ruins it."

"Well." I looked down at my shoes, trying to carefully choose my next words. "I guess it depends on how you look at it."

"And how *do* you look at it, Ashten?"

"He's not always like that, you know?" I hated the way I sounded. Like I barely had myself convinced. "He's only like that when he's here. Back at the Citadel, Finn was the one who showed up and saved the day for me. Multiple times. Both figuratively and literally." I swallowed hard. "He's just stressed about me having to do all of these dangerous things. I mean, it *is* his job to keep me safe."

"And putting bruises on your face when he's angry is keeping you safe?" Sarphi grabbed my arm and turned me towards her. Lyra and Reyland stopped a few beats later, but she waved them forward before turning on me again.

"It's like I said. He's not normally like that. Finn has *never* put his hands on me like that." I thought back to when my father had slapped me. Finn seemed as if he wanted to go right then and give my father a piece of his mind. That had to count for something, right?

It was Sarphi's turn to look down at the ground contemplatively. She opened her mouth several times to speak, but stopped herself each time. I was just about to walk away when she settled on what to say.

"I may be *way* out of line here." She paused for a moment. "But what if *you* are the 'only'?"

"The 'only'?" I repeated back at her. "What does that mean?"

"You said that Captain Finn only acts like that when he is here. To you, this type of behavior is abnormal." She took my hand and only held it tighter when I tried to pull away. "What if this behavior *is* normal for him? What if how he acts when he is with you at the Citadel is only for you?"

"Are you insinuating that he has been putting on a front just for me for the past ten years? I have known him since we were children!" My voice rose as I jerked my hand away from her and took a step back.

"I know what I've seen. The things I've seen him do, Ashten." Sadness filled her eyes, and she exhaled deeply. "I just think that it's easier to be the nice guy behind closed doors. Especially if those closed doors are an ocean away.

"And I just think that, though I appreciate your concern, you have no idea what you are talking about." I let the words sting. I began walking again, starting up at a quick pace. "Finn has always been there for me and I don't see why he would change that now."

Sarphi didn't say anything else, though she trailed behind me the rest of the walk back.

Chapter 42

Ashten

There was a note pinned to our door when we returned. Lyra pulled it off and began reading it out loud.

"Report to the entrance as soon as you have returned. Wear your riding leathers." Lyra turned around to face us. "The Captain left this for us. I wonder what he wants."

"Why would we meet at the entrance?" Sarphi pulled open the door to our chambers. "If we need to be in our flight leathers, then I assume we will be flying. Why not just meet at the dragoncave?"

"I don't know, but we are probably late," Reyland added. "Which means he probably won't be thrilled."

"I guess this means we don't really have time to freshen up." I tossed my dirty jacket on the bed and grabbed a new one. "At least they gave us more than one set of leathers."

We all grabbed what felt necessary and filed out of our room once more. None of us quite remembered how to get to the entrance from here, but our departure must have been common knowledge. We had no trouble getting guards to point us in the right direction. Sarphi, Lyra, and Reyland informed me they hadn't left through the main entrance the entire time they had been here. I let that sink in as I followed them through the halls. Reyland had been here for at least six years, assuming he and I were the same age. He had never left through the front door in all that time.

We passed the alcove where Finn had pulled me aside before we got to the dining hall. My face reddened as the memories of our stolen moments flashed through my mind. Something had definitely changed since then. But what was it? What had caused Finn to act the way he did in the library? Sure, he was jealous, but he had been jealous plenty of times before. We had had arguments about me entertaining suitors that my father had brought for me, but Finn had never laid his hands on me. He had never hurt me before. There had always been a gentleness to his touch, even when he had been making a show of escorting me through this very hallway.

I was thankful to be pulled from my thoughts when we reached the doors that lead to the outside of Asballicuo. Two stone faced guards were posted right in front of it. I glanced over at the daemonfolk woman that still sat at the desk. Her legs were crossed over each other and propped up on the desk. A tightlipped smile graced her pale skin as she waved at the guards. They both stepped to the side, giving us access to the doors.

They creaked as Reyland pushed them open, and we all squinted as the bright sunlight hit our faces. We wearily filed out of the large doorway and onto the sandy terrain at the base of the mountain. Malon and Axilya were waiting just outside the shadow of the doorway.

"So nice of you to finally grace us with your presence." Malon stood with his hands behind his back. "We have been waiting for quite some time."

"Well, the note didn't specify a time." Sarphi crossed her arms. "Be more specific next time and maybe you wouldn't have to wait out in the desert for so long."

Before Malon could respond, Lyra spoke up. "We just now saw the note on the door." She glared at Sarphi, who merely smiled in return.

"Regardless, we need to set out as soon as possible," Axilya cut in. "Call your dragons."

"Bold of you to assume that the dragons belong to us." Reyland took a step forward. "Care to tell us where we are going first? I've spent six years inside that volcano and never once has anyone let me even remotely close to the entrance. Even for my jobs, I was led out of a back exit. So forgive me if I am a little suspicious."

"The four of you have been summoned to the Alterwood Citadel." Malon's face was emotionless as he spoke. "There is to be a celebration honoring the Princess's birthday."

A. Turner

"A celebration?" I questioned. "For my birthday? The one that was nearly a week ago? Why celebrate now?" I threw up my arms. "Why celebrate at all? My father has not thrown a party in my honor since the day I was born and he found out I was a girl. I think that if he could have canceled that one, he would have." A knot formed in my stomach. A week ago, I would have been thrilled at the idea of going back home. Today, I wasn't so sure.

"It's not my job to ask questions. Especially when the question would be directed at the king." Malon still stood at attention, but the command in his voice wavered slightly. "Please just call your dragons. Captain Finn has gone ahead to ensure everything is ready for your arrival."

Gone ahead?

Our dragons could make that flight in a day. It would take a horse at least two, and that would be nearly running it to death. I shook my head, deciding I probably would not get an answer out of this Elf, no matter how many questions I asked. Instead, I focused on the presence of Nyzirth that always seemed to be inside my head, merely existing alongside me.

"So, apparently we are headed out."

"Where?" Nyzirth sounded annoyed.

"To the Alterwood Citadel. My father has summoned all of us." I rubbed a hand down my face. *"That is all the information I can*

318

get out of Malon and Axilya. Please, just come to the entrance of the volcano."

I didn't hear anything else in my head, but soon I could hear the flapping of wings. I turned just as all four dragons crested over the top of the volcano. They made a wide circle before landing one by one behind Malon and Axilya, who nearly failed to keep their balance as the ground rumbled from the sheer size of the four dragons. The two elves looked wearily between us and the dragons. Cyphis leaned in closely. Steam rolled from his nose, causing the loose strands of their hair to blow into their faces. I tried my best not to laugh as both elves took a few all too quick steps away from the dragon, pure fear on their faces.

"We could eat them." It wasn't a question, but a statement. Nyzirth rumbled deep in her chest, as if I needed further proof.

"That won't be necessary." I smiled widely. *"Though I appreciate the offer."*

Malon cleared his throat, schooling his facial features back into neutrality. "I suggest you head out at once. Best not keep the king waiting any longer." I didn't miss the way his throat bobbed as he spoke about my father.

I was the first one to approach the two elves standing between me and my dragon. Though Malon stood nearly six inches taller than me, I felt a momentary rush of confidence as I came to a stop beside him. I crooked my finger, a request for him to lean in closer. He rolled his eyes, but obliged.

"You may fear my father, and rightfully so." The sinisterness of my voice surprised me. I tried not to falter as I continued to speak. "But I want you to remember that, right now, I am the only thing keeping these four dragons from ripping you both to shreds." His face blanched, and I couldn't help but smile.

I gave him a little pat on the shoulder before striding forward and climbing onto Nyzirth's back. She still had to use her head to help me, but that didn't make a difference in the power that I felt sitting atop a dragon staring down at the elves.

My companions all did the same, and we launched into the sky one by one. The sound of wings flapping was soon replaced by the roaring wind as we reached our altitude and began coasting over the ocean. The knot in my stomach returned as reality sank in once more.

I was going home.

I spent the first hour of the flight trying to get all of my thoughts organized in my head. That, combined with trying not to fall off of Nyzirth's back, was proving to be quite challenging. My arms were already burning from the effort.

"Lean forward on your stomach." Nyzirth lifted her head slightly. *"If you make yourself smaller, then the wind won't hit you as hard and you won't have to hold on as tightly."*

"I didn't say anything about holding on." I was still trying to figure out how much Nyzirth could feel without me directly telling her.

"You didn't have to. Until you can learn how to control the link between our minds, I can hear all of your unfiltered thoughts." I couldn't help but notice that she sounded annoyed.

"Everything?" I asked. *"Even when we are apart?"*

"It depends on how far apart we are. When I'm not with you, I can't hear your random thoughts, but I can hear you when you speak to me directly. The normal bond is amplified by your psychic abilities."

"Why can't I hear your thoughts?" My curiosity was piqued. I was beginning to understand just how little I knew about what it meant to be bonded to a dragon. *"Can I talk into other people's minds?"*

"I have control and yes." Her tone softened slightly. *"I do not mean to be short with you, Ashten. All of this is just as new to me as it is to you, but I have the knowledge of generations of dragons before me. I often forget that you are learning it all as we go."* I felt the bond between us soften slightly, something like empathy flowing between us.

A. Turner

"*It's okay.*" I stroked her back softly. "*I don't think that Malon and Axilya knew who I was.*" I changed the subject, hoping that Nyzirth could help me straighten out some of my thoughts.

"*Who you **are**.*" A stream of lavender smoke curled out of her nose and I watched in amazement as it flowed past my head, leaving a trail behind us. I just barely glimpsed Raven's Rest, a small logging town on the edge of the dynasty, through the clouds. "*You are still the Princess. We are headed to a party being thrown in your honor by the king who is your father.*"

"*Don't remind me.*" I sighed.

"*I will continue to remind you until you no longer need to be reminded.*" Nyzirth rumbled beneath me.

"*You said I could talk to other people in their minds.*" I changed the topic of conversation once again. The last thing I wanted to talk about right now was my father or my heritage. I had a feeling there was going to be plenty of that kind of talk to go around when we got to Arvandor. "*How?*"

"*It requires more control over your powers.*" Nyzirth must have felt my frustration because she didn't wait long before adding, "*I can try to show you, if you would like.*"

"*I would,*" I stated quickly, before I could change my mind. I couldn't help but feel hesitant about using my powers after nearly burning out yesterday.

"Don't worry. It requires control of your power, but not large amounts of it. You won't burn out." A wave of calming warmth washed over me. *"It's easiest to speak to someone you are close to for the first time."*

"Well, that might prove difficult." I glanced around at my companions. I had known these guys for no more than a week. *"How do I reach them?"*

"You need to find a connection between you and whoever you're trying to contact. Something you have in common with them. A past experience or a shared interest, for example."

I tried to think about something I had in common with any of the other three dragon riders. I looked around at all of them. Obviously, we were all Drakewardens, but I felt like the connection needed to be something a little more personal.

Lyra leaned forward against Iressei's back, her hands lazily draped across the dragon's neck. I had a feeling that we had a shared disdain for our home life. She never wanted to talk about hers, but I was all too familiar with the look in her eyes any time we mentioned our heritages.

Sarphi was sitting up straight on the back of Cyphis. Her arms were outstretched and her short hair was blown out of her face. I was struggling to find something that she and I had in common. I thought long and hard until something that Reyland had said came to mind.

When we had gone to the library, he mentioned Sarphi liked to read. I wasn't sure if it was enough to support mind speaking, but it was something.

Reyland was relaxed atop the back of Zothim. His arms were relaxed in his lap and he seemed transfixed on the horizon in front of us. As I thought, I began to realize that he and I had more in common than I had originally thought. The nightmares were the first thing that came to mind. Then there was the fact that we both hated our fathers. And then, on a lighter note, we both enjoyed our peace and quiet. Surely, any of those three things would be enough.

"Is it possible to mind speak with more than one person at the same time?" If it was possible, it would be an incredibly helpful skill to have.

"Yes. It is possible." Nyzirth drifted to the back of the group. *"It is also easier if you can see everyone. Hopefully, this positioning helps with that."*

"It does." I scratched behind her wings to show my thanks. She purred in response. *"Here goes nothing."*

As I looked at each of my companions, I tried to focus on the one thing that I had in common with them. Slowly, one by one, I felt a slight tug in their direction. It was like a thin thread of my power connecting each of us. Sarphi scratched her head, as if she could feel it too.

"Can you guys hear me?" I asked cautiously. Not wanting to startle them, I tried my best to whisper in my head.

I was thankful that we didn't actually have to direct our dragons because all three of them whipped their heads in my direction, eyes wide. Lyra said something, but I couldn't hear her over the wind. I dropped my connection with them, focusing on Nyzirth instead.

"Can they talk back to me? Like you and I can?"

"Of course they can. Just like when they speak with their own dragons. It is your magic that is maintaining the connection. It is temporary for now but, with practice, you could establish a permanent one that they could contact you through." She flew forward towards the center of the group. *"Without you having to initiate anything."*

I conveyed my thanks and focused once again on my companions. I found it easier to locate that connection now that I had done it once before.

"Answer me like you do your dragons." I smiled at Sarphi, who was staring at me, mouth agape.

Lyra was the first one to respond. *"I didn't know you could do this. Is it part of your psychic abilities?"* I could *feel* the inquisitiveness in her voice. It was odd.

A. Turner

"Well, this is... interesting." Reyland studied me intently. An emotion that I couldn't quite define started to flow down the connection, but it was pulled back before I could grasp it.

"It is also apparently a group thing, so please keep your thoughts in control." Sarphi cut in quickly. She rubbed her head, looking at me from under her hand. *"As much as I hate this, it could be useful."*

"I have to agree. It gives me a bit of a headache, but being able to talk in private without having to be in private will come in handy once we are inside the Citadel." Lyra's voice was full of amazement, and I could already see the plans forming in her eyes.

"Can you do this when you aren't in the same room as us?" Sarphi asked, finally seeming to calm down from the initial shock.

"I think so. I assume it would be much harder, though." My own head began to ache. *"This is already hard. I don't think I could maintain multiple connections for very long. One connection is probably a little easier."*

"This is going to be very useful." Reyland placed a hand on his temple as well. *"Hopefully, the headache will go away once we are used to it."*

I couldn't help but feel pride as I realized what I had just done. It had taken me only a few minutes to perform a new magical skill. I may not be able to wield a sword, but hopefully this was a sign that wielding my magic wasn't going to be as hard as I had feared.

"Hold on to that feeling." Nyzirth's voice cut through, causing me to lose concentration on my other connections. I realized it wasn't just my pride I was feeling. *"You're almost home."*

Anxiety immediately filled my core as I saw the tips of the spires of the Alterwood Citadel that rose high above the rest of Arvandor came into view. The sun had begun to set and the golden wood shone brightly. It was amazing that I could see those before any of the rest of the city. I had expected to feel happy, but I just couldn't shake the sense of dread that settled deep in my bones as the dragons descended towards my home.

Chapter 43

Ashten

I wasn't quite sure where we were expected to land four enormous dragons anywhere near the Alterwood Citadel without causing panic and uproar. Many people in the surrounding villages had probably already seen us. I directed everyone to land outside the city walls. We slid off of our dragon's backs one by one. My legs were a bit wobbly as I hit the ground.

"We will need to figure out how to get into the city." I motioned to the high walls that surrounded Arvandor. "As far as I know, there is nowhere large enough near the Citadel for the dragons to land without crushing one of my father's ridiculously ornate gardens."

Sarphi chuffed, shaking her head. "That wouldn't be the worst thing, in my opinion." She must not have meant to say that out loud, because her face turned red almost instantly. "I mean no offence, of course."

"None taken." I smiled back at her. "It's not that I would mind doing it. The idea of ruining my father's day actually brings me great joy. It's that I would feel bad for all the servants who would be expected to have it back in perfect condition by the week's end."

"I'm guessing we can't just walk through the city and right up to the Citadel gates?" Reyland asked.

"You guys? Probably. Especially Sarphi. At least to the gates." I shrugged. "Me? Probably not."

"I managed to grab a few changes of clothes before we left." Lyra began rummaging through a backpack that I hadn't even noticed she had grabbed. She pulled out a deep green cloak that matched the color of her eyes. "You could wear this. Do you think that would be enough to keep you disguised?"

I took the cloak from her and wrapped it around my body. Pulling the hood over my head, I tucked all of my raven hair into the collar of my jacket. I spun in a small circle before looking back at Lyra, eyebrow raised in question.

"Maybe if you keep your head down?" Reyland approached. He walked in a circle around me, and I could feel his stare boring into me as he assessed my disguise. "I think anyone would recognize those eyes anywhere."

"I know I would." Finn's voice caused all of us to jump. I didn't miss how Reyland's hand immediately flew to the sword on his back. "Relax. The watchman saw the dragons on the horizon. We were hoping it was you."

"Well, you came woefully unprepared for the slim possibility that it wasn't me." I made a show of glancing behind him at the lack of soldiers. "Unless you were planning to take on four dragons on your own, Captain?" I flashed him one of my signature sarcastic grins, which he matched immediately.

"Of course not, Princess." The way he said that title still sent shivers down my spine, regardless of how he had treated me. "I was planning on running for my life. Which I am grateful is not the case." He gestured to his armor. "This isn't great running attire."

"It can still be arranged." I whipped my head to Reyland, whose gaze was glued on Finn. He was unnaturally still, like a cat poised to pounce on its prey. "I could use the run after the long ride."

"I appreciate the offer, but I will have to pass." Finn looked Reyland up and down. "It wouldn't be a fair fight, anyway."

"I was under the impression that those were your favorite fights." Reyland's eyes found mine for a fraction of a second before returning to trying to burn a hole in Finn's head. He hadn't relaxed in the slightest, but somehow he tensed even more when Finn walked in my direction. Sarphi and Lyra took a few steps forward, though I wasn't sure if that was to help me or stop Reyland.

"I see." Finn's voice was low, and there was a hint of regret as he spoke. "That was a line I hadn't meant to cross." He stood just close enough that he could reach out to touch my face.

He ran a hand across the faint marks that were still there from his own hand. My pulse quickened at his touch. There was such a wonderful familiarity to his touch that I found myself leaning into his hand. Then, as quickly as the familiarity set in, it was replaced by a sense of worry. My earlier conversation with Sarphi came to mind, and I pulled away from Finn just as quickly as I had leaned in. I was torn. Finn lowered his hand back to his side, the sadness in his eyes mirroring the uncertainty in my own.

"I broke my promise to you, Princess." His voice was barely more than a whisper. "I let my emotions get the best of me, and for that, I am eternally sorry. I should never have laid my hands on you out of anger." He hung his head.

I promise I will never hit you, Princess.

The words filled my brain like a soothing song. They reminded me of another promise. One that I had made him at the beginning of the endless week that I had just endured. We had both made mistakes the past few days, and maybe we had both changed a little. But who said that had to be a bad thing? I still had a chance to change a little more before I too broke my promise.

Before I could think better of it, I took Finn's chin in my hand and guided his eyes to mine. "Nothing." I stated, mirroring my earlier promise.

A sparkle filled his eyes as the meaning settled in. He took my hand in his and placed a gentle kiss on my knuckles. A soft warmth filled my chest and I couldn't help but smile. He lowered his hand, still holding on to mine as he gestured to a waiting carriage that I hadn't noticed before arriving.

"This will take you all to the Citadel. The princess will sleep in her own quarters, and the king has had rooms prepared on the same floor for each of the rest of you." He released my hand and headed towards the carriage.

"What about our dragons?" I gestured to the four gigantic beasts behind me. "Where are they going to stay? They don't exactly fit in the stables."

"Well, they have most definitely already been seen and I would be surprised if there isn't a lake at the Citadel gates of civilians trying to warn us of an impending dragon attack. Provisions from the Citadel will be sent to make sure that they are fed and cared for. Otherwise, I would ask that you urge them to stay out of sight as much as possible." He gave me a flat grin that suggested he didn't know how possible that would be.

I turned to Nyzirth, who snorted and flapped her wings in frustration.

"Please? It's just for tonight." I gave her my most apologetic smile.

"Fine." Her voice dripped with annoyance. It seemed that the other dragons felt the same way as they all grumbled their disapproval.

"Well, I guess that solves our problem." I shrugged as I turned back to the group.

I pulled off the green cloak and folded it before handing it back to Lyra. She placed it back into her pack and gave me an awkward smile before walking past me towards the carriage. Sarphi was next to approach me. There was a hint of anger mixed with sadness in her eyes as she leaned in to me.

"You're playing with fire, Ashten." She whispered, her golden eyes meeting mine. "You aren't the only one at risk of getting burned." The words almost sounded like a threat as she waited for me to respond.

I knew without a doubt that she was referring to our earlier conversation about my relationship with Finn. I flattened my lips into a smile and gave a curt nod to relay my understanding. Satisfied by my response, Sarphi walked past me to the carriage, climbing in beside Lyra.

I turned my attention to Reyland. He hadn't moved since Finn approached me, but there was something different about his demeanor now. The anger that had filled his eyes upon seeing Finn was still present, but it was being dampened by an emotion I hadn't seen him wear yet.

Pain.

I opened my mouth to speak, but he held up a hand and shook his head. He advanced, stopping just a few inches short of running into me. We stood there, his eyes locked on to mine, for what felt like forever. It felt like he was searching for something, and he must have found it because he looked away.

"Be careful, Ashten." Was all he said before walking past me to the carriage.

As I walked to join everyone, I couldn't help but have the feeling that I was making a mistake. Regarding what, I couldn't be sure. I just couldn't shake this gut feeling that something was wrong. I took a deep breath and attempted to swallow down my emotions as I stepped into the carriage and sat down beside Reyland.

The carriage ride through Arvandor was now at the top of the "most awkward things I have ever done" list. Not a single word was shared between us as the horses' hooves clopped down the cobblestone road. Sarphi and Lyra shared a few wordless glances, but neither of them even so much as breathed in my direction. I risked a look over at Reyland, whose eyes were trained on his own feet. He didn't even lift his head when Finn pulled the carriage to a stop outside the Citadel gates.

We were only stopped for a brief moment before the carriage started moving again. I opened up the window and looked out at the castle grounds. I had only been gone for about a week, but it seemed as if my father had decided it was time for a renovation. The dragon statues that graced the top of the spires had been replaced. Something that I hadn't noticed when we were flying in. They had been replaced by ravens, as had every dragon statue that lined the pathway from the gates to the main entrance.

Ravens were the symbol of my house, and my father had replaced the dragon winged throne many years ago, but those dragon statues had been here since the founding of this city. My ancestors had erected the statues when the Citadel was constructed as a reminder of what kept them in this place of power. Not of their own power, but the power that the dragons gave them.

The setting sun made it harder to make out many more details, and I pulled the window shut as we came to a stop outside the Citadel doors. A guard opened the door and Finn offered his hand to me. I took it, climbing out of the carriage with the others right behind me. I straightened my jacket and looked expectantly at the guards and Finn.

"It's nearly night. Why don't I escort you all to where you will stay for the evening?" Finn motioned for us to follow before turning and walking through the doors.

Sarphi waved me on, and I could hear them walking behind me down the dimly lit halls. Much like the outside, the inside had been redecorated. I no longer felt the hum of magic as I walked past the newly erected raven statues. I looked up at one as we passed, and couldn't shake the feeling that its amethyst eyes were watching me. The further into the Citadel we walked, the less I recognized my home. The walls were still golden, but they didn't shine like I had come to love. I tried to convince myself that it was just the evening lighting as we came to a stop outside the door of my room.

"As I am sure you are aware, this is where you will stay, Ashten." Finn pointed at the doors on either side of mine that had always been empty. "Sarphi and Lyra will stay in those two rooms, and Reyland will be across the hall." He pointed at yet another room that had always been empty. "All three of your rooms have been furnished to the same standards as Ashten's, so I assure you they will be more comfortable than you are used to. Clothing for tomorrow's festivities has been provided and are in your wardrobes. The other Elvish rulers arrived earlier in the day, and the festivities begin first thing in the morning. I will be here to escort you all to the ballroom."

I tensed momentarily as he leaned in, kissing me gently on the lips. We had never shown any affection in public for fear that someone would tell my father. Sensing my hesitation, he gently cupped my face in his hands.

"I'm done hiding, Princess." He kissed me again, and I kissed him back. There was a freeing feeling in the way he spoke so confidently. He stepped away, and I gave everyone else an awkward wave as I backed into my room and shut the door.

Chapter 44

Reyland

I stood outside my door until everyone else was inside their rooms. I made a mental note of whose room was where in case I needed to find them quickly before morning. Satisfied that I had committed it to memory, I walked into my room and quickly shut the door behind me. It didn't have a lock on it, so I looked around the well-decorated room for something to block the door. I settled on placing the ridiculously fancy desk chair underneath the doorknob.

I pulled off my riding leathers and stood in front of the mirror. The tattoo that Ashten had pointed out just barely crested over my shoulder. I twisted my body to try to get a better look at the nondescript black swirls that made up the tattoo. At a passing glance, my scars were invisible underneath it, but I knew better. I took a shaky breath as I slipped into the black silk nightclothes that had been left for me and leaned my swords against the wall beside the golden bed frame. Something about this place was making my skin crawl, and I wanted to be sure that I could get to them at a moment's notice.

Before I could let myself get into bed, I had to make sure the rest of my room was secure. Surprisingly, the windows actually had locks, and I put them in place with a *click*. I was sure that everyone else had just gone right to sleep, but they didn't have at least two powerful people in this citadel who probably wanted them dead. I began opening every drawer and cabinet, pulling their contents out onto the stone floor. Thankfully, most of them were empty or full of normal desk things. Except for the wardrobe, which contained various changes of fancy clothing.

"How far away are you?" I reached out mentally for my dragon's presence.

"Only a few minutes." Zothim responded quickly. *"Even faster if you need me."*

"Not yet." I breathed a sigh of relief. *"Just making sure."*

"You know I can feel your stress, right?"

"Well then, I feel sorry for you." I shook my head. I could nearly hear him laughing, if dragons could laugh.

"Relax, Elf." A sense of calm washed over our bond. *"The number of people here who want you dead is far outweighed by the number of those who would do anything to keep you safe."*

"I doubt that." I didn't try to hide the disbelief in my voice.

"You don't have to believe it to make it true." I could hear the sleep in Zothim's voice and had to imagine the dragon was quite tired. *"Quit worrying and get some sleep."*

"Yeah. Sure." I glanced around my now trashed room. *"I'll try."*

Somewhat satisfied with my security sweep, I made my way back to the bed, leaving everything out on the floor. This bed was much nicer than the one I had been sleeping on at Asballicuo. As I laid back onto the pillows, I could feel myself sinking into the plush mattress. I should have been exhausted. I had never ridden Zothim for that long, and I could feel the ache in my arms and legs. However, I was practically vibrating with nervousness as I stared up at the ceiling.

Thoughts were rushing through my head like an unimpeded river. Thoughts of the dragons that shouldn't exist considering the last one was killed centuries ago. Thoughts of the beautiful, magical island those dragons had shown us. Thoughts of the hidden history of Xeswal that they had revealed to us, which had no doubt played a role in why the king had sent his daughter to Asballicuo. I was convinced that it was all connected. I just needed to find out how.

Adapting to my situation had been part of my training, but this wasn't something I could just adapt to. The lack of knowledge was driving me insane. My mind was a swirling storm of dread at how this could all end up for us if we revealed we knew all of this information. Information like that is something worth killing over if it doesn't end up in your favor.

Somehow, above it all, were visions of her. Visions of her long, black hair. Her bright amethyst eyes. The way her cheeks flushed any time she drank alcohol. The way she didn't know her own beauty. Her own strength. The way she smiled when I called her Nightshade, as if it was just a nickname. It was so much more than a nickname. It was the verbal decree of how beautifully dangerous I knew she was. How beautifully dangerous I wish she could see herself.

Then another wave of visions flashed through my mind. Unwanted ones. The way she smiled at him that day in his chambers. How her face lit up when he called her Princess. How she melted into his arms when he kissed her. How easily she had forgiven him. How she looked at him like he was her knight in shining armor. I dug my nails into my palms hard enough that I nearly drew blood.

She should be looking at me that way.

Deep down, I knew there was no way that I could convince her. She was stubborn and hardheaded. She didn't need someone to save her. She needed someone to be there to pick up the pieces when she fell apart. Someone who wouldn't judge her, or tell her she was stupid for ever letting herself fall in the first place. Someone who would love her unconditionally and put her back together no matter how jagged the edges were.

I had never felt this way about anyone before, and it was killing me. I couldn't think straight when it came to her. There was one thing I knew with absolute certainty, though. I could be that person to put her back together. I *would* be that person. For her, I would be anything. Even if it killed me.

Chapter 45

Ashten

I thought that being back in my room would be comforting, but I couldn't shake this sinking feeling in my gut as I closed the door behind me. It had been cleaned in my absence, and everything had been put back in its place. I tried to steady my breathing as I walked past where my blankets had been left in a heap on the floor as I headed to the wardrobe to find a change of clothes. I was thankful that my clothes had been left in here as I pulled out my favorite purple silk nightclothes. My hands were shaking, and I struggled to unbutton my riding leathers. It took me longer than I had wanted, but I eventually pulled them off and slipped on my nightclothes. I redid my hair and didn't even bother to look in the mirror before sitting on the edge of my bed.

I looked around at what had once been my safe space. The one spot in this castle where I had honestly felt out of my father's reach. That had all changed when his soldiers had come in here and ripped me out of my bed. I gripped the blankets of my bed in my fists in an attempt to ground myself as the memories came rushing back.

My door flying open.

Being thrown from my bed.

My father slapping me.

My breaths were shallow and quick, but a cold nose in my hand pulled me back from my waking nightmare. I looked down to see Deyka standing on her hind legs as she tried to shove her nose under my hand. I leaned down and picked her up. She was whining in excitement, nearly wiggling out of my arms as I tried to hug her tightly.

"I missed you, girl." A single tear streaked down my cheek, which Deyka quickly licked away.

A knock on my door interrupted our reunion. I stood from my bed on wobbly legs and made my way to the door. I cracked open the door to see Finn standing on the other side. He had ditched his onyx armor and replaced it with a casual white shirt and black pants. He had a plate full of food in his hands.

"Evening Princess." He bowed his head slightly. "The servants were told to deliver all the guests some food, but I wanted to deliver yours personally. I grabbed all of your favorite things." He held the tray out towards me, and I stepped aside to let him in.

I stood awkwardly in the middle of the room while he placed the tray on the desk and arranged two plates and two glasses on the breakfast table. Deyka followed him around, her eyes hopeful as he began filling the plates with little bits of all the different foods he had brought. Crackers, cheese, meat slices, berries, melons, and chocolate. He truly had brought all of my favorite things. He poured what smelled like wine into the glasses and stepped behind one of the chairs. He pulled it out and motioned for me to come sit.

I didn't quite know what to make of this, but I *was* hungry, so I obliged and took a seat. He helped me scoot forward before sitting in the chair across from me. I gingerly took a grape from the plate and popped it into my mouth. Finn didn't say a word as I ate a few more pieces of food and washed it down with a few gulps of wine.

"I figured you were hungry after that ride." Finn sipped from his glass. "Given how quickly you arrived, I assume you didn't stop for lunch."

"Yeah, we flew straight here." I motioned towards his plate. "You know you can eat too. I don't want to be the only one eating in this room. It's weird." I smiled around a piece of cheese.

"Of course, Princess." Finn grabbed a slice of meat and bit a chunk off.

"Thank you for taking care of Deyka." I presented a scrap of meat to the spoiled pup. She quickly took it and strutted off to the other side of the room.

Finn simply smiled at me as he chewed another piece of food. We chewed in silence for a few moments before I couldn't take it anymore. "So, what is all of this for?" I gestured to the spread.

"I figured you were hungry and wanted to bring you some food." Finn shrugged.

"Yes, but this feels like a little more than just bringing me some food." I raised an eyebrow at him over the rim of my nearly empty glass.

Finn swallowed his mouthful of food and looked down at his lap. "Maybe I also wanted to apologize for being a complete jerk."

"A jerk is an understatement." I leaned back and crossed my arms. The wine had hit my blood, and I could feel the boldness of being a little inebriated start to take over. "As far as an apology, this is a start."

"A start?" Finn set his now empty glass down on the table and leaned forward. "What would you have me do, Princess?"

I made a show of thinking, but I didn't have time to answer before he stood from his seat. I tensed involuntarily as he walked over to me. He knelt down in front of me and placed his hands on my knees. The warmth of his hands radiated through my silk pants and my body began relaxing of its own accord. I inhaled deeply as the the scent of pine filled the air.

"Because I would do anything." His deep green eyes met mine. "If the command came from your mouth, I would follow it with zero hesitation."

"Is that so?" This was probably the wine talking, but I leaned forward until my face was inches from his. "Then kiss me."

As promised, there was no hesitation as his lips crashed into mine. He cupped my face with his hand, pulling me up with him as he stood. He guided me backwards until I bumped into the table. The crash of one of the glasses on the floor was enough to sober me up momentarily.

"Wait. Someone probably heard that." I placed my hand on his chest and he took a reluctant step backwards.

"And?" He looked over his shoulder at the door. "The door is shut. They would at least knock once before barging in."

"And if they didn't?" I was thankful that the logical part of my brain was taking the reins on this conversation. All of my emotions were screaming for me to undo the distance that I had put between Finn and I.

"So what?" Finn stepped forward until our bodies were flush again. My breath hitched as he rested his arms on the table at my sides. I could feel his breath on my ear as he spoke. "I meant what I said, Princess. I'm done hiding. But... If you truly want me to stop, I'll stop." What could only be described as a whimper escaped my mouth as his lips skimmed the lobe of my ear before he looked me in the eye. His emerald eyes were dark and searching. "Otherwise, I think I'll get to the rest of that apology."

Words had escaped me and all I could do was nod my agreement. I knew better, but I didn't care. We had spent the past three years hiding from nearly everyone in this castle. Whether it was out of respect or fear, I wasn't quite sure. None of that mattered as Finn gently kissed my neck. I tilted my head back to give him easier access. He promptly took advantage of it by kissing down the front of my neck to what little bit of my chest was exposed by my top. My breaths were already uneven and he had barely touched me.

"I should be mad at you," I breathed.

"You are," Finn purred between kisses. "I'm apologizing, remember?"

He slid his hands under my thighs and hoisted me onto the top of the table. A few more dishes clattered to the floor and neither of us could resist chuckling. He rested his hands on my hips, his thumbs just barely slipping under the hem of my shirt and gently stroking the bare skin they found there.

I pulled on the front of his shirt, causing his lips to crash into mine once more. I could feel him smiling against my lips as I struggled to find the bottom hem of his shirt and pull it over his head. He stepped back and pulled the shirt over his head in a swift motion. I didn't get long to admire his soldier's physique before he was back on me, kissing me roughly while fumbling with the buttons of my blouse. Once it was unbuttoned, he slid it off my shoulders and placed a few kisses on my now exposed skin. I shivered as his lips made their way down my arm. Once he reached my fingertips, he kissed each one before trying to step away. I trapped him with my legs and he chuckled darkly.

"A tattoo?" Finn started at the other shoulder and made his way down that arm as well. "That's new."

"Dragon." I muttered a curse under my breath at my inability to form a coherent sentence.

I felt him smile against my skin and his grip tightened on my bare waist. He leaned away from me, the rise and fall of his chest just as ragged and uneven as my own. He looked me up and down, his face flushed and eyes growing darker.

A soft whine pulled us both to reality. I looked over to see Deyka sitting on the bed, watching us intently.

"I don't know about you, but I don't think I'm the type for an audience." I chuckled, nodding in Deyka's direction.

Finn backed out of the cage I had made with my legs, using his superior strength against me. He only smiled as I grunted in protest. "I'll be right back. I've already arranged for someone to *babysit* for the evening." I opened my mouth to protest, but he cut me off. "Don't worry. They will take perfect care of her." Deyka licked his face as he grabbed her and carried her out of the room.

He was only gone for a few moments before slipping back through the door. He shut it behind him and strolled back across the room. I couldn't help but admire the way every muscle in his body seemed built for a purpose and flexed with every step that he took.

There were bandages wrapped around his abdomen. A small reminder of what had happened between us only a day earlier. I pushed down my apprehensive feelings, easily replacing them with the want that was building as he walked closer.

He wasted no time kissing me as soon as he was within reach. We were instantly in a flurry of exploring hands and mouths. I took my time running my fingertips along each dip of his muscles, and he quickly found all the right places that nearly left me a puddle in his hands. He gripped my bare waist tightly as he pulled me against him. He continued to trail kisses down my neck and chest before leaning back just enough to look me in the eye.

"I mean it, Princess." He inhaled sharply before continuing. "As much as I am enjoying myself already, we can stop right now if that's what you want. I will carry you to that bed, tuck you in, and leave. No questions asked and no hard feelings."

It was my turn to make my intentions clear as I placed a gentle kiss in the center of his chest. I worked my way up his neck, relishing in the way his grip on me tightened as I made my way up his jawline.

My lips brushed against his ear as I whispered, "I would love for you to carry me to my bed, but if you so much as think about leaving right now." I didn't know exactly what I wanted, but I knew I didn't want him to leave. Not now.

"Is that a threat, Princess?" His voice was husky and his breath shaky as he spoke. I grabbed his chin and guided his eyes to mine.

"No. It's an order."

"Yes, ma'am." Finn smiled devilishly.

I yelped when he hoisted me into the air and carried me to my bed, just as I had asked.

Chapter 46

Ashten

I slammed the door behind me and shoved a chair under the knob, just as Reyland had shown me. Blood was dripping onto my dress from a cut on my forehead. I looked around my trashed room for something to fight back with and realized that all of my weapons from Asballicuo were missing. The closest thing to a weapon that I could find was a butter knife that had apparently been left from the previous morning's breakfast. I grabbed it quickly and wiped the blood from my brow.

The sound of boots running down the hall only served to raise my already elevated heart rate. Everything had gone crazy so fast. I didn't know where the others were. I just hoped that they had made it out okay. The various yells and screams that I could hear made that possibility very hard to believe.

I jumped as someone banged on my door. I waited quietly for a moment, hoping they would go away. Instead, I heard a few more voices outside before they rammed into the door so hard that the chair nearly gave out. I didn't have enough time. The chair wasn't going to hold and there was nowhere else for me to go. I backed up to the window and looked out. I was at least four floors high from this room.

I would never survive the fall, but maybe, just maybe, I could be caught. I tried with all of my might to contact my dragon. It sounded like she was underwater as she responded. I didn't quite understand what she had said, but I was going to have to trust that the immediacy of my request had bled through the disrupted mental connection.

My assailants rammed into the doors again, and the legs on the chair cracked. I looked out the window once more. She still wasn't there. I couldn't even hear the sound of her wings flapping. The doors to my room flung open and four armored men stormed in towards me. I was out of time.

I took one more look out the window.

Then I jumped.

Searing pain shot up my arm as I hit it on my headboard. Reality still hadn't quite set in as I jolted upright in my bed. Cool air hit my bare, sweat soaked skin, pulling me a little more towards the present.

Another nightmare. Great.

"I'm sorry. I didn't mean to wake you." I groggily looked over to where I expected to find Finn sleeping, only to find the bed empty.

I rubbed my eyes and pulled the blankets up over my shoulders in an attempt to block the cool air. A quick survey of the room revealed that not only was Finn gone, but so was his clothing that had been piled on the floor next to my own. He left so quietly that I hadn't even noticed. My heart dropped at the thought of him just leaving me. Not because he hadn't needed to sneak out in times past, but because I had thought things had changed.

Regardless, there was no way that I was going back to sleep covered in sweat. I slipped out of my bed and pulled the sweat-soaked sheets off of it. I left them in a pile at the foot of the bed for Evelien to grab in the morning. Then, I made my way to the washroom with my arms wrapped around my body in a poor attempt to keep myself warm and covered.

I didn't want to run a full bath in the middle of the night, so I grabbed a cloth from the rack and turned on the water just long enough to fill a small bowl. I summoned a flame in my hand and used it to heat the water. The warm rag helped continue to calm me as I did my best to clean myself up.

"Nyzirth?" I could feel her presence just at the edge of my consciousness. *"Are you awake?"*

"Well, I am now." I couldn't help but chuckle at how annoyed she sounded. I could nearly picture her narrowed eyes.

"Sorry." I hoped she couldn't hear me laughing. *"I was having trouble sleeping and realized I hadn't made sure that you all had been taken care of."*

"We have been fed and shown somewhere to bed down for the night, yes." Annoyance gave way to amusement as she continued. *"Trouble sleeping?"*

"Yeah." I paused for a moment. *"What's so funny?"*

"Nothing. I just didn't think you would be going to sleep anytime soon." I could hear the smile in her voice.

"What do you mean by that?" I rubbed the warm cloth over my face.

"I can feel your emotions, remember?"

I froze, a blush creeping up my neck as realization set in. I buried my head in my hands. Nyzirth's amusement was an unfortunate reminder that I couldn't hide the embarrassment from her through the bond.

"I'm going to need to learn how to block you out." I was mortified.

"That would be preferable, yes." The mental connection dripped with sarcasm. She waited just a moment before continuing. *"You do know that you aren't the only one he has hurt, correct?"*

"Now isn't really the time for a lecture." I closed my eyes and let the cool air wash over me.

"*Did you have other plans?*" Her voice took on a serious tone. "*And this isn't a lecture.*"

"*Then what is it?*" I was more than a little annoyed at this point.

"*Consider it a reminder.*" Her voice softened a little. "*I just don't want you to forget what he did to the other Drakewardens.*"

"*Well then, I'll do my best to remember it. Not that it has anything to do with me.*" I rinsed my face one more time before grabbing a dry towel from the rack. "*That's between Finn and the others.*"

"*And how long until you become part of the 'others'?*" Concern leaked through the bond for a brief moment before vanishing.

"*I won't.*"

"*I hope you are right.*" A calming warmth washed down the bond. "*Goodnight, Ashten.*"

"*Goodnight, Nyzirth.*" I sat in the silence until I felt nothing but a fuzzy presence from the dragon's side of the bond.

Satisfied, I poured out the water and grabbed a fresh set of pajamas from my wardrobe. I pulled them on and made my way back to my bed. Tossing my pillow, I opted to use Finn's, since he was gone anyway. I grabbed a small blanket off my sitting chair and climbed back into the bed.

No sooner had my head hit the pillow than did I hear the most terrifying howl from outside my room. No. Not a howl. Someone was yelling. My heart began to race, and I tried my best to stay calm and listen closely. A few moments later, I heard the yell again. It didn't sound like the yells I had heard in my nightmares. Those had been much more aggressive. Like orders being given. This sounded like someone yelling in pain. A male, to be exact.

I slid out of bed and walked over to my door. From here, the yelling was louder. I cracked open my door to find the hallway completely empty. There wasn't even a guard posted at my door. I was reminded that that was a later problem, as the same yell filled the air again.

It sounded like it was coming from across the hall. If I remembered correctly, that was Reyland's room. I rushed across the hall and knocked on his door. There was no answer apart from the continued yelling. I tried to push open the doors, but they wouldn't open. I could only assume that he had blocked the doors with something, since I knew that these doors didn't have a lock. If so, there was no way I was going to get in there on my own.

A sense of urgency overcame all logical thinking. I frantically looked around as if someone would magically appear that could help me. If only Finn hadn't left. I rattled the door again, but whatever kept it shut was doing a great job. I expected someone else to have been woken up by his yelling, but no one exited their rooms in the next few moments that it took for me to come up with a way to open his doors.

I placed a hand on either side of where the double doors met. Closing my eyes, I tried to focus all of my magical energy into my core. Just like with Finn, I forced all of my energy out of the palms of my hands. I was rewarded with the doors to Reyland's room flying open, hand shaped burn marks now decorating them.

I didn't even bother to see what had been blocking the door as I rushed into the room. The room was trashed. Clothing and papers were scattered all over the floor. Reyland yelled again, which brought my attention to him. There he was, sheets clinched in his fists, thrashing his head back and forth. He had mentioned having nightmares, but I had no idea they were this bad.

I ran over to the side of the bed and sat down on its edge. He didn't acknowledge me in the slightest as I reached out and touched his arm.

"Reyland." My voice was barely more than a whisper. I wanted him to wake up, but I didn't want to scare him. I tried to shake him, but his arm was so tense that it didn't really move. "Reyland, you need to wake up."

I winced as he yelled again. My hands laid across his abdomen and I couldn't help but notice how muscular he was under his thin, sweat soaked, silk nightclothes. I shook the thoughts from my head and gave his body another rough shake in an effort to wake him up.

"Reyland!" I spoke a little louder. His eyelids fluttered and hope filled my chest. "It's me, Ashten. I need you to wake up now." I gave him one more rough shake and he bolted upright, nearly head-butting me in the process. His eyes were glazed as he looked around the room. He was panting and his shirt was sticking to his body. I averted my eyes to avoid staring at the outlines of his muscular abdomen.

"Ashten?" His voice was raspy but soft.

"Yeah," I nearly whispered. "I could hear yelling from across the hall." He looked at me, confused. "You were having a nightmare."

He looked around the room again, blinking slowly, as if he wasn't sure where he was. We sat in this silence until his eyes became a little clearer and he slicked his sweat soaked hair out of his face. He slid out of the bed and walked to the middle of the room.

"Sorry for waking you." His voice was still raspy from all the yelling. He was looking down at the floor like a child who had just gotten caught by their parents.

"You didn't wake me. I woke myself up," I corrected him gently. "Nightmare." I shrugged. "I guess it's just one of those nights."

"Yeah," he mumbled. "Just like every night."

A. Turner

"You don't have nightmares every night." I stayed seated on his bed as he began fumbling through the pile of clothing on the floor. "At least not ones this bad. I shared a room with you every night for the past week and not once did you wake me up."

"That's because I don't sleep in that room." He didn't look my way as he continued to search for some new nightclothes. "There's more than one reason I bathe late at night. It's not just for the decency of letting you ladies bathe on your own."

My heart dropped at the idea of him sleeping alone on the stone floor of the washroom every night. I couldn't string together a sentence that would soften that statement. Instead, I stood up and began pulling the sheets off of his bed.

"Go clean yourself up. There should be some clean rags and towels in the washroom." I paused to turn and look at him.

Reyland stood silently in the center of the room for a moment. Just when I thought he was going to argue, he turned and began stepping towards the washroom. He stopped just short of the door before turning back to me.

"Every night except for that night in the library."

"What?" I cocked my head.

"I have had a nightmare every night for the past six years. Every night except for that night in the library." His blood-red eyes met mine. "With you. They haven't been as frequent since then." Without another word, he turned back around and entered the washroom. I stared at the doorway until I heard the water begin to run.

At the time, I hadn't thought much of it. I had just assumed he was tired from the day's events. I knew that I had been drained from bonding with my dragon and assumed that he had felt the same. It had never once crossed my mind that he had not had a full night's sleep in a long time.

Six years, to be exact.

I couldn't even wrap my head around the idea as I proceeded to strip his bed. Like I had done for myself, I grabbed him a new pillow and a throw blanket that I was able to find after scouring his mess of a room. Unsure if I should just leave or not, I opted to sit back on the end of his bed until I heard the door to the washroom open.

Reyland stopped in the doorway and watched me wearily. His now clean but still wet hair stuck to the sides of his forehead. He had changed pants, but had opted to forgo a shirt. While Finn had a soldier's stocky, muscular build, Reyland was simply fit. Muscular, but in a different way. He was lean, which made the muscles of his arms and abdomen even more apparent as he leaned against the doorframe.

"Sorry." His quiet voice caused me to snap my attention to his face. "I figured you would be gone. I can go grab a shirt."

"No," I answered a little too fast, my face instantly flushing red. I blinked slowly and shook my head. "It's not like I haven't seen you without a shirt before."

Reyland came and wordlessly sat down on the foot of the bed beside me. He stared down at the floor between his feet and took a few deep breaths. I looked over at him to see that he had bits of his pants clutched tightly in his hands. I placed a hand on his bare shoulder and felt him tense underneath it.

"Everything's okay." I didn't even need to ask what was wrong. I unfortunately could recognize the panic as if it were written out plainly. "You're safe here. I've cleaned up your bed and gotten you a fresh blanket and pillow." I gestured to the makeshift sleeping arrangements. "Why don't you lie back down?"

Reyland nodded sluggishly before climbing into the bed and settling in underneath the blanket. I started to slide off the end of the bed, but a firm hand caught mine. I turned to see Reyland, eyes still slightly glassy, looking up at me.

"Please stay." His plea was barely more than a whisper.

"Of course." There was no hesitation as I knelt down beside his bed. His hand still held tightly to mine. "I'll be right here."

I laid my head on the side of his bed and closed my eyes. His signature scent of peppermint and smoke filled my nostrils. I listened to the sound of his breathing, relieved when it finally fell into a soft, slow rhythm. His grip on my hand had loosened slightly, but I didn't dare move it as I looked over at him. I cursed under my breath as I noticed the dark circles under his eyes that I had never noticed before. He needed this sleep.

I didn't want to wake him, so I laid my head back down. It wasn't lost on me that I was falling asleep beside a second male in the same night. Something I never thought that I would do. There wasn't anything to this one, though. Just me looking after a friend. I just hoped that the first one didn't come back and find me gone.

Chapter 47

Finn

I gently lifted Ashten's arm from my chest and laid it on the bed between us. I held my breath as I slipped out from under the covers and planted my feet on the ground. Thankfully, she barely stirred when I shifted the bulk of my weight onto the floor and stood from the bed. I quietly gathered my clothes from their pile beside hers and pulled them on. Worried that my boots would be too loud on the stone floor, I opted to carry them. Ashten moaned softly in her sleep, and I couldn't resist brushing the hair from her face before leaving a soft kiss on her forehead. I could still feel the soft strands of her hair between my fingers as I gingerly shut the doors to her room behind me.

Once outside in the hallway, I slid my boots on. I was so focused on being quiet that I had almost forgotten about the two guards standing outside her door. They glanced in my direction as I tied my boots. Recognition flashed in their eyes as I stood straight, looking them both over.

"Can either of you tell me what time it is?" I assumed my normal *commander of the guard* posture.

"Nearly midnight, sir," One guard responded quickly.

"Good." I glanced between them. "Are random men usually leaving the Princess' chambers at midnight?" They shared a confused glance with each other. "Because both of you seem rather unbothered by my presence."

There was a long pause before one of them responded. "No, sir. It's just that, well, you aren't a random man, sir."

"Correct answer." I stood in front of the guard that didn't answer. "Keeping that in mind, does the king need to know about what time I left the Princess' chambers?"

"No, sir," The guard quickly answered.

"Right again." I turned to the other soldier. "And who will you tell if anyone else enters or leaves this room tonight?"

"You, sir." I could see a hint of fear in his eyes.

Good.

"Once again correct." I clapped him on the shoulder. "With that settled, I will see you men in the morning." I turned on my heel and left without another word.

As soon as I was back in my own chambers, I bathed quickly, not even bothering to call a servant to warm the water. I decided to get dressed for the day since I was unsure if I would have adequate time after the meeting. Once I had fastened the final strap on my armor, I stood in front of the mirror and studied my appearance.

I ran a hand over my slightly longer but still short hair. Honestly, I missed my shaggy hair. I could eventually go back, but it would take time. This was a small price to pay for how careless I had been. I spoke the command word into the mirror and stepped through.

I once again emerged in the king's war room. The king, as well as Lords Galen and Rael, were waiting around the map table. The king barely acknowledged my arrival.

"Late again, Captain." He didn't look up from the map. "I hope this is not becoming a habit."

"Sorry, my King." I stumbled over my words. "I lost track of time."

King Renlin simply raised a questioning eyebrow at me before looking back down at the map.

"I have faith that whatever has *distracted* you has not delayed our plans?" The king motioned for me to step forward.

I nodded in reverence. "Of course not. The armies of Neron and Andos stand at the ready. Empress Jayde waits for our signal."

"Which is?" Lord Rael asked impatiently.

The king looked back at me. I waved my hand over the war table, causing the image to change from a map of Xeswal to a layout of the Alterwood Citadel. I began to point out different locations.

"There are mirrors now placed throughout the citadel. This includes the throne room, which has been slightly remodeled for tomorrow's festivities." I waved my hand again, and the table zoomed in on the throne room. The image showed an exact replica of the current state of the room. I pointed at the three large mirrors that now sat behind the throne room. "Towards the end of tomorrow's festivities, I will leave to inform the Empress that we are ready."

"And how do you know we can trust your captain?" Galen studied me intently, though his question was most definitely directed at the king. "I personally feel that his *involvement* with the princess has the potential to cloud his judgement."

I tensed at his mention of the Ashten. My knuckles turned white as I gripped the side of the table and stared down at the map. I schooled my features into neutrality before looking up at him.

"The princess has nothing to do with this." I gestured to the map.

"I just think that maybe you and the princess have gotten too close." Rael studied me for my reaction. "I, for one, feel like the princess has *everything* to do with this. The people love Ashten, and that's how this whole thing works."

"Get her name out of your mouth," I snarled as I stepped around the table.

"Excuse me?" Rael turned to face me, muscles flexing underneath his casual clothing as he crossed his arms. "Keep in mind who you are speaking to, *Captain*."

"I'll keep in mind who I'm speaking *to* when you keep in mind who you are speaking *of*." I didn't back down from the Moon Elf lord as he looked me up and down. "She is the Princess and she will be referred to as such."

"Finn is right," The king cut in. The tension in the room was palpable as the king stepped between us. "Regardless of any future plans, the people still view Ashten as their heir. The same goes for Reyland and Lyra. We must continue to treat them as such."

I didn't like how he spoke of Ashten, as if she was something to be replaced. If I had my way, that would never happen. She would always be my Princess. Maybe even my queen one day. However, for now, I had to play my role carefully. I simply nodded in respect to the king before turning my back to the other lords and walking to the other side of the table.

"As I was saying, I went earlier and tested the mirrors myself. As long as the command word is spoken correctly, they will work." I pointed again to the three large ones in the throne room. "These are big enough to move the armies through when the time comes."

"And the dragons?" Galen asked. His tone was less accusing this time.

"The dragons will fit through the even larger ones I have affixed to the back of the castle." They were facing the ocean. The perfect place for the dragons to fly through.

"It sounds like everything is settled." The king clapped his hands together. "I trust everyone will be on their best behavior tomorrow?" He looked at all of us like we were children that needed to be reminded of who was in charge.

I clenched my fists together and nodded curtly.

"Good. Then you are dismissed." The king waved us away as he resumed staring at the war table.

Chapter 48

Ashten

"Ashten."

The whispered word was enough to pull me out of the light sleep I had fallen into. I winced as pain shot through my neck thanks to the awkward position I had been in for way too long. A hand rested on my shoulder, shaking me gently.

"Come on, Ashten." Reyland's voice was a little clearer now. "You gotta get up." There was a hint of panic in the way he spoke.

I was still on the floor beside his bed, but I leaned back onto my haunches to look up at him. He was still in his shirtless nightclothes, and I couldn't help but stare. His shaggy hair was a mess as he looked down at me. I didn't miss the way his blood red eyes darkened before he looked away, rubbing the back of his neck.

"What time is it?" I peeled my eyes away from him to look over at the window. It wasn't any help as he had apparently shut and locked it last night.

"Sometime early in the morning." He extended a helping hand towards me. "Hopefully early enough that no one will notice you missing." I let him haul me to my feet.

The motion was quick and, combined with the remnants of the wine I had consumed last night, it caused me to stumble forward. I fell against Ryeland's chest with a grunt. My magic danced under my skin where my hand touched his bare chest, but I couldn't bring myself to pull away.

"Woah. Someone had some fun last night." Reyland smirked at me. He swallowed hard when his eyes met mine.

"Just a little." I pinched my fingers together. Blush creeped up my neck the longer he looked at me, and I didn't have the alcohol to blame it on this time.

He grabbed me by the shoulders and held me out at arm's length. He looked me up and down, as if something was wrong. I was about to ask him what he was doing, but he eventually spoke up.

"Do you think you can make it across the hall without falling over?" The joke did nothing to dissolve the tension as he continued to stare at me. "It would be in the best interest of everyone involved to get you back to your room unscathed... and alone."

"Uh... yeah." I smiled nervously, suddenly unsure of what to do with my hands. I awkwardly stepped around him and headed for the still broken door.

"Thanks." Reyland's words stopped me in my tracks. I turned to look at him and I could see the worry in his eyes. "For coming over here last night. I know you risked... a lot to do that."

"It was no problem," I assured him. "There were no guards at my door last night, so no one even knew I was gone."

"You were... alone?" I couldn't help but notice that he sounded surprised.

The blush on my neck intensified as his insinuations hit home. To an extent, he was right. He didn't have to know all the details, though. Not when I knew how he felt about the situation.

"There was no one else in my room when I woke up." I tried my best to slink around the truth without outright lying to him. "Makes it easier to sneak out, at least." I hated the disappointment that crept into my voice at the reminder of Finn leaving me in the middle of the night.

"Yeah. It does." There was a hint of anger in his words, but he gave me an understanding look. "I'll see you later."

I nodded wordlessly before turning and walking back across the hall. Relief washed over me when I saw that there were still no guards posted outside my room. I would have to mention the lack of security to Finn, though. I quietly opened my doors and slipped inside.

"You better be glad that I'm the one who came to wake you this morning." I nearly jumped out of my skin at the sound of Evelien's voice. I was beginning to realize just how unobservant I was given that I hadn't even noticed that she was sitting on my freshly made bed.

"Yeah." I sighed in relief. "Just another reason I am so glad to see you." I sat down beside her and gave her a tight hug. "I missed you."

"I missed you too, Ashten." Her smile quickly faded into a scowl. "Next time you are going to sneak out, at least go to a room that doesn't have its door blown off." She sounded like my mother, and I couldn't help but smile.

She was right, though. I had been careless with the door. I had just been so desperate to get in there. To get to him. When it came to Reyland, I couldn't think straight. At that moment, nothing except getting into that room and by his side had mattered. It had been an all-consuming feeling that I had never felt before.

"I'm sorry." I offered Evelien my most apologetic smile. "Finn didn't come back?"

"Thankfully not." She raised an eyebrow at me. "According to some of the other servants, he wasn't in his own room, either. Which is why I was expecting to have to chase him away when I got here. Instead, I open the doors to see the bed stripped, food and plates all over the floor, and *you* nowhere in sight."

I looked over at the table to find that she had cleaned everything from the table and floor. There was a small teapot and a few pieces of fruit sitting in the center of the table. My face reddened at the memory of what else had been sitting on that table just a few hours ago.

A nervous energy settled in me just at the thought of Evelien having walked in and found us. Sure, we wouldn't have been *in the act* or anything, but I know that we both fell asleep naked. Which means we would have both woken up naked. In the same bed. It doesn't take a genius to put those puzzle pieces together.

"What would you have done?" I walked over to the table and poured myself a cup of tea. I leaned against the side of the table as I stirred a bit of honey into my cup.

"About what?" Evelien walked over to my wardrobe and began rifling through the absurd amount of dresses found in there.

"If you would have walked in to find Finn and I..." I was blushing again. I took a long sip of my tea, hoping she would get the hint.

"Found you and Finn doing what, Ashten?" Evelien raised her eyebrow playfully and the heat on my face only grew warmer. She laid a few dresses out on the bed before coming to pour herself a cup of tea.

"You know," I nodded towards the bed, still unable to overcome my embarrassment at even having this conversation. "In bed together." I mumbled quietly.

"I would have just left breakfast on the table and excused myself." She smiled coyly and jabbed me in the shoulder. "Not without a few snide remarks, of course."

"So you wouldn't have told my father?" I could hear the relief in my voice.

"Why would I? You're an adult. He's an adult. You guys can both make adult decisions." She shrugged. "Just like how I'm not going to tell Finn that I found you laying on the side of that Moon Elf's bed this morning."

"Thank you." The idea of Finn finding that out almost scared me more than if the king himself had walked in here last night. I pushed away the part of me that was whispering how messed up that was before quickly adding. "For the record, nothing happened between Reyland and I last night."

"Which is just another reason to be thankful that *I* was the one who found you." She motioned for me to sit in the chair. I obliged, and she began brushing out my tangled hair.

"Why didn't you wake me?" I questioned.

"Because he said he wanted to." She furrowed her brows when the brush got stuck in my hair. "He was already up and said he would make sure you were back in your room as soon as possible. He really wouldn't take no for an answer."

A. Turner

The last sentence didn't surprise me, but the first one sure did. Reyland hadn't said a single word to me since Finn escorted us to the citadel. Since Finn had apologized and I had accepted it. I had assumed that everything that had happened last night only happened because he was delirious from the nightmare. It had never crossed my mind that he truly wanted me there.

"Hmmm." I didn't even know what to say. "Well, at least we all seem to have avoided any true trouble this morning." I gave her a lopsided smile through the mirror as she finished fixing my hair. She held up a smaller mirror to show me the back of my head.

She had braided my long hair and wrapped it around my head in a shape that resembled a crown. Red ribbon had been woven in between the braids and tucked into the back. It was all beautiful, but what caught my attention the most was the purple flower sitting at the back. Normally, I wouldn't have thought twice about a flower in my hair, but this particular flower was still fresh on my mind.

Nightshade.

"Where'd you get that flower?" I asked. I reached up to touch it, but halted once I remembered how dangerous it was. How had she even gotten it into my hair without touching it?

"The Wild Elf you arrived with came by with it before you got back. She said that she made it herself and to assure you it wasn't poisonous." She walked back over to the bed and brought back a dress.

I stepped into the deep red fabric and pulled it up over my waist. My arms slipped into the long laced sleeves and I threaded my thumbs through the holes at the end. I turned back to the mirror, studying my appearance as Evelien laced up the back of my dress. Though red wasn't the color I would have chosen for myself, I had to admit that this dress was stunning. The golden lace that covered my arms extended across the top of my chest before bleeding down into the deep red fabric of the rest of the dress. It fit snugly around my abdomen and waist but was loose enough around my legs that I didn't feel like I was going to have trouble walking like I did in most dresses.

Evelien showed me the back, and I was surprised to see that it was almost entirely lace. I also realized that this was the first time I had seen my tattoo. The swirls and lines seemed to have no pattern to them, but they were oddly beautiful, even through the ribbons and lace.

"I hope you like it." Evelien folded her hands in front of her. "I tried to find something that was the perfect balance between something you would want to wear and something your father wouldn't find entirely repulsive." She smiled sheepishly. "I wasn't aware of the tattoo when deciding on the lace back. When did that happen?"

"Uh, yeah. The dress is beautiful, though!" I realized I didn't know if she knew what had been going on. "A lot has happened in the past week. We are going to have a lot to catch up on after today's festivities."

"I'm not even going to ask about these bruises." Evelien reached over and grabbed a pale paste and began applying it to the sides of my chin. I was going to come up with some stupid excuse, but luckily, there was a soft knock on the door.

"Speaking of today's festivities." Evelien opened the door just as Lyra lifted her hand to knock again. Sarphi stood behind her, but what caught my attention was the wiggling dog she had tucked under one arm.

She lowered Deyka to the ground and the short little dog bounded across the room to my arms. I scooped her up and gave her a quick hug before placing her on the bed. Sarphi and Lyra were both smiling at me when I looked back at them.

Lyra was wearing a long, pale green ballgown. The sleeves of the dress resembled leaves that flowed past her wrist. Flowers of various kinds dotted the velvety emerald corset around her waist. She still wore her hair braided off to one side, but there was a circlet of flowers placed atop her head. There was a sparkle in her eyes as she smiled at me. She was in her element here, and it couldn't be more obvious.

Sarphi stepped out from behind Lyra. She was dressed in a pair of form fitting black pants and shirt paired with a deep red, slim fit jacket. The blue scales on her wings popped against the color of the jacket. Her hair was braided back on one side, while the curls were left to hang down on the other. She stuck her hands in her pockets and leaned against the door frame.

"You both look wonderful!" I petted Deyka's head absentmindedly. "They had that suit prepared for you? It looks great, but I'm surprised they didn't get you in a dress."

"Oh, they tried." Sarphi rolled her eyes. "They pulled this suit together quickly when I refused to wear it. Though it took quite a bit of sewing to get it over my wings." She stretched them out behind her.

I laughed, shaking my head. "I assume you guys were the ones asked to *babysit?*" I lifted Deyka into my arms. "You guys can come inside, you know?"

"Thank you, Princess." Lyra bowed her head and took only enough steps inside that Evelien could shut the door behind them. "I kept Deyka for you last night. Though I wasn't expecting the Captain to show up like *that.*" Her face reddened.

I quickly matched her shade as I remembered his state of undress as he had left the room. "Yeah... Sorry about that. He was a little *late* in deciding to hand her off. I hope she was well-behaved for you." The long-bodied dog smiled up at me in a way that suggested she was anything but. "And please, don't call me 'princess'."

"Yeah. She hates that," Evelien chimed in, though she kept her distance from the three of us.

"Wait." Sarphi smirked. "Lyra watched your dog last night so that you and the Captain could spend some time together?"

"Yeah. He came by late last night to bring me some food and ended up... staying." I looked down at Deyka in a futile attempt to hide the heat spreading across my face.

"Staying?" I could hear the amusement in Sarphi's voice. "The Captain stayed the night?" I opted to nod, not trusting my voice. "Well, well, well. So much for our perfect little princess."

"Mock me all you want. Just please keep this between us," I pleaded. "The last thing I need right now is my father finding out about any of this."

"Don't worry." She smiled at me. "What you choose to do — *who*, if you will — is not something I feel inclined to share with the king." She took a few steps closer and leaned towards me. "As long as we are being careful. In all senses of the word." The threatening tone of her voice conveyed all I needed to know.

"I am."

"We are." Finn's accent carried through the room as he opened the door. He was wearing a simplified version of his normal armor. A smaller and more form fitting onyx breastplate was fitted over a fancy red and gold shirt. He had forgone the pauldrons and bracers entirely. A sword still hung at his hip and a white cloak still graced his shoulder. He gave Lyra a gentle smile. "I really do appreciate you taking care of Deyka for us last night."

Lyra's smile faded slightly and she took a step towards Sarphi, nodding. Sarphi's wings flared and I could have sworn I heard a low growl come from her direction. Finn ignored them both as he approached me and gave me a gentle kiss.

"Your father is waiting, Princess." He extended his hand to me.

"Right. Time to be the perfect princess." I rolled my eyes. "Is it too late to sneak out?"

"I'm afraid so." Finn intertwined his fingers with mine before guiding my arm around his bicep. "Besides, this entire party is for you."

"That is, unfortunately, true." I plastered a fake smile onto my face.

"If you two don't quit looking at each other like that, everyone in this citadel is going to know what went on here last night." Sarphi

A. Turner

grabbed Lyra by the hand and led her towards the door. "We should

probably start making our way to the celebration as well."

"Bye Deyka!" Lyra waved at the dog one last time before

being pulled out of the room.

Chapter 49

Ashten

"So," Finn spoke as soon as he had shut the doors behind us. "How long have they known?"

"Known what?" I scrunched my eyebrows.

"Those weren't the faces of people who were surprised to find that their new friend had their own room in the Alterwood Citadel. They didn't even react yesterday when I called you 'Princess'." He offered me his elbow. "So, how long have they known?"

"Since the day we bonded with our dragons." I shifted my eyes downward. "But I didn't tell them. I swear! They figured it out on their own."

"How?"

"Because I'm not the only one." I shrugged. "The elvish people are divided into three groups and I assume they just made a logical guess."

"What do you mean, Princess?" He rubbed my arm reassuringly.

"Reyland and Lyra are heirs to the other Elven societies." I looked at his face for any sort of reaction. The only hint I was given was a slight tensing of his jaw.

"I see." Finn kept walking, his eyes glued ahead of us. "And they told you this? Do you believe them?"

"I wasn't sure at first, but the more I thought about it... Yeah. I do. I mean, Lyra looks just like Elion." I shrugged again. "It makes sense, so I didn't question it."

"Fair enough." Finn smiled at me. "And they didn't hurt you in any way?"

"No!" I chose not to inform him of how I was the one who had nearly hurt them. "We are all in the same terrible situation. Where we come from doesn't matter." I pursed my lips together. "It still doesn't. Not to me, at least."

"Me either, Princess." Finn came to a stop at the end of the hallway. He leaned over and gently kissed my forehead. "Now your father is just around the corner. Are you ready?"

I closed my eyes and took a deep breath.

"Can I say no?" I chuckled nervously. "You only mentioned my father. Where is mother?"

"I'm afraid she will not be joining us today. She is feeling unwell." Finn gave me an understanding smile.

Something about that didn't sit right with me, but I didn't really have time to question it. "I will have to go check on her after a little while then." Finn merely smiled in response.

I laid my head against his shoulder for a moment, relishing the calm that washed over me simply from being near him. He reached over and placed a tentative hand on my cheek. I leaned into the touch almost immediately.

"Let's go, Princess." He placed another kiss on my forehead. "We can't keep them waiting forever."

"I suppose not." I sighed and interlocked my arm with his again.

We walked around the corner together. My father was waiting just outside the towering doors to the throne room. His black hair was as tidy as ever, and he wore a deep red, nearly black suit.

"You are nearly late, daughter." His blue eyes were calculating as he looked between Finn and I.

"Sorry." I bowed slightly, as was custom when greeting the king. "Two of my friends stopped by my room this morning. We were still talking when Finn arrived."

"Friends?" He raised a brow. "And who might that be?"

A. Turner

"Lyra Windwalker and Sarphi." I wasn't surprised at the lack of emotion on his face as I spoke those names. "They, along with Reyland, are my roommates at Asballicuo."

"I see." He offered his hand to me, and I took it tentatively. "And are they treating you well?"

"As well as to be expected." Confusion crept into my voice. I tensed slightly when he wrapped my arm around his. "In a place like that, at least."

"And have you learned much?" We walked together towards the closed doors.

"I think so." I chose my words carefully. There was much that I had learned in my week at Asballicuo. Much of it I didn't want him to know yet. Not until I understood it better. "I can wield psychic powers alongside my fire ones," I answered.

"So I have heard." His lack of amazement grated on me.

"Have you heard about the dragons?" I couldn't stop myself from asking.

"I have." There was a hint of satisfaction in his voice. "I heard you did well."

"Really?" I had nearly blacked out and then proceeded to fight for my life against regurgitating every meal I had ever had. I wouldn't have called that *doing well.*

"Do not sound so surprised. You are my daughter and I would have expected nothing less." The doors opened wide in front of us.

That was the closest that my father had ever come to saying he was proud of me. It was astonishing enough that I tripped over my own feet as we walked through the doorway. My father tightened his grip on my arm to keep me from falling. He mumbled something that I didn't understand, but the tone was disapproving.

Well. There goes that.

"Now introducing," The herald started. "King Renlin Desai, Ruler of the Desai Dynasty, Sovran of the Solar Elves, and High Lord of Arvandor." My father took a step forward. "And his daughter, Lady Ashten Desai, Princess of the Desai Dynasty, and Heir Apparent of Arvandor."

My stomach twisted into a knot at the number of people in the room before me. They all bowed deeply. We had never hosted a celebration of this size before. There were so many people here that my father had apparently redecorated to accommodate. The thrones had been pushed back, and three large mirrors had been placed behind them. The tapestries that had hung on the walls were gone, replaced with plain black ones instead. I had to admit that it made the room feel a little larger, though I wondered why he had done it.

A. Turner

As if pulled by some invisible force, my gaze shifted to where three individuals were standing in the corner. Sarphi and Lyra were whispering something to each other, but they weren't what I was looking at.

Reyland.

He turned around just as my eyes locked on to him. He was wearing a well-fitted, deep navy blue suit. The fit of his shirt was slim enough that I could see his muscular frame from here. He had opted to forgo the tie that I was sure had been left for him, instead, leaving the collar of his shirt unbuttoned and exposing the top of his chest. I couldn't say I *disagreed* with the choice. His hair was shaggy and unkept, as always, but it seemed to add to the allure. An allure that I didn't quite understand. He was quite handsome, but that wasn't why I couldn't look away. There had to be more to why I wanted nothing more in this moment but to go to him. Something about him demanded every bit of my attention.

Trust me, he had it.

His blood-red eyes met mine, and I felt my face heat instantly. There was something about how he was looking at me that sent shivers down my spine. His gaze dragged slowly down my body and back up, making me hyperaware of what I was doing with my hands. My palms were suddenly sweaty, my chest tight. I wiped my hands on my dress in an attempt to distract myself from this wave of feelings. His eyes were dark when they met mine once more, and he smiled slowly. He shoved his hands into his pockets and bowed his head slightly as we walked past him.

My father cleared his throat, pulling my attention back to what I was supposed to be doing. I peeled my eyes from Reyland to the thrones in front of us. My father's throne was still seated in the center, though I was just now noticing that it was different. The once large, golden throne had been replaced with an equally large one made of an onyx colored stone. Its reflection in the mirror behind it made it seem even larger. My same throne was present, but my mother's was missing.

"Where is Mother's throne?" I whispered to my father. He didn't so much as look in my direction, so I tried again. "Father. Where is Mother's throne?"

"Not now, Daughter." He spoke under his breath as he ushered me to my throne. "Please sit."

"But—"

"I said *not now*," He all but growled.

I swallowed hard, an uneasy knot settling in my stomach. I did as my father asked and walked up the steps to the thrones. He followed shortly after me. He turned to the crowd and began to speak.

"It is my pleasure to welcome each and every one of you to the Alterwood Citadel." His deep voice boomed through the room.

A. Turner

"This celebration has been a long time coming. Not only is this a celebration of my daughter's birthday, but I have something that will benefit the entire realm. But that is for later. For now, let us dance, drink, and celebrate in honor of the Princess." He nodded slightly before sitting down.

I gave the crowd a similar nod as I took my seat. The room was quiet for only a moment before chatter and the clinking of glasses filled the room again. I placed my hands on the arm of my chair and surveyed the crowd. I didn't recognize anyone in particular in the room, though I did see the crests of several influential families.

Hundreds of people in this room and I found myself looking for the Moon Elf heir with messy white hair.

Chapter 50

Reyland

She was going to be the end of me.

I plopped down on the edge of my bed as soon as Ashten was out of the room. I stared at the doorway that she had walked out of for longer than I would care to admit before running my hands down my face in desperation. All I could think about right now was her staring up at me with those sleepy amethyst eyes. I would lose myself in them if I wasn't careful.

I stood from the bed and walked over to the pile of clothes that I had pulled from the wardrobe. A flash of navy blue material caught my eyes. Most of the ceremonial dress of Moon Elves was navy blue. I gathered the scattered silk pieces of what I assumed was my suit and walked back to the mirror. The material of the dark pants was cool against my skin as I pulled them on. I buttoned up the grey shirt just short of the top button. Somehow, the entire outfit seemed tailored just for me. Even the navy jacket fit perfectly, the sleeves ending just before my wrist. My hair fell haphazardly on either side of my head after my poor attempt to tame it by running a hand through it.

I studied my appearance in the mirror. For the first time in six years, I looked the part of a High Lord's son. No armor. No leathers.

A. Turner

No swords. Just the heir apparent to Raath Dorei preparing for a celebration at the Alterwood Citadel in honor of the Princess's birthday. Just as he should be.

If only everything was as it should be.

I grabbed a dagger from my pile of weapons and slipped it into the inside pocket of my jacket. Surely no one would notice, and its presence gave me a sense of security as I walked out of my room. With the direction of a few helpful servants, I eventually made my way to the outside of the throne room, which had apparently been rearranged for the celebration.

A flash of white hair stopped me dead in my tracks. My heart rate spiked immediately, and I fought the urge to turn around and leave. The room was suddenly too small as Rael Dronvakh turned around to face me.

I held my breath as he walked over to me. His dark red eyes scanned me coldly, his ever constant frown present on his face. Every muscle in my body tensed as he placed a hand on my shoulder.

"You look good, son." He nodded curtly before turning away. "Finally put on some muscle."

I stared at him in disbelief. Six years apart and all he could think to say was *finally put on some muscle.* I clenched my fists at my side and took a deep breath. Now was not the time to lose my temper.

"Where's mother?" My mouth was dry as I looked around the room.

"She will not be joining us." My father did not offer a further explanation. Instead, he walked towards the doors, barely giving the guards enough time to open them. A loud voice carried from inside the room.

"Presenting Rael Dronvakh, Sovran of the Moon Elves, High Lord of Raath Dorei." The herald's eyes scanned to me and he quickly turned back to the crowd. "And his son, Reyland Dronvakh, Heir Apparent."

The crowd paused slightly to acknowledge our presence. It wasn't long before the chatter picked up again. My father didn't even glance in my direction before making his way towards the throne, where I assumed the king would sit once he arrived. My heart was pounding in my chest as I scanned the room, hoping to find a familiar face. Thankfully, Sarphi's wings stood out in the room that was filled with mostly elves, and it didn't take too long for me to locate her and Lyra standing off to the side.

I weaved my way through the crowd in the direction that I had seen them standing. The ocean of people seemed endless, and I was sure I would never reach them. I could hear Lyra laughing, and Sarphi nearly took me out with her wing when she turned to look at whatever had Lyra so entertained.

"Woah!" I leaned away, just barely avoiding being knocked in the head. "Watch where you're swinging those!"

Sarphi smiled devilishly as she looked me up and down. "Well, would you look at that! You actually do know how to dress for something other than combat." She reached for my hair, but I ducked out of the way. "Except for that mop on your head."

"Well, I was going to tell you that you looked nice, but I've changed my mind." I turned to Lyra. "You, on the other hand, look wonderful."

"Thanks." She bowed her head slightly, blush staining her cheeks. "Have you talked with your father?" Her voice took on a serious tone.

"Unfortunately." Glancing quickly around the immediate vicinity, I didn't notice anyone who was obviously listening in on our conversation. "What about you?"

"Yeah. I got the same introduction you did." She glanced over to where her father was speaking with mine. "I also made them introduce Sarphi with us. He wasn't too happy about that."

"I've only met him once, and I get the feeling that he isn't happy about most things." Sarphi elbowed Lyra playfully, smiling brightly at her. I didn't miss how the Wild Elf blushed as she nodded in agreement.

"Now introducing!" The crowd grew quiet as the herald began speaking. "King Renlin Desai, Ruler of the Desai Dynasty, Sovran of the Solar Elves, and High Lord of Arvandor." There was a brief pause.

The room remained quiet as we all turned to the entryway. The king stood at the entrance, his eyes cold and calculating as he scanned the room. He wore the colors of his house and his hair was neatly cut and combed perfectly.

"And his daughter, Lady Ashten Desai, Princess of the Desai Dynasty, and Heir Apparent of Arvandor."

Ashten.

She was beautiful. Her purple eyes were bright as they met mine. I didn't even try to disguise my attention as I raked my gaze down her body. Her dress was just long enough to reach her ankles, the red fabric flowing slightly behind her as she walked. The golden lace that comprised most of the top of her dress shimmered in the magical lighting that lit the room. Her tattoo peaked out over the top of her shoulder, the lace barely hiding it. I smiled slowly when I noticed the purple flower that had been woven into her crown-like hair. She looked down at the ground, smoothing her dress with her hands. My entire body buzzed with the need to touch her. To have my hands where she had put her own moments ago. Instead, I shoved them into my pocket and bowed my head slightly in reverence as they passed.

Her father said something that caused her attention to snap to him. They whispered back and forth before the king turned to address the crowd. Everything he said faded into background noise when I noticed the look on her face. She was staring down at her hands, which were folded neatly in front of her. She swallowed heavily as her father sat down on his throne. Ashten followed suit shortly after, holding her head high as the rest of the room slowly came back to life. The musicians played a lively tune, and soon the room was filled with chatter and laughter.

Something was bothering her. Maybe it was just the number of people here, but I couldn't shake the feeling that it may be something worse. I started to walk towards her, but someone grabbed the top of my arm.

I spun around, ready to tell off whoever had decided now was the time for a conversation, but words caught in my throat when I noticed it was Lyra. She smiled shyly, and I held my breath, suppressing my initial anger at being interrupted.

"Was there something you needed?" I tried to hide the bite in my voice.

"I know where you were headed, and I don't think that's such a good idea, Reyland." Lyra glanced over my shoulder at where Ashten was sitting.

I turned around to see Captain Finn approaching the thrones. He bowed at the waist and waited for the king to motion him forward. He stepped up beside the king's throne and leaned down, whispering something in his ear. The king nodded abruptly before standing and walking towards the back corner of the room. Finn then turned to Ashten, holding his hand out towards her and pointing to where several other groups were dancing. I couldn't help but smile when she rolled her eyes as she took his hand. That same smile quickly faded when he placed a quick kiss on her hand before leading her down the steps. I surprised myself when a low growl escaped my chest at the sight.

"That's why I said it was a bad idea." Lyra rubbed my arm reassuringly. "She's gotten under your skin. Into your head, even."

"What would you know about it?" I all but growled at Lyra, who, to her credit, did not flinch in the slightest.

"I've seen the way you look at her. Like the world begins and ends with each step she takes." There was a hint of sadness in Lyra's eyes.

"How do you know?" I asked, my voice a little softer this time. "How do you know when she doesn't?"

"I don't have the answer for why she doesn't know." She took a deep breath before answering me. "But I am very familiar with the way you are looking at her right now." Lyra stared at the ground silently. "Because someone used to look at me the same way." Her voice shook with emotion. "He was my entire life, and I'm the reason his ended." A few tears fell, and she quickly wiped them away.

I didn't know what to say. I looked over at where Sarphi was bugging some poor Wild Elf noble, a glass of wine in each of her hands. She smiled mischievously when the Elf she had been talking to began to nervously tug at his collar.

"But I thought..." I tilted my head towards Sarphi. Lyra shook her head, smiling. "No?"

"No." There was a gentleness in her voice, but the sadness still lingered. "I love her deeply, but not in that way. She's the only person I've ever told about...him." Her face contorted, as if it pained her physically to talk about whoever the love of her life had been. "Since she found out, she has apparently made it her life's mission to make me happy again."

"And is it working?"

"I think so." She looked over at Sarphi. The Dragonfolk was now making her way back to us, juggling three wine glasses in her hands. "It's going to take time, but it's hard not to laugh with her around."

"And what do I do about *him*?" I asked as I watched Ashten and Finn dance in a slow circle, the former laying her head on the latter's shoulder.

"Nothing." Lyra chuckled at the disbelief on my face. "This is one of those things you have to wait for, Reyland."

"And if I'm waiting forever?" My mouth went dry at the thought.

"Then you wait." There was no room for argument in Lyra's voice. "And it will be worth every second."

"Wine anyone?" The cheerfulness of Sarphi's voice cut through the solemn air. She held out two of the three wine glasses, nearly spilling them in the process. I took one before turning back to watch Ashten. I kept my ear tuned on their conversation as my eyes followed the dancing couple across the room, sipping on my wine.

"How much of this have you had?" Lyra asked, grabbing the glass from Sarphi just as the Dragonfolk let it go.

"Enough to make this entire event slightly more enjoyable." Sarphi downed her glass in nearly one gulp. "You should try it." Her words were slightly slurred and I could hear the smile on her face.

"I don't think we should get completely drunk here." Lyra's voice took a serious turn. "We still don't know why we are here and I think it's best that we stay in our right mind."

"Well, it's too late for Reyland." Sarphi saying my name caught my full attention.

A. Turner

"What about me?" I turned back to face them, one eyebrow raised.

"Just go talk to her." Sarphi leaned against the wall. "If you are going to stare at her like a sad puppy all day, just go talk to her."

I looked at Lyra, who smiled and nodded. "There's nothing wrong with asking to dance with the Princess."

"Yeah." The music slowed as the song ended. "I can do that."

I quickly downed the rest of the wine in my glass and headed towards the Solar Elf with the amethyst eyes.

Chapter 51

Finn

"May I have this dance, Princess?" I looked over my shoulder to see the king speaking with Lords Galen and Rael.

"Do you really want me to dance with you?" Ashten looked out at the crowd of people who had broken off into pairs. "In front of all of these people?"

"There's nothing wrong with asking the princess for a dance at her own birthday celebration." I held my hand out expectantly. "Besides, I didn't dress this well to not get at least one dance in with the most beautiful person here."

She rolled her eyes but didn't protest further. I placed a gentle kiss on her hand before leading her down the steps and to the middle of the room. People parted and made room as we walked through the crowd. There were a few whispers, but none of them dared to speak loud enough for us to understand them. The musicians faltered slightly before starting up another song.

I laid the hand that I was holding on my chest, wrapping my own around her waist. She wrapped her arms around my neck, not arguingas I pulled her closer. We began swaying back and forth, the tune soft, slow, and easy to dance to.

A. Turner

"Why did you leave last night?" Ashten whispered as the song grew louder.

"There was some trouble with the guards. I went to go take care of it, but I didn't want to wake you when I came back. I decided to stay in my own room." My thumb softly stroked the small of her back.

"Then why were you not there when Evelien came to wake me this morning?" I could feel her fidgeting with the back of my shirt as she spoke. A surefire sign that she was nervous.

"I got up before sunrise to go over the guard assignments for this celebration." I tried to keep the answer short. No need to dig a deeper hole.

"Is that also why there were no guards at my room this morning?" She glanced around the room. "Because they were at your meeting?"

"No." I gritted my teeth. There weren't any guards at her room because they had come to tell me about the screaming they could hear from outside her doors. When we arrived back at her room, it was empty and Reyland's door was open. It had taken every ounce of my strength not to kill that Elf right then and there when I peeked into his room. "There should have been guards outside your door, Princess."

"Well, they weren't," She stated shortly. "When I woke up, they were gone."

"Well then, I will have to make sure that doesn't happen again." I leaned forward, whispered in her ear. "In the meantime, all I can do is apologize." I loved how her breath quickened at the mere mention of last night.

Not that my reaction to remembering how perfectly we fit together was any better. I played with the lace at the back of her dress, tracing the same spots my lips had been in last night. She bit her lip to stifle a moan, instead exhaling shakily through her nose.

"Not here." She looked around the room nervously. "Everyone is staring, Finn."

"Let them stare." I tilted her chin back towards me. "We are doing nothing wrong. Just the Captain of the Guard dancing with the Princess of Arvandor."

"Nothing wrong? I'm fairly certain you just offered to take me back to my room for a repeat of what happened last night... Which was explicitly against the rules, in case you had forgotten." She looked out at the room again. I could feel her anxiety spike well before I saw the physical signs. She took a deep, shaky breath, and I could feel her hands shaking where they rested against the back of my neck.

"Hey," I whispered. "Come here." I guided her head to my shoulder. "There's nothing to worry about. Nothing bad is going to happen from us dancing." I focused on calming feelings, sending those feelings through where my hands touched her waist. "No one heard what I said. As long as I am here, no one can hurt you."

I felt her relax in my arms. I rubbed small circles on her back and heard her sigh against my shoulder.

"Finn?" she asked, not lifting her head from my shoulder. "Where's my mother?"

A knot of dread instantly formed in my stomach.

"Do you trust me, Princess?" I leaned my head closer to her ear.

"Of course I do."

"Then I need you to do two things for me." I pushed against her waist, creating a little bit of space between us. Confusion laced her features as she looked at me. "First, don't ask about your mother again."

"But—" I cut her off before she could continue.

"Second, when your father comes back in here and offers you and the other Drakewardens a glass of wine, take it, but do not drink it."

"Why not?" Her voice rose. "What's going on, Finn?"

"You said you trusted me, and I'm going to need you to prove that, Princess." I brushed a strand of hair out of her face. "Please."

Out of the corner of my eyes, I could see the Moon Elf approaching. Ashten noticed him too, a beautiful smile gracing her face. I swallowed my pride as he got closer.

"Princess." Reyland bowed deeply at the waist. "Captain." The disdain in his voice was clear as he addressed me. "I was wondering if I could have the next dance with the Princess."

I was just about to turn him down when Ashten nodded.

"Of course." She nodded her head and turned back to me. "It's only one dance, Finn. You don't have to look so sour."

The sour look on my face only intensified as Ashten took Reyland's hand and led her away from me.

"Captain," A gruff voice called out from behind me. Rael was standing a few feet away, arms crossed. "The king has called for you."

"Who's going to watch over the Princess?" I asked. While the concern was a realistic one, it was more for selfish reasons than anything.

"She will be fine in the hands of the assassin," He stated curtly. "Now hurry."

A. Turner

He didn't hear the string of curses I mumbled under my breath as he turned and walked away. I followed shortly, leaving the Princess in the hands of the one person in this room I never wanted her to be alone with.

Chapter 52

Ashten

I took Reyland's hand and let him guide me deeper into the crowd. I looked over my shoulder for Finn to see him walking away with Reyland's father. A twinge of uncertainty settled deep in my stomach as both men disappeared around a corner.

Reyland tentatively placed a hand on my waist, pulling me closer but keeping a respectable distance between us. I placed my hands on his shoulders, letting my arms relax against him. His shaggy hair cast a shadow over his eyes as he looked down at me.

"You look beautiful today, Nightshade." He smiled warmly, his red eyes bright.

"You look better than you did last night." I made a show of contemplating something. "A suit really, well, *suits* you." I hung my head and laughed at my own terrible joke.

"Wow." Reyland shook his head back and forth slowly. "I thought that someone of your standing would be above such a joke as that." He clicked his tongue a few times, and I playfully punched him in the shoulder. "Ow! What was that for?"

"For insinuating that I am any better than everyone else."

"I would like to meet whoever has told you that you aren't." Reyland's voice turned grim.

"What if I don't want to be?" The words left my mouth before I could think any harder about them. "What if I don't want to be better than everyone else?"

Concern filled Ryeland's eyes. "What do you mean?"

"I don't know." I sighed. "Sometimes I feel like people are only nice to me because I'm the princess."

"That's simply not true, Ashten." Reyland met my eyes as he continued to speak. "People are nice to you because you are nice to them."

"Why wouldn't I be nice to them?" I cocked my head.

"Because you don't have to be." Reyland huffed, clearly frustrated. "You're the princess. You don't have to be nice to anyone to get them to do what you want. But you choose to anyway. Even if they aren't nice to you."

"I mean, it's only right." I wasn't sure why I was blushing. "Even if someone mistreats you. Knowing how they would feel is all the more reason to be kind. Everyone deserves kindness, Reyland."

"I don't know about everyone, but you sure do." Reyland scanned the room before focusing his intense gaze on me. "I have to tell you something. You can tell me to find somewhere else to exist once I'm done, but I can't keep this to myself any longer."

"Okay?" I was taken aback by the sudden seriousness of his tone. "Is everything okay?"

"Listen. I know that you and the Captain are... *involved.*" I didn't miss the way he ground out that last word. "And Lyra told me specifically *not* to do this." He swallowed nervously. "But I've, uh, never been good at listening so..." He leaned closer, maintained the distance between our bodies but putting his head right in front of mine. "Did you know your powers can't create new emotions?"

"What?" I had no idea where he was going with this. "What are you trying to say, Reyland? I'm not a fan of riddles."

"Just bear with me. Please." Reyland cleared his throat. "As part of my training, I had to study various magical abilities and their effects. Someone with psychic abilities cannot cause other people to experience specific emotions. They can only amplify emotions that are already present within that person. Like when you panicked that day in our quarters. Your emotions were heightened by your own magic."

"Okay? Yeah, I think I understand that." I furrowed my brows. "But what does that have to do with Finn and I?"

"Do you remember everything I said to you that day, Nightshade?" Ryeland's voice was little more than a whisper.

I thought back to that day. It was my first time using my psychic abilities, and it hadn't gone well. Most of that day was a blur, but I did remember Reyland having to use his own abilities to bring mine under control. My eyes widened as the rest of the afternoon filled my memory.

"Perfect. You're perfect," Reyland repeated, as if he could tell that I had finally made the connection. "Less than twenty-four hours and you already had me hooked. You hadn't done a single thing, and you didn't have to. You never will."

"Reyland..." I fumbled over my words. "I—"

"I know. I know that you have already made up your mind, and I'm not asking you to change it. I've seen the way you look at him." A hint of sadness flashed across his eyes, but only for a moment. "But if you ever change your mind, I'll be waiting. I'll wait forever if I have to."

My first instinct was to agree with him. My relationship with Finn was special to me. It was something I never wanted to lose. He was the first person that I ever felt comfortable with and I couldn't imagine life without him. Even after our recent altercations.

I just couldn't bring myself to say those words. To tell Reyland that he could very well be waiting forever. Every time I opened my mouth to speak, there was a tightening in my chest that took my breath away. I tried several times, but I could never get out more than a few syllables.

"Are you okay?" A concerned look washed over Ryeland's face. "It's okay, Ashten. You don't have to say anything. Really. I just needed to get that off my chest. You know. In case something happens."

"I... I appreciate it." It was stupid, but it was all I could bear to say. "Thank you for respecting me enough to tell me, and thank you for not expecting anything from me. I'm sorry." I didn't quite understand why I felt the need to apologize, but the words escaped my mouth without hindrance.

"No. Don't apologize." He spoke with a surprising amount of gentleness. "Never apologize." I felt his thumb rub against the lace on my back a few times before he froze, seemingly remembering himself.

A loud knocking caused me to startle, and I whipped my head toward the sound. My father was now standing by his throne, a tall sceptre in his hand, topped with a black crystal. He slammed the crystal into the ground a few more times until the entire room grew still and silent. He motioned off to the side, and I watched as Galen Windwalker and Rael Dronvakh approached the thrones. They both held a glass of wine in each hand.

The wine.

A. Turner

"I thank all of you for attending this celebration. I trust that you have all enjoyed the music and festivities, but I did say that I had one other announcement to make today. I would like to ask the three heirs, as well as the Dragonfolk by the name of Sarphi, to join me up here?" He motioned to the elevated platform that the thrones stood on.

I searched the crowd for Sarphi and Lyra. We locked eyes, concern evident on both of their faces. I waved them over to me. As they got closer, I formed a connection to them and opened up my mental communication.

"Can you guys hear me?" I looked straight ahead at my father as we approached the thrones.

"I am never going to get used to that." I saw Sarphi flinch out of the corner of my eye. To her credit, she corrected nearly immediately, keeping in step with me.

"That wine up there? Don't drink it." I bowed slightly at the waist before climbing the stairs. The others followed suit shortly after.

"What? Why?" Lyra asked.

"I don't know why. I just need you to trust me." I turned to face the crowd, giving them the smile of a perfect princess.

"I do." Reyland nodded subtly beside me.

"These four individuals have done something that has not been done here in centuries." The lords handed us each a glass of wine while my father talked. "We sent our heirs to Asballicuo to be trained. While there, they were joined by this young Dragonfolk. Together, they have achieved more than we ever thought possible. Therefore, we are asking you all to celebrate this achievement with us." He motioned to a set of servants off to the side, who immediately began to carry glasses of wine to everyone in the crowd.

"I am proud to announce that my daughter, the Crowned Princess, along with the other three individuals here beside me, have bonded with dragons." An audible gasp echoed throughout the room. Many people began whispering and looking at us with wide eyes. My father slammed his sceptre onto the ground, causing the room to fall silent again. "There have not been true bonded Drakewardens in Xeswal since before my father's birth. This is an amazing achievement for the young riders and something I never thought would be possible. As your king, I ask that you drink with me in celebration."

My father raised his glass, and everyone in the crowd with him. Everyone in the room took a sip in unison. I looked at my companions and was relieved to see them just barely lifting their cups to their lips. My heart dropped when I saw Finn finish the remnants of his glass.

"What are you doing?!" I formed the connection with him quicker than I thought I could. *"You told me not to drink the wine!"*

A. Turner

"What is this, Princess?" There was an unsettling calm to his voice, even in my head. He made eye contact with me, slowly lowering his glass.

"A new trick. Apparently part of my psychic powers."

"I see." A smirk formed at the side of his mouth. *"It's a nice trick."*

I didn't have time to press further as a female Elf standing at the base of the platform fell, clutching at her chest.

Chapter 53

Ashten

No sooner did the elf hit the ground than did foam begin to spill out of her mouth. I watched in horror as others fell, clutching at their chests, foam pouring from their mouths. I could see the blown pupils of the ones closest to me, their eyes wide and mouths agape as they fell to the floor. They barely had time to react before falling victim themselves. One by one, every person who had even the smallest sip of the wine fell lifeless to the floor.

I couldn't move. My feet were glued to the ground as I stared out at the horrible scene that filled the throne room. My hands began to shake, and I could feel my magic surging to my defense of its own free will. I tried my best to steady my breathing, restraining my emotions to the best of my abilities. I scanned the crowd, relieved that I couldn't find Evelien among them. That fact was bringing me a light sense of relief right now.

"Nightshade." I heard Reyland whisper from beside me.

"What?" My voice sounded like I was underwater.

"There was nightshade in the wine."

Horror coursed through me. That could have been us.

A. Turner

"Well, well, well. What do we have here?" A thickly accented voice snapped me out of my trance. Galen Windwalker stepped up beside my father, motioning to the group of us. "Why didn't they drink?"

"I do not know." My father turned to Finn. "Perhaps the commander has some insight?" The look in his eyes promised pain as he waited for an answer.

"Princess. Did you tell the others not to drink the wine?" Finn's voice was unnervingly calm, and he slowly stepped between my father and I. "That information was only for you."

"I told you the Princess would be a problem!" Rael slammed his fist into one of the mirrors. I waited for a spray of glass that never came. Instead, the surface of the mirror simply rippled like water.

"And I told you I had it under control," Finn growled at the Moon Elf Lord. He turned back to me, his movements lethally slow. "I do wish that you would have let them drink the wine, Princess." I saw a flash of sadness in his eyes before he blinked it away.

"It would have been a much nicer death." My father snapped his fingers, and a tendril of shadow snaked from his feet, past me, and towards Sarphi. "Now we are going to have to do this one by one."

Shadows?

The amount of wine the Dragonfolk had consumed had made her a little too relaxed. Her movements were sluggish, and she was unable to step out of the way as the shadows snaked around her leg. She fell to the ground with a *thud*, her face smacking into the stone floor. Her busted nose left a trail of blood as the king dragged her across the floor to his feet. Shadows quickly coiled around her, pulling her upright and restraining her as she finally began to flail and fight back. A string of curses left her mouth before the shadows coiled around her head, silencing her. Lyra immediately began to run to her, but Reyland grabbed her by the arm, holding her back.

"Let her go!" I yelled, my tone frantic. "Finn! What's going on?" He was the only one I trusted to tell me the truth right now.

"Go on, Commander. Tell the Princess what's going on." Galen sneered.

"Princess..." Finn approached me slowly. "It was never supposed to happen like this. Everyone was going to drink the wine except you. They know I would never help them if they took you away. You and I were going to sit on these thrones, Princess. The two of us, ruling together, just like you had always wanted. Just like *we* had always wanted." He reached out to touch my face, but I pulled back instinctively.

I felt a tear fall as everything that he had just said fully registered. "What do you mean? Did you kill everyone?" The look in his eyes told me everything I needed to know. "I told you I would figure it out, Finn! You didn't have to do this!" I backed away from him, but he reached out and grabbed my arms, pulling me roughly towards him.

"Let go!" I fought against him, but his sheer strength was too much for me. My wild eyes found Reyland, and I could see the struggle in his eyes.

"Child," My father cut in. "Your Commander is merely following orders. Our orders. As he has done from day one." The king took a few steps down the platform towards the sea of dead bodies. "This. All of this resulted from centuries of planning."

"Killing your own children took you centuries to plan?" I scoffed, adrenaline overriding the fear that was coursing through my veins. "All that planning and you weren't even successful."

"Only because we needed the dragons first. As I am sure you know, my own father ordered the extermination of dragons on Xeswal. Until recently, we thought he had been successful." He pointed to Rael. "He recently discovered that there was an entire brood of wild dragons living in the caves beneath Asballicuo. Try as we might, we couldn't flush them out."

"I had the brilliant idea to give them someone to bond with," Galen spoke up. "I couldn't have done it without your help, Lyra." Lyra's eyes went wide at the mention of her name. "All that research you did on dragons really came through for me."

"Why us?" Reyland asked, stepping up beside me. "You are aware that killing our dragons would kill us, too?"

"We were honestly hoping to kill you all first." Rael's tone was sharp. "It's a surefire way to lure out a dragon. Killing their rider."

My mind was racing. This couldn't be happening. The edges of my vision began to blur and my heart began pounding in my ears.

"You know, I'm not surprised to hear that from you, *Father.*" Reyland narrowed his eyes at the other two elven leaders. "But I had sincerely hoped that not everyone hated their children as much as you."

"Maybe that would be true..." My father stood at the base of the stairs. "If we were elves and you were our children."

"What do you mean?" My voice was shaking. I turned to look at Lyra. Tears were streaming down her face, her eyes glued to where Sarphi still sat restrained by my father's shadows. Shadows I had never seen him use before. The Dragonfolk was slumped forward, out of breath from struggling against the shadows. "She looks just like you!" I pointed at Galen.

"It would be more correct to say that I look like her." Galen's smile grew unnaturally wide.

"For nearly twenty years, I have strategically withheld information from you, Ashten." My father absentmindedly stepped over a dead body. "There were things I allowed you to learn, and things that I kept secret from you. Things that I wouldn't even allow your tutors to mention to you."

I watched in horror as Galen, Rael, and my father all changed before my very eyes. Their skin rippled and shifted unnaturally, their hair and eyes changing colors as if they were simply changing clothes. In what felt like the blink of an eye, I was looking at exact copies of Lyra, Reyland, and myself.

"You... you're not an Elf." I almost couldn't believe it. I had only heard about these *creatures* in the scary bedtime stories I begged my nannies to read to me as a child. "Is that how you use dark magic? Some sort of special ability?"

"Correct, Daughter." It was unnerving to hear my own voice coming from my own mouth on a different body. "Though I guess I shouldn't call you that anymore."

My head swam with the sudden onset of information. A pounding started behind my eyes and I shut them, shaking my head. When I opened them, the three beings had changed back once more. Now I was looking into the eyes of my father, Axilya, and Malon.

"You see. No true child of ours would have died from drinking that wine. Morphers are immune to most mortal poisons. We are also very capable of wielding at least small amounts of many different magics." The king looked expectantly at Finn as he walked past us. He stood behind the still struggling Sarphi. "Perhaps my son would like to demonstrate?"

Son?

I slowly turned my head towards Finn. He still had a vice grip on my arms, and his grip only tightened as the king spoke. I was met with sad, green eyes. No. Not sadness.

Regret.

"What does he mean, Finn?" The Commander merely stared at me, neither of us moving an inch. Slowly, the truth began to form in my head. "No..."

"I'm sorry, Princess." Dread soaked to my core as Finn slowly changed forms. Nothing drastic, like the others. In an instant, his hair was back to the shaggy length I had always loved. Now, the sight of it made me nearly hurl. His eyes were brighter and I could have sworn he grew a few inches. "I wanted to tell you, but I couldn't risk you mentioning something to the king. It would have put you in too much danger."

"Too much danger?!" Reyland yelled before I could get the same words out. "Your mere presence is dangerous to her! Did that thought ever cross your mind?"

"Every single day, Elf." Finn spat out the last word like an unpleasant drink. "Every single night that I stood watch outside her doors, it was the only thing on my mind. I wasn't even supposed to like you, Princess. Yet here I am, completely in love with you."

"In love with me?" I shook my head. "You're trying to tell me you did all this because you are in love with me? I have just discovered that I barely even know what you are, yet I anticipate that you expect me to return the same feelings?"

"In time, yes." Finn's eyes softened, and I felt a warmth begin to spread throughout my body.

I don't know if it was the adrenaline or the sudden lack of trust, but I did not immediately calm down as I had in the past. This time, I had the innate response to fight it. My own magic recognized a version of itself and fought hard. I let it happen. Slowly, Finn's magic dissipated and my magic settled back down. I locked eyes with Finn, utter shock lining his features.

"Psychic magic?" I breathed. "This entire time. Every comforting touch. Every kind word. Was any of it real? Or was it all just a cover so you could use your own abilities to make me like you?"

"Psychic abilities can't make new emotions, Princess." Reyland had said as much to me, but I still couldn't shake the feeling of being used. "I just helped you realize them."

"No!" I fought against his grip. "I may have loved you once, but now I can't. Not anymore." Power gathered at my fingertips and I let just a little bit of it leak through into the physical world. "I told you not to touch me like this again."

"But you will again in time." Finn's tone was matter of fact. He did not loosen his grip on me one bit, despite my threats.

"Please, Finn. Please tell me you are lying. Please tell me I'm misunderstanding this. Tell me this is all some elaborate way of protecting me," I pleaded. I summoned a bit more of my psychic powers and lavender smoke danced at my fingertips.

"Come on, Finn. Just let her go." Reyland stepped away from Lyra slowly, the Wild Elf still pleading with my father. "You guys have already won. There's no use in scaring her any further."

My eyes met Reyland's and there were no words needed to explain the pleading look on his face.

Play along.

"I can't control my powers yet. I don't want to hurt you!" I held my palms up defensively, lavender smoke swirling around them.

"I don't mean to scare you, Princess. I just don't want to lose you." Finn's grip on my arm loosened a little.

I didn't dare step away, but I did let my shoulders relax.

"You already have." I watched all hope drain from his face. It was quickly replaced by anger.

Those three words were enough for Reyland. Shadowy tendrils snaked from his arms and wrapped around my waist. Finn's physical strength was no match for the dark magic, and I was pulled from his grip with ease. I slammed into Reyland. The force of it knocked my breath away, but the shadows steadied me and kept me on my feet. The look in Finn's eyes turned murderous.

"You shouldn't have done that." A chill ran down my spine when I looked over at the king. He stood behind Sarphi, a sinister smile stretched across his face. He palmed a shadowy blade, dancing it through his fingers. "I guess it's time to get started."

With a flick of his wrist, a sharpened shadow painted a red line across Sarphi's throat.

Chapter 54

Reyland

I shot a shadow towards the king's hand, but I wasn't fast enough. I couldn't look away as Sarphi's eyes widened in surprise. The only thing I could hear over the pounding in my ears was Lyra's blood-curdling scream as Sarphi slumped to the ground. I pulled my shadows from Ashten and wrapped them around Lyra to keep her from running to her fallen friend. We all needed to stay as far away from these males as possible. A pool of red formed around Sarphi's lifeless form, her eyes already dull. I had enough experience in this area to know that she was likely already dead. I hoped Lyra could at least find solace in the fact that it was quick.

"You didn't need her!" Lyra screamed. "She wasn't an heir! You could have just left her out of this!" The Wild Elf's voice was raw with emotion as she fought against my restraints. Vines began fighting against my shadows, and I had to double my efforts to keep her in place.

"Get them," The king commanded. "Now. I want them each alive." An animalistic smile crept across his face. "I plan to have a little fun since they have inconvenienced me so much today."

"I guess death is a spectacle, after all." Rael's smile matched the kings.

A. Turner

"Run!" I shouted, grabbing each of the females by the arm. I heard the drawing of blades, but didn't bother looking back.

Ashten was quick to respond, though I could still see the shock on her face. Adrenaline was in control right now, which I was thankful for. Lyra's movement was sluggish, her eyes dull. Her body was in survival mode, which I could work with. At least she hadn't shut down completely. I led them down the only corridors I knew in this place. The ones that led back to where we had slept the night before.

We ran as fast and hard as we could through the Alterwood Citadel. I heard shouting behind us and turned to see a few Elven guards running our direction. One of them lifted his hand, and a bright orange flame formed in it. He hurled it towards us, just barely missing our moving forms. I sent my own shadows in their direction, slithering along the floor and wrapping around their ankles. Once in place, my shadows froze, cementing the guards to the floor as we rounded the corners.

Dark shadows danced along the walls, but these weren't mine. I could hear more footsteps behind us and they were gaining fast. I pulled the one dagger I had hidden on the inside of my coat and shoved it into Lyra's hands as we came to the outside of Ashten's room.

"Here. You can have this. I can use my shadows." Lyra regarded me numbly, but nodded her head. I turned to Ashten. "Is there a quick way out of this castle? Preferably one your fa — the king doesn't know about."

She thought for a moment. I knew we didn't have long, and an easy escape route was our best chance. Lyra and I were trained, but nowhere near as strong as all four of those males combined. Even if Ashten could wield her powers effectively, it was still a fight we may not win.

"In here." Ashten perked up, running towards her room.

Lyra and I followed quickly. I shut the door behind us and we all worked together to pull over as much furniture as possible to cover the door. Mere seconds later, there was a heavy pounding on the door.

"I won't let them hurt you, Princess!" Finn's gruff voice sounded from the other side. "As long as I am here, no one can hurt you, remember? You just need to let me in." If I didn't know any better, I would have said he sounded desperate.

I watched Ashten for a reaction, but she gave none. Instead, she walked over to her window, throwing it open. She leaned out, looking both directions.

"Enough, Finn," The king's voice boomed. "Just break down the door." The pounding on the door became incessant. The wooden furniture cracked with every hit.

A. Turner

"What's the plan here?" I walked over to the window and looked out. I saw nothing other than a ledge. It looked like midnight outside, though I knew it couldn't be any later than midday.

"Do you trust your dragon?" Ashten asked, looking at both Lyra and I. Lyra nodded wordlessly.

"Uh. Yeah. Now isn't really the time for a trust exercise, though." I gestured to the door just as the hilt of a sword busted a hole in the wood.

"Do you trust *me*?" Her eyes turned fierce. Lavender smoke danced in them.

"Always." I nodded tightly.

Trepidation filled me as she stepped out of the window and onto the thin ledge. I didn't know what she had planned, but falling to our deaths had to be better than whatever they had in store for us, anyway. I stepped out behind her and then helped Lyra out the window. The holes in the door were larger now, hands bursting through them and pulling the wood off.

"Call your dragons," Ashten looked to the sky.

"What?" Lyra spoke, her voice raspy.

"Call your dragons." Ashten repeated. "We are going to jump and they are going to catch us. Chances are they are already nearly here. Cyphis probably lost it when Sarphi—" She choked on the words, but I understood her meaning.

I took a deep breath and focused on the bit of frost that had settled deep inside of me.

"Zothim? Some bad stuff has gone down and we need a way out immediately." I paused for a second. *"How fast can you get here?"*

"We can see the lights of the citadel from here." I was surprised to hear the panic in his voice. *"What happened? Cyphis said—"* I cut him off.

"Cyphis is right. I don't have time to explain right now." The faint sound of wings flapping filled the air. Ashten nodded. *"If we jump from this window, can you catch us?"*

"Catch you?" Zothim questioned. *"Why would we need to catch you?"*

"Because the only way out of our predicament is through this window, and I don't think any of us have spontaneously learned how to fly in the past hour." Annoyance laced my inner voice. I could just make out the forms of the dragons in the unnatural darkness that had surrounded the city of Arvandor.

"Understood. Jump on the count of three."

"On three?" Ashten asked, inhaling deeply.

A. Turner

"On three." Lyra and I confirmed at the same time.

We stood in a straight line on the ledge and began counting in unison.

"One."

"Two."

"Three!"

The end of the last word caught in my throat as we launched ourselves into the unnatural night.

Chapter 55

Ashten

This is how I was going to die.

My hair whipped at my face and stung my neck. My stomach was in my throat as the ground got closer and closer. I could just barely hear the flapping of wings over the roaring of the wind in my ears. We had not been that far up, so why did it feel like we had been falling forever? It still wasn't going to be long enough, though. I could nearly make out the statues in the courtyard garden. The dragons weren't going to make it in time. I closed my eyes and braced for what I hoped would be a quick death.

I'm sorry.

I slammed into something solid. My arm had been positioned between my body and whatever I had landed on, and I heard the snap before I felt it. Nauseating pain coursed through my body. Enough pain that I realized I was still alive. I splayed my good hand out against the surface I had landed on. It was cool and jagged.

And breathing.

"We are going to have to work on your landing if we are going to make this a habit." I had never been so relieved to hear Nyzirth's voice.

A. Turner

I jolted my head upward and scanned for the others. Immediate relief washed over me when I spotted Reyland and Lyra atop their dragons. They were both alive and breathing, which is all I could ask for. Like my arm, anything else could be fixed. Even Cyphis still flew with us.

"What is the plan?" Nyzirth asked as she ascended higher into the air. I looked down to see dozens of soldiers pouring out of the entrance.

"I don't know. We need somewhere to gather our thoughts." I opened my mind to each of the elves and dragons present. *"Head to the cliffs behind the citadel."*

"Isn't that a bit close to them?" Reyland questioned.

"It takes a while to scale those cliffs on foot. It should give us enough time to decide where we can go safely." I directed Nyzirth downward. *"The citadel has no defense against dragons."* It seemed that was the only useful information I had ever gotten from Finn.

There was no other discussion until we had all landed in the soft sand at the base of the cliffs. The normally calming splash of the waves on the shore were nothing but drowned out background noise as I slid from Nyzirth's back. I couldn't help the few choice words that left my mouth as pain coursed through my broken arm. I held it close to my body, supporting it with my other arm as Reyland came running over to me.

"Are you alright?!" His eyes frantically scanned me up and down. "Your arm! What happened?"

"I landed on it," I stated flatly. I had no more energy for explanations or witty comebacks. "I think it's broken."

"I didn't even think about you having to make that landing." He muttered a curse under his breath. "I was able to use my shadows to soften the fall, and Lyra her vines. I..."

He pulled off his jacket and tied it around my neck, making a makeshift sling. I did my best to breathe through the pain as he slowly lifted my arm until it was settled nicely into the jacket. A splint would have to wait. I smiled my thanks and turned to Lyra.

She stood quietly beside Iressei. The male green dragon's massive head was slung over her shoulder, and she stroked his green scales slowly. There was no light in her eyes, but she registered me staring. I couldn't even begin to think of what to say, so I chose to say nothing instead.

I felt a warmth at my back and turned, expecting to see Nyzirth. Instead, I was met with Cyphis's large golden eyes. Sorrow laced every one of the red dragon's features. He exhaled against me, likely searching for any lingering scent of his lost rider.

"I know," I muttered, though I truly couldn't understand what the dragon was going through right now. I slowly reached for his nose. He did not pull away, but instead closed his eyes as my hand touched him. "I am so sorry." The large male dragon exhaled slowly before lumbering over to Nyzirth, who greeted him with a soft nudge of the nose.

"So." I didn't realize that Reyland had stood silent beside me. "I know that a lot just happened, and I know it is a lot to process." He took a deep breath. "But we need to make a decision. Where can we go that is safe?"

"I don't know if anywhere is," I mumbled. "We can't go to the Mistymoon Glades or to Raath Dorei. They would expect it. Besides, they probably have spies everywhere."

"And we can't go back to Asballicuo." Reyland ran his fingers through his hair. "And we obviously can't stay here."

"I never thought Xeswal would feel so small." A defeated chuckle escaped my lips. "All I've ever wanted was to leave the citadel, and now I can't even decide where to go first."

I hated making these kinds of decisions. It was a big reason why I hated my station in life so much. I didn't want the weight of everyone's lives resting on my shoulders. I didn't know how to make these types of decisions. That indecisiveness made me so bad for this position.

A sound that resembled thunder emanated from where the cliffs were behind us. Reyland turned around immediately, ice forming at his fingertips. Nearly thirty feet away from us was a swirling cloud of fire and smoke. From the corner of my eye, I could see vines wrapped around Lyra's arms. I felt a heavy presence behind me and looked up to see all the dragon's heads positioned over us protectively. A low growl emanated from each one of them and anger quickly flooded my bond with Nyzirth.

It felt like forever before a lone male figure stepped out of the fire. As soon as he was clear of it, it disappeared. I couldn't make out any discernible features, but I could see that his hands were raised up over his shoulders.

"I mean you no harm, Drakewardens." His voice was smooth and low. I didn't recognize it. "It's just that I hear you may need somewhere safe."

"Take a few slow steps into the light," Reyland commanded with an icy tone I hadn't heard from him before. Sharpened icicles floated in the air in front of him. "Too fast and I won't hesitate to put a few new holes in you."

The man took a few hesitant steps forward, stopping only when the dampened light of what I assumed was still the sun hit his face. He was nearly as tall as Reyland. He had pale skin and pointed ears. The top half of his long black hair was tied up in a bun, though the rest of it hung well past his shoulders. He wore simple red and gold armor that reminded me of some that had been described in my history books. It was obviously Elven in nature, but definitely not from Xeswal. No weapon hung at his hip, though there was no doubt the male was a warrior.

"You're a Solar Elf." I took a few steps forward. Reyland grunted his annoyance, but I ignored him. "But you aren't from here. That armor is nothing the king would have commissioned."

"You are correct." He smiled at me. He slowly lowered his hands, and I could feel some of the tension in the air lift away. "I have been sent here to bring you home, cousin."

"I don't have any cousins." Confusion washed over me. "Neither of my parents have any siblings."

"That is only partially correct." The Elf shrugged. "Your mother does not have any siblings. Your father, on the other hand, had five."

I had barely had time to process the fact that Renlin Desai was not my father. It hadn't even crossed my mind that I may have another family. I stared speechless at the Elven male.

"And say we believe you." Reyland stepped up beside me. "Where would you take us?"

I was thankful for his ability to think straight right now. I, unfortunately, was too overcome with a mixture of guilt and paralyzing indecisiveness to get anything done. I turned to Reyland and Lyra, forming our mental bond.

"Home. That is all I may say until you agree to come with me." He looked past us at the four large dragons loomed overhead. "The dragons are more than welcome, of course."

"And if we didn't?" Reyland asked.

"I don't feel like we have much of a choice." I could see the disagreement on Reyland's face, but he said nothing.

Lyra remained quiet, and I had a feeling that she didn't care one way or another at the moment. Her mind wasn't here. Her mind was still in that throne room. Where her best friend lay dead on the cold stone. A wave of nausea washed over me as a not so gentle reminder.

"I go where you go, Nightshade," Reyland finally responded. *"There is one thing you are forgetting, though."*

Before I could ask what was so important, he was gone in a swirl of shadows. He returned in an instant, a black bundle of fur in his arms. Deyka leapt from his grip and bounded across the sand to me.

"How did you—?" I scooped her up with my good arm, tears threatened to escape as I hugged her tightly.

"You talk in your sleep, Nightshade." Heat spread across my face as Reyland smiled.

A. Turner

"So." I turned back to the mysterious Elf, who had made no further advance towards us. "Where are we going?"

"Follow me." He turned his back to us and threw up his hands. He muttered a few words and the swirling mass of fire and smoke reappeared. "Don't worry, even the dragons will fit through." With that, he disappeared into the flames.

I stepped in after him before I could change my mind. The fire didn't burn, but I could feel my insides being twisted. It felt just like when Reyland had moved us to the library using just his shadows. Within just a few steps, warm sunlight filled my vision.

My arms were full or otherwise indisposed, so I resorted to blinking rapidly until my eyes adjusted. I realized we stood at the top of a cliff. Before me was a beautiful, lush forest made of golden trees with white leaves. The trees looked just like the Alterwood trees that used to grow around Arvandor. I could just barely make out the tops of a few tall buildings at the edge of the horizon. I turned around to make sure the others had followed to find them all, dragons included, standing behind me, their eyes wide.

"I never thought I'd see the day." Nyzirth's voice was full of amazement.

"It's beautiful," Lyra breathed her first words since encountering this male.

"Where are we?" Reyland asked, his eyes never leaving the beautiful sight before us. He scooted closer to me, ignoring Nyzirth's grumbles.

The Elf walked to the edge of the cliff and turned around to face us with arms open wide.

"It is my pleasure, Drakewardens, to welcome you to Hyria."

A. Turner

www.ingramcontent.com/pod-product-compliance
Lightning Source LLC
Chambersburg PA
CBHW020519110726

47899CB00004B/1174